STUART CLOETE

The Fiercest Heart

Futura

A Futura Book

Copyright © Stuart Cloete 1960
Kind permission to reprint this edition was granted by
the Estate of the late Stuart Cloete and INPRA

First published in Great Britain in 1961
by Collins, London

This edition published in 1984 by
Futura Publications,
a Division of Macdonald & Co (Publishers) Ltd
London & Sydney

ISBN 0 7088 2626 1

Reproduced, printed and bound in Great Britain by
Hazell Watson & Viney Limited,
Member of the BPCC Group,
Aylesbury, Bucks

Futura Publications
A Division of
Macdonald & Co (Publishers) Ltd
Maxwell House
74 Worship Street
London EC2A 2EN
A BPCC plc Company

TO TINY

CONTENTS

CONTENTS

I

THE WOMAN

IT WAS dusk. The pale lilac dusk of the African evening. In the distance low red clouds of dust moved towards the kraals and stables. The animals, driven by their herders, were coming in. Horses, cattle, sheep and goats, each according to their kind. But they were still far away and the little world of the farm was wrapped in a blanket of silence, pierced only by the song of a Kaffir maid going to fetch water and, from farther away among the small hills, came the cry of a hunting jackal that was answered by its mate.

On the stoep, immovable as a rock among her pot plants, a big woman sat staring at the lilac sky and the moving clouds of dust. They were a mile or more away but she saw into them. Into their very hearts, for she had certain gifts and could see into the hearts of both men and beasts. Into the future too at times, so that it became as real as to-day. She knew which horse would be leading the troop and that the newly foaled brown mare with her blackish colt would be bringing up the rear. She saw into the future too, seeing the colt turn into a dapple grey and then become white like a man with age. His sire was Bloubooi, Francina's pet. She knew the big spotted kapater, the castrated goat standing as high as a small donkey, who led the stupid bastard Kaffir sheep. The sheep, their blotched coats a mixture of hair and wool, their tails fat with the accumulated nourishment of summer, were her delight, for fat was a luxury. Their was little fat to be found on game except about the kidneys and most of the game that had fat—giraffe, zebra and eland— had been killed off in these parts. Of course there were her pigs. She loved her pigs and got much fat from them. Fat for spreading on bread when there was no butter, for making soap and candles, for greasing the axles of the wagons and the barrels of the guns; for cooking, as a base for many of the unguents of her *bossiemiddels*—medicines made from the wild fruits, leaves and roots she collected in the veld. Some sheep had such large fat tails that they had planks with wheels like little carts fastened to them to keep them off the ground.

She was thinking of fat as she listened to the Kaffir girl's song, as she heard the cry of the jackals. Thinking that without fat there could be no soap, and without soap there could be no civilisation. She thought of the big, three-legged iron pot, of the rendered fat simmering, of how she added the lye slowly, testing the mixture with a wooden ladle. She thought of the soap, snow-white, run out to cool, of it cut into bars. She thought of the other womanly arts— of the making of candles from wax berries, of preserves, konfyts and jams, of medicines, of her pleasure in collecting wild herbs. She thought of the planting of vegetables, the saving of seed, the setting out of an orchard, of growing plants on the stoep, of setting hens and raising chicks, of plucking the living geese for their down, leaving them more naked than sheared sheep A woman on a farm had to be a midwife and a doctor. She must know how to cast lead bullets and be able to load guns and fight with her man.

But all this was over for her now. This was no longer the frontier. It had been once, not so long before her time. But much of her life had been led far beyond these now tame parts. Much of her life. All of it, perhaps. All that had been real had been lived with her husband, Jan. Groot Jan—the hunter, the trader, the farmer, the lover, the father of her children, of whom none survived to-day. Only Francina, the daughter of her daughter Melani, was left. Cina—fifteen, wild, untamed as a filly running in the herd, her long tawny hair flowing out behind her like a horse's tail. This was something that continued to distress her. A maid should keep her hair braided and covered decently, for hair was a temptation, an incitement to the eyes and hands of men. Slim, supple as a wand, her almost golden brown-flecked eyes eager, sultry and sullen by turn, but never still, always seeking the road she would take, always looking for some gap in the fence of her monotonous days.

The old woman's belly began to quiver, her hands folded on her lap moved up and down as her laughter mounted. The idea of Cina and the fence took hold. Ja, she was looking for a gap, for a way out. And what would she see framed in it out there in the beyond of to-morrow but a man? What else was there for a woman? The child was almost a woman now. The wheel of her life had made another turn. That was the way it went. Infant to child, child to girl, girl to woman, woman to wife and wife to mother—after that only death or widowhood remained. This was the design of a woman's life. The pattern inevitably embroidered on the fabric of her days. Sometimes she wondered if death was not the best choice—if one could choose. Better than the emptiness of widowhood, better than a life that was like meat without salt or pepper. Only a man could flavour a woman's life.

Now the cattle were passing in front of the house. A flood of sleek, multi-covered hides and white, black-tipped horns as sharp as spears. The bulls, with their thicker horns and massive humps, towered over the more passive cows. They

stared with wild angry eyes—defiant, restless. They were
like men, never content, always challenging each other,
fighting for mastery, for the leadership, which meant the
possession of the cows. Men and women, male and female,
were as God had created them, all—both animal and
human—seeking increase, driven towards it by God's command, for had he not said, " Increase and multiply "? But
somehow the devil had got his finger into this pie. The finger of cruelty, of jealousy, of hate, for these were also a part
of love—the obverse side of the coin.

These thoughts were often in Tante Maria's mind as she
watched Cina. The girl was opening like a flower. Soon the
bees would be coming for her honey. But she was not an
ordinary docile Boer girl. She had wild blood in her. Ja,
before God, that child was not easy to manage. Groot Jan
had been a bold man and Melani, more than her other children, had inherited his nature. It was this wild streak that
had drawn her daughter to Dirk Marais, the ivory hunter.
A fierce, dark-haired, golden-eyed young man of Huguenot
descent. These were the loins and wombs from which Cina
sprang. Knowing those who had had the making of her, her
grandmother had no difficulty in recognising their characteristics as they appeared in the child. They came out like
those of a fast horse or a good hunting dog. They had been
bred into her blood and bones. And life here, isolated on
her great-uncle's farm, had done nothing to tame her.
Groenplaas had been their home since she had brought
her here as a tiny child, a child who had just begun to
walk.

Tante Maria got up and went into the house. She moved
majestically, rolling forward slowly like a great black rock
that would crush any obstacle in its path. The room was
nearly dark. Sara and Eva, two coloured girls, were working by the open fire burning in the hearth. Barefooted,

silhouetted against the glow, they bent over the pots hanging from chains in the chimney.

Only when her eyes became used to the gloom did Tante Maria see Francina sitting on a bench with her back to the wall. The girl looked up. The light caught the whites of her eyes, her teeth, and lit up the honey of her hair. She sprang up.

" Do you know what they are saying, Tante Maria? "

" Who says and what do they say? "

" That many are thinking of trekking, of leaving their farms and going to the North. That some have already gone."

" I have heard, Cina. But what kind of men have gone? The fools, the feckless, the useless. Those who would sooner hunt and adventure than work like honest men."

The two now stood close to each other.

" Horses," Tante Maria said, wrinkling her nose. " You stink of horse sweat."

" Ja," the girl said. " I rode fast."

" That is all you ever do. Ride about the veld like a boy."

" And she rides as well as a boy," Willem Prinsloo said. He had come in for his supper. " And since this is a horse farm and it will one day be hers, it is as well that she should know horses."

" Horses," Tante Maria turned on him, " are not for girls. Is it seemly for a girl of fifteen to have a pet stallion and gallop about the world on his back? "

" Food," Willem said. " Magtig, I came in to eat and not to argue." He sat at the table. One of the coloured girls brought a candle.

Cina and her grandmother waited on the man, the master of the farm, as he ate. They served him roasted buck flesh, its quarters presented like a child for a whipping. With the meat he ate sweet potatoes, pumpkin and rice. They cut him slices of homemade bread, spreading it with strong, almost rancid homemade butter. They poured out coffee for him. They brought him watermelon konfyt—a sweet preserve—and mebos—peaches dried with salt and sugar—to end the meal. When he had lit his pipe and risen from the table the woman and the girl sat down. The coloured girls brought their food, which they ate in silence, for once again there was war between them.

Tante Maria saw the girl astride her stallion, riding like a man, free as the air. Uncontrolled. Capricious. Ready for any mischief the devil might put into her mind. The mind of a young girl was a favourite receptacle for the devil's mischief, which she saw as some kind of concoction that he poured into Francina's empty skull. Cina would be a more than usually welcome object of the devil's attention, with her wild good looks. There was something unnatural about her, about the way she moved—like a buck, but also like a tiger. About the way, though she seldom wore a sunbonnet, her skin remained as white as milk on which the cream has set. Almost colourless, like the petals of some waxy bloom. She never blushed with either shame or anger. If her lips had not been so red and her eyes so bright, one might have thought her ill. There were other things too. She showed her hair—wore it long instead of drawn back parted in the middle and hidden under her kappie, like a respectable girl. She never wore anything upon her head except at Nagmaal. She never wore a dress except on Sundays. Till you saw her shape, which was very apparent, you would have thought she was a boy. That was only in the distance, of course.

Why, her grandmother thought, had God seen fit to leave her only this child? The last of her blood and her race.

Francina knew what was going on in the old woman's

mind. But it was nothing to her. She loved her Ouma. Yet
this love was separate from what she knew to be her life,
something apart from it. Her life was her own. As a man
might follow a star in the night, so did she follow her in-
clination towards some special end that had not, as yet, been
revealed to her. It had to do with her youth, with what she
felt when she rode with her horse's mane blowing in her face
as she leaned over his neck, while the wind tore at her hair
as if it would pull it from her scalp. In her ears as she ate,
she still heard the thunder of Bloubooi's hoofs, felt the sweat
that first blackened and then curded the lovely dapple of
his neck upon her hands. In her mind she slipped from his
back and stood looking into his face, into his big, dark, excited eyes, into his blowing nostrils. This horse had become
part of her, his pride her own, his shrilling neigh the cry of
her own heart, that her throat could not bring forth. This
horse was a king horse, a stud, the father of two hundred
foals, but like her he remained somehow alone, inviolate—
isolated by a quality which she had recognised from the first,
from the day her Oupa had bought him from the British
soldier. Also she had known—even then as a small child—
and Oupa had known too, that he was stolen and the soldier
a deserter, making his way to join the lawless men who
lived hidden in the hills. Scattered about the country there
were many men, soldiers and sailors who had deserted,
renegades, criminals and runaway slaves who, with women of
ill repute, stolen girls and native women, formed wandering
groups that preyed on the lonelier farms and travellers who
were not prepared to defend themselves.

Francina's thoughts went back to the purchase of the big
grey horse, to the mounted man—a soldier from his bearing
but dressed as a farmer—who circled it around them, showing off its paces . . . to her grandfather saying, " I'll give you
twenty pounds for him," and the man's laugh. " Fifty is the

price." Oupa said, " That's an English blood horse. He's
worth five hundred, but he's stolen and you're lucky to get
twenty pounds for him. You fool," he said, " leave him
here. Take your money and make for the hills." Then
he said, " I'll throw in an old horse for you to ride so
that you can make a good impression on the brigands."
The man had laughed again, showing his white teeth.
He had taken off his hat and the sun had glinted on his
bright red hair. Francina had never seen a red-haired
man before. His eyes were grey. "You win," he said, and
threw his right leg over the horse's neck, sliding to the
ground.

" Ja," Oupa said, " I win, and I remain honest, for to
buy a horse stolen from the English who stole our land, who
press down upon us, is honest, for we have never made
peace with them in our hearts."

" They flogged me," the soldier said. " They tied me to
a wheel and flogged me."

" If they catch you they'll shoot you."

" They won't catch me."

He had taken the gold her grandfather had given him in
a small rawhide bag and had ridden away on an old bay
horse.

That was how they had got possession of Bloubooi, five
years ago when she was ten.

She looked up from her plate and said, " You began it,
Ouma."

" Began what? What are you talking about now?"

" Horses," Francina said. " It was you who first put me
on a horse. Ja," she said, " when you saved me from the
Kaffirs when Pa and Ma were made dead. Do you think
I can forget that? The terror. The shouts. The assagais.
I remember it all. Your hand about me, the horse's mane

twisted in my fingers, the way his shoulders moved under my legs."

"How can you remember all that, Cina? You were only two."

So the child remembered what she had tried so hard to forget. But she never could, not in its entirety. There was always something that reminded her. The sound of a galloping horse, a sudden shout, blood on the ground where a pig had been killed. The gleam of sunlight on a black skin wet with sweat. These were the things that had marked the end of her life, though she still lived on. But to the child that she had carried in her arms these terrible events had evidently only been a beginning, something so vivid that all that had gone before it was lost with the milk of infancy. Francina seemed to remember the feel of the horse's neck better than that of her mother's breasts.

"Ja," Francina said, "I remember, and that was the beginning of my horse love. Then there were no other children here, only dogs and horses, only the beasts, domestic and wild, so it was with them that I always played."

It was true. Cina had had a lonely childhood. Looking back on it her grandmother saw her walking about the farm, followed by her dogs and hand-reared lambs, carrying a kitten or a puppy in her arms. She had grown up like an animal with the animals, talking to them as though they were people because she was so alone. She had talked, too, to the coloured girls and women, to the menservants, Hottentots and tame Kaffirs who worked with the stock and on the land. What she knew of life she had learned this way, her only addition to it being what she had picked up from the Bible. Twice a day, in the early morning and again in the evening, all the household were gathered together for prayers. The white people sat about the table, the servants squatted on their heels against the wall. A Psalm was sung slowly.

Then came the reading from the Bible. Then came another
Psalm and finally a blessing. On Sundays a sermon was
added. So that the Scriptures were well known to all
and continuously quoted. The Bible, apart from collec-
tions of sermons, was the only book they read, or half
read and half recited, so well did the older people know
it.

Of course Francina had her letters and could read and
write with some facility. She could also multiply, add and
subtract, and knew some other odd facts which might or
might not be true, since they had been taught her by the
Englishman Oom Willem had seen fit to succour when he had
staggered into the farmhouse, instead of employing a wandering Meester like other people. But Willem Prinsloo could
be counted upon to be perverse. The man said he was an
English officer who had been hunting in the interior where
he had been gored by a wounded buffalo. His boys, who had
brought him to Groenplaas, confirmed his story. But it had
never made much sense to her. Anyway, before he died—
he had lingered on for some months—he had taught Francina English and figuring. He had given Willem his guns,
which were beautiful, engraved with pictures of birds and
buck with many-pronged horns. Cina was, in fact, therefore, well educated—better than most girls—but her loneliness had bred a strangeness in her. The Old Testament
grafted on to the superstitions and fables of the servants and
imagined conversations with her pets made her difficult to
understand, and hard, if not impossible, to manage, particularly as her Oupa encouraged her wildest escapades. With
his sons dead, he was turning this girl into a boy, against the
will of God who surely knew what He was doing when He
created the children of men.

As a family this branch of the Prinsloos had been unfortunate. Their children had been too bold, too adventurous. They had fallen beneath the spears of savages, been killed by the animals they hunted, died in epidemics, of fever, or drowned in the rivers they tried to cross in flood. Reckless, driven by some hidden urge, they had all gone north into Kaffirland to hunt and trade. Willem had gone too in his youth, but had returned, and he alone of the men survived, not because he was less reckless but because for some reason the Lord had seen fit to protect him instead of his brother, Jan, to whom she had been married. Nor had the next generation been more fortunate. None of Oom Willem's children had survived the smallpox that had struck them, killing Gertruda his wife, Petrus, his eldest son, also Cornelius and Adolfus and the three girls, Susanna, Anna and the baby Catalyn, still at her mother's breast. Only one boy had survived and grown to manhood. Ryk had been a fine man, standing six foot three, one inch taller than his father, and he had fallen to the spears of the Kaffirs while on commando on the eve of his marriage. Thus of the Prinsloo blood only Francina, the granddaughter of his brother, Groot Jan, who had been Maria's husband, remained.

Tante Maria pushed back the bench on which she sat and went over to pat Francina's shoulder. " You are a good girl," she said. " It is just that I forget that you are young." She began to laugh as her mood changed. " You would not believe it, my child, but I was like you once. Young, slim and full of fire."

Francina looked at her with wide eyes.

" I was not always a mountain," she said. " Do not think I was this size when we rode away from Sterkwater? Do you think there is a horse alive that could carry me to-day? My man was killed," she said, "and my daughter and my daughter's man. When a woman's man is dead her life is over and she becomes very fat or very thin, according to her nature, or she dies. She is never the same again. That is the will of the Lord."

Going to a shelf recessed in the whitewashed wall, she fetched a great brass-bound Bible which she put on the table. She lit a second candle from the first and set them on each side of the Book. Then she went to the double door, the lower half of which was closed, and stared up at the stars that pinpricked the velvet cloak of the night. They were like holes in it. Perhaps what one saw up there were not really stars at all but glimpses of the lights in heaven.

" Willem," she called, " Willem, we are ready. Come in and read to us from the Book."

He had gone out when he had done eating and now he returned—a big man with long grey hair, and beard that was almost white, whose bulk filled the doorway.

He too had been looking at the stars and listening to the stillness of the African night that was almost a sound.

2

THE GIRL

THE HORSE KRAAL was built of limestone and the walls were high enough to shelter the stock from wind and rain and even shade them from all but the midday sun.

This circular enclosure was a second home to Francina. She felt secure here. Invisible to the human world, hidden by the masonry, she could be completely herself, swimming like a fish in the water of her animal life instead of gasping on the bank of human loneliness as she did among her own kind. Or not her own kind. Perhaps that was it. Everyone was old. Or was coloured. The old lived among their memories and the coloured had a complete world of their own where they worked, loved, suffered, laughed, and bore children that were like little fat, brown berries. The circle of their lives and those of their masters barely intersected. There was a tiny elliptical area where they met, but the rest for each was separate and utterly irrelevant. Sometimes Francina wished she was a coloured girl and could know some kind of completeness, could live as a girl among girls and boys and children. Have a mother who was young enough to bear more children, and help her with them, and a father—active, alive—a model for the man with whom she would one day choose to mate. Instead there were only the animals. The two pet sheep and the dogs that she had left waiting at the gate. The horses that came towards her with cocked ears, snorting gently with wide nostrils as they advanced over the thick carpet of dry, powdered manure. It was four feet deep, soft, springy and still wet with dew under her bare feet.

Bloubooi was in front of the others, looking at her as if he wondered why she was here so early, before the grooms and herders were astir, before the blue smoke of the cooking fires rose into the still night-sharp air.

For some reason unknown to herself, Francina had come to the horse kraal at cockcrow, as the first streaks of dawn marked the grey sky with pink, as in fact the cocks crowed, first one then another, then all the cocks, in a vast chorus of awakening masculinity as if it was they, in their proud virility, who were calling the sun to rise and shine in the east. And thus was the sun greeted in the hour of its rising all over the world. This was a strange thought that came to her. That the sun should be so greeted in the world of men. For wherever there were men and houses, so were there cocks to greet the sun. And in the wilder places, in the wilderness of the veld, there were singing birds, tremblingly eager with bursting throats waiting for the day.

She put her hand on the horse's iron neck. It arched at her touch. His muzzle pressed into her side, pushing between her arm and breast. His eye was level with her own so that she could count his grey eyelashes as she looked into the soft brown pool of his eye, as she noted the whirl of hair that made a white star on his grey forehead below the long forelock, which lay like the hair of a girl in a splendid tassel between his ear and eye. His mane, still jewelled with dew, hung in a curtain from crest to withers. Under it Francina's hand was warm and dry as she stroked the silken coat.

To have, to hold, to see, to touch, to smell, to know. All of her was going out to the horse, for her heart was still in her eye and hand. In her breath as she breathed into his

nostrils. This was love, the culmination of her fifteen years
of life. The high point of its living. One day she knew it
would not be a horse. But till that day came it was a horse.
It was Bloubooi. She slid her hand down over the great
rounded bosses of his chest on to his forearms, his knees, and
the clean hard fleshless cannon-bone below it. Her hand
cupped his fetlock, felt for ticks on the underside of his
pastern, and finding one pulled it off, squashing it between
her fingers where it burst like a bloody grape. She went
over his other legs, and between them. Later she would
smear his dock with fat to kill the small brown ticks that had
congregated there. And all the while the great horse stood
as the girl went over him inch by inch. No man could have
done it. But there is a sympathy between male animals and
girls, and from that first day when Oupa had bought Bloubooi there had been this friendship between them.

When the soldier had ridden away towards the hills on the
old bay horse Oupa had given him, they had stood watching him. She remembered the look of amusement on Oupa's
face. He had bought a fine horse for nothing from the
enemy. He had helped one of the enemy to desert. He had
said: "Sometimes there is justice, Cina. The hand of God
is visible here."

This remark had been beyond her then and still was. But
grownups were very curious and if they believed that God
was concerned with improving the breed of the Prinsloos'
horses with a stolen race horse stud it was simply another of
those things which could only be understood by people much
older than herself—people who were not children and had
attained the age of reason.

She had not argued about the hand of God. His hand was
in it all right. But what He had seen was a small lonely
girl on a farm in Africa, and had sent her a thing of beauty
to look at and to love.

When Klaas, the head horse boy, had led the stallion away she had followed. She watched him put into a loosebox, standing back with her forefinger in her mouth. When Klaas left she tried the door, but the bolt was too high for her. She then had gone round to the back of the stables. They were a long low building and here she could not be seen from the house. There was a window in the loosebox, not very high up, and unbarred. She found a bamboo ladder and a moment later she was staring down at the horse. He had raised his head to look at her. She got on to the window sill and sat on it with her bare legs dangling against the inner wall of the stable. The horse smelled her feet. She still remembered the feel of his nose. She had put out her hand to touch his head and then had slid, half falling, into the deep straw of the box. The horse had gone up into a rearing plunge as she landed, but had become calm as soon as she touched him. For an hour she had stroked him and then, exhausted by the excitements of the day, had lain down beneath the manger at the stallion's feet and slept. How many times since then had she listened to him eating, heard the rhythmic crunch of his jaws on the grain, the tearing sound as he ripped hay from the rack? That had been where they had found her much later and still asleep, when Klaas had come in to fetch the horse to water him. She had been beaten. She had been told that stallions were dangerous.

"Ja," she had said. " Perhaps they are dangerous to men, but Bloubooi will not hurt me."

No one has ever heard of a bull or a horse hurting a woman. The women fear them because they are male, and run away. The men challenge them, male to male, eye to eye, strength to strength. Francina did not think in these terms but she knew it in her heart.

They had not been able to keep her from him. To be

near him or to watch him became her life. It was not decent
for a girl to see a horse mounting the mares to serve them.
Very well, it was not decent, but she watched. It meant
nothing to her. It was merely another of his activities. He
now came as soon as he saw her, and they walked about
together. It had taken a year of growth and effort before
she was able to scramble on to his back. This had been
achieved by getting him to stand near a big rock and then
pulling herself up by his mane.

She led the horse out of the kraal by his forelock. At
the stables she saddled and bridled him. Then she tied him
to a ring let into the wall, gave him a truss of oat forage and
went to get her own breakfast.

The girls would be up by now. Still heavy with sleep and
thoughts of the men who had just left them; they moved
slowly about their work, for the rhythm of the night was yet
upon them. Fresh kindling of dry branches was thrown on to
the glowing embers of the fire and burst into flame. Water
from the well was brought in, slopping from the bucket on to
the stone-flagged floor of the kitchen. Milk was poured into
saucers for the cats that wove about their bare legs. The
dogs that had followed them into the house were chased out.
"Voetsak! Voetsak!" they shouted together, and then fell
laughing into each other's arms.

The cocks had stopped crowing. They led forth their
harems of hens to feed and tread them. The flies that had
blackened the ceiling began their buzzing search for food
and excrement.

The night was over. The day with its routine of cleaning,
washing, polishing and cooking had begun. The girls would
do as much of it as they could outside, where they could call
in their high female voices to the men working in the kraals
and stables.

The kombuis or kitchen and sitting-room were combined

into one great chamber that was illuminated by the double stable doors that led to the front and back stoeps and by the small glass window in a wooden frame that was Tante Maria's pride. There was not another piece of glass within fifty miles. There was a great table on posts let into the stamped ant-heap floor, two folding tables, some folding rawhide stools, two benches and several rusbanks furnished the room. A sixteen-foot bamboo ox whip, its thong neatly wound about it, lay across the rafters. A couple of leather haversacks hung from bushbuck horns that had been fastened by their frontal bones to the whitewashed wall and painted blue. A saddle and bridle were slung by riems to the beams. In the bedrooms the kartels or beds of the wagons rested on four forked posts let into the stamped earth floor.

This was a Boer home, easy to defend provided the reed thatch was not set on fire, and easy to evacuate. Everything in it could be folded up or taken to pieces and packed on to the wagons in a couple of hours. Even the great stinkwood armoire, with silver hinges and yellowwood panels, was fastened together with pegs and could be taken down. The two brass-bound mahogany chests that had been brought from the East Indies by a Prinsloo ancestor were, with some blue and white china, the only objects of beauty or value on the farm.

It was into this big kitchen, that was also the living-room of the family, that Francina came, demanding coffee, mealie porridge, eggs and bread and jam. She was hungry for food and for the day. Hungry for her breakfast, for the feel of her horse between her thighs, for the wind in her hair, for life that was slipping away from her so fast. Everything took so long. It took a long time to eat, so one gulped one's food. A long time to go from one place to another, so one ran if on foot or galloped on a horse. It took so long to grow up. It was so long from one birthday to the next. So long for the fruit on the bough to ripen in the sun. Everything took so long that one had to hurry, to be up before the sun, to stay up late if one could, to try and keep awake. For Francina life was a river into which one plunged naked, not a lake shore where one paddled with raised timid skirts.

Her dog, Wolf, came in with her. The other, Wagter, a year old but still foolish, had been behind the others. He leaped the half door with a crash. The tame sheep pattered on the great flat entrance stone and then stood up on their hind legs, bleating and looking into the room in which they, being motherless, had been raised, and still considered to be their rightful home.

The two coloured maids, stimulated by the presence of their young nooi, now became very active. They were, in addition, hungry themselves. Soon eggs were frying in a great flat pan. The smell of coffee joined the other smells in the room—of old meals, of rancid fat, of wet dogs—and mastered them, absorbing them all into its own aroma. For, as the crowing of cocks was the sound of the dawn, so was the smell of coffee the smell of breakfast. Soon, Francina knew, Oupa and Tante Maria would appear from their rooms with their hands outstretched for their cups. But she would get away before they came. Be up and away. She gulped her coffee. She had no explanation for to-day's urgency— only that she had waked with the first light and sprung out of bed so filled with life that she had felt as if she would burst out of her own sleek skin, burst like a plum overripe in the sun or a rosebud from its sheath of green. Her room, the house, even the farm, were too small to contain her to-day. She jumped up and ran out of the door with the dogs leaping beside her. The sheep joined her, bleating happily, thinking they were going to play as they did sometimes—butting at the dogs and being chased by them. But not to-day. Francina reached her horse, undid the rein and, mounting, galloped off followed by her dogs.

Tante Maria and Oom Willem breakfasted and went about their business. Willem mounted Soldaat, his rooiskimmel, roan being his favourite colour—you never saw a bad one either red or blue—and rode out to watch the grazing cattle. Often a sick beast could be seen more easily in the open than in the kraal. It would be standing apart, neither grazing nor chewing the cud. Its head low, its eyes dull, its coat staring, its quarters stained with scour. These were the symptoms of illness in man or beast, all of them or one alone must be looked for. And the way an animal moved—freely, boldly, not favouring itself in any way—had to be watched. These animals were his life, an extension of himself. Many of them he knew intimately, as if they were friends. He had doctored them, cut them, branded them, trained them. He knew their fathers and grandfathers, their mothers and grandmothers. He remembered even further back—to Kornet, the big bull he had bought in Bredasdorp, and that was thirty years ago. It was this bull and his get that had made the herd what it was. Truly men were right when they said the bull was half the herd. A bull could serve thirty or forty cows—more if he was well fed. In a few years the impress of his blood was there, apparent everywhere. That was the way it had been with Kornet. That wide forehead, those great horns and powerful forehand had been transmitted. Which was why it was so widely recognised that his trek oxen were the best within many miles, as good in fact—or perhaps better—than any in the land. He pushed his horse into a tripple—a slow pace—where he moved both near and both off feet alternately. A very comfortable gait, natural to many Boer horses, but which could be improved upon or even developed by fastening the horse's legs together on one side when it was a foal.

As he rode past the vlei a heron rose on majestic flapping wings, its legs outstretched behind it, its head back between its shoulders on its folded neck. Some small, neat ducks—geelbek or yellow-billed ducks—paddled away and lost themselves in reeds. Stopping to let his horse drink, he saw the round spoor of a rooikat, the red lynx that preyed on hares, small buck, and on sheep, too, if they were not protected. This was a world he understood. His own world. Not only did the land belong to him as it had to his father, he belonged to the land, to these flats and sand dunes and marshes, and the mountains that hemmed them in on three sides. On the fourth side was the sea, where the wild waves from the south beat in never-ending fury against the rocks and strand.

At the house Tante Maria sat still on her great chair. It had been specially constructed for her of stinkwood, a dark heavy wood used for furniture and those parts of wagons that took the hardest wear. Never could she forget that last day on the farm. Their first warning had come from Jacob, a herdboy, who had come galloping in, riding bare back using his belt as a bridle and shouting: " The Kaffirs! The Kaffirs!" and had fallen dead at her feet from a spear wound in his back. This had given them a few moments' grace. Groot Jan had saddled the horses, hoping the men would be able to fight their way out with the women between them, but the Kaffirs had come too fast and only she had got away with the baby.

A week later she had been back with a commando led by Oom Willem who rode at her side. Nothing was left but the blackened walls of her home and the mutilated dead. They had loaded the bodies into the wagon they had brought for the purpose and taken them back for burial at Groenplaas. She saw it again as she had left it. The dead dogs and poultry. The white cat that had been dashed against the wall. Only the pigeons were left alive. They had fluttered down and, tame with hunger, had been caught and put into a bag. But that was all over, all long ago—though it seemed like yesterday—it was no use going on thinking about it, and she set about reviewing the day that was before her like a general reviewing troops. She called out the hours in her mind. They fell in in front of her, were inspected and dismissed. The poultry, the garden. Vegetables to be picked. Laundry to be counted and checked for holes. Coffee beans to be roasted. Three chickens to be killed. The maids' rooms to be looked at, checked for cleanliness and traces of men.

It was the custom to do this. As if girls only became pregnant in bedrooms. Why, she herself . . . Her eyes closed and she began to shake with laughter. But when she had done, when the mountain of her body had ceased to quiver, she had to wipe away a tear that her memories had brought forth. Girls, girls, she thought, white, brown or black, were just girls, but some were cleverer and greater hypocrites than others.

And that Eva—there was a girl for you! Two years ago there had been a baby. Ja, that she would never forget— a breech delivery that would have puzzled a midwife. But she had brought it forth alive. How Eva had screamed and moaned. Then two days later the baby had died. She had never thought he would live, so small was he. No bigger than a puppy. And the father? Ja, before God, when she had said: "Eva, who was his pa?"—not blaming the girl at all for she was young and coloured, scarcely Christian, and the child had been born in September and therefore conceived in the Christmas season when all barriers and clothes are somewhat loosened by the festivities and the summer heat—what had Eva replied? "His pa, Misses? His pa was a man who came in the night."

When she thought, Tante Maria sat very still, her hands folded in her lap. She was now thinking of men and women. Of how men went out fiercely to meet life, to challenge it, while women waited passive at home for the news of what they had done. Men were free like birds, women rooted in the soil like trees or rocks. Like trees they could whip before the storm. Like rocks the waters of disaster could sweep over them. But this only if they were strong. The weak trees were uprooted or snapped, the unstable rocks rolled in the current, coming to their final rest with strange companions. She knew herself to be a rock. Immovable and unmoved, drained of emotion, sucked dry by her tears. Once she had been like a young tree trembling in the winds of love, stripped by gales of passion. That it seemed was the fate of women. The sapling into the tree, and the tree into the rock. She began to laugh again. There was a fable here —a story. The story of the old stump watching the young tree grow, unable to advise it. Unable to say: "I was a supple young tree once, nubile with green leaves and rich with coursing sap." "Ja, what a story that is," the young tree would say, "for how could you, an old fat stump, have been as beautiful, as alive, as I?"

This sudden shaking laughter of hers, starting from nothing like the standing jump of a buck, always frightened the servants. No one was there. There was no joke, nothing funny had occurred. At such times they thought she must without doubt be possessed. It was terrible to hear her laughter sometimes as she sat alone. When they heard it, the girls ran out into the yard till she had done and crept back, sneaking in on tiptoe, cringing as if they were beaten dogs. They did not know that Ouma, as they called her to each

other, was never alone. That the memories of her dead
never left her and that of the circle of those about her only
Francina had reality. Everything else was nothing, often a
joke, which was why she laughed. Many years ago she had
decided it was better to laugh than to cry.

Francina rode over the veld in a dream. Her grey race-
horse was her way out of her ordinary life into one of beauty,
of grace, of speed. Coming to a stretch of short, sheep-
cropped turf, she loosened Bloubooi's reins as he shook his
head asking for freedom. They both knew this place. He
thought of it as the galloping place. To the horse it brought
back memories of the turf, of the race track, the feeling of
other horses competing with him, of shouting men, of the
feel of whip and spur. With springy turf beneath his hoofs
and an open space in front of him, the horse would hardly
contain himself. His great muscles contracted and expanded
like springs under his satin skin. But she knew. He had only
to shake his head from side to side, to shiver and tremble, and
she let him go, leaning over his neck, her cheek against it,
her hair mingling with his mane in the wind of the gallop.
Intoxicated by his own speed, hearing imaginary hoofs
behind, the stallion raced on, shaking the ground with the
thunder of his gallop.

And then it was over. Cina sat back in the saddle. There
was no need to touch the reins. The horse slowed to a canter, to a walk. He came to a halt. Francina patted his neck.
She was breathing hard. The blood flowed through her
swiftly. Her cheeks were rosy as ripe apricots, her nostrils
wide open as she sucked in the perfumed air, for here almost
every bush was fragrant, its scent carried to her on the strong
salt breeze blowing in from the sea. This was what she had
sought. Something she described wordlessly to herself as her
moments of happiness. These were very special and were

what made life worth living. They could come as now, violently, as if she and her horse and the land had been welded into one by the fury of their gallop, or gently, with the wet nose of one of the dogs in her hand, or the tiny white star of a flower beneath her nose as she lay on her belly in the veld, with her head in her arms. These were moments when she was one with all living things.

At home the two older people would be going their way, following the circular rut of a long established routine, each day resembling the one that had preceded it. Everything they did was known to them, everything they saw had been seen before. Yet they, being man and woman and not wed, had no common ground. For it is only in bed that men and women would meet to weave the subtle mesh of perfect understanding. So they were diverse, bound only by the name of a dead man who had been a husband to the one and a brother to the other—Groot Jan Prinsloo, her grandfather. Bound only by this and their love of her in whom their blood was merged. It was strange to be alone in a country where big families were the rule. Strange to be the last of a line and be looked at as if one held some strange fortune within one's womb. They never said this, but she could feel it. You, they seemed to say, are our security. Only through you and your seed can we live on. Being old, of course, they were near to death and so thought more of it—and of life too—hers and the new lives that lay within her.

So ten miles away they, the old, went about their work— man and woman—utterly separate and alone. And she was alone too. Not only here by distance, but by her youth and girlhood. She was still virgin—thus divided even from the coloured girls, Sara and Eva, who had known men since childhood and might even now be pregnant. They had that look in their eyes that she had seen in other female things that had been taken.

She wondered if everyone was lonely. She knew she was loved, but it did not help her, for somehow she felt this love was not for her, not for Cina, not for the real girl but for the things she represented to them. Not a girl, but a mixture of memories of the past and hopes for the future. Only the animals loved Cina. The horse she rode. The dogs that followed her. The idiot lambs she had raised into great fat stupid rams, that she had refused to have cut because she knew if she had, her Ouma would have wanted to eat them.

3

THE HILLS OF THE HUNTER

FRANCINA NEVER knew what made her turn her horse's head toward the hills, or she might not have turned him. She often rode with the reins loose on his neck and let him have his way. He seldom stopped to graze but walked on with pricked ears and wide staring eyes as if he owned the world. He was an adventurous horse, interested in everything he saw. The dogs put up a pair of steenbok. The ram had little black needle horns and both had ears like small wings. They ran, leaping over the bush, easily outdistancing the dogs who, knowing they could not catch them, gave only token chase.

Francina's dogs were Boer hounds, big rough-haired mongrels standing twenty-six inches at the shoulder and showing traces of great Dane, foxhound and Scottish deerhound blood on a foundation of the native Hottentot dogs that the first settlers had found at the Cape of Good Hope when they landed. These dogs were all that could be desired on the frontier as guards and hunting dogs. Brave, tireless and with good noses to follow the blood spoor of a wounded beast.

A pair of tall grey secretary birds moved out of Francina's way and then rose, flew a couple of hundred yards, landed and resumed their search for any small living thing that crouched in their path—snakes, frogs, mice, the young of birds or hares. For these birds were eagles that walked on stilts instead of circling the sky in search for prey.

There was no sound save the brushing of the horse's legs through the heath. Sometimes it was so tall that it touched the girl's thighs. One kind she loved particularly. It had pale green flowers. The flat land between the hills was watered by a stream, its water brown from the peat and roots it ran through. The air was sweetly perfumed by the heavy fragrance of the *fontein bos*—a fragile, feathery bush covered with pale blue sweet-pea-like flowers. They grew only in damp, sour soil.

All these things, the birds and game she saw, the flowers she rode past, the very soil she rode over, Francina noted and accepted. They were like the pages of a well-known book where loved phrases caught the eye and were repeated once again. There was often a tortoise to be seen at one place and green malachite sunbirds were almost certain to be drinking nectar from the orange-coloured wild dagga blossoms in another.

The girl drifted slowly up the kloof that opened up into little grassy patches, white with arum lilies, and then closed again, narrowing into a passage where the horse had to walk in the bed of the stream before the hills opened out again into another of the glades that were strung like pearls on the string of the little river. In winter they were flooded and the small gorges up which she rode so pleasantly now were raging torrents, ten feet deep, as the water poured down from the mountains on to the foothills and ran from them into the valleys that divided range from range.

Still dawdling along, talking to her horse who cocked his ears back to listen, patting him, picking such blooms as she could reach from her saddle, Francina was lost in her dreams till she was brought back to reality by the horse stopping, raising his head and neighing. There must be other horses nearby. She tightened her rein and looked about her Four horsemen were coming towards her. She knew them at once

—the four Beyers brothers. She was, in fact, on their land. But what were they doing all together like this? She pulled her horse to the side of the track and waited for them.

They were all big men, loose-limbed and powerfully built. Daniel had a full dark beard. Barend and Flip were fair — bearded too, but their upper lips were shaved. Louis had a golden fuzz on his cheeks whose growth he encouraged with lotions his mother had made him. They were all armed and dressed in their best moleskins—trousers of the klapbroek type with a flap that buttoned up in front, that were held up by the heavy leather belts on which their long-bladed sheath knives, called *Hernhuters*, hung. They wore jackets of brown duffel. Flip, who was a dandy, wore a waistcoat made from the black and white spotted skin of a newborn calf. They all wore wide-brimmed, high-crowned, homemade felt hats. Flip had a short white ostrich plume stuck in his hatband. Each carried a buffalo powder-horn that held a pound and a half of powder and wore wide leather bandoleers over his shoulder with pockets for bullets and wads. The bullets were round to fit the barrels of their guns but the slugs were either set in cylinders of hard fat or sewn into little oiled buckskin bags, known as *vet lappies*, that slid down the barrel easily.

The men's horses now raised their heads and shrilled the greeting that was also a challenge, for they were all entire— no Boer ever rode a mare or a gelded horse. They cantered towards her, and Barend, who was in front, said: "We are on our way to visit Oom Willem."

"Oupa?" she said. "All of you? And dressed like that? What do you want of him?"

"It's private," Flip said. "But he may tell you."

She looked at Daniel, the eldest. "Ja," he said, "he may tell you, but at the moment it is secret, something we do not wish to discuss."

Francina tossed her head. " Secrets," she said. " I love secrets."

She joined Louis, the youngest of them, who was only a year older than she was herself. She said: " What will you bet that I find out your secret before you leave?"

" I'll bet you a Boer bull pup. I've four now at home. I'll bet you the white bitch with a brindle spot over her left eye."

" Ja," Francina said. " I'll take her. I'd like to cross her with one of my hounds." She looked down at them as they walked beside the horses.

" And what will you give me if you lose?" Louis said.

" I had not thought of it. I shall not lose. What would you like?" She smiled into his eyes.

" A kiss," he said.

Francina laughed. " Why," she said, " you are growing up and acting like a man."

" I am a man," Louis said. " And do all men want to kiss you?"

" I do not see many men but they might if I did," she said. Then she put her heels into her horse, " I'll tell them you are coming," and galloped back home.

Tante Maria was waiting on the stoep when Francina arrived, windblown and dishevelled. " The Beyers men are coming, Ouma. They are on their way."

" All of them?"

" Ja, all four of them. They are armed and in their best clothes. They are coming to consult Oupa about something. They would not tell me what it was."

Tante Maria smiled. " It is man's business then. Something to do with hunting or war."

Francina's mouth drooped open with surprise. " There is no war."

" With men there is always some chance of it. I do not

mean a real war, but they may have lost stock to thieves and want to get together a small commando to recover them. Men always want to fight something."

"Oupa is too old for commando," Francina said.

"You may think so and I may think so, Cina, but will he think so? It is my belief that no man is ever too old to fire a gun at another man if he has any excuse to do so. Men are like that. All men. They like to hunt, to take risks, to kill."

"I hate killing," Francina said. "Ja, even the killing of a pig or a chicken."

"That is because you are a woman, Cina. The female creates. She makes things. Babies, homes, food. The man is the destroyer, often even the destroyer of his own happiness."

"We must have coffee for them," Francina said, "and there is a fresh milk tart. I will get everything ready. Will you send a boy for Oupa, tell him that they come?"

Francina went into the house to set the table with cups and plates. She also put out glasses and from a built-in wall cupboard brought out a bottle of homemade peach brandy. It was as clear as water but very potent and sometimes known as tiger's milk. It was a great loosener of tongues and likely to make the men talk with more than their usual loudness.

Her plans now made, Francina went out of the back door and round to the east gable where stone steps led up to the loft. The beamed ceilings of the rooms below were covered thick, varnished stems of Spanish reed. On these was laid a four-inch floor of clay known as a *brandsolder*, or fire ceiling. In the event of the thatched roof catching fire, this insulated the rest of the house and delayed its burning for long enough to enable the inhabitants to save themselves and their furniture. The loft was used to store bags of grain, spare riems, saddlery and harness, odd boxes and chests, old guns and trophies of the chase. Other oddments of all kinds littered the floor. Things no longer in use but too good to throw away. The accumulation of almost a century.

But the centre of interest to Francina was always Oupa's coffin. Immense, to fit his great frame. Expensive, Ouma said, and too good for such a man. Imported mahogany, as if stinkwood was not good enough, and oiled twice a year. Ja, twice a year her Oupa climbed the steps to the loft and lovingly oiled his own big coffin. Death was always in the mind of the old while she, before God, was not yet fully alive. What had yet to come for her was behind them and gone for ever.

Picking her way through the dusty collection, Francina wiped a section of the floor that was considerably cleaner than the rest of it, as if it had been swept before, and lay down with her eye to a small hole through the clay and the reeds that supported it. She was exactly above the table she had laid. All she had to do now was to wait for the Beyers brothers to arrive. So she lay waiting, thinking of the Boer bull pup with one brindle eye.

Klaas, the boy Tante Maria had sent to fetch the master, met him a mile from the house. He was on his way back.

" Baas," he said, " men come to visit. I was sent to call the baas."

" What men?"

" Baas Beyers. The three big ones and the little baasie."

This was curious, Willem thought. Of course visits were exchanged between the neighbouring farms. Once every month or two one saw someone or called on someone. But for four men to come at one time was something of an event. Something serious must have taken place. He pushed his roan to a faster pace. Klaas swung in his horse, following a few yards behind it.

Maria greeted Willem from the stoep. " So you've come," she said. " Do you know what they want? And why they should all come?"

" I do not know, Maria I have no idea, but we shall know soon, for there they are." He pointed to the four horsemen who were now in view.

They were in no great hurry but rode slowly towards the house. They were well mounted but had no servants with them, which was unusual and meant that they did not want their mission known. A few minutes later they pulled up, dismounted, tied up their horses, and came on to the stoep to shake hands with Oom Willem and Tante Maria.

" Well, how goes it, Oom Willem?" Daniel said.

" Good, very good, and how goes it with you?"

" Very good. But we have something to discuss with you, Oom Willem."

" I guessed it. I said to myself, all these young men would not ride out like a commando for nothing. They want something. Come inside. Come in." He opened the door.

The brothers followed him in.

" Sit," Willem said.

They drew up the chairs. Tante Maria brought coffee, poured it and left the room.

Willem poured brandy into the glasses. " Try it," he said. " I do not think anyone around here has a better brandy or finer livestock." He stared at his guests to see if they would deny his assertion. It was good to see them. He would now tell them about his cattle and horses. Being here and drinking his brandy, they would be forced to listen.

But they did not follow his lead. Instead Barend, the second brother said, " Oom Willem, we have come to talk to you of the North, of the interior. We know that you were there as a young man."

" Ja, kerels. Thirty years ago I was there hunting ivory. A fair, far land. There was one place . . . " He paused. His face changed as it all came back to him.

" Tell us," Flip said. Flip was the third brother and the wildest of them.

" Tell you? Tell you? Ja, I'll tell you. The North, my North, is a thousand miles away. More than a hundred days' trek if all went well. But you would be lucky to reach it in a year. Deserts, mountains, rivers, wild beasts and wilder men all stand in your path. But when you get there—what a country! Rolling hills with beautiful trees of kinds we do not know down here. Herds of game that cover the veld like great moving carpets. Sweet grass by the thousand morgen. Waterfalls, rivers. Verily I tell you that that is the land of Canaan, the promised land that one day will be found by others. This place of which I speak I called the Hills of the Hunter. Set in the plain there were five small hills among which not only elephants but all game abounded. Giraffe, eland, swartwitpens, rooibok—sea cows in the vleis and birds, ducks and geese by the million so that sometimes they darkened the sky . . ." He paused for breath. Now it all came back. It was many years since he had spoken of it or even thought of it. Now it seemed like yesterday.

Barend said : " That is the way we remembered your speaking of it, and that is why we came."

" Why you came?"

" Ja, we are going to trek. We and some of our other neighbours. The Van der Merwes, Cronjes, the Bokmans, the du Plessis family and others."

" You are all going to leave the Colony—leave your farms?"

" We are going to trek. Our minds are made up and that is why we are here. We need a leader. We want you to lead us. You have been there. You know the way."

Oom Willem seemed to pay no attention to what they said. He continued his own train of thought.

"I was a young man then," he said, "a hunter. That was the best hunting veld I have ever seen before or since. But later, as I grew older and looked back, I have seen it differently. I have seen it as a garden, as lands and fields. I have seen the ploughs turning over the rich, black soil. I have seen the lands under water. There is plenty of water for irrigation. I have seen crops of mealies and tobacco and great herds of cattle. But this is all a dream. Something possible only when our people have tamed the veld, creeping forward over it like snails, an inch at a time."

"We are not going an inch at a time," Flip Beyers said.

"We will go a thousand miles and take even two years if you say it will take that long. But you must lead us."

Barend echoed his brother: ". . . lead our trek, Oom Willem."

Daniel said: "I am remaining behind. I will care for your farm as if it was our own."

Above them, Francina squirmed on her belly in the loft. So this was man's talk. This was the thing they had come to say. Well, she knew it now and the bull pup was hers. How surprised Louis would be. She could hardly restrain her giggles.

Oom Willem said: "But why are you all going?"

"We are going because some others have already gone. Not many, but a few, and we wish to be among the first and to pick the best farms. Then, we want our freedom. We want no more taxes, no quitrent, no laws but our own which are the laws of God. We wish to build a republic in the wilderness where we can live in our fashion as farmers and hunters. Just look at what the English have done. They have freed our slaves. They have allowed servants to testify against their masters. They have taken away our language and tax us for the land which we have tamed. And this is only the beginning. First one law, then another, and then before we know what has happened we will find ourselves knee-haltered and our freedom gone."

Barend sat back. He had had his say.

" But you and all these people who go with you have good farms," Oom Willem said. " You are all solid men with many beasts and rich lands."

" We are the subjects of the English and we would be free burghers."

" Many will die on the road, kerels. Much stock will be lost because there is a biting fly which kills all tame animals, though wild remain alive and increase in abundance. And men will die from wild beasts and illness. Women will die of hardship and in childbirth. Babies will die. Your trek path will be marked with the graves of men and the bones of beasts." He jumped up and banged the table with his fist. " But despite all this," he shouted, " if I were ten years younger I would go with you. Ja," he said, " I would lead you to the Hills of the Hunter, to the the fairest land that I have ever seen."

" Then you refuse?" Barend said.

" Ja, I refuse. But I say this, Barend. I say it to all who wish to go—to Flip and Louis and our neighbours—that I shall be with you in my heart and mind. It is only my body that is too old which holds me back. Ja, I say go. God bless you, and all in this household will pray daily for your success and safety."

Flip said: " We should have had a greater chance of success with you to lead us. A young pack needs an old dog when the scent is bad."

" Do not fear, kerels. I will begin to-morrow to make a map. It is all clear in my head. The distances may be wrong, but the mountains and the rivers will be there. These things do not change. The world remains the way God made it."

The stools and benches were pushed back.

Francina stood up, brushed the dust from the front of her frock and the cobwebs from her hair, and tiptoed out of the loft and down the stairs. She must see Louis before he mounted. She went up to his horse, a dun with a black tail and mane, and patted it. She heard the men saying good-bye to Oupa.

" Tot siens . . . Tot siens . . . till I see you . . . good-bye. Good luck . . . It's a pity about your decision . . . You are not too old . . . Think it over . . . The map . . ." Words and half sentences came to her as she stood among the horses.

Then the men came. " So there you are," they said. " We wondered where you were."

Francina laughed. " That is something you'll never know," she said. " We women have our secrets too."

" A woman?" Flip asked. " You're just a girl. Last time I saw you you had a doll in your arms."

" It was a kitten," Francina said. " A dressed-up kitten."

They all laughed again. Louis began to tighten the girth of his dun.

Francina kicked his leg with her bare foot. " Is she weaned yet, Louis?"

" Weaned? What? Who?" He stared at her in surprise.

" My white bull pup with the brindle eye."

" Yours?"

" Ja, I know what you discussed. You are going to trek and want Oupa to lead you."

" How did you find out?"

Francina said: " You promise to tell no one?"

" Ja, I promise."

" Very well. You know what they say about Ouma—

that she is a witch, that she can see things before they happen? Well," Francina said, "I am like that too." She clasped her hands together in front of her and looked down. " I see things," she said, " I hear voices. To-day I heard them clearly. Barend said young dogs need an old one to lead them ... Sometimes it frightens me, this power that I have. I have told nobody before." She put her hand on his wrist. " You won't tell? You promise? And when can I have the puppy?"

" Anytime. This week, next week. She is yours. I'll bring her over or you can fetch her." His brothers had clattered off. Louis mounted, waved to the girl and followed them. She had really frightened him with her mysteries. Everyone knew about Tante Maria and her gift had evidently been handed on. Why indeed should it not be?

Everyone at Groenplaas was very quiet that evening. Tante Maria evidently knew nothing. Francina could not discuss what she knew with her without explaining how she knew it.

Oom Willem was very silent, his blue eyes vacant as if he were staring into space—the vast space of Africa, the space of the days he had lived, and the roads he had travelled. Francina, too, was lost in a dream, a new dream of what it would be like to trek. To live in a wagon—not for a few days as they did when they went to Nagmaal, but for a year or more. To live among other people—young men and women. To be able to play with children and nurse real babies instead of dressed-up kittens.

When Oom Willem had read from the Bible, when the last sonorous words had been said, the Book closed and hasped, he went to the rack where his guns were hung across buck horns fastened to the wall. He took one down—the biggest—the four-pounder that he had used for hunting elephant when he was young. That was the way Francina saw him when she said good night—standing in the candle-light holding the gun at the ready in his gnarled hands. Later she heard the sound of a fiddle. Who, before God, could be playing it here? Playing " O vat jou goed en trek, Ferriera "—she opened the door of her room softly. It was Oupa. Oupa, who she had never even known possessed a violin.

4

THE SMOUS

SOLOMON ROSENBERG was a small wiry man with curly black hair and a hooked nose. He had a face that might have come off an ancient Eastern coin. Assyrian, Phoenician, Arab, Jew. He had come to Africa from Prussia as a baby with his father and mother in 1815—twenty-three years ago. His only memories were of Africa. Disdaining his father's little business in Cape Town, he had branched out into an adventure of his own. He had become a smous, one of the wandering peddlers who, with a string of pack donkeys, traded between the border and the interior with anyone—white or black—who needed their goods. He sold soft goods—dress material, needles and thread. He sold cook pots, tin cups and kettles. He sold lead for bullets and powder. He sold beads, axeheads, knives and hoes. He sold purgatives—senna pods and jalap from Mexico—and medicinal bark from Peru. Bachu and Haarlem olie for the treatment of wounds and diseases of the skin. Camphor against the inroads of moths, and also such luxuries as sugar candy, red cayenne pepper, vinegar, tea and coffee. For what the Boers called coffee was often only roasted grain—mealies or wheat—sometimes even acorns. He traded them for the valuable skins of leopard, jackal, lynx, lion and wild-cat, for ivory—the teeth of both elephant and sea cow—for rhinoceros horn and whips, riems cut from the skins of rhino, hippo, giraffe or buffalo. He traded for beeswax, for fragrant gums. Sometimes he got a little gold dust packed into vulture quills. This he tested with acid, for the Kaffirs had learned to collect fool's gold—iron pyrites to be found here and there on the rocks. It was amazing how quickly the Kaffirs became civilised and acquired the crooked tricks of the white man.

At the moment he was homeward bound to Cape Town, to see his father and mother and dispose of his trade goods, exchanging them for cash that would be reinvested in such things as were required in the North. He had come a few miles out of his way in order to deliver a letter to the farm Groenplaas in the district of Bredasdorp. It came from a widow on the frontier. She had asked him to deliver it to her sister, also a widow, who lived on this farm with her brother-in-law and her granddaughter. The writer of the letter, Magdalena Retief, was a woman of some renown, being the widow of the trek leader, Piet Retief, who with his party was slaughtered treacherously by Dingaan, the Zulu chief.

Retief had left the laager at Kerkenberg and crossed the Drakensberg with four wagons and fourteen men to visit the Kaffir chief, Dingaan, in the hopes of obtaining a grant of land from him on which they could all settle. Dingaan promised him the land if he could recover some cattle that had been stolen from him by Sikonyela. That was the beginning. Later he returned again with sixty-seven armed men and thirty mounted servants. His own small son, Piet, was with him. They took Dingaan the stolen cattle and arranged a sham battle for the entertainment of the Zulus. The Zulus then danced for them. An agreement was come to and the land between the Tugela and the Umzimvubu Rivers was ceded to the Boers. Since no weapons were allowed in the king's kraal, the guns were stacked beside two trees at the entrance. In the middle of the dance the Kaffirs fell upon the Boers at the king's command and beat them to death.

Solomon was a man who combined a good heart with an insatiable curiosity about people. He was always ready to go out of his way to meet new people who always became his friends and usually his customers. Everything you ordered from Sol you got, though it might be a year or more before he passed your way again. But he was a welcome man, a bearer of letters and verbal news, one who seemed to know every living man on the frontier and have trodden every path that tied farm to farm and kraal to kraal in a net of little trails. Solomon was a happy man. He was fond of his twenty donkeys and the life suited him. He thought he must be a throwback to some ancestors who had traded for tin in Britain, or gold in Sofola.

Leading his favourite, Salome, a black Catalonian donkey mare with a white nose, that was loaded with gunpowder— he felt that this was safer in his personal charge—with the others pattering on neat hoofs behind him and his boys bringing up the rear, Solomon Rosenberg climbed the hills and slid and slithered down into the valleys that confronted him. He was very interested in what was happening in the Cape Colony, in the leakage of its people into the emptiness beyond its borders. First it had been men alone—a few hunters, adventurers, renegades and failures. But now all that was changed. Respectable men, men of substance, were moving with their families, servants, flocks and herds.

The sun was overhead when he reached Groenplaas, where he was welcomed by an immense woman dressed in black who sat on the stoep, overflowing her throne-like chair. Arranged on either side of her against the wall were two sea-cow skulls and a dozen oxskulls, all much polished by use, to be used as seats. She was surrounded by plants in pots and jars. Ferns of various kinds, lilies and geraniums embowered her. She sat unmoving, like a great black spider embedded in the greenery, till he was within a yard of her.

Then she said: " Don't let those beasts eat my flowers." She reached behind her and produced an immense whip.

"*Pas op!* Look out, Salome!" Solomon pushed his favourite's inquisitive nose back. She had stretched her neck to sniff at a geranium.

" Salome! What a name for an ass, Meneer."

" Are you by any chance Mevrou Prinsloo, the relict of Groot Jan who was slain with his family on the border?"

" I am. And what do you want with me?"

" I bring a letter from your sister, the Widow Retief."

" That must be the reply to the one I wrote her two years ago. She is well?" she asked.

" She lives," Solomon said, " but is swollen with dropsy."

" That is possible," Tante Maria said. " She was always fat."

Fat, Solomon thought. This mountain calling the other fat. Why he doubted if—and he was a good judge of weight —there was a difference of five pounds between them. " I am on my way south," he said. " To Kaapstad, and will buy cattle if you have any slaughter stock for sale."

" You must ask Oom Willem. I have no place here. Just a roof over my head, but no rights, no say, about anything. That is the fate of a widow woman. So I sit here and think. Sometimes I see visions. I have the gift." She held out her hand. " Give me the letter. Unload your donkeys and send them out to graze. I will make you coffee and warm up some food. You will stay the night," she said, " and show us your goods. Perhaps you have some India muslin for my granddaughter. Magtig," she said, " Salome—the donkey that danced before Herod." She began to quiver with laughter.

Leaving her, a black-clad jelly shaking in her bower, shaking even the fern-pots so that their fronds waved about her,

Solomon turned Salome away and shouted to the boys, telling them to off-saddle and bring the packs on to the stoep. There he would make them into a heap, a bed on which he would sleep with his head on a pillow of gunpowder.

There was not much gunpowder left now but he never sold it all because often he came upon men in dire need of some. But, full or empty, he slept on the powder bags and led Salome, who loved him as much as if he had been an ass, himself. This was his joke—one that he often told against himself, for he was a humorous man and invented jokes to pass the time as he trekked about the country. Part of his love for Salome was due to the fact that, apart from being very pretty for a donkey and very dainty in her ways, she seemed to like the stories he told and indicated her pleasure by twitching her ears this way and that when he talked to her. As to the muslin and other goods, he had a little left. There was always a little of everything left and he would be glad to let it go cheap, even cheaper than usual, if the granddaughter was a mooi meisie. He had a weakness for pretty girls. He also liked flowers, sunsets and other beautiful things.

Tante Maria decided to save the letter till later. She had waited so long that to wait a little longer would make no difference. To-night when they were all assembled at the table for prayers would be the best time. Then Cina could read it aloud. She had good eyes and read well. At her age and with so little practice, Tante Maria had got out of reading script. The Bible she read easily but knew much of it almost by heart. Of course she could have asked the smous to read it to her, pleading her eyes, but he would have sold her a pair of spectacles, and then her secret would be out. No, the best thing was to wait for Cina. To say she would read it aloud. This would please Oom Willem who was always proud when he could show her off as if she was his own granddaughter instead of great-niece, and impress Solomon Rosenberg, the smous, who could then spread the tale of her erudition far and wide on his journeys. There were not so many girls who could read at all, much less read script. She certainly hoped Cina could still read script and had not forgotten.

Tante Maria Prinsloo sank back in her chair among the foliage of her plants. Everything that needed to be done today was done. The setting hens had been seen to, the butter made, the bread baked. The girls were dishing up food for the smous who was no doubt pinching those parts of their anatomy that they offered to his fingers, for this was the way of men, all men, till their dotage and even beyond it. Sometimes she even wondered about Oom Willem, a man of sixty. Why, if I had not been his sister-in-law, she thought, he might even have wished to wed me. But a man could not marry his deceased brother's wife. Only this had saved her from this lecherous and domineering old man who, because he put a roof over her head and food into her belly, behaved as if he was God. Or, if not God, one of the prophets. Moses, Abraham, St. John the Baptist. Now she became angry with the smous for putting such thoughts into her head with his donkey called Salome.

For Francina it had been a day of excitement. First the Beyers brothers riding out with their guns as if they were going on commando. Then their news. Their talk with Oupa. The way he had spoken of his youth, of the North, of the wonders he had seen and the dangers he had survived. How dangerous he made it all seem! How utterly desirable and romantic it would have been if he had been willing to go! Though he had refused, she knew that he had been moved. That his heart was in the trek and that only common sense held him back. She knew because she was a woman, because she had seen that look in his blue eyes as if he stared into the infinite distances of Africa. And from the way, later, when she said good night to him, he had stood holding his gun with its barrel glinting in the candle-light. Adventure was not dead in him, old as he was. And was he too old? He still rode and shot as well as ever. And then on top of all this there was the Boer bull pup. She had always wanted one. And now the arrival of a smous with a letter, with news of the great world beyond the mountains that hemmed them in, and with dress material and other wonders—buttons, combs, town-made shoes and even corsets in his packs. How she longed to wear a corset! The symbol of full womanhood.

She watched the smous's boys herding the hobbled donkeys. She saw them pile the packs and saddles on the stoep. Above her an aasvoel swept in wide circles. How wonderful it would be to fly like a bird, to circle like a vulture or an eagle, to be free, to go untrammelled. Wonderful to be a man like the Beyers boys, to be able to travel and see the world.

She saw the smous looking at her. He came toward her, a small, neat, dark-haired man, very sunburned, with black, friendly, snapping eyes.

" A mooi meisie, I see," he said. " I am Solomon Rosen-berg, a Jewish merchant whose packs contain many pretty things that a pretty girl could use. Lace handkerchiefs and perfume. Wicked tempting things. Silks, muslins, poplins."

" You think I am pretty, Meneer Rosenberg?"

He looked at her carefully. He thought, if she was properly washed and dressed and her hair combed she would be beautiful.

" In Kaapstad you would not have to ask me," he said: " You would know."

" How would I know?"

"Every man would have told you. Have you not looked in your mirror?"

"I have no mirror. A mirror is a vanity."

He came close to her. "We will have a secret. I will give you a small mirror. You can keep it hidden."

"Oh," she said, "then I shall really see myself. I have only seen myself reflected in the water or in a shining pot, but such images are not clear."

"You are a pretty young meisie," Solomon said. "When you are older you will be beautiful if you are not ruined by hard work, poor food and child bearing."

Francina blushed and looked down. "To say such things to me, meneer—a young girl."

"I apologise. They escaped me. I was just thinking of what would happen to you in the town. You would be a toast, my dear. Men would drink to you."

Francina laughed. "Do not apologise, Meneer. I like what you said. I like to be told I am beautiful. I like presents. I think I should like men if I knew any. Also other girls and little children to play with. Meneer, Groenplaas is a lovely place but I have only the birds of the air and the beasts of the field for my friends." The golden eyes filled with tears. They hung like crystal dewdrops in the corners of her eyes.

Solomon Rosenberg was enthralled. What a girl! What gifts he would give her! But it would have to be done when he was sure they would not be disturbed. He would watch her face when he unpacked his goods to see what excited her.

Oom Willem heard of the arrival of the smous from one of his herders who had had it from his child who had been told by his mother and brought the news into one of the outlying kraals with her father's lunch. The news was disturbing. So many visitors were disturbing. The four Beyers brothers yesterday and now this travelling Jew with his tales of the outside world. He had given up thinking of the world many years ago, with the death of his wife and children from smallpox, with the loss of his brother, Jan, and his brother's girl and her husband the savour had gone from his life. Only his stock and his grandniece were left to interest him. They were superimposed on the memories of his hunting adventures which the thought of his neighbours' trekking had revived, giving them a new vitality. It was as if a flower pressed in his great Bible had suddenly regained its shape, colour and perfume. More and more incidents were remembered. He had already begun the map, secretly, when the others slept. Last night when he had put his four-pounder away, he had sharpened a new quill and begun to plan the route the trek must take. How it came back to him! The rivers, the hills, the mountains. The great trees and boulders that were landmarks. The kopjes shaped like the head of a man or the breast of a woman, with small nipples on their rounded tops. Rocks balanced upon each other—sometimes three of them one above the other—arranged like toys by some giant hand.

He hoped the smous had a little powder and shot left, for he was short. He thought it would be nice to buy some clothing material for Cina. She could then occupy herself with some dressmaking. Perhaps that woman, his dead brother's wife, was right. He was turning her into a boy. And what a boy she would have made! It was strange to think that Maria, that old bag of suet incased in black bombasine, had once been almost as slim and sweet as Cina. That was the way she had been when he and Groot Jan had first met her, more than thirty years ago. Well, he would not like to see this child go that way, swell into a female barrel that spouted venom from her bung. And all because he did not make advances to her—his dead brother's widow

—as if such a thing was possible. Yet from the first she had tried to tempt him, tried to lead him into the sin of lust with her smiles and wriggles. Magtig, a sea-cow could smile and wriggle too. And now she hated him. Jeered at him. At me, he thought, me who house, feed and clothe her. Insinuating that I am finished, an old and impotent man. Well, she would see. If she was not careful, if she did not keep a civil tongue in her head, he would find himself a young wife and make new children—not because he wanted to but just to spite her, Maria, who by some accident of fate was the grandmother of his brother's granddaughter. A woman who could well have been taken instead of spared. But the ways of God were strange and wonderful. Perhaps she had been left to plague him like the fleas on the back of a dog. A great three-hundred-pound flea who might yet drive him into marriage with some stranger which, of course, might be God's reason for allowing her to survive.

The day's work was done now, the stock had been counted and their calves checked. He turned his horse homeward and left the lowing cows behind him. Their calves had been separated for the night and would only return to them when they were milked in the morning. The cows would not let down their milk without the calves and so while they sucked at one teat the milkers milked the others. It was a kind of race between a man and a calf, in which the honours were more or less evenly divided.

The smous remembered having met Willem Prinsloo in the past. They had mutual friends. Oom Willem knew many of the farms that he visited and the men talked as they ate a saddle of mutton served with rice, sweet potatoes and pumpkin—there were no other vegetables—and drank coffee.

Rosenberg said he had some fine coffee he would sell;

also sugar and some spices. Everything very cheap. It was
no good taking it back to Cape Town. He showed Oom
Willem some ivory he had bought—tusks that went from ten
to twenty pounds. The price was the same per pound and
he preferred smaller tusks. They were much easier to
transport on donkeys. The big tusks had to be carried by
men, he said, by slaves, which was why the two trades of
elephant hunting and slavery went hand in hand in the
Northeast. He spoke of the Arabs and half-caste Portuguese
slavers he had met, of the coffles of slaves he had seen carrying ivory, fastened neck to neck and whipped along by
brutal guards. He also showed them great, curved sea-cow
tushes that were carved by dentists into teeth—plumpers
that filled out the sunken cheeks of the toothless.

Francina waited on them, wide-eyed and open-mouthed.
She had never heard such talk before. When the women
had eaten, Tante Maria brooded in her great chair which
had been carried in from the stoep. Her letter was in her
hand.

At last prayers were said and a chapter of the Bible read.
Solomon Rosenberg had listened attentively and had
informed Francina when it was over that he had enjoyed it
all very much, for the Old Testament was the history of his
people. Something she had not known.

Now was Tante Maria's moment. She called: " Cina . . .
Cina . . . take this letter to the light. Sit by the table and
read it to us. Show us how well you can read." She folded
her hands on the mound of her belly and closed her eyes.

Francina broke the wafer of wax that held the sheet of
paper folded, and began to read:

" Dear sister,
　　At your request I shall write to you how many children
I have had and how many I still have. Of the late Jan

Greijling I had nine children. Three died in infancy, six I have brought to maturity. Of these, my Gertruidja was dead in childbirth, my second daughter, Maria, had palpitations . . ."

Tante Maria opened her eyes and said: " She was named for me. I remember her well. A beautiful child." She closed her eyes again and said: " Continue, Cina. You are reading very nicely."

". . . both were married," Francina continued, " and my son, Jan, was murdered by the Kaffirs. He and his late father had to lose their lives there in the interior and their bodies were left to the wild animals. And here again I had to give the bodies of my brave husband, Retief, my youngest son, Pieter, and my eldest son, Abraham Greijling, to the wild animals because of the savage Dingaan. Of Retief's children—two others died in infancy. Of Greijling's children, I still have Piet and Barend, and of Retief's Jacobus, François—his wife and children are also dead—Debora, Jacoba—her husband and children are also dead. So I have of my fifteen children, five still left alive."

Francina was weeping when she put the letter down. These were her unknown cousins and their little babies who were dead. So many dead. Oom Willem patted her back and fondled the mane of her hair as if she had been a frightened horse. Tremors shook her body.

" Mevrou Retief is a fine woman," Solomon Rosenberg said. " A brave Boer vrou."

" I always said she was a fool to marry those men," Tante Maria said. " Adventurous men who could come to no good end, for ever in Kaffirland and thinking they could trust the Zulus."

To Oom Willem the reading of the letter had brought back every story he had ever heard of danger on the frontier. He had tried to persuade his brother Jan to remain here with him. But he, too, had been too bold a man. Groenplaas had bored him. He turned on Tante Maria. " You insult the memory of your dead husband, my brother. The memory of your daughter and her husband. Heroes," he said. " The true voortrekkers, the first of them, who did not only live to hunt and trade but built homes. Men who drove the first plough furrows into that northern veld. And that is the only conquest that can endure," he shouted. "The conquest of the plough."

" You are mad, Willem," Maria shouted back. " What advantage is there in death? How does it help my sister that of fifteen carried in her womb ten are dead and five are quick?"

Solomon, taking advantage of the distraction, slipped a small flat package into Francina's hand. Then he went out of the door. No one saw him go. Ten minutes later he was asleep with his head on the pillow of gunpowder.

Inside, the old man and woman were still talking— arguing—but the girl had gone. He had peeped through the window to see. This was a night she would never forget. The night of the mirror. The beginning of that curious relationship which must always exist between a woman and her glass and only ends with death.

5

THE REDCOATS

CAPTAIN JOHN CEDRIC ROBINSON was in a temper. His normally red face was purple under the hot brass of his helmet, his scarlet tunic black with sweat under the arms and on his back. The whole thing was a disgrace. Here he was riding over the African veld with a half-baked cornet of horse for company and followed by two batmen, a farrier corporal and a coloured sergeant of the Cape Mounted Rifles. That was all that had been allowed him. He had wanted to bring at least a troop with their lances and pennons flying. That was what he liked—to ride with the jingle and rattle of troopers behind him. He wanted people to say: " There goes Captain Jack Robinson with his dragoons. One of the smartest soldiers in the service."

It was said of him that he had been the original Jack Robinson. The " before you can say Jack Robinson " the job was done. He never denied it. He even tried to live up to it and so was hated by the men he drove as a martinet, and despised by his brother officers who thought his efficiency contemptible and ungentlemanly. He had money, he had a fine appearance. Why, then, did he not leave the soldiering to the non-commissioned officers and content himself with hunting, gambling and whoring like every other respectable cavalry officer? Instead, he behaved like the officers of the East India Company—professionals, mercenaries, who studied strategy and tactics, thus bringing disgrace upon the regiment whose officers were very jealous of their outstanding reputation for those vices which were the science of gentility. Of course, in battle, officers had to ride in front of their men in that British fox-hunting method of charging, and were expected to die as they had lived, like gentlemen. But anything else, any interest in discipline, in men, in horses or equipment, was regarded as a sign of ill-breeding and an attempt to obtain promotion through efficiency rather than purchase or influence.

Captain Robinson's only consolation was that this adventure would bring him even closer to the governor, who was already his friend. And it had all happened so simply. Once again his intelligence and quickness had borne fruit.

Three weeks ago, when he had been looking at the last remounts that had just come from upcountry, he had been struck by something. Three of the horses, two greys and a strawberry roan, had been outstanding, taller than the others by almost a hand and differently topped. He'd thought, I've seen them before. But he knew this to be impossible. For an hour he had watched them. Then it had come to him. He had them caught and led by three mounted troopers to Government House, where he had audience with Sir Benjamin d'Urban.

The governor would see no one without an appointment. Robinson pushed past the A.D.C. and made his way upstairs. Holloway, another officer of the staff, asked him his business.

" It's urgent," he said. " If His Excellency does not see me, if you turn me back, you'll hear about it when everything comes out."

" You mean that? You mean he will not mind being disturbed?"

" Quite the contrary, Holloway," Robinson said. " His

Lordship will be delighted and I'll bet you a case of port that within fifteen minutes Sir Benjamin comes out of that door with me."

"Done, my boy. I could do with some port. Good stuff mind you. No slops or rubbish!"

"The best!"

"Then come on." Holloway flung open the door. "Captain Robinson, your Excellency. He says it's urgent."

"Can't I have half an hour without some interruption? What is it, Robinson? What's so urgent?"

Robinson brought his spurred heels together with a click and saluted. "It's Lord Denton's grey, sir," he said.

"Denton's grey. You mean you've found him?"

This was a horse the previous governor, Lord Charles Somerset, had imported at great expense and which had been stolen by a deserter. There was a whole file about the matter. He would be glad if it could be cleared up.

"No sir."

"Then what's all this about?"

"His get, sir. I've got three of his get in the yard for your Lordship to see. They came with our last draft of remounts from the interior."

"Then he's there? Is that what you mean?"

"If these are his colts, and I think your Excellency will recognise the stamp, then he's there. Or was there, at stud to get them."

Sir Benjamin jumped up. Holloway opened the door. As Robinson followed the governor, he turned back and said: "Remember—no slops, no rubbish."

Robinson followed the governor into the upper hall and down the stair. The troopers were leading the remounts up and down.

Captain Robinson said: "What does your Excellency think of them?"

" Think? I don't think. I know! They're by an English blood horse all right. You're quick, my boy, very quick, to have spotted them."

" Have I your permission, sir, to go after him? To take some men and see if I can get him back? I know where these horses came from. And if he's still alive he'll be there. If he can get colts like that on common mares he'd get some real beauties with blood stock."

" Go? Certainly you can go. Come back and I'll give you a note to your colonel. I will also recommend you very highly for your perspicacity and initiative. That's what we need. Men who see things, particularly in the cavalry of the line. The eyes of the army. But by God, sir, unless it's a girl they can lay or a beast they can hunt, they all seem to be blind."

Robinson followed the governor back upstairs and stood waiting by the desk as he wrote the note to his colonel and sanded it. He saluted and turned away. The first move was completed. Everything had gone according to plan.

But the horse had not been the whole thing. The recovery of the governor's stolen blood stallion could lead to advancement but, added to this was a private feud, a vengeance. By tracing the horse he was also tracing Trooper Harry Bates of the Tenth Dragoons. It was he who had stolen the horse and disappeared with him three weeks after he had been flogged. By God, he should have been strung up for what he had done. Because Bates, a common soldier, had done something that he had been unable to do himself.

It was incredible, quite unbelievable, that a woman—a girl really—should have preferred a common soldier's attentions. Of course the story was that he had forced himself upon her because if it had been generally known that she had sought him out every day for weeks—and this while he had been paying her court—the scandal would even have reached London. So Trooper Bates had been tried by court-martial for rape and condemned to be hanged. Then, by some miscarriage of justice, the sentence had been commuted and changed to a flogging—not the usual forty less one, but sixty—with the cat. With a lesser man this might have been fatal, but Bates had the resistance of an animal. He had not died. He could see him now, fastened by the wrists and ankles to the wheel of a gun carriage. In his mind he could hear the whistle of the cat, the whipping thud of it on the bare flesh of Bates's back. He could see the blood running down and coagulating above the trousers where they were held up by the man's belt. He had wished he could seize the cat and lay it on himself. That would have taught him something.

The Honourable Amelia Fenthorn of Houghton Park, Surrey, was in Africa visiting her brother, Lord Francis Benting, who commanded the 200th Foot. To this day, even knowing it to be true, he could not bring himself to believe that Amelia, dark-skinned, fiery, with a Spanish pride that came from her mother, had not only permitted liberties but had sought intimacies from this coarse soldier who stank of sweat, beer and the stables, that he had lain with her among the bundles of hay in a disused loosebox. And all the while she had acted so high and mighty with him, sending him off with flashing eyes if he laid so much as a hand on her. Utterly shameless, she had remained at the Cape. Why should she go? She had done nothing. To run home to England would imply fear, would suggest guilt and the inference that she had been in some way to blame. She was not the first girl who had been taken advantage of in a stable, and she would not be the last. The fact that she was a lady, the daughter of Lord Benting, made the story sound even more improbable and much easier to laugh off, which

she did with a charming blush, than if she had been a
governess or some poor relative. brought out to the colonies
in the hope of finding a husband. Amelia could take her
pick and everyone knew it, which made this escapade more
inexplicable than ever.

Robinson knew that if he found the horse he would see
more of Amelia, because he would then be asked to every
function at Government House. He still wanted her and
pretended to believe her when she said that nothing had
happened, that the man had seized her arm, drawn her into
the loosebox and that she had screamed at once and been
rescued from the clutches of the lecherous soldier who had
suffered for his temerity. She looked down, blushing as she
spoke of it, her long, dark lashes lying on the roses of her
cheeks. Then she had looked up at him, her brown eyes
limpid as summer pools. " You believe me, don't you,
Jack?"

" Of course, of course," he'd said.

But he'd get her yet. She sent him mad and the knowledge
that Bates had known her first infuriated him so that his
always doubtful love had turned to lust, jealousy, and the
desire to both possess and humiliate this proud and capricious
girl. Interwoven with these emotions which rocked him was
an insensate hate for Harry Bates who had partaken of this
fruit that still remained forbidden to him.

One day he would get him and he would pay. Having
traced the grey to the Bredasdorp mountains, he was sure
that Bates had joined one of the roving bands of brigands who
lived in the vicinity, moving from Hangklip to the Winter-
berg. If he had had a troop with him it had been his inten-
tion to smash the band and capture Harry Bates. This time
he would be hanged for horse stealing and desertion, but
he'd flog him first. Flog him personally. Flog him to death.

Why not? Who would know? Who would tell? Who would care? He licked his sun- and wind-burned lips in anticipation as if he already held the renegade prisoner. Yes, that's what I should have done if I'd had my squadron with me, he thought. The possibility of failure did not occur to him. But since he had been allowed only this handful of men he'd made another plan and was offering a reward of one hundred pounds, dead or alive, for Trooper Harry Bates—a reward of his own money, and his man carried printed hand-bills to that effect in his valise which would be distributed when they reached the district.

Now, after four days of riding, they must be approaching their destination. Prinsloo's farm could not be far away. The first day they had slept comfortably enough at Somerset West. Then they had climbed the Hottentots' Holland Mountains and camped by the Palmiet River. Stanford had been the next stop and now they were on what the Cape Mounted Rifles sergeant, who had been sent to interpret, said was the last lap.

To left of the horsemen was a low range of hills. To their right were sand dunes and the sea. They rode along a rough track bordered by pink-flowered protea bushes which at times closed over their heads. There were patches of evergreen forest where ancient trees climbed up into the mountain kloofs, filling them with a dense canopy of shiny leaves. Where there was water near the surface, there were reeds and arum lilies by the hundred, their white kid chalices open to the swarming insects. There were other flowers and flowering trees. There were brilliant sugar birds sipping the nectar of the wild Cape honeysuckle.

But Captain Robinson had no eye for beauty unless it was that of a woman or a horse. For him a thing was beautiful only if it could be touched, held, caressed and also possessed, owned and punished. His mind now was on Willem Prins-loo's farm, on the governor's grey stallion, on Harry Bates, the fornicating thief and deserter, and on Amelia, who was now no doubt busy with some new intrigue.

It was difficult for him to understand his colonel's view. Colonel the Honourable Robert Aiken had not been sympathetic. He had refused him even a troop. He had seen through him.

" A troop, Jack, to bring back a horse?"

" There might be trouble, sir. Those farmers up there don't like us much."

" No danger of trouble unless you make it. But I know what you're up to. You think that Bates may be up there, that he may have joined up with a band of robbers and renegades—after all, what else could he do?—and you want to get him. For desertion and horse stealing. This time it would be death. I couldn't save him again, could I?"

" So it was you, sir." He had never been able to find out who had pleaded for clemency with the governor.

" Bates was a good boy, Jack, one of the best. I had my eye on him for troop sergeant. Smart, quick, a good man with his weapons, and one of the best horsemen and horse masters in the regiment. That was why we seconded him to Government House as Lord Charles's orderly, and put him in charge of the grey." The colonel looked at him queerly. He had said, " Yes sir," wondering what all this nonsense was leading to.

" Do you know what was wrong with Bates, Jack?"

" No sir, except that he was a bad 'un. That he went wrong and paid for it and bolted like a cowardly dog and thief with the most valuable horse in the colony."

" No, Jack," the colonel said. " That was not the reason. He was too good-looking. Too full of life. And that high-class whore . . ."

" Sir!" Robinson said, " you are my colonel but I cannot permit . . ."

" Don't be a fool, Jack. I know you want her but I also know a hell of a lot of men who've had her. Do you think because a girl's the daughter of an earl she must be good? Leave her alone, Jack, and leave Harry alone. You hate him because he's the only one of her lovers who's helpless and you want to take out your revenge on him. But what chance had he alone in a loosebox with her hands on him? A woman like that, a society beauty in her rustling silks, powdered and perfumed? What chance had a poor hot boy with a girl like that? Pushing herself on to him, rubbing against him like a cat . . ."

" He raped her," Robinson said.

" Rape? With a hundred people within call? He took what she offered, what she had given him time and time again; it was only rape when someone came in."

But it was all a lie. It wasn't at all the way the colonel saw it. It was rape. It was desertion. It was horse theft. He wanted no revenge—only justice—only the maintenance of the regiment's discipline. Well, if he could not catch him one way he might another. There were more ways of killing a cat than choking it with butter. He had had notices printed. He was going to distribute them. They offered a hundred pounds reward for the capture of Harry Bates, horse thief and deserter from the Tenth Dragoons. It was his own money, and would be well spent if it was ever claimed.

That would show her—the beautiful, maddening bitch —what happened to men who . . . But of course it didn't and it couldn't. He knew some of the other men, officers like himself. He would have challenged them except that he had no rights, nor could he have even if he had had them, because of the scandal and the ruin of her good name. Sometimes it seemed to him that a well-born woman was free to sleep with whom she wished because a man defending the honour she held so lightly would bring dishonour both upon her and himself. If he had to duel her lovers it had to be for some other trumped up reason.

And she had jeered at him. Before he left on the " reconnaissance " as it was described in the *Gazette*. She had laughed in his face.

" I shall miss you, Jack," she said. " I was just beginning to find you very attractive. You should have realised that I would find a man who would have another man whipped almost to death because he touched my arm most interesting. And he stood it so well, poor boy, and didn't die after all. Sometimes I wonder if he thought it was worth it. Just those few minutes—and then that. But of course there were the other uninterrupted times . . ."

" You mean he did—that there were other times—that you lied?"

" Do you think I'm mad, Jack? A sweet boy, a hot lover, but a groom. A horse boy in uniform. I think that was what excited me. The smell of his sweat and horse, and of course he was a very good lover—a kind of redheaded Greek god. Don't you think so, Jack?"

She had said *and he stood it so well*. He had been flogged in the castle yard. Perhaps she had seen it—had watched.

" You saw him flogged?"

" Of course. I watched from my maid's room. She was with me. We both went nearly mad with excitement."

With one part of his mind he knew all this, knew what she said was true. That she was cruel, a bitch, a whore, a Circe who delighted in turning men into swine for her own delectation, for it was swine that she loved—men driven to madness by her teasing. He knew the names of some of the men with whom she had slept. He guessed at others. But at the same time he refused to believe any of it. It was untrue, impossible. Why, if she was like that, did she refuse him? He was more personable than most. That she refused him proved her virtue, for no woman had ever refused his attentions before.

He jerked up his horse's head. They must hurry. He must get back to her. By God, he thought, if I could get her alone in a loosebox . . . What she needed was a whipping herself to teach her who was master.

From what the Cape rifleman said they were not far away now. They would camp and push on early in the morning, so that if they found the horse, and he was sure he was there, they would be well on their way home before dark. He had had some experience of these Boers. They were determined men who resented interference, and it might be as well to get clear of the place as soon as possible.

6

THE ESCAPE

FRANCINA LOOKED into the mirror as soon as she had closed and bolted the door of her room. The light was not satisfactory no matter how she moved the candle. At one point, as she was trying to get a closer look at her eyes, she set a few strands of her hair alight. The bedroom now smelled like the back stoep when a chicken was being singed. After this adventure Francina decided to wait till daylight, and wrapping the mirror in a cloth, put it under her pillow. The sooner she slept the sooner morning would come. So she slept, too tired even to dream.

Up with the dawn's first glimmer, Francina sat holding her mirror, seeing herself more clearly every minute, seeing her golden-brown eyes, her tawny hair, the colour of a lion's name, her creamy face and red lips, the teeth white as mealie pips when she smiled at herself. The girl she looked at, whose eyes searched hers, smiled back. She had a friend at last. A confidante, someone who would understand her. Francina had a friend—herself.

From her window she could see the peddler opening up his packs. His box of wonders, of things made in distant towns and transported over the sea for sale in Africa. Often when she rode down to the beach and looked at the rollers coming in from the south, she thought about other lands and their peoples, of other races. Often in the winter storms strange things were washed up on the beach—kegs, oddly shaped boxes, planks and baulks from smashed bulkheads, each with a story if one only knew it. Most of the doors and beams of the farm were flotsam—the fruit of some disaster collected on the strand.

The longest journey Francina had ever made was the two hundred miles her grandmother had carried her after the massacre of her parents. She remembered little of it except the feel of the horse. The farthest she had been and remembered, therefore, was thirty miles, to Bredasdorp. A fine place with a big church, more than a hundred houses all with gardens and fruit trees, and the people all beautifully dressed, walking about as if every day was Sunday. She had been there twice and it remained in her mind as the very core and centre of the world. Its heart, as it were.

She combed her hair quickly, tied it with a voorslag—a whiplash—and ran out through the big living-room on to the stoep, where Meneer Rosenberg was occupied sorting out his goods.

He smiled at her.

He was nice. He was not old. Not so old, that is, and she liked his eyes.

He looked round quickly to see that they were alone, leaned towards her and said, " You saw?"

" Saw what, Meneer?"

" The girl—the pretty girl?"

Now she was bewildered and looked about her. Where was there a pretty girl? What did he mean?

" In the glass," he said, and began to laugh, slapping his thighs and holding his sides.

She laughed too. The dogs ran up barking. The tame rams followed the dogs, their playmates. A tame goose hissed at her feet.

" I have other things for you," the smous said. " Small gifts of no value, but things that will amuse you. A necklace of beads that resemble pearls. Two bracelets. A silken scarf, a small workbox."

" Oh!" Francina said, " those are all vanities. I am not allowed such things."

" Take them," he said. " Times will change. You will grow, you will marry, I should like you to remember me as your friend—to be able to think as I trek about the veld that there is a pretty girl at Groenplaas who thinks well of me and remembers me with affection. Ja," he said, " I miss that. Sweetness, affection, love. These things are not for a wandering Jew."

" Then why do you wander?" Francina asked.

" I wish I knew, my pretty maid. It is my heart that calls me to the distant hills, my feet that carry me. I think it is in my blood. I think that for thousands of years my people have traded in far places. That this is the price one may have to pay for belonging to such an ancient race."

" Is it true, as some say, Meneer," Francina asked, " that our Lord Jesus was a Jew?"

" Is it true," he said.

" It is an interesting thought. Ja," she said, " that you may be of the blood of Our Lord. That you are also one of the chosen people as we are."

With the Boers there was some confusion of mind about this chosen-race business. They lived by the Old Testament. It was their inspiration but they despised the Jews.

She supposed that the Lord Jesus might have looked a little like this man. She stared at him with new respect. Her thoughts were interrupted by one of the boys from an outlying kraal galloping into the yard on a horse that was white with sweat, shouting, " Baas, baas, the Rooibaadjies come—the Redcoats are here!"

As if he had been expecting the news, her great-uncle burst out of the house like a charging bull.

"How many?" he cried. "How many are coming?"

"A thousand, baas, a regiment. The valley was full of them—a sea of scarlet and shining steel. They come to destroy us."

"We will resist. Ring the big bell. Get me the guns. Arm the men. Smous, bring out your powder and shot. I will pay any price you ask."

A few minutes later some ten coloured boys and men were being handed out arms and ammunition.

Willem Prinsloo now stood on the stoep, with his elephant gun over his arm, surrounded by his servants. The women were behind him. Tante Maria was ensconced in her ferny bower, also with a gun across her knees. Francina, wide-eyed as a buck, with Sara and Eva clinging to her, crying out that they would sooner die than be raped but that they did not want to die.

Solomon Rosenberg tried to calm Oom Willem. "This is nothing," he said. "You will see. A false alarm. There is no war, you have no cause for alarm."

"Before God, I am not alarmed. I am merely ready to resist. And how can the report be false? Either a man sees Redcoats or he does not. Are Redcoats something a man invents when he is cooking his breakfast over a fire in the veld? Andries is a good boy, a reliable herder."

"I saw them, baas," Andries said. "Ja," he said, waving his gun, "I saw them by the hundred, by the thousand. They were like sand upon the seashore." His gun went off. Fortunately it was pointed at the roof of the stoep.

"Be careful, you fool," Oom Willem said. "And reload. Save your shots for the rooineks."

Solomon shrugged his shoulders, sat on one of his packs and stroked Salome's white muzzle. These Boers were simple people who took things very literally. It was probable that the boy who had brought the news had seen some English soldiers, a patrol of some kind. He had no seen thousands. But any story of Redcoats was enough to bring this reaction at once in almost any part of the back country.

So they sat and waited, grouped like a curious frieze, a set piece about the stoep of the farmhouse. Oom Willem wore a smooth brown corduroy jacket, blue moleskin trousers, a white shirt, a black tie and waistcoat and a furry grey bell-shaped tophat. The servants were in leather held up by belts or suspenders, over their ragged shirts. Only Klaas wore a jacket. It was made of leather, and an old wide-brimmed straw hat with a green lining.

Then the English came into view.

Oom Willem saw them first, the glint of light from a brass helmet and then the red of their tunics.

" They come," he shouted, and stepped out into the open to meet them. " You will cover me," he said. He looked back. " Be careful, Andries. I said cover me. I do not wish to be shot in the back."

The English were nearer now. Two officers rode in front. Behind them came four men riding stirrup to stirrup. Three white men in scarlet and one coloured sergeant in green.

Oom Willem called Francina. " Come and stand beside me," he said. " You are the daughter of the house. Listen to what they say but do not let them know you understand their tongue. They have brought a man from the Cape Rifles to translate. But magtig, that Andries gave me a fright. Englishmen in hundreds, he said." He laughed grimly. " We can deal with this handful unless there are more behind them."

To Captain Jack Robinson the Boer group presented a curious spectacle. In front of the house in the open yard stood an enormous man, white-haired, with blazing blue eyes and an elephant gun in his hands. Beside him was a slim, girlish-looking boy. Only when he got nearer did he see it was a girl in boy's clothes—a girl who, in a country-bumpkin way, was quite beautiful. Two large dogs and two fat-tailed rams stood near them, watching him approach. A goose sat at the girl's feet, pecking at the odd blades of grass that grew near. Behind them was the house, thatched with reeds, long and low, whitewashed, surrounded by kraals and outbuildings. On the stoep were assembled a number of coloured servants, all with guns in their hands, who stared coldly at him—and a great woman dressed in black among the greenery of her house plants, also with a gun across her knees, whose looks were really malevolent—her eyes dark-hooded like those of a snake about to strike. She awaited his approach impassively. He was glad he had come early. This was no place to spend the night. Overhead a flock of white pigeons wheeled, glistening in the sun.

The only person who seemed to offer any welcome was the Jewish peddler who came to his horse's side, removed his hat, bowed, and said in English, " And what can we do here for your Lordship?"

" Tell them I want to come in. I have business to discuss."

He translated.

" I have no business to discuss," Oom Willem said. " Let them bait their horses and rest them. I will give them food because hospitality is our custom, and then let them go forward or return whence they came."

Again the smous interpreted and then, not wishing to become involved as a middle man in a quarrel, he excused himself. He said, " I think your Lordship has brought his own official interpreter, so I will leave you and go about my manifold affairs. Your Lordship has no idea of the problems that confront a peddler. There are sick donkeys to doctor, packs to mend, accounts to balance. Endless," he said, waving his hands. "It is endless, so that although all men wish to be themselves I have at times wondered if it was not better to be an English lord and ride about in a brass hat than a Jewish peddler trekking over the veld with his donkeys." He swept the ground with his hat. "The choice in my mind is not yet fully resolved. The appearance of your Lordship has reopened the matter and I will meditate upon it while I perform my humble but interesting tasks." He winked at Francina, and dragging Salome behind him, went off towards the veld where his boys were grazing the other donkeys. Salome was more a friend than a donkey and they were seldom parted. She got special food and treatment, a reward for her love of him and the risks she took as his gunpowder donkey.

Robinson looked after him angrily. A bloody Jew who, now that he had gone, he suddenly realised had been pulling his leg. "Sergeant Coetzee," he said, "come here."

"Sir?" the coloured sergeant said, and rode forward.

"Tell these people that there is nothing wrong. This is just a reconnaissance. I am just making certain inquiries."

For a moment Willem Prinsloo and the English captain stared at each other. Then Prinsloo said: "Very good. Tie your horses."

To his people he said: "Put up your guns. Fire them off." He set the example himself, pointing his four-pounder to the sky and pulling the trigger.

This set the captain's big black charger up on his hind legs, nearly unseating him. The other horses also reared and plunged. The ensign fell off as the other guns were discharged in a ragged volley.

"What the hell are you doing?" Robinson shouted.

"What does he say?" Oom Willem asked the sergeant. He did not have to know English to understand the gist of the remark, as he picked up the ensign.

" The officer asked what was Meneer Prinsloo doing? "
the sergeant said.

" Magtig, man, we were unloading. How else does one
unload? Does the rooinek want to sit about with a dozen
loaded guns in the parlour? Tell him to dismount and come
in." Oom Willem turned and led the way. " Coffee!" he
shouted. " Coffee and food for these Englishmen."

Feed them—ja, sure she must, but it should not be good
food. Mutton stewed in sheep's-tail fat and a soup of boiled
wheat and mealies. Food for the servants and the dogs was
good enough for the Redcoats. Too good for them indeed.
Too good for murderers and assassins.

Tante Maria, who had not fired off her gun with the
others, now decided to do so, which frightened everyone, as
she omitted to point it upward.

" Coffee," she said. " Ja, I will make coffee, but it goes
against the grain. It is true that we are commanded to turn
the other cheek, to suffer little children and aid those in
distress. But there is no mention of the English in the Book
unless they could be the Philistines whom we should smite
with the jawbone of an ass." Her laughter now shook her
so that she could hardly stand. She put out her hand and
grasped Captain Robinson's arm to steady herself in a grip
that made him flinch. With her other hand she pointed to
the donkeys grazing on the veld. " There they are," she said,
" twenty jawbones. But they are all in use." Recovering,
her expression changed again and she shot the English
officers a look of hatred as she waddled off into the house,
closely followed by Francina, the dogs and rams.

Tante Maria turned on the girl and said: " Get them out!
Are not the English vermin enough to have in the house?
Must it also be a dog kennel and a sheep kraal?"

Francina chased out the animals.

The officers and coloured sergeant came in. The troopers

tied their horses to the rings in the wall. The men now all sat at the table, their spurs clinking and their sabres rattling as they dragged them on the floor.

Captain Robinson removed his plumed helmet. Ensign Hartley followed suit. The sergeant alone stood, cap on head, waiting for orders.

Captain Robinson pointed to a chair, said: " Sit down, Sergeant," and looked round the room.

What a place! What barbarians! Mealie cobs in pairs and bundles of tobacco leaves hung from nails in the rafters. The half-tanned skins of beasts lay on the floor. The room buzzed with flies that a half-naked coloured child kept on the wing by waving a whisk of horsetail fastened to a stick. Above his head swallows darted in and out of the clay tube that led to their nest—a ball-shaped structure wedged into a corner. They came through a smallish hole that was meant to be a window in the wall. There were other similar holes, only one of which was glazed.

Francina came in with cups. She was followed by Sara with the coffee, sugar and milk on a tray. As Francina poured out the coffee, the English captain pressed against her. She moved away from him. His body had been hot against hers, hard, with a strange smell of soap and perfume mixed with that of sweat, scarlet cloth and leather. She was watching Oupa. She knew what was in his mind. He was thinking: all these people. There was no peace in the land any longer. One day four Beyers brothers, the next the smous and now, before he has even left, these verdompde soldiers—six of them—strangers and alien in every way.

" Well," he said, " what is it you want?"

The officer said: " First, I must introduce myself." He stood up, bowed and said, " I am Captain John Cedric Robinson of the King's Dragoons. This," he pointed to the ensign who rose at once, " is Mr. Hartley." The ensign bowed. They both sat down, their spurs clinking.

Oom Willem said: " I am Willem Prinsloo of Groenplaas, known to all men as a breeder of fine horses and cattle."

" That is why we are here," the captain said, speaking through his interpreter.

" To buy stock? Cattle? Horses?"

" No, we have some of your horses. Remounts you sold to a dealer who sold them to us. We traced them back to you. Your brand," he said, " is a double *O*, is it not?"

" Ja, that is my brand."

" Well," the captain said, " there is a man we want. We think he came this way."

" Why do you want him, Meneer Captain? And what has my brand to do with him?"

" He's a deserter, a rapist and horse thief. That is why we want him."

" He stole a horse?"

" Yes, a grey horse, five years ago. That is how we traced him. We bought some of that horse's get—some of his sons. They bore your brand."

" That is most remarkable," Oom Willem said.

Francina felt herself turn pale. She held on to the table. Now it was she who pressed into the captain. Anything to distract him, to hold him while she made a plan. It was Bloubooi they had come for. Her horse. Her life. She said in the Taal language to the sergeant, " About the man? What will they do to him?" She saw him again in her mind—red-haired, so gay, so debonair, on the great grey horse.

" Hang him," the captain said. He had understood the gist of her question. " We'll hang him. And if we don't get him to-day it will be to-morrow." He slapped a printed notice on the table.

£100 reward for Trooper Harry Bates
Deserter of the Tenth Dragoons
Age 26, Height 6 ft. 1 in., Weight 180 lbs.
Grey eyes, red hair. Back scarred by flogging.
Wanted for rape, horse theft, desertion,
and possible murder

CAPTAIN J. C. ROBINSON
King's 10th Dragoons

" Someone will betray him," he said. " If the reward is big enough there is always someone to betray. Judas is a common name—the name of almost every man, given the right conditions."

The plan had come into Francina's mind. She turned to the captain, looking down into his face. She made her golden eyes wide and soft. She half opened her mouth, showing her teeth in a smile and ran her tongue tip over her lips to moisten them. Those were the expressions she had practised before her mirror this morning, only a few hours back. She had copied them from the looks she had seen Sara and Eva give to men when they thought they were not observed.

The captain's face flushed, he smiled back at her and touched her wrist with his hand. She flounced away from him, flinging up her skirt as she turned. She went to the wall cupboard and brought out glasses, setting one before each man. Then she poured the white peach brandy, giving it first to the captain and leaning over him so that he could peer down into her breast.

She was quite surprised at what she knew instinctively about men, and how naturally it all came. Then she slipped away from him with the bottle hidden under her arm. Swinging her croup, she went into the kitchen and called the girls.

"Sara! Eva!"

They came quickly, for they had been watching everything.

"The men," Francina said. "The men outside with the horses. You must get them away. Take glasses. Show them the brandy. Flirt with them—anything—but get them away, all of them. Get them into the storeroom."

"Anything?" Eva asked. She was the prettier of the two. Her eyes became big and black. She shook out her long hair from the purple doek that held it.

"Ja, anything," Francina said.

The girls ran out with the brandy and glasses, laughing at each other.

Francina went out, too, but turned to the left instead of the right, going round the house the opposite way and standing where she could see the horses and the men beside them.

She saw Eva waving the bottle. Sara danced forward, raising her skirts higher and higher, and then ran back looking over her shoulder.

This was too much for the soldiers. For a moment they hesitated, then they followed the girls.

Now she was safe. Those two could deal with three men, even without brandy. She ran along the front of the house, creeping on her hands and knees past the half door of the voorkamer where she could hear the men talking. Reaching the troopers' horses, she untied the reins and left them running free through the middle of each ring. The chargers, accustomed to being tied, all stood resting, half asleep on three legs. Francina now made for the horse kraal. Because of the excitement of the smous's goods spread out in the yard and the news of the English, the horses had not been let out. She went in, called Bloubooi, mounted him and galloped him round the kraal, forcing the others—the mares and colts—to mill about with excitement. Then she opened the gate, leaning over the grey's neck. Out they went, streaming after the stallion that she was urging with heels and hand past the front of the house. As they swept by, the troop horses reared, pulled their reins free and joined the stampede.

A moment later there was not a horse on Groenplaas. Behind her, as she lay flat along her horse's neck, hidden in the cloud of dust, tossing tails and manes, Francina heard the English captain shouting. At the heels of the last horse her dogs ran, barking with excitement.

7

THE PLAN

CAPTAIN ROBINSON had his mouth open to speak as the horses stampeded. His mouth opened wider still as he heard them thunder past. He jumped up and ran to the half door in time to see the troop horses plunge, break away and be swept and lost in the eddying swirl of manes and tails. He caught, or thought he caught, a glimpse of a big grey horse that might have been the missing stallion. His mouth closed slowly. His face became suffused with angry blood. He was, for a moment, unable to speak.

He was not going to be able to recover the grey. He could not even prove he was here. True, there had been a high percentage of greys and roans among the horses that had galloped past. But he could make nothing of it, whatever he believed to be the cause. There would be no chance to do anything about the capture of Harry Bates. If he had found the horse it would have been impossible for the authorities not to proceed further in hunting down the thief. He did not quite know what he had been going to do, but it was now impossible even to distribute more leaflets. They had disappeared in the saddlebag of his orderly. So had everything else. His silver-mounted pistols, his clean stocks, his great cavalry cloak and his horse—a valuable Irish hunter. By God! By God! He put his hand to his neck, almost choking now. Everything was gone and in all the world there was nothing so utterly stupid, helpless and absurd as a dismounted dragoon. He saw himself leading his men, dragging their sabres, hardly able to walk in their jackboots. Walk—dragoons were not meant to walk. They had not been created by God or the War Office for this function. Someone was going to pay for this!

The troopers now stood staring, first at the dust made by the escaping horses and then at the wall where their chargers should have been. There were the marks of their hoofs, the neat little piles of dung behind them. There indeed, in their minds, still stood the horses as they had last seen them. But they were not there, only ghost horses, memories of horses. Dimly—their minds bemused with brandy and girls, their bellies burning with the tiger's milk they had drunk, their hands still aware of the satin skins they had been touching—dimly, as through a fog of sound, they heard their captain shouting.

" By God, I'll have you flogged for this. Neglect of duty. Desertion in the face of the enemy! Loss of government property—and my property! My black! My pistols! By God! I'll—I'll . . ."

He lowered his voice. " Do you mean," he hissed, " that with five years' service you still can't tie up a horse?" He pointed to the rings. " How did they get away? If the reins had broken they would still be there. How . . . ?"

He never finished. Solomon Rosenberg had grasped his arm. " My lord," he said. " My lord, they have stolen Salome from me."

" Who has? Who is she? Let go of me, you fool!"

" Your horses, my lord. The governor shall hear of this. It will not end here. That my virtuous Salome has been abducted by the horses of the licentious soldiery. Like man, like horse," he said. He stood back, pointed his finger as if it was a pistol, and poked the captain in the ribs. " Sir," he said, " if I recover her and she is pregnant, there will be trouble. Ja," he said, "I will carry it to the King of England himself."

"Arrest this man," Robinson shouted.

The dragoons, delighted to do something, dragged off the Jew who was now laughing hysterically.

As soon as they had got him behind the house, he said: "Let me go, you fools. I got you out of it, didn't I?"

In the house Captain Robinson turned on Willem Prinsloo. "Well," he shouted. "Well, what are you going to do now?"

"Niks," Oom Willem said. Then he shouted, "And magtig, I will not be shouted at in my own house. No one shouts here except me. Ja, I shout to my heart's content, but no one will shout at me."

Tante Maria thrust herself between them. "No one shouts at the Oubaas," she said. "He is master here. Before God, this is our home, our woonplek, our living place. And you . . . you have no right here." An idea struck her. "Have you a warrant? If not, by what right do you thrust yourself upon us, frightening the life out of our maids, bolting our horses, arresting the good Jewish smous who attends to our small wants. Ja," she screamed, "a warrant. Show us your warrant."

"I am not a policeman," Robinson said, somewhat taken aback. He was also pushed back as Tante Maria forced her soft bulk against him.

"Not a policeman? You are worse than a policeman. They only put innocent men into the lockup. You soldiers, you Rooibaadjies, are murderers. You cut men to pieces as if they were strings of sausages, with your sharp swords, you tramp them under the feet of your horses. Well, now you have no horses. It is a judgment. God has swept them away."

"He swept away ours, too," Oom Willem said.

"The ways of God are inscrutable," was Tante Maria's answer.

"Get food," Oom Willem said. "Get food, woman. We must feed these men and set them on their way."

"I must have horses," Captain Robinson said. "We must go after our chargers."

"Horses?" Willem said. "There is not a horse within ten miles."

"You mean you cannot mount us?"

"Mount you?" Oom Willem roared with laughter. "Meneer Officer," he said, "I will feed you and your men. Then I will have a team of oxen inspanned and send you to the Bay in a wagon. You should be there by dark. From there you may be able to get a boat. One is lying there, they say."

By now Oom Willem had guessed what had happened. Francina had realised that the grey stallion had been traced to Groenplaas. Somehow she had got rid of the troopers who were standing by their horses and had bolted the chargers with the horse herd. He knew, as well as if he had seen her with his own eyes that she had been riding Bloubooi bareback and that he had led the others as he always did. He was proud of the girl. What a boy she would have made! This was something Tante Maria could put in her pipe and smoke. If he had not brought her up as he had, would she have had the brains or the courage to save the stallion that was her pet, and also the cornerstone of the new breed of horses he was getting together? The hardy Boer mares had a great deal of Arab blood in them, but the effect of this cross on them was unbelievable—it added a hand to their size. It added speed and nothing was lost in hardiness or endurance. Ja, he'd tell the old fool. He'd say, If you'd had it your way and brought her up like a girl, who was fit for nothing but the kitchen or the bed, do you think she could have saved my horses? No, he thought, a boy could have done no better. It all just went to show how right he always was and that of course was what really infuriated that great bladder of lard who expected him to treat her as if she were a princess in a fairy tale. Leaving the Englishman, he went to the back. He wanted to talk to the coloured girls.

" Come here," he said.

They followed him out into the yard, close together, giggling but looking down at the ground with simulated modesty. The rough soldiers were still in their minds. They had been a pleasant change. Strong men who had understood no word of protest. They now certainly had plenty to discuss together. Those few minutes would give them conversation for years. Whenever men came up or foreigners or soldiers, they would be able to speak from practical experience. Eva looked down at her ankle which was still bleeding from the wound of a spur rowel.

" Now," he said, " now, where is the girl?" Their master had turned so suddenly that they almost ran into him.

" She is gone."

" Ja, she is gone. But where?"

" On the blue horse. Ja, baas. She led the bunch of horses, lying flat on his back, her hair mingling with his mane."

" It was a fine sight," Eva said.

" And you? You girls? What were you doing?"

" We were with the soldiers. The young mistress told us to go to them. We gave them a bite to eat. She said we could do anything. Ja, baas, the nooi gave us permission."

" And I have no doubt you did."

" Nee, baas, there was not time." The girls fell into each other's arms again, giggling and laughing at their memories.

" You should be whipped," Oom Willem said.

" We are not slaves," Sara said.

" You are still children and will still be whipped when you misbehave. But this time I will buy each of you a new doek from the smous."

" Silk?" Sara asked.

" Ja, of silk."

The girls smiled at each other. They had a good master. These talks of whipping were a joke. Neither of them had been whipped since they were children. Now they must decide on the colour of the headcloths they wanted. Would it be better to have the same colour or be different? Would the Jew have a big variety of colours? Life was certainly very interesting. So much had happened in the last few days and there was much to look forward to. Great events were in the air. There must be with all this coming and going.

Once well away from the farm, Francina slowed down her horse. The mares and colts swarmed around her as she sat looking over them. She knew them all, knew their names and breeding. They were her friends. A blue roan colt pushed his nose against her knee, almost unseating her. Then she saw Salome, looking rather forlorn, her long black ears cocked towards her. She began to laugh. What would Meneer Rosenberg do without her? Why, she thought, he loves her as I love Bloubooi.

The horses had now settled down. They had opened up and were grazing, the foals beside their dams. Some were in family groups, old mares, grandmothers, with their progeny grouped about them. She had halted in one of the grassy glades among the hills that she had ridden through the other day when she had met the Beyers brothers. She would take Bloubooi and the mares to their farm. They would take care of them till all danger was past. They would lend her a horse to ride home on. She would lead Salome. But first she must off-saddle the troop horses.

She had no trouble. They let her walk up to them. She took off their saddles and bridles, setting them in the crotch of an old melkbos. Then she went to the officer's horse. A splendid black gelding, beautifully accoutred. She transferred his saddle and bridle to Bloubooi. He looked very handsome with a gold-embroidered saddle cloth. There were silver-mounted pistols in the holsters. There was a silver flask and sandwich case in a leather container fastened to the dees. Behind the saddle a dark-blue cloak was rolled.

Smiling to herself, Francina shortened the stirrup leathers by the three holes and remounted. To get them started she drove the horses in front of her. Salome, apparently fascinated by Bloubooi, trotted happily at his side.

The Beyers farm, situated in a mountain valley, resembled most others in the district—a main house with stables, outbuilding and kraals distributed somewhat haphazardly about it. They had never been planned but had been put up where they had seemed to be most needed; behind the house, and visible before you saw it, were a group of tall bluegums—eucalyptus—whose seeds had come from Australia many years before. In the walled garden there were also magnolias, camellias and gardenias, and many other shrubs, flowers and herbs. Francina knew the farm well. She had come over here several times a year for many years. These were their nearest neighbours.

Riding at a walk now, followed by the herd of horses, Francina came through the kloof and into full sight from the house. The Beyers dogs ran out, barking. This brought Mevrou Beyers from the kitchen. She was followed by Daniel's wife. Young Louis came out of the stables, and recognising the visitor, came to greet her.

" How are you?" he said. " And why are you bringing all your horses here?"

" I want you to keep them for a few days till all danger is past."

" Danger? What danger?"

" The English, Louis. They came for Bloubooi. So I came away with all the horses, including theirs, so that they could not follow me."

" That was clever," Louis said. He was walking beside her with his hand on Bloubooi's neck. " Of course we'll keep your horses, and you can have my yellow horse to carry you home. He is a very good little horse. Come," he said, " we'll take your beasts into an empty kraal." He flung open the gate of a large walled enclosure and they drove the horses in. Francina dismounted and led her grey towards the house.

" That is a very fine saddle," Louis said. " You are certainly very well equipped, with horse pistols and a flask."

Francina smiled at him. " I stole them from the English officer. At least I stole his horse and they were on him."

" You stole an English horse, Francina?"

" I stole six. They are in your kraal. I had to do so."

Only now did Louis realise what Francina had done.

" And what will the English do?"

" I don't know. Walk home, perhaps. But they do not know I stole them. They think they ran away." She put a hand on Louis's arm. "You can ride Bloubooi but keep him stabled alone. He will fight if he is near another entire."

" I'll take care of him for you," Louis said. " It is nice to think that you are riding my horse and I am riding yours.

" You will eat with us," he said, " and I will give you your bull pup. She is a beauty, white as snow on a mountaintop, with a brindle patch over her left eye."

The women now came forward to greet her. Mevrou Beyers was not old—not much over thirty—dark-haired, dark-eyed and vivacious. She had been married young. Louis was her son. The other sons were from a previous wife. There were dead children—both sons and daughers —from both women in the farm graveyard, lying beside their father. Dora, Daniel's wife, was still a girl but growing plump with matrimony.

They embraced Francina and oh'd and ah'd when she told them her story. How daring! How brave she was . . . and bareback too?

But she got the feeling that Dora did not approve. That she felt that such things were not for women. For two pins, she thought, I'd spit in her eye. Did one have to live as if one was already dead to be a woman? Had women then no brains, no feelings, no sense at all? Must they be driven like cattle before the wind of every circumstance? That was not the way her Oupa had brought her up. Be free, he had said. Do what you must and pay the price. For each thing there is a price—in risk, in pain, in joy. Life is something you must buy with your blood and tears, with risks and chances. Yet such women as Dora, married and mothers, knew less of life than she. Understood it less or its necessities.

She ate what they put before her and drank coffee. She asked them if they were going to trek too. Dora said she was remaining with Daniel. Mevrou Beyers said she would go with her son and stepsons. " How can I not go? They are all I have."

Francina liked Mevrou Beyers. She thought there might be a bond between them, for she also had Huguenot blood in her veins, that came out in her love for clothes and a certain style of dressing foreign to most Boers but instinctive to her. Sometimes she carried a little green parasol to shade her from the sun. In winter she wore a muff to Nagmaal and a white shawl with a long silk fringe. We are Boer women, but French, she used to say when they talked about clothes. It had surprised Francina to learn that in Europe the fashions changed continually and that even in Cape Town they were many years behind, while on the farms in the backveld they were wearing clothes that had gone out a hundred years ago.

Magdalena always wore shoes and stockings. Her hair was not drawn back into a tight bun but worn in little plaits kept in place with a ribbon or a comb of tortoise shell. On Sundays and for Nagmaal, when Francina put up her hair, she tried to do it in a similar way.

Louis brought in the Boer bull pup, a white rolypoly with a brindle spot on her face covering her left eye like a patch, just as he had described her. She had a round bullet head, and long wet pink tongue. Louis also brought a leather haversack in which Francina could carry her slung over her back. He fetched his yellow horse. Francina put her grey in a loosebox and kissed his nose. " I love you, Bloubooi," she said. " I'll die before they get you."

Then, with the pup slung in the bag, she mounted and rode away. But not to Groenplaas. She must find Harry Bates, the English soldier, and warn him that he was not forgotten, that the authorities were still after him. No one knew where the bandits hid but she had heard that they kept a lookout on one of the mountains seven or eight miles away. She must find this man before dark and send him for Bates, the red-haired soldier.

8

THE BRIGANDS

FRANCINA LED Salome on a riem. The donkey did not care for Louis's yellow horse. The dogs followed, keeping well away from his heels.

The track that led to the mountain was not well defined, it was so seldom used. It did not occur to the girl that she might not find the sentry, nor did she worry about her safety alone with the brigands, supposing she did find them. She was interested in the road that snaked up the hills, winding around them. There were nice flowers here. Mountain bluebells and giant proteas with great pink and white flowers as big as the head of a child. She saw a black eagle and a number of dassies—the rock rabbits on which it must have lived. She heard the bark of a baboon. If there were men about they would now know that someone was coming. She began to sing. She had a high clear voice that was caught up in the sounding board of the hills. The track came round a shoulder where the great tumbled rocks that had rolled down from the berg above almost blocked it.

A man with a gun stood in front of her. A coloured man with a dirty, evil face and snaggle teeth. She pulled up her horse. The dogs advanced and stood growling on each side of her.

Francina said: " I have a message for a man you have with you."

" What man? And who are you?"

" I am Francina Marais and the man I seek is Harry

95

Bates, the English deserter. It is important. Either take me to him or bring him here to me."

The man adjusted the blue and red bandanna he had wrapped round his head. He was stripped to the waist. He had a gun over his arm, a pistol stuck into his belt; a powderhorn hung from a wide bandolier that went over his shoulder—it supported a brass-handled cutlass in a sheath of zebra skin. His feet were bare, the soles horny. His greasy hair was long and tied with a dirty black velvet ribbon.

If she had not had the dogs with her Francina might have been frightened of him, never having seen his like. A man who quite obviously was a criminal—a murderer who would stop at nothing and who, if taken, would certainly swing as food for crows on a gibbet. She had never met evil before or seen a man who was less than an animal. Her will hardened against him. Her eyes never left his face.

She said: "Fetch Bates. I will wait here."

"Who are you to give orders?" he said. But after a moment's pause he turned away and went up the mountain in great strides.

Once he had gone, she off-saddled her horse and knee-haltered him. The donkey showed no signs of running away, and stood beside her. Francina now sat down in the shade of a big rock and got her puppy out of the bag. The big dogs investigated it. She said to Wolf, " You do not know it yet but she is going to be your wife."

She thought: Somewhere there is a man, too, who does not know that one day I shall be his wife. The surprises that life held in store for everyone, for dog and man, for every living thing, were beyond number. Then she laid her head back on the saddle, set the white bull pup in the crook of her arm, and slept.

Harry Bates followed his man down the mountain. This

man, de Vries, was not one of his favourites—a coward, a cruel man, who killed and tortured because he enjoyed it, but always left others to take the risks. Still, men were men. He was a good shot and since he had been born in this district he knew the mountains hereabouts better than any of them.

A girl to see him. What girl? A white girl. It had been years since he had spoken to or even seen a white woman. They had women certainly—he had one himself, and a son by her, a half-wild coloured girl born in the hills of run-away slave parents. They all had their doxies, their wenches and whores, and most of them wanted no more. Most, in all their lives, had had no dreams. Certainly not one of them had ever thought of becoming, after twenty years of service, a sergeant major of dragoons.

" She's down there," de Vries said, pointing.

The dogs heard him speak and barked. The yellow horse looked up. The donkey, not wishing to be forgotten, extended her white nose and brayed. Francina woke, stood up with the puppy under her arm struggling to lick her neck, and moved towards the men who were coming down the mountain towards her.

Bates was in front. There was no mistaking him. Tall, still ramrod straight, his eyes as grey as she remembered them, his hair still flaming. But his face had changed. It was harder. It looked as if it were no longer made of flesh and bone but of rock—of some hard, brown, polished stone. He was wearing a wide-brimmed felt hat with a high crown made of tiger skin. Blue corduroy trousers with a flap in front and a coat of brown woolly duffel worn over a white linen shirt. He wore no waistcoat. He carried a gun with two barrels and two pistols and a sheath knife in his belt. He had the usual bandolier over one shoulder and buffalo powderhorn ornamented with carved devices. On his feet he had veldschoens in good repair.

He came forward, his hand extended. "I am Harry Bates," he said.

His man was at his heels, wishing to miss nothing of this adventure and hoping it would end in rape. In fact, in his mind he saw no other end. They could easily dispose of the dogs. We'll each kill one, he thought, fingering his pistol.

"My name is Francina Marais, Meneer Bates," Francina said. "You do not remember me?"

"I don't remember you."

"It was a long time ago. Five years is a long time."

De Vries leered. What a man their leader was! He must have had this child five years ago, and now she had escaped from home to come and join him. What a man! This made rape less likely or at least postponed it, but there would be interesting complications. Gertruda, the leader's woman, for instance—would she kill this girl? Or would Harry throw her out? Would he keep them both?

"I was ten," Francina said.

"Ten?"

"It was when you came with the big grey horse. When you sold Bloubooi to my Oupa—Oom Willem Prinsloo."

"The grey," Bates said. "Then you're the little girl who stood watching. I've often thought of you and the way you looked. I remember thinking, there's a girl who loves horses."

"I love him," Francina said.

"Who do you love, my pretty maid?"

"Bloubooi."

"So that's what you call the grey—Blue Boy. And you love him."

"Ja, Meneer, and that is why I am here."

Bates took off his hat and ran his hand through his hair.

"You do not make yourself very clear," he said.

"Oh, it is clear enough," Francina replied. "The soldiers came for him—the Redcoats."

"They were on your farm?"

"Ja, they had traced him. We sold some of his colts. They were so like him that a man who knew Bloubooi recognised them as his sons."

"Everyone knew that grey," Bates said. "Didn't you know that he was famous? That he cost the governor five thousand guineas?"

"No," Francina said. "I did not know. I only know Oupa gave you twenty pounds for him and I love him and I rode him away with all the other horses when the Redcoats came. I also took their horses, one of them a splendid black with a white star on his face, and one white sock."

Bates said: "A white sock on his near foreleg?"

"Ja," Francina said. "You know him?"

"That's old Nick, Captain John Robinson's black hunter," Bates said.

"That is the name of the captain. I did not care for him and he hates you. He was asking for you. He called you a deserter, a horse thief and a murderer. That is why I came," she said simply. "To warn you. Now I will go. They will wonder where I am at home."

She picked up her saddle and bridle and moved towards her grazing horse. Then she turned back. "There is one more thing," she said. "He is offering a reward for you—a hundred-pound reward for your capture."

Then before she could turn back, an event which, when she thought about it afterwards seemed to have taken a long time to happen, took place. Actually it was all over in the winking of an eye. But then she had never seen a man killed before.

At her words, a curious expression had flitted across de

Vries's face. He was thinking that now he'd get the girl and the reward.

Harry Bates's face changed too. In an instant, all in one movement, his hand fell on his pistol butt, he drew it and fired. De Vries, an evil smile still on his lips, put his hand to his bare chest as if to stem the blood and fell forward, dead.

The yellow horse stood, head up, on three legs. Surprised by the shot, the donkey brayed again.

Bates took the saddle from Francina's arms and led her round the shoulder of the hill. "You will stay here till I fetch you," he said.

She said: "Ja, I'll stay. But why?"

"Why, my dear," he said, "how long do you think I should remain free if my men knew I was worth a hundred pounds?"

"So I might have been the end of you?" Francina said. Tears filled her eyes. "I came to save you and I might have killed you."

"You saved my life," he said. "Now rest till I come to fetch you." He took her hand, bent over it and kissed it.

When he had gone Francina began to tremble. She had just seen a man killed. Before God, how easy it was to kill a man. She had never thought of that before. And her hand had been kissed. A man's lips had been there. She looked at the top of her hand. Then her knees gave way and she fell, crying, in a heap.

That was how Bates found her a moment later when he came back. "You forgot something," he said, and put the bull pup into her arms.

Then he left her again. No wonder she was crying. But it would do her good. When it was over she would be well. A woman's tears were like a countryside swept with rain. After it the sun came out and it was refreshed, more beautiful than before. Sometimes, he thought, it was a pity men could not cry. Then he laughed at the thought of someone crying for that devil de Vries, whose body he must now dispose of and whose death he must explain to a band of men who would be in no way surprised at his end.

Returning to de Vries, he turned the body over with his foot. In death his face looked even more evil than it had in life. Here lay a man who had had nothing to recommend him, who in his whole life had probably never performed a single act that had not been to his own benefit and the detriment of another. It was known that he had killed two women, a mother and daughter, in a robbery. He had been taken and had escaped. Then he had killed a man in a brawl, shooting him as he sat at his wine. After that he had taken to the hills, living like a beast till he had joined up with the band, creeping up to them humbly like a whipped dog, begging admission to their company. It had been a mistake to let him join them. He had caused nothing but trouble, and now the error was rectified. He pulled the pistol from the dead man's belt and divested him of the bandolier and cutlass. The weapons were good ones.

Bates now half carried and half dragged the corpse to the edge of the krans that edged one side of the hill and let it go. The body rolled a few yards, then bounded out away from the cliff and plunged into the rocky gorge at the bottom where the jackals, hyenas, vultures and crows would soon make an end of it. A very suitable end, he thought.

The story he would tell was simple. De Vries had tried to kill him and take the girl who had come to warn them of the dragoons in the vicinity. There were two other deserters in the band, one of them Fred Carter from his own regiment, and they well knew that anything—including death— would be better than recapture by the military. Death, anyway, would be the fate of them all if taken, but by hanging—a relatively merciful end compared to the flogging which the soldiers would receive or the keelhauling of Navy Jack, as they called the naval deserter.

Justice. There was no justice for their like. That was reserved for gentlemen. He spat into the void below him where already the crows were assembling, so quickly were they cognisant of death. A gentleman. He had once had some such pretensions himself. How astonishing it was to think that he and Jack Robinson had shared a father. He would never forget the day when, as a recruit, Jack Robinson had come up to him and said, " Is your mother's name Nancy Bates?" and he'd said, " Yes." " By God," Robinson had said, " fancy a by-blow of the old man's in the Tenth Dragoons." He had nearly struck him then. But to strike a commissioned officer was a most serious crime. One that could be punished by death, they said. Now he wondered if Robinson had known it and tried to get him to hit him. But there had been something else that held him back. His mother's words. It was she who had told him to enlist in the Tenth. " Your father's regiment." That was just before she died. She'd never talked about his father except to say he was dead and that she was a widow. But John Robinson's father, Sir Douglas James Robinson, Bart., had once commanded the Tenth. He was not dead, he had merely retired.

It was hard for him to believe Jack Robinson's implication that he had been born out of wedlock, the illegitimate by-blow of a cavalry officer and a whore. He knew his mother better than this. He knew that she was a country girl, the daughter of a parson in Little Wently in the Midlands. This was Robinson country. Was that why she had said enlist in the Tenth? But she could not have known that his half-brother had a commission in the regiment. How he hated him. How he had tried time and time again to break him. And at last he had succeeded. But evidently it was not enough to have driven him to live with wild men in the hills. He must still come after him. Must put a reward on his head so that he would be hunted down like vermin. What was the cause? Was there a cause and would he ever know it?

" We will go to the camp now," he said. He took the puppy from Francina's arms. Finding a new face to lick, it set about, making every effort to plunge down Bates's throat.

" It is many years since a pup has licked my face," he said. " That is one of the little things that make life sweet. Puppies, kittens. The sound of milk squirting into a pail, a garden of flowers. It is many years since I have seen such things. One even comes to forget their existence. Yet it is they which keep a man sane, and his heart tender."

Francina looked down on the man from her horse. He was carrying the weapons of the man he had killed. How sad he seemed to be. What a terrible life he led. People talked of the freedom of such men, of outlaws and pirates, but they were so free that they had nothing. No homes, no lands, no families, no stock. Less than snails and tortoises that carried their homes upon their backs.

The track they followed led on over the foothills across deep valleys till they reached a small flat-topped mountain from a narrow, easily defended neck that linked it to a lower range.

Here suddenly there were men about them. They sprang up from behind every rock and heather tussock, ragged, wild-eyed, unkempt men pointing their guns.

One came forward and said: " She can't go back, Harry. She must stay or die."

" She'll go back," Bates said. " She'll sleep here and go back to-morrow."

" A spy," someone shouted. " It's a trick to send a woman spy."

" You fool! She came to warn us. I know this girl," Bates said. " She came by herself to tell us that there are troops about. Dragoons," he said, " who are looking for us."

He threw de Vries's pistol, gun powder horn and cutlass on the ground. " He's dead," he said. He could explain later.

They moved forward, the band grouped about them. The mountain had a flat top that sank into a saucerlike depression which was filled with water and surrounded by reeds.

The brigands' village, for that was what it was, consisted of a row of huts and small houses that ran round the curve of the rim but well below it, facing north to catch the sun. Immune from the gales which roared over them, the trees and bushes scarcely stirred. Wild-looking women—many pregnant, or carrying a child and with children hanging on to their skirts—came out of the huts to stare. Dogs barked. A shortish, thick-set, fair man, with almost white eyelashes and pale grey eyes, came up to them and was introduced by Bates. " This is Fred Carter," he said, "also once of the Tenth."

Carter was fair-haired with a reddish face, very powerful looking, with a barrel chest and slightly bowed legs. Francina did not like the look of his eyes. They were a very pale, unwinking grey; like Bates he was clean-shaven. Most of the other men were bearded.

Someone took away the yellow horse and donkey.

Bates said: " Don't worry," as she looked after them. " They'll be taken care of," and led her to a house that looked rather cleaner and larger than the others. The white-wash was peeling off, but it had been whitewashed once.

The thatch was neat and new. A woman met them at the door, erupting fiercely, spitting like a cat. With flashing eyes she turned on Bates, pouring out a torrent of words in a language Francina could hardly understand, so great was the mixture of curiously pronounced English, Dutch and native words.

Bates pushed her back. " She's not here to stay, you fool. She spends the night here and returns to-morrow. She brought us warning of the troops."

This changed matters and Gertruda became friendly, made coffee and proceeded to cook a meal.

Bates showed Francina where she could sleep and went out of the house.

He had a lot to think about. He was going to send Fred Carter back with her. The best of a bad lot. English too, a Kentishman, but he did not trust him. He had seen the look in his pale eyes as he flicked them over the girl, feeling her with them as if they were hands. There was only one answer. He would have to send someone else with him, a second man whom he could trust. Kleinbooi, his Zulu servant, must go with them. He went to find him.

The procession down the mountain began. Fred Carter led the way on foot, then came Francina riding her borrowed horse or leading it where the descent was too steep. Salome followed the dun to whom her affection had been transferred. Francina carried her puppy and her dogs followed. Kleinbooi, Bates's Zulu so called because of his immense size, was close behind. No one knew how he had arrived in these parts. No one knew anything about him except that he was unbelievably powerful and devoted to Bates. He carried a gun and a heavy, long-shafted knobkerrie made from a white rhino's horn.

They went down a different way. Carter said they were

going to a farmer who kept their horses for them. She gathered that his situation was more than usually lonely and that he also ran the cattle they stole and in general acted as a link between the bandits and the outer world. When they had been going about two hours, Carter left her with the Zulu and continued on by himself. Kleinbooi built a small fire and put on a pot to cook.

Francina sat with her dogs about her and the puppy in her lap. She had decided to call her Meisie. The donkey and dun horse grazed near her. Life had taken a strange turn. It had suddenly become most interesting. The events of the last few days would give her plenty to think about for a long time. She realised that it was not just people and friends she missed or thought she would like to have, but ideas, things to think about. What a lot there was now! The idea of the trek, the Jew who had become her friend and had given her a mirror, the coming of the Redcoats, her escape with Bloubooi and the wild gallop with the horse herd. The wonderful sensation of all those manes and tails and bodies pushing against her. The thunder of their hoofs, their snorts and neighs. Then there was her Boer bull pup. She was glad to have thought of a name that would suit her, Meisie—little girl—for big head and all, that was what she was like, so sweet and loving. Then there was the terrible sentry that Bates had shot before her eyes. And her astonishment that his death had not upset her. Inside her, from the moment she met him she had known he was dangerous. Bates had shot him as he would have shot a mad dog.

Francina had no great respect for human life. As she saw it, men and beasts were born, lived for a while, and then died in one way or another. Though of course God cared for human beings and saw to it that if they were not evil they went to heaven after death. She thought of people in heaven being rather like old horses pensioned off and turned out to grass.

By the time Kleinbooi's stew was ready, Carter was back. He rode a chestnut mare and led a powerful dark brown entire. He looked slow, Francina thought, but it would be impossible to get a fast horse to carry the big Zulu. This was the kind of beast that could have carried her Ouma, even to-day. A horse that could carry three hundred pounds on his back.

Carter sat down with them and they ate. The dogs licked up the scraps and crunched the bones. Then they mounted and rode away, taking short cuts across the hills until they emerged into country that Francina knew. Now she took the lead and they soon broke out into the little valley where she had halted in her gallop away from the farm. She rode toward the tree where she had hidden the troopers' saddles. They were still safe, straddling the horizontal branches of the old melkbos, as if they were in a saddle room, their stirrups hanging on their leathers, the girths thrown back over the seats. The headstalls hung from the stubs of broken branches.

" What's all this?" Fred Carter swung his horse in beside hers. " Saddles and bridles in a tree?" He dismounted in a flash and went up to them with his horse's reins hooked over his arm. " Cavalry gear. By God!" He began to laugh. " It belongs to the Tenth Dragoons," he said. " How did it get here?"

" I put it there," Francina said complacently. She was seeing things a little differently now that Bloubooi was safe. Ja, she was in her way something of a heroine. She had stolen six cavalry horses, one of them of unusual quality, complete with saddles and gear, from the English. After all, how many other Boer girls of fifteen had done as much?

Carter was examining the saddlebags. They contained

spare clothing, socks, drawers, stocks. Behind the saddles there were rolled cloaks. There were pistols in the holsters. What a find! He'd take them back with him. Meantime they were safe enough here he supposed.

" They're safe here, aren't they? he said. " I mean no one will pinch them?"

" No one comes here," Francina said.

" I'd like to take them when I go back."

" You can have them, Meneer. What use would they be to me?" But she was glad she had the officer's saddle and gear. That he had not seen it.

Carter opened another bag. It was full of printed forms. Proclamations. " Here," he said, " what's this?" He pulled one out. " My God, it's about poor Harry. Harry Bates. There's a reward of a hundred pounds out for him, and it's offered by Captain John Robinson of the Tenth. He always hated Harry, did Captain Jack."

" That's why I went to find him," Francina said, " to tell him there was a price on his head."

The picture was clear to Carter now. That was why Harry had shot de Vries. " No one must know about this," he said. " We'll burn the lot of them."

He told the Zulu to collect some sticks. A fire was kindled and the proclamations burned. Soon, in a few minutes, they were all gone and the light flat sheets of ash scattered by the wind. All gone but one, which Carter had secreted in his pocket. A plan was forming in his mind. There was more to this than met the eye. Why was Jack Robinson so keen to run Bates to earth? There were other deserters. He was one himself and no one worried about them much. Once they got clear away everyone knew it was impossible to catch them in a country as big and wild as this. Big. By God, no one knew how big it was. No one had ever got to the end of it. And besides, most deserters came to a bad end anyway. They were murdered by Kaffirs or died of starvation and disease. Sometimes he wished he'd never left the regiment himself. He'd got fed up with the discipline, the spit-and-polish. But at least he'd always had a roof over his head, enough to eat and a bob or two—beer and girl money to jingle in his pocket.

They remounted and rode on.

9

THE DECISION

WILLEM PRINSLOO was not worried by Francina's absence,
now that he knew what she had done and why she had done
it. She could take care of herself. She was strong, quick and
clever. No man would take advantage of her because she
was not yet a woman so that with her there would not be
that moment of weakness, of hesitation, when a woman
wonders whether she will fight, fly, or give in, and her dogs
were with her. So without this worry, and his grey
horse safe, Oom Willem smoked with some content. A
decision had now been forced upon him. He would lead the
trek. This would be his last act, last, for certainly no
matter how long he lived up there—he looked towards the
North—he would never return? His body would lie there,
unless he died on the way, separated from those of his
parents, his wife and dead children. But why should a man
cling to the graves of his race? Remain like an ox in a kraal
when the world lay wide and open before him?

He thought of the English soldiers he had loaded into
the ox wagon, of their officer's fury. The wagon had not
been tented and they had sat on the benches he had put
into it, across its bed, like little children in a school. This
was something that man would never forgive him. How
everyone had laughed when the wagon started! The
servants, the smous, all of them. A blow might be forgiven,
a cross word forgotten, but laughter never. No man forgave

being laughed at. Laughter made a festering wound that was only healed by death.

When they had gone, the smous had said: " With your permission, Meneer, I will remain here till the young lady brings back the donkey that she stole."

" Stay, stay," Oom Willem said. " Everything is now so disturbed that one person more or less makes no difference. I have lost my great-niece and I gain a Jew, but at least the English have gone."

" Meneer Prinsloo," Solomon said, " is it not true that there are many families about here who are determined to trek to the North?" He knew this was true but he wanted to bring the matter up.

" Ja, it is true."

" Then I would like to remain a while and trade in livestock. It will be wise for these people to part with many beasts and travel with only their seed animals, the very pick of their stock. They should turn the others into gold. Meneer," he said, " I have seen some of these trek Boers on my journeys so I know what I'm talking about."

" Your words make sense, Jew, and you can remain here. Since God has seen fit to surround me with strangers, to send them to plague me as if I were an Egyptian, I would sooner have one that I know than others whom I do not."

" Meneer, I am overwhelmed by your hospitality and will be of as much help as I can to you and yours." Of course his host did not know that he had Francina in his mind. Why, if she really wanted her, he would give her Salome—the very apple of his eye. This decision shocked him. It showed how deep his feeling was for this Boer chit. " At any rate," he said, " I must wait for my donkey." He did not add that he assumed the girl and the donkey would return as they had left—together. How he wanted to see Francina, see her golden eyes light up, see her long tawny hair swing behind her, look at her long legs in boy's trousers. How he wanted to touch her hand. This was love. It was also madness, but a madness that he enjoyed.

Oom Willem sat on a sea-cow skull near the house, smoking his pipe contentedly. It was one of a pair that had been put in position by his father and on which he had sat since childhood. Ja, he and his brothers and sisters, and his children too. Many people had sat upon them. A great diversity of bottoms, all polishing them a little. Everything was now in the hands of God. He had made his decision. It was based on the firm foundation of his desire to adventure once again, to have a last fling, and to annoy the old woman. These two ideas gave him great pleasure. He knew Francina would enjoy it. He knew that the Redcoats had been suspicious and would come back in greater strength. Magtig, that was something. Bloubooi belonging to the governor—a horse worth thousands of guineas, the price of a score of farms, just running half wild in the open veld. The pet of a Boer maid. If they took him, the girl would be hurt. She might even try to kill one of them. She might succeed, for she knew the use of firearms. He refilled his pipe from tobacco he had grown. The pipe was one that his dead brother, Groot Jan, had carved out of soapstone for him many years ago in the form of a horse's head.

He realised that he had always wanted to trek, that for thirty years the northern bushveld had called to him. He had been like a loaded gun. The Redcoats had done no more than pull the trigger. God damn them! These men from over the sea who squeezed the Boers as if they were oranges for the tax juice they could extract from them. Who fenced them in with laws, who . . . There was no end to the reasons for his hatred. The language they spoke. The way they dressed and looked. Their manners. The fact that they were not respectable or God-fearing but gambled and drank and whored, turning Cape Town into a Sodom and Gomorrah.

And who, after all, was he to refuse a direct order from God? If God had not wanted him to lead this trek would He have sent him north thirty years ago to spy out the land? Would He have permitted him alone to survive? Because of all those whom he had known in the old days only he had lived to tell the tale. Was it not God who had inspired the Beyers boys to come to ask him to lead them? Was it not in this way that the prophets of old had received their instructions? He thought of Moses and the fiery tablets. He thought of Saul on the Road to Damascus. He thought of all these. And was he, Oom Willem Prinsloo of Groen-plaas, less than they or different from them, in this, his own sphere?

He rose slowly to his full height and stared about him as if seeing the farm on which he had been born and raised for the first time. By God, he thought, I'm sick of it. It is too tame, too mak. Too small. Why sit here and wait for death?

He smiled. He would go and tell the old sea-cow, the old hippopotamus, tell Tante Maria his good news.

"Go? Trek? Oom Willem, are you mad?" Tante Maria screamed. "You would leave a good farm and trek into the wilderness because you think a headstrong girl will die before she gives up her horse? Magtig, who gave her the horse? And is it even decent for a girl to love a horse like that?"

"It is not for the girl." Willem's face had fallen into deep repose. His blue eyes were expressionless. "Nee," he said, "the girl is only part of it. She is but the outward and visible sign of an inward call that has come to me. Out of the mouths of babes and sucklings," he said. " That is in the Book, is it not?" He looked at his sister-in-law and, not waiting for an answer, said, " Ja, it is in the Book and it was the Lord God who inspired her to love the horse, thus forcing me to do my duty."

" Your duty?" Maria shouted. " Your duty is to stay in your own place on your own farm. I am too old to move. I have taken root here. Groot Jan, your dead brother God rest him, said if anything ever happened to him I should have a place here in his old home."

" You are not too old to trek," Willem said. "You are in your full strength, but you are fat and lazy."

" That I should hear this from my brother—oh, if Groot Jan were here! Ja, there you stand, smoking the stone pipe he made you which, as his heir, should be mine, and make statements that brand you mad . . ."

" If Groot Jan were here you would be absent. So listen, woman," Willem Prinsloo raised his voice, " I am inspired. I am directed. I must lead this trek. That is why I went to the North as a boy, to spy out the way to Canaan. That is why the British tax gatherers came to oppress me—the Egyptians from whom we shall flee into the wilderness."

" Magtig," Tante Maria wailed, " how shall I get into a wagon? It's bad enough at Nagmaal four times a year. But every day, several times a day, every time I want to go outside."

" I will make you steps," Willem said, " strong steps. Also you will get thinner. Sometimes there will be little food."

The man was mad. There was no doubt about that. But all men were mad. Even Groot Jan, when she looked back on their life together, had been mad. Not as mad as most perhaps, but mad. She wondered if it was the lack of this madness that had made life so dull since his death. Still, this was going too far. Her mind went back to her sister's letter. Surely he had not forgotten it.

"The letter," she said, "the letter I had from my sister, and all that she had endured. Have you forgotten it? She is less far than you would go from civilisation."

"I forget nothing. I have thought of all. All last night I prayed to the Lord my God. I walked over the veld and thought of our land, our people. Others feel as I do. Some have already gone. Many more are going. This is the only way. What have we seen but oppression? Wars in which the English took more cattle than the Kaffirs? Our language is taken from us and our lives when we try to protect our property. The Bezuidenhouts were brave men and they hung."

He sprang to his feet and thumped the table so that it jumped. His white hair was wild as he ran his hand through it. His eyes blazed. "No!" he shouted, "we will take no more of this oppression. We will make a new land. This time it will be ons land, for ons volk, a free land for free Boers where we will worship God and live as brothers. This is our mission for we are a chosen people."

Tante Maria got up to face him. They stood with the table between them.

"Ja," she said, "you will go and you will drag me behind you like the tail of a kite. But I warn you Oom Willem, I who am a wise woman and see hidden things as all men know . . ."

"All men, woman? You with your fortune-telling and visions! All men, indeed! Some coloured girls and tame Kaffirs whom you frighten with your spookeries."

"Nevertheless, Willem." Tante Maria closed her eyes and pointed her finger as if she were describing something that she saw. "Ja," she said, "ja, this is what I see. Blood. Ja, blood and fire and water. The plagues of Egypt will strike us down." She gave a scream and sank back in her chair. "The laager," she said, "the laager. I see the Kaffirs swarm over the wagon. Ja, like bees with the bloody stings of their assagais." She came to. "Go, Willem, go if you wish to, but the trials of Job will be as nothing to what we must suffer. All the perils of the wilderness and the plagues of the Egyptians besides."

"God will protect us," Willem said. "God's hand will be over us. I have no fear. If some die it will be God's will. For the Lord gives and the Lord takes away."

"Willem," Maria said, "stay here. The Lord has been good to us here. He has given us much and taken little away."

"I will go. My mind is made up. It is the will of the Lord. He has directed me to lead our people, all such as wish to join us from Bredasdorp. This being the case there is no more to be said." He puffed a great cloud of smoke from his pipe and demanded coffee.

He was drinking from his big cup, thinking about the trek when Eva and Sara burst in on him. The nooi, the nooi is here with two strangers—one white and one black. She is riding Baas Beyers's yellow horse and leading the Jewish donkey. "Kom, baas, kom kyk!—come and look!"

Oom Willem got up. Tante Maria joined him and, followed by the girls, they went out into the yard.

Francina let go of the donkey's riem, put her heels into the yellow horse and cantered forward.

"Who are these people?" Oom Willem demanded. "They do not look like Boers to me."

"They are bandits," Francina said, laughing, "and look at my new dog." She put the bull pup into his arms.

Fred Carter said: "We mean no harm. We merely

brought your girl down from the mountains and will ride on. It is in my heart to see the sea which I have not done for many years."

"You will eat first," Oom Willem said.

"Ja, dankie, we will eat and then ride on."

The two men dismounted and followed the coloured girls into the house.

The smous, who had been resting, awakened by the noise, came out yawning. He saw Salome and ran toward her, flinging his arms about her neck. "You faithless beast," he said. "You daughter of the horse leech, or worse! That you, who have been so well brought up and cared for, should allow yourself to be seduced by a great grey horse!" He bent down and kissed her white nose.

"You have Louis's dun horse, Cina," Oom Willem said.

"He lent it to me. To-morrow I will ride over and return him."

"That is good," Oom Willem said. "It is inconvenient here without horses, but that was a good trick you played upon the English."

"It was a good trick, Oupa, but when it was done, when I had left the horses, I had to warn the red-haired man who brought us Bloubooi. Bates," she said, "Meneer Bates. So I rode until I found him. I spent the night in his camp and he sent these two men to see me safely home, for I was lost up there in the mountains."

Tante Maria stood with her hands on her hips. "You slept with the brigands? You stand there before us and say that? How many brigands, may I ask?"

"About fifty," Francina said.

"You slept with fifty brigands. You, a virgin! And come back brass-bold to brag of it. Fie!" she said. "Perhaps after all it is a pity the Kaffirs did not kill you, too. My granddaughter a harlot on a mountain top, and now we are going to trek. Ja, a harlot and a madman. These are the people with whom I am condemned to live."

"Nothing happened to me, Ouma," Francina said. "I slept in a house with my dogs beside me."

"Thank God," Tante Maria said. "Thank God. So my prayers were answered. You are home safe and still a virgin."

Francina felt that there had been aspects of her adventure which had escaped her. She had feared de Vries. She did not like Fred Carter much, but she had never thought of herself as being in any real danger.

The smous joined them, leading Salome. "It is good to see you back," he said, "and to regain my lost donkey." He thought how beautiful Francina looked. Her presence illuminated the farm for him. It was wonderful to be staying on for a while. He would be able to observe her.

Tante Maria said something more about trekking.

"Trekking? Who is trekking?" Francina asked.

"We are," Tante Maria said. "But don't ask me. Ask him, your Oupa. Ja, that madman, my dead husband's brother, has decided to trek, to leave all this . . ." she waved her hand—"to leave Groenplaas, our home, my dead husband's birthplace, and trek as if we were paupers." She burst into sobs of rage. "Imagine it! Imagine me climbing up and down out of a wagon, many times a day, for weeks, for months . . ."

Francina imagined it and burst out laughing. "You will get thin, Ouma. Thin as if you were a girl again." Then, as the full significance of what had been said dawned on her, she cried, "Trek? Us? We are going?" She jumped up and down, clapping her hands.

The gate of the kraal was open. The wide world lay before her. To-morrow when she went to get the horses there would be much to discuss.

" Do they know, Oupa?"

" Does who know?"

" Do the Beyerses know you will lead the trek?"

" How could they since I have only just decided?"

" Can I tell them, Oupa? Can I give them the good news?"

" Ja, you tell them. Tell them to come back here. I will show them the map I have made and we will begin to plan on the number of wagons we will take, how much gear, guns and livestock. But when you bring the horses back leave them the English horses that you stole."

Francina laughed. " I'll leave them," she said. " They are all geldings and no use to us."

Tante Maria raised her hands to heaven. " That a young girl should talk like this!" But it was not her fault. It was Oom Willem's. How strange that brothers should be so different.

Next morning when Francina got ready to leave, she found the smous at her side. " May I come with you?" he asked. He had Salome saddled and bridled.

They rode slowly. Francina was interested in the Jew's conversation, in his knowledge of native peoples and their customs, in his talk of beauty. She had never heard anyone speak of beauty before. Coming to an open valley, he said, " Stop. Look about you. This is beautiful. The arum lilies, the maidenhair fern, the dark trees, the bright flowers of the proteas. Look at the sky, at the shadow of the berg."

Francina said, " I always liked this place—it made me happy—and now I know why. Thank you, Meneer Smous. You have shown me something new and of great value."

" Many things are beautiful. Women—you, for instance, are beautiful; also animals, flowers, mountains, rivers, houses. Beauty consists in the proportions of each object, its form and colour and its relation to other objects."

Francina said: "Ja, I see." And she did, though she felt what he meant better than she understood it with her mind.

Once again she was greeted by Vrou Beyers. Once again Louis came forward to ask how she was. He patted his horse and took its bridle when Francina dismounted.

"I've come for our horses," Francina said. "All but the English horses. Those you had better let run with yours, for no Englishmen will ever come as far as this."

"I'll see to it," Louis said, "and will bring you Bloubooi myself."

Barend joined them "So you have come for your horses," he said.

"Ja, Meneer, but also to bring news. Oupa has changed his mind. He will lead the trek and he wishes you to come over to Groenplaas to discuss the details and look at the map he has made."

"That is good, very good. Everyone will be pleased."

"How many are going?" Francina asked.

"About ten families," Barend said. "If all come who say they will there will be more than twenty men and boys and forty women and children."

"Oh!" Francina said, "a great company."

"Ja," he said, "we shall be strong. You have nought to fear."

Louis came leading the grey stallion. Salome trotted up to him, braying loudly.

"See, she loves him," Solomon said.

"Thank you for looking after our horses," Francina said.

"It was nothing," Barend said, "and Bloubooi has served one of our mares."

The smous laughed. He clapped Barend on the back and said: "Magtig, they talk about us Jews being smart, but a Boer is a slim man, too."

Francina was stroking her horse's neck as he pushed his head into her, nuzzling her with his lips. How fine he looked in his officer's saddle and headstall! How very fine! But she would have to hide them when she got home in case the English returned or sent someone to spy upon them. Ja, she would hide them. She would keep everything under her bed. No one would think of looking there.

10

THE COMPACT

FRED CARTER was in luck. Captain Robinson and his party of soldiers were camped in the cove waiting for the return of the boat—a small coasting vessel that called each week. They had collected, by commandeering and by purchase, a canvas sail that served them as a tent, some blankets, cooking vessels and food.

All this was learned from local sources, for the whole scattered community was agog with interest and delight at the Redcoats' ill fortune. *You should have seen them come riding in a wagon. You should see them walking about in their great jackboots.* This was something that would make talk for years. Dragoons on foot. Their horses stolen—— No one believed the story about the runaway horses. How could they have run away if they had been tied? And surely horse soldiers would know how to tie a horse. No, there was more in this than met the eye.

That, too, was Fred Carter's impression. He was thinking about the horses and he liked the idea of the dashing Captain Jack Robinson tramping about on foot without a razor or a change of linen. By God, that was a joke. But it was the reward that interested him. Why a hundred pounds? Why so much? And if so much, why not more?

He was not afraid of seeing Robinson. He had never served in his squadron and he had changed a great deal since he had deserted. He had grown out, thickening into manhood. He pulled a black patch out of his pocket and clapped it over his left eye. He popped a dozen dry peas into his boot. Now crippled and half blind, no one would be able to place him. Leaving the Zulu with the horses, he made his way down a small patch into the thicket of milk bush where the Englishmen were camped beside the cove.

He had no difficulty in recognising the captain. Though it was hard to stop laughing at his appearance. Unshaved, uncombed and filthy, he still tried to strut as he came over the rocks that edged the cove. His sword scabbard was rusty, one spur was rowel-less, the brass helmet dull.

"Hi!" he shouted. "Hi! Come here. Do you bring news of the sloop? By God, it had better come soon. Sergeant," he cried, "come here and translate. There's a man here . . ."

A sergeant of the Cape Mounted Rifles came running out of the trees. He had discarded his boots and was barefoot.

Carter took off his hat. He had almost saluted. What a mistake that would have been! He took the crumpled proclamation from his pocket and handed it over. "Does your Lordship know aught of this?" he said.

"You speak English?"

"I am English, my lord. A man of Kent."

"Then what are you doing here?"

"I'm farming, sir. I work for a farmer on shares."

"You're a deserter. I'm sure of it. I lay six to four your back is marked by the cat."

Carter laughed. "A soldier, sir? Me? Blind Joe? Blind and lame. Oh sir, how I wish I could have taken the king's shilling. Me a soldier? Lord!" he rocked with laughter. "The paper, sir," he said. "I could do with a hundred pounds, my lord. It would set me up."

"You could lay your hands on him—on Bates?"

" Not me, my lord. Not a cripple like me. But maybe I could arrange something."

" You could?"

" I might."

" Then why don't you? Bring him here. Bring him, by God. You'll get your gold."

" It's an idea I have, sir," Carter said. " Simple Joe, Blind Joe is a great man for ideas, my lord."

" Well, what's the idea?"

" The idea, sir, is a question. And the question is, my lord, if your Lordship is ready to pay a hundred pounds of his own money—because the government offers no reward for deserters—for Harry Bates, how much would he pay for Harry dead? Would he pay a thousand pounds for him dead, sir?" He turned away. " I'll be back, sir. I'll be back, for a sum like that needs to be carefully considered, sir. A capital sum, my lord."

" Stop!" Captain Robinson put up his hand. " There is something I must know. How do I know you even know this man? That you ever even saw Trooper Harry Bates?"

" Six foot one, sir. Red hair, grey eyes. One hundred eighty pounds."

" It's all in the proclamation."

" Yes, my lord, But there's one thing that is not in it."

" And what is that, may I ask?"

" The little finger, sir. The little finger of the left hand has no nail and no top joint. Would you pay me a thousand pounds for it, my lord? For Trooper Bates's left pinkie preserved in a little bottle of white peach brandy. Then there's the ring, m'lord—a ring with a flying bird upon it and the motto: UBI CRAS which I am informed by an educated friend means: Where to-morrow?" He paused and gazed at Captain Robinson—a one-eyed stare. " A thousand pounds," he said, " for the little finger and the ring thrown in." He said no more but turned away and rejoined the Zulu who held the horses at the outskirts of the wood.

Captain Robinson watched him go limping off down the path between the trees. There was something familiar about the man. If he had not been blind and halt. Where had he seen him before? But one did not forget lame, one-eyed men. It must be some chance resemblance. Some man somewhat like him that he had seen somewhere. But he was certainly a rogue. There was no doubt about that. He also knew Harry Bates or had met him and thought he could lay his hands upon him. It would probably be easier to kill him than take him alive. A clever man this Blind Joe—if that was his name. A thousand pounds was a high price but not too high. No, by God, it was a cheap price for Harry—there was much more at stake than that. But how had that rogue guessed it?

It was eight years almost to the day since he had had that last row with his father. That Sir James hated his son was commonly known. Still there it was. He was his son and heir. That was what he had told him. " Whether you like me or not, sir, is neither here nor there. I am and I remain your son and heir. When you die I'll be Sir John Robinson of Pockenham Hall."

" You will, will you, you young dog?" The old man had laughed till the tears ran down his cheeks.

" I don't see the joke, sir," he had said.

" No, no, you wouldn't. In fact until about a month ago there wasn't one. Remember I told you that my old friend, Charlie Malone, was coming to stay with me? Major General Sir Charles Malone, once of the Tenth. We served together as young men. A rakehell, he was. Wine, women, horses, gambling, a dueller. Killed three men. Spitted them like partridges on his sword. Cuckolds, the lot of them, and foolish enough to challenge him. With Charlie a man had to choose between his wife and his life, if he was chasing her. And most men became very blind—very blind indeed."

How the old devil had drivelled on, drinking more port and getting redder and redder in the face. Gobbling like a turkey cock in a barnyard. God damn his eyes! What had Major General Sir Charles Malone to do with him? "And what has all this to do with me, sir," he had said. "What's the joke?"

"You remember my telling you of a half-brother of yours that I had out of a parson's daughter? A redhead she was, pretty as a picture. Nancy. Small, very small, but game. Nancy Cimmaron . . . Queer name Cimmaron, isn't it, Jack? I've never heard it before or since, have you?" He paused and said: "Then one day you told me he had enlisted in the Tenth, and you didn't even know you were related till I told you. You just showed a list of recruits. My by-blow," the old man said. "My bastard," A smile had spread over his face. "Jack," he said, "it's you, not him."

"What's that?"

"You're the bastard, Jack."

He had stood up, pushing back his chair. It had fallen with a crash behind him.

"Sit down and behave."

He sat down.

"That Nancy was a hot little filly," his father said. "Hot as they come, but she wouldn't let me near her without a ring and all that goes with it. But I was mad about her. She sent me mad with her love and her teasing."

"And what's all this got to do with me?" he'd said.

"I'm coming to it, Jack." Sir James filled up his glass and held it to the light. "Pretty," he said. "Port is a very pretty wine. The colour of a ruby. Charlie Malone always said that. A great judge of port and fond of rubies. Came back with a lot from India. Was seconded to the East India Company for a while. Yes," he went on, " Charlie was a man of very catholic tastes. Knew all sorts of people. A very knowledgeable kind of man. So of course, being such close friends, he knew about me and Nancy. Used to laugh about it, because in those days neither he nor I were used to not getting what we wanted from women. And one night when we'd been talking about her, he said: ' Well, you'd better marry the bloody girl.' ' Marry her?' I said. ' You're mad, Charles.'

" ' She's a lady,' he said. ' Her father's a parson. Oxford and all that. It's a good name but dying out. I remember my grandfather mentioning a Cimmaron, a redhead too, served with him if I remember rightly.'

" ' Marry her, my boy?' I said. ' When I marry it's got to be money,' And when I did, it was. Your mother was a great heiress, Jack. An unpleasant woman, but rich. Very rich.'

" Charles said, ' In that case I've got the man for you.'

" ' You mean . . . ?' I said to him.

" ' Yes,' Charlie said. ' Run away with her and I'll meet you with the parson—a man that'll look like a parson, anyway.' And he did.

" I lived with Nancy off and on for twenty years. Lived with her till she found I'd married your mother and that her lines were valueless, a fake, a forgery, and that my name wasn't Bates. Somehow she never seemed to blame me. She just said good-bye. I'll never forget her turning around and walking off down the street. Straight as a bloody little arrow, Jack, proud she was . . . a blood 'un. Raining a bit. Cold and raining, and a bit of her hair showing under her hat. She was dressed in dark green, Rifleman green. And a brown fur tippet I'd given her. Never saw her again but I

might have been better off with her and no money than with
your mother. Better off with that little redheaded brat
she bred me than with you."

" That's a nice thing to say to your son, sir."

" It's true, Jack. At least I think it's true. Your mother,
God rest her, was a hateful woman, and you take after
her. Vain, arrogant, stupid, cowardly, cruel. Oh yes, Jack,
you're a real beauty. But that isn't what I was going to say.
I was going to tell you what Charlie told me when he came
to stay here last month. He said that man who did the job
was a real parson and Harry Cimmaron Bates is in the book.
He'd met him again. So you see, Jack, you're the bastard
and your dear mama the whore. It must be queer to find
the boot on the other foot. Very queer indeed, I should
think."

Robinson stared out to sea. A thousand pounds was
cheap. There was proof of the marriage. There were the
lines. The register had not been a dummy. There was the
ring. The ruby ring that General Malone had given his
father after he had had his crest engraved on it. That was
the ring Harry Bates now wore on his finger. Of course
Bates knew nothing of all this. He knew that they shared
the same blood and believed that his mother had been
tricked. But when the old man died things would come out.
Sir James had said he would see to that, and then what lay
ahead for him? For Captain Jack Robinson of the king's
Tenth Dragoons? Disgraced, penniless and without friends
or position. The only possible safety lay in Bates's death—
safety and revenge for the woman he had taken from him.
Now he was in no hurry for the sloop to come. If it did
come, he must hold it up. He must see Blind Joe again.

Carter's thoughts when he left the captain were on money,
on the reward, on plans. How was he to kill Bates? He

must get him alone. Away from the others. They liked him and would protect him. He was a good leader. The best they had ever had. Of course if they knew of the reward they would give him up. So it must be done before they got to hear of it. A hundred pounds would be a lot to them, even divided up, and he was not good at dividing things. He must get him away from the others. But there was still his Zulu. Kleinbooi never left him. This was the first time in years that he had left Bates's side. And he knew why. He knew that Bates was afraid of leaving him alone on the veld with that little tawny-haired filly. Must have an eye on her himself. And why not—they'd been alone on the mountain, hadn't they? He knew what would have happened if he had been alone with her. And by God, Bates had been right to send the Zulu. She had excited him. Her wild good looks, her innocence, her trust, the way she had looked into his eyes. He had wanted to take her in his arms, to crush her to him, to kiss those red lips, those eyelids, to bury his hands in her hair, to touch her, to have her. The very thought of her inflamed him. Well, he might still get her one day. The farm was isolated. If the old man was killed. If . . . But first there was Bates to dispose of. I've got to kill Harry, he thought. That meant the Zulu too. Suppose he killed Kleinbooi now on the way home. It would not be hard to shoot him in the mountains. He could send him forward and then shoot him in the back. But Harry would want to know how it had happened, would come back for the body. No, he'd better wait. With Harry out of the way, he'd take over the band and raid the farm. They would kill everyone and carry off the girls, both white and coloured. Of course he'd have the money then, too. He'd hide the gold and then, when he'd broken the girl to his ways, abandon the hills and go back to England. Perhaps he'd buy a little pub. With a thousand pounds a man could do a lot. And how little stood between him and the realisation of these dreams? The death of a few men— nothing more than that.

It was dusk when Fred Carter returned to Captain Robinson's camp. He stood in the dark of the trees and waited till the captain passed near him. Then he called, " It's Joe. Poor Blind Joe."

" So you're back."

" I'm back for my answer."

" I'll pay your price."

" A thousand pounds, my lord, for a certain finger pickled in tiger's milk and a ring thrown in."

" That's it."

" And what have I got but your word, my lord? Suppose you go back on it?"

" That is not my reputation," Robinson said.

" So you say, my lord. But how is Poor Joe to know?"

" You'll have to take my word," Robinson said.

" I'll take it," Joe said, " but let met tell you this, my fine gentleman. Cross me and you'll die. Cross me and I'll find a way to poison you. Cross me and no bite of food or sup of wine will be safe for you. It may take a month or two, or a year or two. You might even get back to England and still die there. Or die at sea and be buried in the briny with a shot at your feet. Cross me and you'll die," he said, his one eye blazing.

" God damn it. I've given my word," Robinson said.

" And damn me, sir, so have I." Carter held out his hand. " The word of Crooked Joe, of Poor Joe, of Blind Joe. Shake it," he said. " Don't just stand there looking at it. It's the hand you've hired to kill, my lord. It's yours and at your service."

He felt Robinson's hand tremble as it grasped his.

Captain Robinson was a coward and he was afraid. He would pay.

Now they would sleep in their cloaks and go back to the farm in the morning. The Prinsloos would feed them again. He'd see the girl and be able to look round for the best way to attack the farm. On the way back they'd load up the saddles, lashing them together by their stirrup leathers and ride for their home in the hills. All in all this had been a profitable business. He smiled up at the stars, thinking of Harry Bates. He was fond of him in a way. He would try not to hurt him. Then he wondered what had happened to the captain's saddlery.

I I

THE GREAT GOOD-BYE

To EACH PERSON going on the trek leaving the farm that was their home meant something different. For each it was both the end of one thing and the beginning of another.

Tante Maria wanted no new beginnings. Rooted in her fat, she rolled around the house and yard like a marble in a rut. She was a woman who was attached to things. She was fond of certain saucepans, of the blue and white china, of an ornamental china pig. Having lost her own home and all in it in war, she had come to love everything here, and now, owing to an old man's foolish whim, all this was going to melt away—to be left behind. But some things she would not leave. The great stinkwood armoire with silver hinges and yellow wood panels. This had belonged to Willem's wife's father. The two brass-bound chests that had come from the East. The blue and white china. The copper cooking vessels and the tin dishes they used every day. Ja, and in addition to the losses she must sustain, there were the dangers and the discomforts of travel. It was all very well for Willem to say he would make strong steps that could be put against the wagon for her to ascend and descend from it. But suppose there was no one to move the steps—that she was left there screaming like a child before a door it could not open.

Then there was the matter of food. She liked good and plentiful food. She would get neither. Not merely on the trek, but when they arrived—if they ever arrived. Houses would have to be built. Lands and gardens made. It would be months, years, before any measure of comfort was achieved. All this time they would live like hunters, which was to say like animals, like bushmen, on game and wild fruits when their grain ran out.

There was only one bright spot in the firmament, one glimmer of blue sky. She would be the oldest and most experienced woman in the trek. She had her gift of second sight which would impress them all. She had lived for many years on the frontier. She had seen war and wounds and would once again take her rightful place among the people. Ja, old Willem might lead the trek, but she would manage it.

The china pig she would take even if she had to carry it a thousand miles in her lap. Around it she would build a new home, and if she died she wanted it buried with her. This might not be a very Christian idea but it was a comforting thought.

She must also take some of her pigs. Since they could not walk, they must ride, since she could not take the big ones she would take the small. Ja, she would take six little gilts and two small boars. Without them she would not move, and if she did not move, Willem could not go either. Me and my pigs, she thought. Both or neither.

Oom Willem was excited. Though he refused to acknowledge it, feeling excitement unseemly to one of his years and experience. So with difficulty he controlled his feeling and gave what he hoped was an impression of calm indifference and of merely leading the trek because he felt it was his duty to do so. The Beyers boys had just left. They had thought his map wonderful, as indeed he did himself. He had described each mile of the way, illuminating them with tales

and anecdotes of adventure. Then they had made their list
—the names of the trekkers. There were six family groups,
including his own. The Beyerses, Van der Merwes, the
Bokmans, the du Plessises and the Melks. Between them
they could muster ten fighting men and boys. The total of
married women and widows was six, of marriageable girls
four, of other children sixteen, and some of the women were
bound to be or become pregnant. This made a total of
thirty-six souls. Ja, in addition there were nine young
adventurous men who might or might not join them, and of
course the servants—both male and female. They would
probably amount to forty people. To lead such a trek as this
might make a man famous, might even leave his name alive
for centuries.

Oom Willem walked round the yard and kraals. He
looked at the buildings he had put up or enlarged, at the
roofs he had thatched. Everything was in good order but
suddenly it bored him.

The smous joined him. " You are saying good-bye,
Meneer," he asked. " is it not so?"

" It is so. I have lived here all my life except for one trip
to the North. I was born here and expected to die here, to
lie with my loved ones in my own graveyard." He looked at
the walled enclosure and the cypresses that pointed their
dark fingers at the sky.

" What does it matter where we die?" the Jew said. " It is
where and how we live that counts. That is what men
remember of us. Dead, all men are equal, and there is no
honour in equality. All babies are equal," he said, " for
they are born and made in a similar manner. All corpses are
equal though the deaths they die are diverse. But in the life
that lies between the one and the other—between birth
and death—men are not equal. In life, Meneer, there are
some men who live like lions, and some like dogs. To lead a

trek is a great thing," he said, " and if by chance you die
on it, each man who follows in the spoor of your wagons will
raise his hat and offer up a prayer. Strangers, even men
perhaps not yet born, Meneer. So that by some strange fate
you may get more prayers by the roadside and be thought of
by more men that if you lay in your own graveyard at
Groenplaas. Home," he said, " home is a word. For me
all the world, all Africa, is home." He raised his hat, bowed
and left Oom Willem to his thoughts.

A strange man, this Jew. A wise man like those who had
followed the star to the birthplace of the Infant Jesus. They,
too, had been travelling merchants, and no doubt Jews, for
that was the land of the Jews.

Francina looked at her home. The house, the stables, outbuildings, servants' quarters and kraals. At the big pale-
leaved bluegums whose great trunks gleamed as white as
bones in the moonlight, at the line of paper-barked cypresses
that also came from Australia—that fabulous land of
criminals and kangaroos. The ships that went there
stopped at the Cape of Good Hope to refit, both on the
outward and return voyage, which was how such seeds had
reached the country. The captains brought them and gave
them to friends. In the walled garden there were other
Australian trees. Myrtles and scarlet bottle brushes. All
this must be said good-bye to, must be left behind. The
thought of it tore at her heart, which beat faster as she pictured the adventures that must now befall her. So, divided
between sorrow and anticipation, caught between the past
and the future, she rode toward the sand dunes and the sea.
She would say good-bye to the ocean first. She wondered if
she would ever see it again.

This was the most beautiful part of the farm. The shrubs
and heath ended abruptly in a solid mass of ancient melk-

bos, a miniature forest of twenty-foot evergreen trees sculptured into a sylvan cushion by the savage winds of centuries. Their branches were interlaced as if they were people holding on to each other's arms to resist the pressure of the storms. Through this tight little wood ran a tunnel-like track wide enough to take a wagon. In here the filtered light was green and the atmosphere mysterious. It was almost like being in church. Beards of grey moss hung from some trees, bright green moss almost covered the trunks of others. A small stream, spotted with patches of maidenhair fern, ran toward the sea. The white chalices of arums shone like silver cups in the gloom. The horse's hoofs made no sound on the soft moist soil, which was black with rotted leaves. Their scent rose as the stallion stepped nervously upon them, as if he too felt the strange beauty of this small forest.

Francina had always thought there must be fairies here, little men and women clothed in green. The Englishman who had taught her had told her many fairy stories. She had always wished he had been well enough to be brought here to see this place for himself. The track was not straight but wound about, following the little stream. Then the trees ended, as suddenly as they had begun, in a sharp line as if they had been cut off with a knife. Beyond them was short, sheep-cropped turf, as smooth and green as a lawn, and beyond the grass lay the golden sand of the strand where the waves, in long lines like charging white-maned horses, flung themselves against the edge of Africa. The sea was the eastern boundary of Groenplaas.

Three tame ostriches looked up as she rode near them, a great black and white cock and two grey hens. She watched a pebble go down the cock's long throat. She looked at his pink thighs and long scaly legs. He could run as fast as a horse and kill a man with a kick. If you were attacked by an ostrich the only thing to do was to lie flat. They could not kick along the ground. Then, when it got tired of attacking and squatted beside you, you should grasp its neck and try to break it. She wondered if she could break an ostrich's neck. An ostrich egg was equal to two dozen hen's eggs. The hen sat on the eggs by day and the cock by night. God had arranged it this way because by day the hen was hard to see and at night the black and white cock invisible. Francina's mind was filled with knowledge about the ways of the beasts and birds among which she lived. But soon they would be off. The animals and birds in the North would be different. There would be no more Vaal rhebok and grysbok or bonte-bok. Everything would be new and strange. She would see for herself the great wonders of which she had heard so much, see herds of game that were uncountable, see lions and elephants. She would also be among people. Having wanted this so much and for so long, she now wondered how she would like it. She would not be able to get away on her horse the way she did now. There would be too many dangers from savages and wild beasts. She might even get lost.

Then there was this business of men. So many men in so few days. A week ago she had known nothing of men, felt nothing in their company. Now—she dropped the reins on her horse's withers and counted them on her fingers. How many had there been? First the English officer pushing into her. Then the man Harry Bates had killed. Harry himself, and other men up in the bandits' mountain camp—she had felt them to be aware of her. And Fred Carter who had made her afraid. The Jew and the Beyers boys—even Louis betting her a kiss against his pup. With them all she had felt something strange, new ... Something that passed between them and her, from their eyes to hers, from the touch of their hands, without spoken words, and she knew that she had responded to them with her blood. She had felt it kindling like a fire in her veins. She knew that now suddenly the time had come . . . as it did with other female things . . . to mate, to love. That somewhere, soon, there must be a man for her. Was he one of those she had already met? Or would he be among the strangers on the trek . . . ?

She snatched up her rein and put her heels into the horse, galloping him along the sands and then turning him into the water so that the yellow storm suds that bordered the beach like soapy water covered his hoofs and fetlocks. Here they stood, horse and girl, staring out at the great waves that broke on the rocks beyond them, at the rolling seas which reared themselves black against the blueness of the sky, and fell roaring as if with rage upon the jagged reef. Beyond her, where the mountains came down to the sea, great caves, once inhabited by Hottentot beachcombers, and filled with the mounds of shells they had eaten, indented the coast—cavities eaten out by the storms of long ago in the rocky fangs of the shore. She would not see any of this again, at least not with the same eyes, for this was the time of change for her. Not only of place but change in herself, in the realisation of her femaleness, and with it of her oneness with all life. She might never see the sea again for, from what Oupa had said, they were going deep into Africa, into its very womb. Far, far from its edges where land and sea met in this endless and fascinating warfare. Looking back, she could see the sand of high dunes blowing as if it were smoke and they were on fire. Beyond her there was nothing. This was the end of Africa, of the world, nothing but the raging seas of the Cape of Storms. Strange things were washed up here. Great planks and masts and bulkheads, chests and hogsheads. And sometimes the bodies of drowned men and beasts. Every few months a wagon was sent down to collect the flotsam. Much of the mystery of the big winter fires into which she had stared so often came from the copper nails used in the construction of ships, nails that burned with a beautiful green colour as they were consumed.

A string of duikers flew across the horizon. It thickened into a rope. There must have been several thousand of them, cormorants that were called duikers because of the way they dived for fish.

She swung her horse round. This would be a good way to remember it all. The beach, the rocks, the great seas roaring in, and above them the birds flying home to some sea-girt rock as they had done for a thousand years, and would continue to do, though she was no longer here to see them. That seemed strange to her. That things should go on and on. That the parents and grandparents of these birds had flown as they did now. That their descendants would do the same long after she and they were dead.

To-day she was close to mystery, had glimpsed secrets which she would never either understand or forget. Once again she had a feeling of being at one with everything, part of everything alive. She knew she owed much to the Jew who had put what she had so often felt in her heart into words. Ja, she thought. I owe beauty to the smous and beauty was in some way related to God, was consonant to His creation.

She turned her horse and rode back through the vleis where she stopped to watch the birds—green shanks, sand pipers, sand plovers, sanderlings, ringed plovers, stints, rails and coots—all busy about their affairs. Walking, swimming, preening themselves. There were many yellow bills and some white-backed ducks. In the distance a company of pink flamingos walked like soldiers, shoulder to shoulder, feeding with their heads upside down in the water.

Some of these pans were brackish and in the summer, when there was no rain, collecting the evaporated salt was a

source of income to her Oupa. Then, empty of water, the
pans shone like snow in the sunlight.

None of this would she see again. They were not moving
for a month. It would take that time to organise the trek,
but after to-day she would not see it even if she looked at it
once more. For she had said good-bye. She had parted
from it. In her heart she was already distant, her feet on
the road of the future.

12

THE NOAH'S ARK

TANTE MARIA looked at her poultry. There were many
and difficult decisions to be made. Some hundred and fifty
birds were pecking about her feet—chickens of all ages. From
these she would select a dozen, ten hens and two cocks.
It would be best to take young birds. But she decided on
six young hens and four old ones that she knew to be good
and reliable mothers. She would take one young vigorous
cock and one older one who was wise to the ways of snakes,
hawks and other vermin. She was going to take three mus-
covy ducks since they could breed without swimming water—
two ducks and one drake. She decided to take no geese.
They were too big. The poultry would ride in the crates
slung beneath the wagons—only the pigeons would ride
inside, two pairs in a wicker cage. These were the descendants of the birds she had brought from Sterkwater in the
same wagon as the remains of her loved ones. With everything—cattle, horses, pigs or poultry—these selections had
to be made. The best breeding stock had to be selected, the
beauty and vigour of the young balanced against the experience and foraging ability of the older beasts.

Having reached these conclusions, Tante Maria went into
the shed where she kept her setting hens. She had six, each
sitting on twelve eggs in boxes filled with soft, dry grass.
They had to be removed from their nests and fed and
watered every day by hand, for they forgot about their own
needs in the passion of maternal brooding.

She filled a dish with clean water. She put a heap of meal-ies on the bare earth floor. Then she picked out the protest-ing hens, holding them two feet above ground level and letting them fall, making them use their wings as they fluttered down, an action which opened their bowels. The hens walked about slowly, clucking with ruffled feathers and lowered heads. They held their wings away from their bodies as if to shelter their as yet unhatched chicks. They dusted themselves in the wood ash that Tante Maria had spread for this purpose. They ate their mealies. They drank and returned to their nests. One of them was due to hatch to-morrow. She had sat for twenty days. Tante Maria, bending with some difficulty, squatted on a small stool near the nest boxes and stroked the necks and backs of the hens. She was going to take two of them with her. The white one with black hackles and the yellow one. She would divide their chicks among the others. Four of them were due to hatch within a day or so of each other. Like all Boer women, Tante Maria had kept poultry all her life and still remembered being taken into the chicken pen the first time by her mother, as a tiny child.

Her mind now turned to other things. There were the medicines to see to. She must take plenty, for up there—she looked towards the North—Willem said all the plants and shrubs were different. She wondered how they would discover which were useful. Then there were the seeds. The seeds of pumpkin, melons, cabbages, carrots and turnips and pits of fruits—of peach and plum. They must be packed in sand to prevent their drying out. And salt. Here where they harvested salt for sale, it was easy to forget how necessary it was. They must take several bags—and the other things, things without number. Blankets, pillows, feather mattresses, karosses, cups, beakers, plates, knives, spoons, cooking vessels, baskets and other receptacles.

Casks of brandy, water casks, sewing materials, cotton, material for repairs, needles of various sizes. There was no end to what must be collected, sorted out and packed. She was not going to abandon her big chair or her *konfoortjie*—the little charcoal stove that warmed her feet in winter. Nor was her little window going to be left behind. The tableware—copper jugs, plates and dishes of pure tin, which were in use, must be kept out with the cook pots. A box was found for the china pig and other small ornaments and was packed in Oom Willem's coffin. Tante Maria had decided to use this as a seat in the wagon and thus keep secure all her best things that were packed within it.

She had won her battle about the pigs. She was taking six small ones that would be weaned shortly. They would travel in a two-wheeled Scotch cart tied on behind one of the wagons. When they stopped, the pigs could forage about until they were old enough to follow the wagons. She was sure they would soon learn to do this. She had the greatest confidence in the intelligence of pigs.

Oom Willem was also busy, checking the stores he would take. More powder and lead had been sent for from the Cape. The old guns were all cleaned and had been fitted with new flints. Yokes, pegs, riems and traces had to be prepared, carpenter's and blacksmith's tools collected. Garden tools, spades, hoes and axes, were ready. A plough had been fully reconditioned, strengthened and fitted with a new sharp shear. For the plough was his favourite weapon. It was with the plough that he intended to conquer the North. But he was also going to take a new English iron plough on the advice of the smous. His guns were to protect his ploughing spans and hold the lands he broke. Let others hunt and trade and adventure; he was a real Boer, a farmer, to whom nothing was more beautiful than the shining, folded lines of the newly turned up rich earth—except, perhaps, his herds of cattle and horses. For without the one the other was not possible. It was the oxen that drew the plough, the mounted men who discovered the best land and protected it. Other things were also in his mind—his long, ox-horn trumpet that he would use to call his people. Big round cooking stones that he would take from the beach here, so as to have something of home with him, for in many places there were no stones—nothing upon which to set the pots to cook.

When he returned to the house, he heard Tante Maria and Francina quarrelling again. Truly there would be no peace till they were off.

" And what is it now?" he shouted.

" It's her," Francina said. " First she wants to kill my tame rams. Ja," she said, " she is seizing this opportunity for murder. And then she says I cannot take my goose. Magtig," she said, " if her pigs can ride, why can't the goose?"

" Why?" Tante Maria said. " Why? Because he is a gander. Because he is big and fat. Because he will have nothing to do with any other goose since he thinks he is a human being. Ja," she said, " if he had a wife we would take them both, but he is a bachelor goose and a disgrace to his species."

" Oh! Oh!" Francina gasped. " How can she say such things about my goose that I brought up like a baby."

" Sheep, pigs, geese, bull pups," Oom Willem cried. " What is this—a trek or a Noah's Ark with all the animals riding in carriages like men, or fat old women." He looked at Tante Maria. " No goose," he shouted. " No goose. No useless animals."

" Useless," Francina stamped her foot. " Useless—and

how are you going to write if you have no goose quills? Magtig, are we going to use the feathers of an aasvoel?"

"Quills," Oom Willem said. "I had forgotten quills. Take the goose."

"And that Boer bull pup?" Tante Maria said. "Are we to take that destructive beast? What will become of us, are not wild Kaffirs and lions enough without a pup that never ceases to destroy everything within reach?"

"The pup goes," Francina said, "and if some accident happens to it while I am absent I will kill your little pigs. Ja," she said, "I will stab them to death with my new big knife."

"So you have a knife now?"

"Ja, I have a knife—a man's knife, a real Hernhuters from the mission at Genadendal."

"And where did you get it, young lady, may I ask?"

"From a man," Francina said, tossing her yellow mane. The smous had given it to her, but she would let her Ouma think the worst. "Those bandits would have given me anything," she said.

Tante Maria shrugged her shoulders. What were children coming to to-day? Where would all this end?

Solomon Rosenberg was killing a number of birds with the one stone of the trek. To begin with, he had sold everything he had left in his packs at a good price instead of a near loss. He had also arranged the purchase of all the goods that were needed for the trek—powder, lead, flints, coffee, tools, soft goods and so on—through a friend in Cape Town —and had sent three hired wagons down to fetch them. Goods had to be bought in quantity. Every family required 300 pounds of powder, and 500 pounds of lead was not too much when one remembered that an elephant gun fired a pound in four shots.

No one knew how long it would be before they would be able to buy another needle or a bolt of cloth. This was not a toggie or trip—though sometimes such trips took a year or more they always returned to their point of origin. This was a trek, an exodus.

The Prinsloos, for instance, were taking three wagons, one with clothes, materials, bedding and foodstuffs, another with furniture, lead, powder and tools.

However, there was only a commission to be made on Solomon's three wagonloads, which he hardly regarded as a profit, merely a stipend to cover the expenses he had been put to in organising everything. But still it was something as the total amount involved was large. He had also bought a great number of cattle, horses and sheep and goats, and sent them off for sale. This was the Boer surplus, stock that they could not take with them. It would put gold into their pockets and give him a handsome return. At times he wondered how these simple people would have got along without his help.

Of course to do all this and cover so much ground, going from farm to farm, he had had to buy a horse—a slightly pregnant chestnut mare no longer in her first youth, but with a beautiful intelligent face and very soft eyes. He had bought her because of her face and because she was cheap— only three pounds. He called her Susie and when he had been informed that she was in foal he had been delighted. This made her no cheaper but gave him more for his money, and the baby would make an interesting pet. Susie had put Salome's white nose somewhat out of joint. She detested the mare, but her master had never forgiven her for running off with Francina's grey stallion, and showed her no sympathy.

Solomon was delighted with all his new friends and had more or less promised to follow in their spoor and bring them up new supplies. He had never been so far before, since there had been no customers to serve, but the demand always created the supply and it was always interesting to see new country. He recognised in himself the same taste for wandering as the Boers'. All men of any race who went to far places had this unease in their blood, and seemed to transmit it to their children, so that no matter where they settled they put out only surface roots.

He thought Tante Maria had made a mistake in refusing to buy his Peruvian bark, never having heard of the cinchona tree or its uses. But Magdalena Beyers had been wiser, taking his word for its value. She had also bought dress materials of the gayer kind, saying that if they met with disaster money would be no use to them, while if all went well she meant to be smartly dressed . . . " for good clothes affected one's mood and courage, Meneer Smous," she had said. " In pretty clothes I could even face a lion . . ." And he had believed her.

Solomon now prepared his final present for Francina. His business here was almost completed. So far he had given her a mirror and a fine hunting knife. He selected two strings of imitation pearls, one bottle of perfume, a Spanish comb, two ordinary combs for her hair—he had told her she should comb it more often—a hairbrush, and a small silken shawl. Also there was a small package of flower seeds. He had written on it: *In this little parcel, Beauty sleeps.* He wrapped all these things in a piece of linen and tied it securely. With the parcel under one arm and leading Salome on a riem, he went to find Francina.

The girls, Sara and Eva, could not make up their minds about the trek. One day they were going. The next they were not. It was Francina who made up their minds for them.

"Idiots!" she said. "That's what you are."

"Why are we idiots?" the girls asked, standing with arms akimbo, staring at her with insolent eyes.

"What do you talk about all day? What do you think about when you are silent?"

The girls dropped their eyes.

"Men," Francina said. "That is all you ever think of. Very well then, trek, or you will regret it when all the young men for a hundred miles around have gone. Ja," she said, "all the men, both white and brown. All that will be left will be old toothless men, and babies—also toothless."

"We will go," Eva said. "Ja, we will go. We could not bear to be parted from our nooi. Were we not all raised together as if we were sisters? Are we not also orphans?"

"Ja," Sara said. "It is to be with you that we will suffer these dangers and hardships. It has nothing to do with men." She tossed her head so hard that her long hair fell out of her headcloth.

Francina laughed. The girls laughed and linked arms with her. "We will all stay together," they said. "We will stay together till we die. All three of us. Ja, we will never leave the nooi. When we marry, our men must work for her."

Francina kissed Eva. "You are good girls," she said, taking their hands. "Yes," she said, "let us all stay together like sisters."

"You are our little white sister," Eva said, dancing away from her as she saw the smous approaching.

"Meneer Smous," she called, "are you bringing us more presents? You have no idea, Meneer, how nice we can be to those who bring us gifts."

"Ag sis," Solomon said, "you are naughty girls. That is not country talk."

"Girls are girls everywhere, Meneer," Sara said. "They

all have love to offer. Some for a headcloth and some for a ring."

The smous put the parcel he was carrying into Eva's hand.

"For me?" she said.

"No, not this time. Take that to the nooi's room secretly and hide it. She can take it in more easily than you," he said to Francina.

When the girl had left he took her hand. "This is good-bye," he said. "My donkeys have already gone and I must follow them. In the parcel Sara has are some small gifts that will, I hope, make you remember me when you look at them."

"I remember you every time I look in my glass, Meneer Rosenberg. For it was you, Meneer, who were the first to tell me I was beautiful. Now I begin to see it for myself. But I owe it all to you."

"To God," he said. "Never forget that all beauty belongs to God and is a gift of God. Whether it is that of a pretty maid, a rose, or a jewel." He paused. "You know, I suppose, that I love you. That I am consumed by a mad passion for you. That you are in my mind by day and my heart by night. But no one knows better than I that this passion is hopeless and beyond comsummation, for what have I, a wandering Jew old enough to be your father . . . Ja," he said, "I could have been a father at the age of twelve—in common with a Boer maid of fifteen."

"I shall soon be sixteen," Francina said. "I am a woman."

This was her first proposal. She was not going to let it slip away between her fingers without a scene worthy of such an event. "I . . ." she began again.

"So," Solomon went on as if he had not heard a word she said, "I make the supreme sacrifice. I will give you something that I have sometimes thought I loved more than life itself." He put Salome's riem into her hand and turned away from her. "Good-bye," he said, "good-bye, or perhaps tot siens, for it is in my heart that our paths will cross again." There were tears in his dark eyes—whether for her or the donkey, Francina could not decide. They might have been for both of them.

13

TO CANAAN

SLOWLY THE MOMENTUM of the trek was built up. Preparation piled upon preparation. Three layers of extra canvas, each layer painted white against the rain and the heat, were fastened to the hoops that supported the wagon tents. The hoops were strengthened—no assagai could pierce these tilts. The wagons, by agreement, were all painted one colour—bright blue with yellow wheels. On each farm the spans of draught oxen were being rested, fattened up and admired. They were all matched, broken-coloured spans. Oom Willem's beasts were red with white blazes, legs and tails. The Beyerses went in for black with a white stripe along the back and belly and white markings on the face. A Boer's oxen were his pride and delight. A matched span took longer to collect than a wife to court. His gun, his horse, his span were the passion of a Boer's life. Without them there could be no lekker lewe—or good life—or indeed any life at all in the vast emptiness of the African interior.

The wagons had four kists or chests in them. One in front on which the driver sat, one behind and one along each side. They were lashed in position. Nothing in a wagon was nailed. Everything was held by pegs, wedges and riems to make running repairs easier and to enable the wagon to be taken apart and carried plank by plank and wheel by wheel over any obstacles that proved impassable, and rebuilt the other side. The kartels fitted across the boxes at the back or were suspended by riems from the framework of the tent.

Now the trek had almost begun. Their homes, their past, even their tenuous ties with Europe, would soon be utterly severed. It was only a matter of minutes now. The long whips clapped, echoing like rifle shots in the hills. The oxen lowered their heads, taking the strain on their yokes. The trek tous and chains clipped over their sleek backs, straightened out, and the great wheels began to turn. In a long line the tented wagons rolled over the rough road like ships at sea. They were off.

Beside the wagons ran the herds. The horses and cattle, the flocks of sheep and goats. Beyond them, to prevent their breaking back to the farms where they had been born, were the horsemen—the Boers and their mounted servants, all armed, each carrying his gun across his saddle or riding with its butt upon his thigh. The horses—stallions still strange to each other—plunged, fought for their heads and screamed defiance at each other. And of all the mounted people, Francina on Bloubooi was the only woman. Not fully a woman yet, nor a girl, but a tomboy just awakening to men, sitting her grey horse as if she were part of him.

In a few hours they would be in new country among scenes that would be strange to her. Already her life had changed. Not only was the farm behind her but she was part of a great company of men, other women and children. Loneliness was behind her too. Before her were adventure, hardship and danger, but these would all be shared. She was at present unaware of the sensation she caused by being mounted on such a horse, of being mounted at all in fact. And wearing boys' clothes with her hair loose upon her back. Nor had anyone ever seen such saddlery—its brass and silver buckles and decorations flashing in the sun. She did not even know that all the young men were eyeing her and that even the older and the married watched her and saw in her a disturbing factor. She was too happy, too excited to-day, to think of men.

The men knew the trek to be something special, a historic event. But the women, more concerned about treasured objects that had been abandoned, and with the difficulties and hardships that lay before them, failed to appreciate their point of view.

They were leaving their homes and many of their kin. They were leaving two hundred years of history behind them, cutting the umbilical cord that bound them to their mother countries in Europe—the Nederlands, the Low Countries. The authority of the Dutch East India Company, and the later authority of the alien British Crown, were also left behind. Authority, any authority except that of God, was unbearable to these people who had lived alone in a world almost empty of men for so long that they refused to recognise any form of government. Riding alone on the veld, sleeping out in the silence under the stars, the Boers more than any other European people had made themselves one with both the soil of their land and its Creator. Theirs was a mystic bond that transcended patriotism. All Africa called to them.

The empty North had called and they had inspanned their wagons, saddled their horses and gone. The excuses were the English pressing upon them, new taxes, a shortage of game and old farms farmed out, that their slaves had been liberated. But these were not the only reasons for the trek. This was to be found in the Boer heart. These farmers were inspired, or believed themselves to be. Nothing but their belief in God could have persuaded them to give up what they had in order to gain so little for themselves. They were the first, and bound to suffer most. They paid the price. They sowed the seed for their children's children, who would reap the crop of new free country that they were going to create in the wilderness.

The trek had a biblical flavour. It was not only a flight from Egypt. It was also the wandering of the desert nomads with their flocks and herds, their tents, their menservants and maidservants. It was a mass movement of many treks separated by time and distance, spread over ten years and hundreds of miles of country, each unit different in size from any other, but all enclosed within the same frame in which escape from the past was balanced by a drive into the future. These were the voortrekkers—those who went in front knowing that their people were behind them, that if one fell two others would take his place. They were at once driven and inspired. Driven by an inner urge that forced them forward. Inspired by the belief that they were God's chosen people whose duty it was to conquer and civilise a continent. That they were only a handful did not deter them, because they had no knowledge of greater peoples. They had no cities, and the towns that they had, few Boers had ever seen or even desired to see. It was Africa—ons land—with its vastness, its unknown grandeurs and dangers that called to them. Ranges of mountains to be crossed, rivers to be forded or swum, waterless deserts to be faced. These were the challenge. The tests set before them by the Lord their God to try them, to temper the iron of their natures into steel. For them the ploughshare and sword were interchangeable. Farmers who had beaten their ploughshares into swords for the conquest of a wilderness would later beat their swords back into ploughshares for its cultivation.

Mounted on small hardy horses, armed with guns, carrying Bibles, accompanied by their women and living in covered wagons that were houses on wheels, they moved with their servants and stock into a savage wilderness, to tame it, watering it with their blood, leaving the graves of their dead beside the spoor of their wagons—a testament of sacrifice.

14

THE MIRROR

TANTE MARIA stood poised at the end of her wagon. Hendrik, the only boy she could count on, had arranged the wooden steps against its tail. She was about to descend. She did this only by an act of will that was brought about by necessity. Still, she thought, things might be worse. She was certainly being appreciated and looked up to. This was a pleasant change. Even Groot Jan, her beloved husband, had not fully appreciated her. Of course the trek was not as strong as they had hoped. Two families had changed their minds when they had heard of the great massacre at Weenen. And the nine young men who had been going to accompany them had decided to go off on their own and not be embarrassed by the company of women and children. This left them with the three Beyers boys and their mother, Magdalena, a woman who, she was now beginning to think, had been aptly named. It was certainly a strange thing that a woman of thirty-three should bloom in such discomfort and act as if the trek was an endless picnic. Tante Maria was against happiness—no good ever came of it.

Then there were the Van der Merwes—Johannes and Lysbet. She was not surprised that they had trekked. He was a lazy man, good only at procreating an endless chain of children. His wife, Lysbet, said she was pregnant and would, no doubt, be brought to bed before the trek was over. Still, she had helped to bring so many children of all colours into

155

the world that Tante Maria thought no more of it, deciding to cross that river when she came to it. The four children, Carl, Ryk, Sophie and Louis, were strong and healthy and looked as if—if they lived, that was—they would become fine men and women, an improvement on their parents of whom she had a low opinion.

The Bokmans were a different kettle of fish. Jappie was a big man. She liked big men. And his wife, Selina, a good mother and housewife. The only woman she had ever seen who could make soap that almost equalled her own in texture and whiteness. She also was pregnant and the mother of six children. Frikkie, the eldest boy, was almost a man. Then came Miemie, who was fourteen, Christina who was twelve, Klienie eight, and two little boys, Koos and Boetie.

This gave them only seven guns. Not counting those of the servants, who could not always be counted on, to protect six women and girls, and eight children—for you could no longer call Miemie a child. Sometimes it seemed to her that pretty girls were never children, even when they were small, and she was large for her age, with ideas that went beyond her years.

Tante Maria came down slowly, a step at a time. All the wagons had halted and lay like ships anchored at sea. It was midday. Cooking fires were lit and the oxen outspanned. To keep well, working cattle required eight hours to graze and chew their cud and eight to sleep. The voorloopers were driving the spans down to water. Women were already bent over their cooking pots. Children ran, followed by their dogs. She heard a shot. One of the men had found a buck.

She told Hendrik, who was still near her watching her descent with some anxiety, to loose the chickens. Their wicker crates hung under the bed of the wagon, but already they knew what was taking place and had thrust their heads

out between the bars. As soon as the crates were opened
they ran out and began to scratch and peck about. Tante
Maria was delighted at how adaptable they had proved.
People said chickens were foolish but this was not true.
They did not have strong nerves, that was all, and lost
their heads if they were chased or frightened.

Now the pigs had to come out. They, too, knew what was
about to happen and were squealing in their Scotch cart.
It was tied by the disselboom to the end of the wagon.
She had been right about them too. How clever they were
at digging and rooting out food as soon as they were put on
the ground, and as soon as they saw the oxen being inspanned
again they came to be caught and waited to be lifted,
squealing, into the cart, where they slept or sat resting their
heads on its sides watching the scenery go by as if they were
Christian people. Once, when they had been hard to catch,
she had left them and on finding themselves alone in the
veld they had run screaming after the wagons. After that
there had been no more trouble. There was a great deal to
be said for animals, Tante Maria thought. They never lied.
They only ate things that were left about and sometimes it
seemed to her that they had higher moral standards than
most people. Moreover, they were not stupid. Whoever
heard of an animal leaving a place where it had every
comfort and going off into nothingness for no reason?
Allewêreld, one didn't see animals trek. No, only men did
that. Pigheaded fools who would listen to no wisdom.

She watched her pigs root and her chickens scratch with
pleasure. They made the wilderness almost homelike and
secure. The crow of a cock in the morning made up for the
roar of a lion in the night. They were not in lion country
yet, but they would be soon. Not only had she been told
about it, but she had dreamed of it and, in a trance, had
seen lions devouring cattle in a kraal of thorn—and fright-

ened the coloured girls out of their wits by her description of the scene. Her married youth had not been devoid of lions. The farm Groot Jan had carved out of the wilderness, had been the roving ground of several till they had been killed.

Tante Maria sat on a stool with her back against the wagon wheel to watch the girls cooking and shout advice and instructions. She wondered if she would ever be able to teach them to wash their hands, or at least just dip them in water, instead of wiping them on their skirts or their hair. But they were good cooks and if she had been unable to train them at Groenplaas, what was the good of trying to do so now, here in this verdant wilderness? Still, she shouted at them.

" If you will not wash you hands, at least wipe them on a clean lappie, a cloth that has been laundered, and not on your filthy skirts."

The girls turned back from the fire to smile at her. " Ja," they said. " Ja, ja." And wiped their hands on their skirts.

The next and nearest wagon—it was a hundred yards away—belonged to the Beyers family. She could see the woman, Mevrou Beyers, walking round it on her toes, as if she were a young unmarried girl, and singing! This really shocked her. Of all things that a widow could do, this was the worst! Particularly if she sang loudly and well, like a bird. And she did not like being called Tante Magdalena. What did she then want to be called, with a son who was almost grown up? Who in a year or two would marry and give her grandchildren? Ja, the day that happened she would call upon her to congratulate her and call her Ouma. She would say how strange it must be to be a young girl one week and a grandmother the next. She would certainly do this, provided they all lived and that Mevrou Beyers did not settle too far away to make the journey convenient.

Another thing disturbed her—a dream she had had

about hell. It had to be hell because there was much smoke and a roaring fire. In the firelight devils leapt and shouted. She had great confidence in her dreams and was disturbed by them. They were always bad and always came true if she waited long enough. First lions, and now devils. Perhaps people without her gift were happier, living in ignorance of what lay before them.

Magdalena Beyers remained composed. She was unperturbed by Tante Maria's dislike of her, which she understood most clearly. She was thirty-three years old and had been a widow for three years. The trek, therefore, had been a solution to her difficulties. As soon as she had heard rumours of it she had decided to go, with her son Louis and her two stepsons, leaving the other, Daniel, to take care of the farm. By the time they had reached their destination, whatever it was, she would have found a new life and a new place. She had loved her husband, but she was still young. Three years of mourning was enough. Tears would not bring him back, nor did it help to live in her old home and be reminded every moment of the day as well as the night of Pieter Beyers, who lay peacefully in the farm graveyard while she tossed, sleepless, in the great bed that they had shared. She had known that she must leave this place sometime. She had known it almost as soon as she had realised that Pieter was really dead. That she would never see him come in through the front door into the house again. That she would never set another plate of food in front of him or hear him call for coffee. That had been in '34. At that time there had been no excuse for going, nor even a place to go. It was merely that she had left Verloren Vlei in her heart and mind. She had gone about her work in a dream, suspended between the full and happy past she had lost and a future which she could not yet envisage but which she knew would not be spent here. Then came the talk of the trek. Some men—a few—had already trekked.

The Lord, to whom she prayed twice daily, had shown her the way. They would trek. Me and Louis, she thought, and the two big boys. So slowly she had built up the idea in their minds. To Barend, the serious one, she had built up a picture of a great stock farm with a thousand morgen of sweet grass for the cattle. To Flip she had talked of hunting and ivory. Yet, when they had come to her and spoken of trekking, she had shown great surprise and only after much discussion had she let them persuade her into coming.

The news of the massacre in Natalia had not disturbed her unduly. It was sad. It was terrible. But it would be avenged one day. In the meantime she was happy, happier than she had been since her husband's death. She knew that the women disapproved of her, because she was still pretty —a disgrace at her age—had remained slim and was quick as a girl on her feet. They also disapproved of Francina. They disliked their freedom. Maria Prinsloo was imprisoned in her fat. The other two were pregnant and surrounded by children who were a continual anxiety, and always in trouble or danger of one kind or another; yet nothing ever happened to them more important that a cut finger or a barked knee. She enjoyed watching them run and play and was amused at Miemie Bokman's sudden assumption of womanhood when a man was near her, and Francina's alternate forwardness and fear. This was how women always caught men—coming towards them to show their beauty and then running away demanding pursuit and capture. She knew also that she could do so. That she was still young enough, and pretty enough—much prettier than many younger women who were already worn out at her age with childbirth. Louis had been her only child. There had been one miscarriage and then nothing. Though it had not been for lack of trying. Her Piet had been an amorous man, very sweet and loving in his ponderous way. A man like an elephant, if one could imagine a loving elephant. And she missed him greatly. Still, she was happy with her son and her stepsons, and the changing scene, which was why she sang. Round her were the other wagons. The trek oxen grazed or lay chewing their cud. The blue smoke of the cooking fires rose into the still air in little columns that went up like pillars and disappeared into nothingness. Away in the distance she could see the great herds of cattle. This was one of the trek's difficulties. To be safe, the wagons must stay as close as they could to each other. To secure water and grazing for the sheep, horses and cattle, they had to scatter. But that was the men's business—Oom Willem, their leader's. He was a man whom she had always admired. It amused her that the other women did not like Cina either. She saw her riding in on her grey horse and greeted her.

Francina waved and cantered towards her own wagon. She was hungry. She had been out with the herds and when she had done eating she would return. She had arranged to meet Barend Beyers. He wanted to show her a new calf that had most curious markings, being white with both red and black marks arranged upon it in symmetrical spots. Ja, she thought, that is what he says with his mouth, but his eyes say something else. Her heart beat faster in her breast. She gulped her food, told Hendrik to put her saddle on another horse, a bay with black points that she often rode to rest the grey.

Barend was waiting for her. He was sitting with his back to a tree eating shavings of biltong, the dried game meat of which he was very fond. His horse was knee-haltered and grazed nearby.

Cina dismounted. Barend rose and took her hand, his

arm encircled her waist as he pulled her against him and kissed her.

Francina had been kssed before by older men as they kiss a child, by Louis as children kiss. But this was different. She was being kissed savagely, almost angrily, as a woman. For an instant she fought against Barend's grip. She felt herself trapped like an animal. No one had ever held her against her will since early childhood. Then her strength left her. Her legs became too weak to support her and she clung to Barend's shoulders with her arms about his neck. She felt his lips still on hers. She returned his kiss. At that instant her whole life was in her mouth. This is me, she thought. She felt as if she was being swallowed, as if she was about to disappear into this man's mouth. As if he grew larger and larger as she diminished in size, like a tick-bird in the open jaws of a crocodile. Like the bird, she was at his mercy. She had become suddenly his, by this kiss, by the way he held her. His hand sought her breast and cupped it. She felt them harden and grow heavy. A bridge had been crossed. She was a woman now, with a woman's feelings. The fairyland of childhood lay behind her. All that was lost. The door to the garden of her dreams had closed behind her. She could never again go back. She did not want to. She wanted more experiences, more life, more danger—not less. Before her now, in the near future, lay the act of love and the child that would be its outcome.

They rode back to the camp together, parting as they reached their own wagons. They had not spoken after their embrace. Barend had broken away from her, shaking her off as a dog shakes water from his coat. She had been trembling under his hands. She had wept swift hot tears like none she had ever shed before. She had cried from neither fright nor rage. Nor from happiness, but from some strange relief that something was now over. That the chrysalis of the girl she had been was broken, and the woman she would become about to emerge. Her tears were born of the wings of beauty drying in the sun of love.

"And the spotted calf?" Tante Maria said. "Was it so wonderful? Was it worth riding all that distance to see?"

"Calf?" Francina said. She had forgotten that she had told her grandmother about it. "I saw no calf, but I am going to marry Barend."

"He is a good man," Tante Maria said, "and you get a better bargain than he does, for I cannot see why anyone should want to marry you."

"You cannot see, that is why."

"I cannot see?"

"No, you are blind. Barend wants to marry me because I am beautiful." Francina stamped her foot. "Ja, I am beautiful, beautiful and he desires me."

"Who told you that?"

"Meneer Rosenberg, the smous."

"That Jew!"

"Ja, Jews are not blind. No, they see very clearly. Which is why they are so successful in their affairs. Moreover, Meneer Rosenberg comes of the family of our Lord who was also a Jew."

"What things you believe, Cina. Truly a young girl will believe anything. It was the Jews who slew our Lord and had Him crucified."

"Ja," Francina said, "there are good and bad among all people." She was thinking of the man Bates had shot down before her eyes. A very evil man.

"Before long I shall no doubt hear you say that there are good Englishmen."

"Ja, you will hear it, Ouma. I say it now. There are good Englishmen." She was thinking of Harry Bates now.

"And I am beautiful. I am like a lily dripping dew in the first light of the dawn."

"Barend did not say that. No God-fearing Boer man would say such things."

"No," Francina said. "It was the Jew who has eyes to see. Is it not in the Book? Have I not heard it read out many times? How Solomon, the King of the Jews, spoke of the beauties of women, of how their bellies were like heaps of mealies in the sun? And their breasts like . . ."

"Mealies!" Tante Maria shouted. "It was wheat, and though it is in the Holy Book I have always thought it must have crept in through some error. For no man could think of a woman like that—certainly no Boer."

Francina looked down at her breasts and the flatness of her belly. One day they would change, become rounded, filled with milk and the seed of a man.

"Stop staring at yourself!"

"Why should I not? I am fair to look upon. Ja, fair all over; my belly is like heaps of mealies, my breasts . . ."

"Fair? How do you know? You have never seen yourself."

"But I have, I have," Francina cried, dancing up and down. "I have a mirror."

"From the Jew, I suppose?"

"Who else? Who else would tell me I was beautiful and give me a glass to prove it?"

"Well, see that that belly of which you think so much stays empty till you find a preacher to marry you. We have had enough disgrace from you already—a girl who rides about the veld alone on a stallion, dressed like a man, exposing her hair and with pistols in her saddle like a brigand. Now all that is required is that you become pregnant like a Hottentot kitchen wench. Ja," she said, "what good is it that each day I rise in the estimation of all through my perspicacity and talents, that Oom Willem is revered—rather stupidly, I think—as the leader of the trek and a wise man, if you undermine the importance of the family by your antics? Riding and love-making instead of praying that we should reach our destination, wherever it may be, safely with all our company."

15

THE BROTHERS

BAREND AND FLIP BEYERS were very close to each other. The calm steadfastness of the one was balanced by the recklessness of the other. Flip could not understand, though he respected, his brother's caution, and Barend was continually afraid lest Flip, through lack of foresight, come to trouble—even death—for he was both an ardent and a reckless hunter. Louis, their half-brother, admired them both. To him each was a hero in a different way, and he was delighted when Barend told him that he was going to marry Francina, for he loved her, too, as a friend, a playmate and a sister. If there was more in his feeling for her, he did not know it. All he knew was that he was glad she should come into their family and that he would not be parted from her. Flip, too, was pleased but somehow annoyed that his staid and solemn brother had got there before him, surprised that he had not noticed the sudden blooming of this girl into a woman. It was the trek that had done it. Away from her home, her past, among people—some of whom she scarcely knew—Francina had been forced to grow up. He saw now how pretty she was. How beautifully she moved, how gracefully she rode. And all this had been there under his eyes, ready to his hand, for he knew she liked him and he had let it go. Still, like Louis, he was glad she would marry his brother and not a stranger.

For Barend, the whole picture was different. He was not

a ladies' man like Flip. He had never felt anything for any girl he had ever met before. Not even the faintest flickering of desire. And now, suddenly, he was overwhelmed by his love. He could think of nothing else. He was with Francina whenever he could spare the time. He watched her, experiencing a strange pleasure in her every movement. It was wonderful to see her eat, and surely no one had ever sneezed in such a charming fashion. He loved to kiss her, to touch and hold her, and she responded to him, purring like a kitten in his arms. So his days passed in a kind of bucolic idyll of herding, hunting and seeking out his love wherever she might be. He spent many evenings sitting at the Prinsloo fire, listening to Oom Willem's tales, to Tante Maria's complaints, but hearing neither as he courted Francina with his eyes and touches of his hand when she passed near him.

The trek was now passing through heavily timbered, hilly country. Some of the yellowwoods were immense—fifteen feet in diameter and two hundred feet high. There were other big trees, too, in the forest. Assagai, black stinkwood, black ironwood, white stinkwood, hard pear, white pear, Cape chestnut and Cape beech. This was Neisna, the land of the Outeniquas, where a man named Rex—said to be a bastard of the English king—held dominion over the white and coloured woodcutters who lived in great poverty, barely making a living. It was by the greatest yellowwood anyone had ever seen that Barend made love to Cina. Leaving the stock, which would not stray from the narrow track through the forest, they had made for this giant. Without a word they had turned their horses toward it and had dismounted at its foot. The great trunk rose like a wall in front of them.

" I wonder how many men have seen this tree? How old do you think it is?" Francina asked. " Five hundred or a thousand years?"

Barend said: "I do not know—but long before our fathers landed at the Cape this was a great tree, almost as great, perhaps, as it is to-day."

The forest was green about them. Dark green with filtered light. The boles of the trees stood resembling the pillars of an ancient church. Lianas hung like rigging from the branches above their heads. The leaf mould on which they lay was black with age, deep with the fallen leaves of centuries, perfumed with a heady, fecund scent. It was bed-soft, and in her hands as she held the rotted loam, Francina could feel its life. This soil was alive, elastic, almost palpitating, as she clenched and relaxed a handful in her fist.

Tante Maria had talked of waiting for a predikant, but where was he? Where was the church? Surely this—she stared up through the dark canopy of leaves above her at the distant sky—was church enough?

Once again there had been a struggle. Then Barend had kissed her and she had kissed him back, lost in his embrace. He had become more urgent. She had fought him once more, struck him. She had bitten his hand. As he flung her down, her strength failed her when she felt his hands upon her, his weight pressing on her body, and then—nothing. It had all ended without reason. It was as if a great storm had brewed up clouds of blackness, as if she had heard distant thunder and the roaring of the wind in her ears. But the lightning had never struck, and the sky which had been black was clear, blue, empty as a baby's eyes.

Suddenly Barend had stood up and stared down at her. He looked very big, standing above her, and she had hated him. Why had he not finished what he had begun?

"Get up," he said. "We are not animals or Kaffirs to lie together in the fields."

It was when he had said that that she hated him, hated him for his caution, for his fears. Above all for what he had said, putting it into words. It seemed to her that it was words that made reality. Things that were not mentioned never happened, though they had happened, and Barend acted as if they had done something evil when they had done nothing. He had dirtied something that had been clean. She hated and loved him at one time, and wondered how one could do this.

Now she stared at him as he sat beside her in the light of her grandfather's fire. This was her man, her lover, her husband to be, the father of her unborn children. She laughed suddenly at the thought that had he been different she might already be a mother. She wondered when motherhood began. Did it begin when a woman was pregnant or only after the child was born?

"What are you laughing at?" Barend asked.

"At a joke, Barend. At what else does one laugh? Ja," she said. "But it is a very private joke." Then she began to cry.

So far, though the Prinsloo Trek, as it was called, had travelled far, there had been no incident or adventure that was in any way out of the ordinary. They had seen no new game though the game was more plentiful. Now for the first time they were in elephant country and saw their sign. Great balls of dung in which twigs, the size of pencils, from the branches they ate were embedded. There was the immense spoor. The great circle of the front feet with the ellipse of the hind cutting into them. For they walked this way, as if the front and hind ends were two men stepping into each other's footprints. Several of the Boers had been out after them but had not seen or even heard one. As they approached, the great beasts had moved away, silent as ghosts, along their forest paths.

The forest was not continuous. It lay like a great dark

green carpet in the valleys, climbed into the kloofs and sometimes reached the hilltops. But much of the land was grass and open veld so that there was ample grazing for the beasts. Before long Oom Willem said they would reach open country that was almost desert but where the succulence of the bushes replaced water so that the stock could go for a day or more without it. Then, after crossing a great river, they would come to the high veld, vast rolling plains covered with game, where in winter the cold was bitter. After that again, after crossing more mountains and rivers, they would descend into the low country. Here the game changed again as did the nature of the land, for this was bush country, a land clothed with spiky thorns, some no taller than a sheep, others the height of the giraffes that fed upon them. There were many lions here, and fevers that killed those unable to resist them. But on the way they would pass through country that was occupied, though only sparsely, for the road led past the London Mission Station at Bethelsdrop to the village of Uitenhage and then across the sour veld to Grahamstown, a city of four thousand souls and only two hours' ride from the Great Fish River, the boundary of Kaffaria, the land of the wild Kaffirs. Then to Cradock, Graaff Reniet and Colesberg, all country settled to some extent but ravaged within the memory of man by wild Kaffirs as far south as Mosselbaai.

With this talk of Oom Willem's in his mind, with the thought of the adventures that lay before them, Louis Beyers rode out of the woods into the more open rolling country that separated the forest from the karroo, as the desert they were approaching was called. He was riding his yellow horse and led a pack horse loaded with the two bushbuck he had shot.

He had been about to turn back when he saw the mouth of a large cave in the hillside and rode towards it. The veld outside it was trodden bare of grass and several narrow paths led to it. This surprised him. He wondered what animals could use this cave. At first he thought the spoor was that of small horses or donkeys, till he saw there was no mark of a frog. Whatever they were, they appeared to use the cave as a stable, for its floor was deep with the piled manure of years. They must come here in cold wet weather, he thought. It was something he had never heard of before. He had thought only beasts of prey, lions, leopards, hyenas and the like, ever lived in caves.

Leaving the valley he rode up into the bare rolling hills, for Oom Willem had told him to look for more grazing while he hunted meat. The land here was high. At first he rode through fynbos scrub and then came to the rooigras and matted finger grass. This was the kind of grazing he had been looking for. Oom Willem would be pleased. This grass was good and there was water—a strong stream that burst out of the hillside.

As he sat looking about him from his horse's back, he heard a kind of barking scream. It sounded like the noise a hunting dog makes when it is galloping at the heel of a wounded buck. He looked round, wondering what a dog was doing so far away from any human habitation, and saw a zebra stallion, its ears laid back, its teeth bared, charging at him. Behind it stood a small herd of mares with foals at foot. Louis drove his heels into his horse and galloped off. Circling away, he brought up his gun to shoot. But he was too late. The zebra's bark merged into the scream of his pack horse as the zebra's teeth caught it by the throat and tore out its windpipe. Then it reared and chopped at the horse as it fell to its knees. The zebra now swung round and delivered two terrific kicks at the dying beast. As it turned again to savage the still quivering horse, Louis shot it through the chest. Blood spurted from its mouth, staining

its stripes. It reared and fell beside the horse that it had
killed. The mares, seeing their champion down, and frightened by the shot, bolted with their foals. By the time Louis
reached the pack horse, both it and the zebra were dead.
Unwilling to leave the buck he had shot but unable to carry
them all on his own horse, he cut the hind quarters from
them, skinning them along the backs, which he tied together
and slung over his horse's shoulders so that they hung level—
a bushbuck on each side of his saddle.

This was the first adventure of the trek and he, Louis
Beyers, had had it. The loss of the pack horse was not
serious. They had plenty of horses.

Everyone was interested in his tale and Oom Willem told
him that these were mountain zebras that the Boers, who
hunted in these parts, called wildeperde or wild horses.
They lived in small herds and the stallions became savage
when the mares had foals. The caves in which they took
shelter were known as *wildeperde stalle*, or stables.

Two days later they were among the wild-horse hills and
then passed through them into the flat karroo country, out
of which flat-topped, rocky hills rose starkly without preparation, straight out of the plain. Here the land stretched out
like a dirty cloth of yellow-brown and grey, dusty soil which,
for a few moments as the sun rose or fell, assumed an
unearthly beauty, becoming tinged with rose and lilac light.
The dry water courses were bordered with dwarf willows
that gave no shade, and mimosas, whose long savage thorns
stuck out like pairs of thick white bone needles. Succulent
bushes, neither green nor black, seemingly neither dead nor
alive, fought for existence in this strange empty world.
Stones, polished by the wind-driven sand, lay shining
between the bushes. Dark ridges of ragged rocks, like the
backbones of buried monsters, stood up, cutting the plain
into strips. Little hills, some rounded, some as flat-topped

as if they had been cut off with a knife, broke the monotony of the skyline, and in the distance the mountains were pink, blue, purple or black according to the time of the day.

There were stones everywhere, and baked earth as hard as stone and swept clean by the wind. More willows, mimosas and karee bush marked the dry river beds. There were banks of dusty, drifted sand. This was a land that went months—even years—without knowing rain or feeling the flow of water. When it rained, the veld bloomed, was suddenly carpeted with grass and flowers and the dry rivers ran. And then, as suddenly as this land had come to life, it died.

Wood for fuel was scarce. Food had to be cooked on fires made of dry game dung or thorns that crackled under the pots, flaring up and dying down in a moment or two. Oom Willem now began to train his people in the art of making laagers when they camped, and in the stratagems of war. For soon, in a month or two, they would reach the highveld and might run into wild Kaffirs.

It was the men themselves, rather than what they did, that interested Francina. Whether they made laagers or no laagers mattered very little to her. She liked to watch them, to listen to them shouting, to see their eyes change when they looked at her. Barend had done something to her in the forest. Perhaps, she thought, had he done more, the change in her would have been less, for then she believed she would have been stilled and satisfied. As it was, the blood ran through her more swiftly than ever before. Her smooth skin felt too tight for her body and her eyes burned with the sombre brooding flame of inquiry. It was as if, galloping madly, she had reached the edge of the precipice of life, and there had been pulled up by a cruel bit, pulled up and flung back on to her haunches. But still she pawed the air, still sought the leap that would carry her into the future. There was a lock to a woman's life and men held its key.

Miemie Bokman had become her friend and they talked together about life and men. With Miemie, she assumed knowledge she did not have, speaking with the authority of an engaged girl. Miemie listened with wondering wide dark eyes, neither believing nor disbelieving. Often both girls came near to truths that they felt but could not put into words.

One day Miemie said: " I shall be your sister, for it is in my heart to marry Louis Beyers."

For a moment Francina was jealous. Then she flung her arms round the other girl and kissed her. " How lovely that will be," she said. " And Louis is a lucky boy for you are very pretty."

" You think so?" Miemie asked. " I think I am pretty too, but it is nice to be told."

" Ja, you are pretty with your dark hair and brown eyes," Francina said. " And your shape as smooth and sleek as a buck."

The girls spent much time together and were usually joined by the Beyers brothers when they had finished their work. Francina worked almost as hard as a man with the Groenplaas herdboys, counting and doctoring the stock. So far there had been more births than deaths, many of the cows and mares had young at foot. So all lived well with plenty of meat, bread and milk. They had butter, too, making it by the simple process of fastening a churn to the spokes of a wagon wheel which churned the cream as it turned.

In the afternoons, while the laager was being made, Francina and Miemie, under Tante Maria's direction, taught the younger children their letters and some simple sums to the girls. They sat on little folding stools grouped about their teacher and wrote on their slates or read from the Bible. The older ones used ink made from vinegar, rust and gum collected from the thorn-bushes.

Everywhere the farmers welcomed the trekkers and sped them on their way. Francina was amazed at the largeness of the world and the number of people in it. She had never conceived the possibility of a place the size of Grahamstown and could not believe that Cape Town was much larger. Grahamstown had four churches and was almost entirely inhabited by the English people who had come here eighteen years ago and their children. It was a military town and filled with the soldiers who defended the frontier. Criminals were hung in the open streets. She saw a soldier being flogged in front of the Drostdy, lashed to an eight-foot wooden triangle, the cat-o'-nine-tails being dipped into a bucket of salt water before each stroke. So this was what they had done to her friend Harry Bates. She had not realised its full horror before.

Wild dogs and jackals screamed round the outspan at night. There were drunken Kaffirs everywhere. Brandy was only a penny a tot.

A deputation from the city came to see them off when they left, with a military band playing martial airs, and presented Oom Willem with a Bible as a token of their goodwill.

But the Boers were glad to leave. They did not like the bustle of the town or the soldiers. Though now that they had met English farmers, they were prepared to acknowledge that there were some decent folk among them.

As there had been a routine on the farm, so was there one here. The oxen were inspanned with the first grey light before the dawn, in the hour that the tame Kaffirs called the hour of the horns. This was the time when, by kneeling on one knee, a man could see the horns of his sleeping oxen black against a greying sky. Seeing their horns, he knew them, their names and places in the span, for each ox had his accustomed place and yokemate. The leaders were chosen for their intelligence and quick walk. The wheelers —the pole oxen—for their great weight, experience and courage, for on this pair sometimes the safety of the wagon might depend. The laziest oxen were put on the right side where they could be struck more easily with the long giraffe hide wagon whip—fifteen feet of bamboo and sixteen feet of whip with its two lashes, the first as thick as a willow twig and the second thinner than a bootlace A good driver could take a piece out of an ox's side with his whip. He could flick a fly off its neck. He could kill a bird on the wing as it flew over his wagon. But a good driver did none of these things. He clapped his whip over the backs of his span, exploding it an inch above them. Once trained, he seldom hit them. In training them, every time he called them by name he struck them so that when they heard their names the oxen moved inward. Those on the near side to the off. Those on the off to the near. So that a man who knew his oxen well could drive them by words alone.

The wagons rolled on till the sun was high. Then near midday they outspanned near water if there was water. The distance travelled was known as a skof. A skof was three to five miles. They seldom went more than two skofte in a day —ten miles at the most. And on Sundays the Boers did not move, nor would they hunt or even fight unless attacked. When freed, the oxen grazed lay chewing their cud. The women prepared a meal, for all were hungry, their bellies empty of food since they did not eat before leaving. Two hours later they inspanned again and the trees and bushes, instead of standing in the pools of their own shadows, began to throw them to the east. Later these shadows would lengthen so that a tussock of grass might have a shadow a full yard long, and that of a tree stretch halfway across a valley.

This was the time to laager. Oom Willem blew his horn and drew up. The other wagons came up one at a time, beside him, passed him, and taking a turn inward, stopped. Each was a link in the chain of wagons that would form the protective ring of the laager. One lightly loaded wagon that could be moved by hand was kept as a gate. The working oxen and horses were now sent out to graze. As night fell they would be driven in and the gate closed. The other stock rested out on the veld, held by the older, tamer beasts. Some of the older cows wore bells. Some of the horses were knee-haltered. And the rest stayed more or less grouped about them in their respective herds.

For Willem Prinsloo, confident in his power to lead his people, with God's help, to the promised land, life seemed to have begun again. It was not merely that he felt younger. This new life had made a new man of him. Each day there were plans to be made. The road they were taking had to be explored—water, grazing and camp sites found. He was astonished at how well he remembered everything, at how in thirty years there had been no change. Trees that he had camped under seemed no bigger, nor were they, for some thorn trees only grow an inch in five years. Time passed this ancient land by. No more could be written here. It was too old. The hills exposed by the erosions of millennia were the backbone of Africa. Only the hardiest trees and shrubs could live. So hardy were they that if they did not seem to grow, they were also unable to die. The droughts did not kill them. They withstood the occasional floods that swept over them. Veld fires, set by the natives hunting game, scorched their foliage but they recovered from their burns. And this was the Boers' land, the indestructible Africa of which they were a part.

They were now on the trekpad, the road to the North. Three days ago they had picked up the spoor of two wagons that had preceded them. For them, one spoor was enough to make a road. When their own wagons had passed, those who followed would call it a highway.

Willem on his roan horse rode alone ahead of the wagons. He could see their dust five miles behind him. He kept his horse between the marks of the wheels where the oxen had beaten out a path with their hoofs. Suddenly he stopped and turned off the road to look at a heap of rocks. A cross was painted on it with whitewash made of wood ash and milk. He took off his hat. Someone had died here. A child, from the size of the stone heap. Ja, he thought, children die. There were his own dead children in the cemetery at Groenplaas. But at least there they were walled in and lay with their own blood. But to die here and lie alone in the open veld was a strange fate for a child. Ja, and when the dead arose at last on the Day of Judgment, what of this little one isolated and alone in the veld?

He did not want to think that they had been lucky so far or that before they reached the end of their march they were bound to bury some of their own dead. This thought he thrust behind him.

16

A PLAN FOR MURDER

FRED CARTER's difficulty was how to kill Bates while he was surrounded by the rest of the band and never parted from his big Zulu servant. The only plan was to detach him permanently, to say, " Come on, Harry, let's get out of this. Let's think of some other way of living." He thought Bates would agree because both of them were getting tired of a hunted life. But if they cleared out on their own he would lose his chance of taking over the bandits and raiding Groenplaas. Francina was continually in his mind. He had not believed that he could ever feel this way or that a young girl could send a man so mad.

After seeing Robinson, Kleinbooi and he had come back to the farm where they had been well fed and spent the night. He had not been able to take his eyes off Cina. The way she moved, the way her heavy hair swung over her shoulders. The looks she gave him—as if she was afraid but could not help wondering about him. Her strange, almost golden eyes. Used for years to taking what he wanted when he wanted it, he had had the greatest difficulty in keeping his hands off her. This had increased his desire till it had become an obsession. The following day he had said good-bye and had taken her hand. It had been as firm as a boy's. It had lain in his, passive yet alive as a young bird, warm and afraid—poised for flight. As if she knew what lay in his heart. That she felt this only inflamed him more.

He had tried to put it all out of his head. As they rode

back to the mountains, with the troopers' saddles fastened together by their stirrup leathers hanging over their horses' shoulders, he had concentrated on the reward for Bates's death and the various ways of achieving it. The thought of murder did not deter him but it had to be a safe murder. Safe for him.

Then the situation changed. The brigands received news from one of their spies that the Prinsloo family had trekked. She was no longer here. The nest was empty. The pretty bird he coveted had flown. This simplified everything. He must follow her. He would persuade Harry to come with him. They would join the trek. Say they were reformed characters. That they now wished to hunt and farm, to become Boers. They would point out that two men like themselves, used to a rough life, to guns and horses, well mounted and armed, were an acquisition. No, by God, he thought, coves like us don't grow on trees. They would not be refused.

There being no time like the present, he decided to visit Harry Bates at once. He took a bottle of dop with him. This was real brandy distilled from wine and not peaches or other fruits. His pipe was going well. He was, he knew, a picture of contentment. And why not? Why should he be dissatisfied? Everything was going his way. The birds were no longer in the bush. They were almost in his hand.

Harry was sitting on a bench outside his cottage when he arrived.

" Well, Fred," he said, " you're the kind of visitor I like to see. The kind that brings their own liquor instead of drinking me out of house and home."

" It's good, too." Fred Carter held up the bottle.

Gertruda brought out another bench and three beakers. For an hour they sat drinking and smoking. Kleinbooi joined them.

This is getting us nowhere, Carter thought. He put his hand on Harry's shoulder. " 'Arry," he said, " I got something to tell you." At times, though he could speak good English having had some education and been a clerk before enlisting, Carter lapsed into Cockney when moved by emotion.

" Tell me then."

" It's private like. An idea that I got."

Harry got up. " All right, we'll go down to the water." Fred threaded his arm through Harry's.

" 'Arry," he said, " I'm sick of this. We'll get nowhere here unless it's the gallows."

" Well?"

" Wot about getting out of it? Wot about joining some of these Boers that's getting to hell out of it to the North? We're good men, 'Arry. Good men with swords and guns and horses. They'll take us, 'Arry. I'll swear they'll take us."

" And the boys here?" Harry looked around him. " Who's going to take care of them?"

" That drunken scum?"

" Drunk and scum they may be. But without a leader they'll be taken. They're stupid, Fred."

" That's right, 'Arry. Stupid. Let 'em swing. It's my hide I'm worrying about. Mine and yours, 'Arry. There's a rumour, you know, that there's a reward out for you—a price on your 'ead." That's clever, he thought. By God, that's clever. " And if it's true, 'Arry, how long do you think you'll last? I'd stand by you, 'Arry, by God, because I'm English, because we've lived side by side and fought side by side in the Tenth. Sailor Jack might, too, and your big Kaffir. But they'd pull us down, 'Arry. The weight of that coloured scum would pull us down."

" Your idea is that we join some Boers?"

" That's it, and there's some Boers we know, the Prinsloos. You sold them that big grey 'orse and I spent a night there. Decent people, 'Arry. Very decent and God-fearing." Fred raised his eyes to heaven. He was much attached to God-fearing people, having preyed on them all his remembered life.

Harry Bates struck his flint with its steel, blew up the punk in his tinderbox and lit his pipe.

" I'll think about it, Fred," he said.

He did think about it. There was a great deal in what Fred had said. This was a dead end, the final paragraph in the story of life which must end with a bullet or a gibbet. Why not turn a new page and start afresh? A new man in a new land. Forget he was an English soldier. Forget his blood, his mother, his past. Forget the regiment that had been his life.

That was the hardest of all. Though he had lost it now, though he could never go back, it had become part of him. The smell of the stables and the horse lines, the troopers riding knee to knee. The jangle of the bits, the rasp of the sabres as they were pulled out of their scabbards. The scream of the trumpets, the rattle of the kettledrums. The shouts, the orders, the neighing horses, the whole of it that went to make the life of a cavalry regiment. And he had been a part of it. A living part of its body. And here, by God —he began to laugh—he had licked a ragged bandit band into a kind of military unit with some semblance of discipline, order and even drill. Sailor Jack could take them over. He was a good man as long as he stayed sober. Drunk, like most drunken men, he was without judgment. Yes, he would go. But Fred was wrong about one thing. He was not going to sneak off like a thief. He would say goodbye to them. He would hand over to Jack. There would be a last parade. Leaving the woman, Gertruda, did not worry him. It would not worry her. Before he was out of sight she would be in some other man's bed. When he thought it over he discovered that he would regret nothing here, and wondered why he had stayed so long, Fred, his friend and comrade of the Tenth, was going with him, and Kleinbooi, the only person in the world whom he loved, would never leave him.

Kleinbooi, when he was told the news, said he was glad to be going. "Baas," he said, "I do not like it here."

"Then why did you remain?"

"Why, lord, does the hyena follow the lion? I remain because you are my lord and a man cannot be separated from his shadow except by death."

"What don't you like, Kleinbooi?"

"The climate. I do not like rain in the winter when it is cold. In my country it rains in the summer. I do not like the people here—dogs, scavengers and mangy jackals, robbers who are afraid of war and steal by night. And finally, I am sick of my name. I will no longer be Kleinbooi. My name is Nzobo, the Zulu, of the Zulu clan. Lord," he said, "I am all Zulu. I am of the blood. I," he tapped his chest, "I can wear the skin of the leopard and none can say me nay, for the blood of Senzangakhona runs in my veins."

Bates looked at his servant, now transformed into a savage warrior, the descendant of kings.

"But what happened, Nzobo? Why did you leave your land where you were held in honour?"

"I left because of a maid, lord. One of the three hundred concubines of the king. *Aaie*," he said, "that was love. Our spirits burned together, our hearts were bound as the blade of this assagai is bound to the haft." He raised the spear he carried. "Nor were we to blame. It was the king, lord, who tempted us and many died that day. Would it please the lord to hear this tale?"

" Tell it, Nzobo."

" Very well. But the lord had better sit, for it is long."

Bates sat down.

His servant, with his change of name, had acquired a certain majesty. Always big, he now seemed bigger as he stood before him—black, immense against the sky of Africa.

" Our impi had been at war for eight moons, lord. I was a captain. This regiment was called the Destroyers and many of the captains were Zulus of the blood. Our induna was Umtaso, a brother of an uncle of the king's. He died that day. In eight moons we had travelled far, lord, and killed a multitude. *Aaie*, our spears had drunk blood till they were full. Their bellies were full. It dripped from their butts. Men, women, and children were dead. Their kraals in flames. Their cattle taken. So great was the herd that we brought to the king that the dust of its coming darkened the sky." Nzobo paused. He drew air into the great bellows of his chest.

" But this was not for nothing, lord. Some of the nations we ate up were men. Many of us lay dead. My brother among them." His eyes flashed. "*Aaie*, lord. It is in my heart that we were meant to die. That this was the plan of the king. The task he had given us he had thought impossible, beyond our strength, and had none of us come back he would have been free of many whom he feared, their blood being as good as his own. This is what is in my heart to-day, since I have had time to think, and through living with so many evil men I have learned how treacherous and wicked men can be.

" So, lord," he continued, " we came back, the proud remnants of the Destroyers, the handful that had once been a legion. But we were men, lord, hard with marching and scarcely one who was not scarred with wounds. Eight moons, lord, for men in the height of their glory and no women. We had killed them, lord. Killed and passed over them, treading them beneath our feet, for these were the orders of the king. And now he lined us up and sent his dancing girls naked against us, belly to belly, to tempt us, and those who were tempted, whose flesh rose to the challenge, he slew. Setenga was the girl who danced before me. Our eyes met and through them we leaped as though they were windows that led into each other's souls.

" Lord," Nzobo said, " has the lord ever loved a maid like this? *Aaie*," he said, " the heart of a girl is not reached between her thighs. The passage to one womb is like that to another, as one egg is like another in a wild bird's nest. No," he said, " it is the eye, the man's and the maid's through which they give themselves to each other, plunging the spear of their looks into each other's hearts.

" The girls had been told what they must do. They had been given beer and they, too, were starved. How many could be used by the king, who had also many wives? And here, naked before them, were the finest in the land, great warriors still smelling of sweat and blood and war.

" ' Close your eyes and live, fool,' Setenga said. For she knew I could not have looked upon her charms and remained calm. So I closed my eyes, but even then it was hard, lord, for I felt her near to me. Her belly a hairbreadth from mine, for this she dared not simulate, but it did not touch mine. I smelled her sweet sweat and her breath. The ground on which I stood vibrated from the stamping of her feet as she danced. And the air moved as if the wings of a bird had passed very close as she clapped her hands, and sang.

" At last it was over. We who had stood the test were called to the king's chair and praised for our self-control.

But still I saw death in his eyes. One way or another the Destroyers were doomed. I saw it in the face of our brave induna.

"So this was the end. I had lived twenty-five summers and this would be my last. The king promised us wives as a reward. Now we could wear the beeswax ring of married men in our hair. But I wanted no wife. I had lost my heart to a dancing girl whom I would never see again, for to touch a woman of the king meant death for both. Yet that night an old crone came to me and guided me to a corner of the king's kraal where there was a small hole concealed by a hanging mat. Here Setenga was waiting and I lay with her, matless in the dust, as the old woman kept watch. *Aaie*, lord, that night I knew her—my heart, and for many nights. Till they caught her. For they found a baby growing in her belly and the king had never touched her. So she died slowly, lord, impaled upon a pointed stick, never speaking my name. But I was suspect, for all knew that she had danced before me, so I fled, lord. *Aaie*," he said, "I fled and I am here. But I will be glad to go back to a land where it does not rain in winter."

It took Harry Bates three days to make his preparations. Then he called the band together and told them of his decision.

They stood round him, ragged but confident and well fed, the women and children on the outside of the group.

"I called you together to say good-bye," he said. "Fred and I and Kleinbooi are going to leave you. We are going to hunt elephants in the North. Sailor Jack is a good man to be your captain."

The men cheered him and wished him luck.

Gertruda's eyes flashed over the men. Which one would she now choose for a master?

Fred Carter thought how easy it had all been. No persuasion had been necessary.

Nzobo looked at Carter. He was not sure about this man. There was something about him he did not trust. Why, when they had delivered the girl, had he gone on to speak to the English captain? Why had he disguised himself with a patch over his eye and peas in his shoe? What had he said?

17

THE HUNTERS' CAMP

THE WAGONS had passed through the karroo without adventure or accident. For weeks they had moved through clouds of red dust as fine as flour. Everything was red. The wagons, the livestock, the people. There was dust in the food, dust in every clotheschest. Nor was there enough water for laundry or any point in washing had there been water. But there had been enough for drinking. Though sometimes the stock would have been short had it not been for the succulence of the karroo bush which oozed moisture as soon as its stems were broken.

Almost the only game here were springbuck which swarmed in herds of hundreds, leaping and playing. Sometimes they manœuvred like regiments of cavalry, at others they played like children, jumping over each other in some inexplicable game. Fawn-coloured, with a white mane down the centre of their backs, a dark streak on their flanks, they were almost invisible in the brilliant sunlight. Their horns were lyre-shaped and heavier in the rams than the ewes. They were so plentiful that the servants and the dogs became almost useless from the meat they gorged. There was one curious thing about these buck—at the moment of death they exuded a most sweet perfume from some gland on their backs.

Then at last the country changed. It became more hilly as they climbed towards the high country. The karroo bush and tall aloes were left behind. There was grass. Such grass as these men from the Colony had never seen before. Grass stirrup-high that swayed and rippled like water in the breeze. There were few trees. This was a world of grass and flowers. Game was plentiful here too. Wildebeest and zebra grazed in great herds. Eland were common, the fat bulls easy to ride down and herd back to the camp as if they were cattle for the slaughter. This was a new Africa for people who were accustomed to live among the jagged horizons of the Cape mountains. Here the world seemed endless; it rolled out before them like a vast grass carpet enclosed only by the bright blue sky. In all the world there was nothing else—only grass and sky, and the birds and animals that peopled this flowering paradise. There was plenty of water, great flat pans upon which ducks and geese swarmed in such thousands that when they rose the sky was blackened.

Day after day the scenery was the same. The tall virgin grass going down before the hoofs of the leading span and the wake behind the last one stretching out till it disappeared as a thin thread on the horizon.

Through this new bright world Francina rode between Barend and Flip, laughing first with one and then the other. It was fun to be riding with two men, to know that one of them knew her with his eyes and hands. That he could have had her had he not been afraid. While one part of her cried out for him as her desire mounted, another resented him, not for what he had done, but for his omissions. Her knee brushed against Barend's. He put a hand on her thigh as he looked into her eyes. She turned away so sharply that the long switch of her hair brushed across his face. She laughed at Flip when he said he wanted to be the godfather of their first child. " Ja, Cina," he said, " there is no law that a man cannot be both an uncle and a godfather."

" Not that I know of, Flip, but of course I am only a young girl, ignorant of such important matters."

Flip leaned toward her. " Only one thing would be better —to be its father," he whispered.

Francina felt herself growing hot under his eyes. But she smiled. " Brother-in-law to a girl who is not yet wed, and godfather to a child still unconceived," she said, recovering her composure. Sometimes, she thought, Flip did more to her without touching her than Barend had ever done. I must not give him the chance, she thought, for he would have no scruples about time or place. Any thinking he did would come afterwards. She leaned forward to stroke her horse's neck.

She turned to Barend and said: " In two days it will be Christmas. How strange that will be, to spend it like this, homeless in the wilds."

Everyone on the trek was thinking of Christmas. Thinking of what they could give each other, of what they should eat, of what hoarded dainties they could partake to the glory of the Christ Child's birth. For Francina, most of the other children and many of the men, it was their first Christmas away from home. The women had left their own homes to be married. But for all it would be a strange festive season, a time of uncertainty tempered with hope.

Tante Maria would have liked to kill Francina's goose. It annoyed her, riding in the Scotch cart with her pigs, sticking out its long neck at her and hissing like a snake. The sheep were too old to kill now, their meat—being rams— would be too strong. These pets were something she never quite forgave the girl, and now there was that damned bull pup, that was so indefatigably destructive. It was no use Francina's saying that she had her pigs and her poultry. She did. Ja, she loved them—but she ate them. " Like a cannibal," Francina said. "A woman who eats her own children is a cannibal. They trust you, they put their lives into your hands, and then you wring their necks or chop off their heads with an axe!"

The girl was mad, but what else could one expect of a child brought up by a madman?

Christmas returned to her mind, fluttering in like a pigeon into its cote. At last she had become really important. Her position was assured. Everyone looked up to her. They said, "Ask Tante Maria. She will know." And they were right. She did know. At last she had a social stature that was worthy of her talents. And this would justify her great sacrifice. She would kill the small black and white boar. Who else would do a thing like that? Who else had a pig to do it with? "A young roasted pig," she said. "That is what we will have for our Christmas dinner." This pig was not very well but she was sure it would live two more days if she kept it in the cart and fed it by hand; fattening it up she would call it. Ja, I do not want him running round getting thin. That had been the pig's problem, he could run no more. Well, now he would not have to.

Johannes Frederick Ullman, with his wife, Sybella, and their two small boys, two herders and three hundred head of mixed stock, had been camped for a month. The grass and water were good and there was plenty of game. Long strips of drying salted meat, the results of his hunting, were hanging from the trees. This biltong became iron-hard and would last a year or more. It was eaten shredded, cut into dark-red marbled shavings. The meat that could not be cut into strips he abandoned to vultures and hyenas. He took no skins except those of the giraffe which could, when breyed, be made into wagon whips. He was busy with one now, cutting the immense skin, working his way round and

round it, into one single strip from the outside with his boys
clearing it away from him as he attacked the oval island of
hide that got smaller and smaller beneath his hands.

Looking up to wipe the sweat from his eyes, he saw the
dust of a trek in the distance. He recognised it at once for
what it was. After all, he had been part of one himself a
couple of months ago, but had decided to leave it since its
leader, Piet, one of the great clan of Potgieters, had been
impossible to get on with. Everyone had said so but only
he had had the courage to branch out on his own. If the
others wished to be led like oxen to slaughter, that was their
affair. He enjoyed this solitude but Sybella had become
dissatisfied. She had been fond of several women in the
Potgeiter trek and found it less interesting to cut up the
game he shot than he did to hunt it. Being a reasonable man,
he saw her point of view and said if another trek came by he
would ask to join it, and there was no reason why he should
be refused. He was a God-fearing man in the prime of life.

"Sybella," he called. "Sybella! There are wagons
coming."

His wife climbed out of the wagon, followed by a small
boy. When she was on the ground she turned back and
picked a still smaller boy off the kartel that filled its end.

It was Flip who saw the outspanned wagon first. He had
left the lovers to hold hands as they rode side by side,
amazed that Francina, who had for one instant seemed so
close to him, in whose gold-brown eyes he had seen a
promise, had turned away from him so suddenly.

Turning his horse he galloped back, shouting: "There
are men camped a mile away."

"Men?" Barend said.

"Ja," Flip said. "Boers. There are cattle and some
horses."

"They must be hunters," Francina said, "or perhaps someone is sick. Kom, kom," she said, driving her heels into Bloubooi's flanks and setting off at a gallop. Men, people, new faces, change. All this at Christmas time—it was as if God had sent them as a present.

She saw the wagon drawn up beside a big kameeldoorn. She saw the oxen grazing and the toy figures of a man and woman, some servants and children, grouped together staring at them with their hands raised to shade their eyes. She saw a servant bring the man a saddled horse. He mounted and rode towards her. Then she slowed down. Barend and Flip came up on each side of her.

The figure of the man was clear now—a middle-sized black-bearded man dressed in the moleskin and leather clothes of a trek Boer. They saw at once that he was one of the Doppers, members of the Reformed Church who wore short jackets and used neither belts nor suspenders to hold up their trousers. A buckle at the back and a drawstring served this purpose somewhat inadequately. But they had seen them before and had heard no ill of them. His horse was a bay trippler—a pacer—with a white blaze. When they were two lengths apart he pulled up and raised his hat. "I am Johannes Frederick Ullman. I am camped here with my wife and sons," he said.

Barend said: "We are the Beyers brothers—Barend and Flip—and she," he nodded at Francina, "is Francina Marais, the great-niece of our leader."

"Come to my camp," Ullman said. "It will do my wife good to see strangers. It is curious that no man is ever enough company for a woman. They all need other women with whom to gossip if they are to be content." He looked doubtfully at Francina.

Sybella Ullman looked at Francina with some astonishment. A young girl, hatless, her hair down her back, and wearing trousers, mounted on the finest horse she had ever seen. Sitting on a splendid saddle with pistol holsters in front of her thighs and an embroidered saddlecloth beneath her. The horse's bridle was ornamented with brass plates that shone like gold, a scarlet foxtail dangled swinging to and fro beneath its throat. A half-naked girl—for this was how she saw her—accompanied by two wild young men, who threw her leg over her horse's neck and slid to the ground. Never had she seen anything more disgraceful. Such lack of modesty, even taking the conditions under which they met into consideration, was unbelievable.

Francina held out her hand. " I am Francina Marais," she said. " And you must be Mevrou Ullman."

" Ja, I am Sybella Ullman."

" Give them coffee, vrou," Ullman said, dismounting.

Francina picked up the smallest boy.

" I'm Dirkie," the child said.

" Ja, Dirkie," Francina repeated. " That is a fine name for a man."

" I am not a man but one day I shall be one. Ja," he said, " a man and a great hunter and fighter in the Kaffir wars."

Francina kissed him. He was good to hold—warm, with firm solid flesh. His silky hair was fair, almost white.

The men were looking at the giraffe riems that were being breyed. The long single strip of skin that had been peeled from the giraffe hide had been passed over a branch of the thorn tree and through a wooden handle lashed to a stone which was mounted on a table. The strip went over the branch, through the eye of the stone and over the branch in loops. The boy who was working on it now took away the table. The stone fell a foot, stretching the skin. A long pole was now inserted into the eye of the stone weight and the boy began to walk round and round with the stick in his hand, twisting the riems till they came to rest against the branch. Then he withdrew the stick and the stone came down, unwinding the skin strip as it came, twisting down like a great top. The stick was inserted again and the process repeated. This would go on for two or three days. At intervals a mixture of fat and wood ash would be rubbed into the strip to help the softening process.

The Boers watched in silence. This breying was one of their life functions. They had no ropes. Everything was tied with riems—with rawhide strips that had been cured in this fashion. The trek tous of their wagons, the riems that tied the oxen and knee-haltered the horses, the strops or loops that held the ox yokes, the bridles and harness of their horses, many of their clothes, even their shoelaces, were all only removed by this one process from the living beasts that roamed the veld. This was one of the mysteries of their craft, one of the means by which they lived, a strand of the tenuous web that supported them in the wilderness. With guns and ammunition they killed their meat. With knives they flayed it, eating the flesh and using the skins for riems and clothing. They also needed flint and steel for fire. With these essentials and the simple tools they carried in the wagons that were their homes, they were self-sufficient.

Francina was telling Sybella Ullman about the trek and of how her Oupa, having no sons, had brought her up as a boy. She told of the other women and children.

Sybella pressed her hands together before her and said: " I pray you will let us join you, for here I am most lonely and afraid." She looked at her husband. " Suppose," she said, " just suppose, he was killed by some wild beast or had an accident? What would become of us? Of his wife and children?"

"You can join us. I am sure of it," Francina said. She looked to the south and saw the leading wagons. "Let Meneer Ullman ride back with us now to meet Oom Willem."

Johannes Ullman held out his hand. "Ullman," he said. "Johannes Frederick Ullman, once of Swellendam."

Oom Willem took it. "I am Willem Prinsloo," he said. "Of Groenplaas in the District of Bredasdorp." He was glad he had been riding near his wagon and had been able to get out his furry grey bell topper to greet the stranger.

"That is near the sea," Ullman said.

"Ja, it is near the sea."

"We would like to join your trek," Ullman said. "We were with Potgeiter, a difficult man, with whom I did not see eye to eye when he decided to turn east."

"What is wrong with the east?" Oom Willem said. "I have heard that when you cross the berg into Natalia the land is fair."

"The land may be fair, Oom Willem, but the Kaffirs are not. That is the land of the Zulus."

"Ja," Willem said. "That is true, but if one is strong one need not fear them. They killed Piet Retief, the brother-in-law of my sister-in-law, and his men, but Piet and his party were unarmed and unprepared."

"That was in February," Ullman said.

"Ja, in February."

"But that was not all, Meneer," Ullman said. "Perhaps you do not know what else happened—in February they also swept down upon the Boers camped in the sweet grass near the Blou Krans River. This was on February the 16th," he said. "I had the tale from a man who escaped. The attack was not expected and came at night. In that night of terror perished the Liebenbergs, the Rossouws, the Bezuidenhouts, also the Engelbrechts, the Greylings and the Bothmas. Meneer," he said, " on that night forty-one men, fifty-one women, one hundred and fifty-six children and more than two hundred servants were killed, and twenty-five thousand head of cattle stolen. The veld was red with blood and fire. Of the wagons and the gear nothing was left but smoke. The Van Rensburgs' laager did not fall nor did that of Gert Maritz, for they were warned. No," he said, " it is not in my heart to go into that land, nor do I deem myself a coward to fear the Zulus."

" This is terrible news indeed," Oom Willem said.

" Ja," Tante Maria said. " It is indeed fine Christmas news to hear that so many of our loved volk are dead and that we are like to follow them. In my dream I saw all this and more. I saw . . ."

" Hold your mouth closed, woman," Oom Willem shouted. " You and your dreams that are fit only to frighten the tottie maids."

" Then why will you not listen? You will not listen because I am always right and you do not wish to know. But I will tell," she screamed. Her hands were on her hips. " I saw black devils dancing and a great fire."

" Shut up!" Oom Willem shouted again. " Silence, I say!"

She closed her mouth. " Very well," she said, " if you will not be warned, if you will not listen to reason and turn back while there is still time. Turn back before we have lost a single life. The blood is on your head. Ja"—she raised her hand and her voice—" the blood of the little children who will die is on your head and the girls and women raped and the men and the servants slaughtered. For all who die you are to blame as God is my witness, and as those gathered here about me will testify when the last trumpet is blown, and we rise from the dead, that I, Tante Maria Prinsloo, who was born Maria Nell, have warned you."

Later Johannes Ullman spoke more of the Zulus. His friend Carl Espach, who had escaped, had told him of their organisation into regiments, of how each carried a great oxhide shield of a different colour. Those with black shields were recruits—young regiments—and the white shields made from the skins of the white royal cattle denoted the guard regiments of the king—the picked warriors of the nation. There were also regiments with red shields and red and white shields, and black and white shields. Each regiment wore a special headdress. One wore the feather of a crane, another those of a widow bird. They all had names —the Crocodiles, the Wanderers, the Sticks, the Blue Horizon, the Bees, the Gadflies and so on. No man could marry without the king's leave and this was seldom given except to veteran warriors, men already in their thirties. This system of regiments and distinctions, it was said, had been learned from a white soldier who had fought in the Wars of Napoleon and had told it to Chaka, Dinagan's brother and predecessor, whom he had murdered.

The king's round hut was twenty feet in diameter, its roof plaited as finely as a basket, and supported by twenty-two pillars, each entirely covered with beadwork. The black mud floor was so highly polished with beeswax that a man was reflected in it, as if he walked upon a mirror.

He told them about Dingaan's wives and his dancing girls, of his town of nearly two thousand huts with storerooms for shields and grain and spears. To all this, sitting round the fire, they listened open-mouthed, the men angry, the women clustered and afraid. The children, only half under-standing, clung to their mothers' skirts.

" Ja," Ullman said. " This is all hearsay. I have seen no

more than you, but my friend made it all so clear to me, for it was he who brought the news to the Potgeiter trek, that I see it in my mind as clearly as if I had been there myself. For this Espach has the gift of tongues. He knew the Zulus and traded and hunted with them. Many were his friends among them."

Sybella Ullman sat with the women, her little son Dirkie in her arms, listening to her husband. The bigger boy squatted at her feet. She had heard it all before but the story lost none of its terror. She felt safer now among the people, but was still fearful, for they were going on into the unknown. And Tante Maria had upset her, prophesying disaster, speaking of flames and devils. Why did they not take her advice and return to the safety they had left? To Swellendam, to Bredasdorp, to the sweet security of the Colony where life was ordered and under the law? What did it matter if the English ruled? One never saw them. Surely the English were better than the Zulus?

But these were strange people, mountain people from the coast, and not at all like Potgeiter's Swellendamers who had been her lifelong friends. She thought of Francina again. A girl who lived like a boy. Though when you were close to her she certainly did not look like one. Quite the contrary indeed, and this was something to ponder over. Why should a girl in a man's clothes appear more feminine than if she wore a skirt? She looked at Francina standing by Oom Willem with her hand on his shoulder as he sat by the fire. Her hair glowed in the flame light. There was a dark shadow between her breasts in the opening of her shirt, a wide belt carrying a great sheath knife defined her narrow waist. Dressed as a man, as a boy, the girl looked half naked. That had been her first impression. She saw no reason to change it. She did not think she would be happy among these people but at least her little family would be safe.

18

THE CROWS

MAGEBA, the Induna of the Zulu regiment known as the Crows, because of their great white and black oxhide war shields, was talking to his captains.

He was a powerful man, his body scarred with wounds, some of them quite newly healed. The shield on his left arm almost hit his body. In his right hand he held his short, wide-bladed stabbing spear.

"It is many moons since we ate up the white men by the Tugela and the bushman's river," he said. "Many months since the great elephant, the Buffalo whose tread shakes the earth, whose cough silences the lions' roar sent us forth to kill. And we killed. Our assagais drank blood that night. The blood of men, of women, of children, of dogs. Now our scouts come in with news of other white men who will become meat to our spears." He pointed to the west. "They are there. Their cattle are as numerous as the leaves of the trees in the forest."

The captains sitting on their shields looked up at him "*Aaie*," they said, moving the spears they held in their hands and shifting their feet.

Behind the captains were the warriors in their hundreds. As they heard the induna's words they began to stamp their feet and chant. A man leaped forward from the ranks and began to dance. Others joined him as the drums began to beat.

Mageba strode over to Naguni, a grizzled veteran, the

oldest of his captains. "We are men, Naguni. *Aaie*, we Zulus are men. We are the children of the sun."

"You have a plan, lord?" the old captain said. "The scouts say that they are strong and well armed. As we have learned, O Mageba, whose blood is that of the king, spears and courage are no match for guns."

"I have a plan, old one. The plan is fire. The gods are with us. The grass is high. There has been no rain and the wind is blowing from the east. *Aaie*, we will use the old fire and they will use the new. What good are guns against flames?"

"And the cattle, lord? What of them?"

"Enough will be left, Naguni. For we are not going home. The king has fled. Mgungundlovo, the royal town, has been burned at his orders. The white men with their guns and horses have eaten us up. *Aaie*, old one, we are now homeless men, lost ones who must start our lives again."

"And our women and children? Our herds that covered the hills like the feathers of a moulting bird?"

"Gone, gone, Naguni. All is gone!"

"Then . . ." The old man's face was blank. This disaster was unbelievable. The Zulus had never been defeated.

"Then," Mageba said, "then, old one, did you not say it? Are we not Zulus? Not men? Not the children of the sun? Our homes are gone but our spears are honed and sharp. We will go into the land of the dying sun. The dawn we will leave behind us. But first we will take our revenge. We will eat up this handful of white men. We will take as many of their cattle as we need. We would not drive them all, and collect new women as we go. For Zulus the world is full of women and cattle. We will join Mosilikatze in the North. Forget the past, old one. The past is smoke. It is dead."

" How do you know all this?" Naguni said.

" You saw the messenger who came to-day? The runner from the king?"

" I saw him. I spoke to him, but he told me nothing. He told me all was well."

" I told him to say nothing. I said if he spoke I would cut out his tongue and feed it to the dogs, that when the time came I would tell the men. I will tell them when they are roused and their blood is up and crying for revenge. I will tell then when we attack. Now leave me, old one, for I must mourn my dead. Go you and do likewise, but silently and alone. For a space we will think of our sleek wives and our fat children rolling naked in the dust. Think of our herds grazing on the hills, of our king, Dingaan, sitting in his kraal. And then it must be over. Then we must forget and go on, for we are still Zulus, and we have our spears."

Dingaan's great kraal, Mgungundlovo, was the biggest in all Zululand. He had built it after he had murdered his brother, Chaka, on the Mkumbane, a tributary of the white Umfolozi River. The name meant " The Secret Conclave of the King," for this was the spot where Dingaan—meaning ". The Needy One "—had conspired to kill Chaka and take his place.

In his mind Mageba saw it all. Once more he built it up in his mind as it had been, as if to impress it on his memory, for neither he nor any other would ever see it again. It was gone. The kraal was set on a slope that led to the river. Beyond it was the rock-strewn hillock that they called Kwa Matiwane. To the east flowed the Nzololo that joined the Mkumbane in the North.

The great kraal was oval and the public entrance was nearest to the stream. The king's dwelling place—the

Isigodlo—was opposite the entrance. Two great hedges surrounded the kraal. Between them were the rows of round huts, to the number of seventeen hundred, occupied by the soldiers. A special guard was assigned to the king's quarters. Here were the king's hut, his mother's and those of his multitude of women and servants. There were also lesser kraals where animals were slaughtered, one for washing and, attached to it, a milking kraal. He thought of the Zulus of Chaka, the great one, sons of Senzangakhona the Zulu king and Nandi the daughter of a Langenia chief. When Dingiswayo died, Chaka became king of the Mtetwas and also of his father's nation. Then blood had flowed. Chaka had conquered the world and had died as he had lived, by the spear. Dingaan and Mhlangana, aided by Mbopha, a trusted bodyguard, had killed him. But as he died, Chaka had cried, " My brother, you think you will rule the country when I am gone? But you are wrong. I see the sky full of vultures. I see the country covered with a network of roads. Not you, my brother, but the white men will rule the country."

And now it had come to pass. To-day he had received news of it from the runner of the king. These had been his words:

" I, Dingaan, king of the Zulu nation, greet my brother Mageba, prince of the blood and induna commanding the Crows, with this message. Chaka's words are true. Mgungundlovo is no more. The cattle are gone, the impis broken and scattered. I, Dingaan, have fled and am pursued by the white men. Go you, therefore, toward the dying sun, follow in the path of Mosilikatze, greet him Zulu. Say Dingaan, the King, has sent you. Reward the runner. Take him with you, for he has served me well. Farewell, Mageba. Do not fight guns with spears. This is the last word of the king."

The runner had led him away from the others to give his message. " It is for your ear alone, oh lord."

He had stood as straight as a spear to deliver his message. The king's words had rolled like drums from his lips. They were the last words he would ever hear from the king, and must be well spoken. Then, before Mageba could catch him, the runner had swayed and fallen.

The message he had brought still buzzed in his head like an ibungwane round a flame. For no beetle buzzed louder than a flying dung beetle. As he stared at the sinking sun, Mageba's mind was on blood, on revenge, on glory, on newly captured cattle and freshly taken women. He spat on the ground and tramped the spittle in. The past was dead. It was gone with the spittle. He sent for the scouts again. These were the hounds he sent out almost daily to seek for kraals to be destroyed. Moving fast, from bush to bush and tree to tree, creeping through the long grass, following water courses to look for spoor, these men missed nothing.

It had been this way since they left the sweet, softly rolling hills of Zululand. Hills that were like the green breasts of recumbent women, rich with the milk of captured cattle. How often had the scouts gone out and brought in the news of a village dreaming its peaceful life away? They told of the girls and women going to water with their great pots balanced on their heads, of the men building huts, hunting or drinking beer. Of the children and the dogs playing, of chickens scratching in the veld, and cattle lowing in the kraals.

Then suddenly all this peace was ended, broken like a pot cast against a rock. For with the dawn came the shouts of the Zulus and the cries of the dying. Then all was peaceful again and the vultures fell like stones from the heavens to feast undisturbed upon the dead. Dead men, women, children, dogs, goats, cattle, poultry. Nothing was left alive. Nothing was taken away. The coming of the vultures was a sign to the hyenas and the jackals, who watched them and came up from holes in the ground and the distant hills.

It was always the same. In front of the Zulus lay a beautiful land. Behind them only bones and the ashes of burned-out kraals.

Three men stood before the induna.

"Tell me again what you saw," he said.

"Ten wagons, five times ten people, men and women and children. And great herds of cattle."

Mageba said: "We will eat them up. We will destroy them."

"They are strong," the scouts said. "They have many guns and good horses."

Mageba told them to call the captains. He told the captains to assemble their men and sent for his finery which was carried by a boy. He put on a great war bonnet of black ostrich plumes with leopard earflaps. A necklace of lion's teeth. A cloak of black ostrich feathers. He bound bands of long white hair from cattle tails above the elbow and below the knee. He put on a kilt of leopard tails. When the men saw him come toward them dressed like this, a cry went up, "The chief! The induna! The blood of the king!" For only those of royal blood could wear leopard skins.

He held up his assagai for silence. A hush fell upon the regiment.

"I have news for you," he said. "Ill news. You saw the runner who came. He has come far and fast, for that is the way ill news must travel." He paused. "Prepare yourselves," he said. "The Crows are homeless. The tree upon which we perched has fallen. The shade of the king is no more. Mgungundlovo has perished in the flames. The impis lie dead beneath the white men's guns. Dingaan, the king, is fled."

The men groaned. One stood up and began to shout.

" Sit!" Mageba said. He sat down.

" We are homeless," he said. " Our nests are destroyed. We have no wives. No children. No cattle. But we are men. We are Zulus." he paused.

" We are Zulus," the men shouted.

" *Aaie*," he said. " We are Zulus. We are the Crows. We have wings and spears."

" We are Zulus!" the men echoed his words. " We have wings and we have spears!"

Mageba raised his hand to silence them.

" And these are the words of Dingaan, the King, by the mouth of his messenger. ' Go forth, Mageba, my brother,' he said. ' Take new cattle, new women, and build a new nation.' This we will do," he said. " And according to how things go we will remain alone or join Mosilikatze in the North. But first . . ." he paused, ". . . first comes revenge. The scouts tell me of white men only a day's march away. Boers with many cattle. And these will be the beginnings of the riches of the Crows. So go now and whet your spears. Sing them the song of blood. Let them thirst for blood as men do for water who have taken too much salt, for before the sun has risen twice they will have drunk their fill."

With that he turned and left them. The Boers had guns. But he had fire. He looked up at the cloudless sky. As long as it did not rain he had fire. The breeze was from the east and it would not rain.

19

THE CHRISTMAS LAAGER

WHEN THE wagons pulled up by Ullman's camp, Oom
Willem ordered a strong laager to be made at once. Natalia
was a long way off—some hundreds of miles to the east—
but the Zulus were not confined to Natalia. Mosilikatze's
Matabeles were somewhere in front of them to the northwest.
They, too, were Zulus—renegade regiments who had broken
away under their chiefs and formed a new nation with
stolen girls and cattle. They also lived by the spear—war
was their sport and only occupation.

From now precautions must be redoubled against surprise.
Laagers must be made early in the afternoon so that they
could be strengthened before dark. All this Oom Willem
told them beneath the ancient kameeldoorn that came to
be known as Ullman's tree, and their camp site the
Christmas laager.

He stood beside the giraffe riems that hung from the
branch above him. The great stone suspended from them
swung like a pendulum when he touched it and went on:

" My brothers," he said, " to-morrow is Christmas Eve.
All over the world at this time rejoicing and prayer com-
memorate the birth of our Saviour. Here, isolated and alone
in the wilderness, we cannot rejoice. We can only pray for
God's guidance. We can pray for our dead, murdered by
savages as they slept in the night. Pray for the men dead and
tortured, for the women raped, the little children slaugh-

tered, their throats cut like lambs. Pray, too, for God's help and protection, for this and our guns are our only hope. We shall stay here for three days to praise the Lord and rest our beasts. Our new friend, Johannes Ullman, tells me that grazing is good and the water strong. For this, too, we must thank the Lord our God, from whom all mercies flow."

But Oom Willem was not prepared to leave everything to God or put his trust in the peacefulness of the Christmas season, and the great laager was begun. Before this, they had laagered each night, but now with the coming of the New Year, with their being well into the grasslands where the cattle-loving Kaffirs roved, he felt the time had come for greater precautions and he had felt this even before he had heard Ullman's news, and besides they would be here for several days.

So with much shouting and clapping of whips, the wagons were drawn into a close circle and the spans went out to drag in trees and bushes that the Boers and their servants felled. These were stuffed into the spaces between the wagon wheels and used to strengthen any other place that seemed weak.

All the old guns that were beyond use—even blunder-busses that he had told the people to bring with them—were now loaded with anything that came to hand. Nails, odd bits of iron, broken iron pots, even small stones. In each wagon a tray of such material was set ready for reloading the guns after they had been fired. These old guns were for use at close quarters. The women were to hand them to the men and reload them again. The damage they did at point-blank range was unbelievable.

There was not, Oom Willem told them, any likelihood of attack. But one day there might be, and it was as well to be ready for it. " Ja," he said, " for it would be too late to learn.

So let us act from now on as if danger was always in the offing."

While the men got the wagons ready for battle, the women prepared the Christmas feast.

Tante Maria's spotted pig was killed and scalded. Bobotie was made. Milk tarts were baked. Louis brought in two giant bustards that were roasted. There were still some sweet potatoes and smoked fish left from the Cape. And how strange it was, the women said, to be serving them so far from the homes where they had been grown and cured. There was a small barrel of wine and brandy of several kinds, also dried salted apricots, raisins and other fruits and konfyts of many sorts. This Christmas was going to be a feast—something they would all remember.

There were some fine ant heaps near the wagons which were hollowed out and used for ovens to bake the bread, tarts and biscuits they were making. In fact, once the laager was completed and its purpose forgotten, the trek settled down to enjoy itself—this was a Christmas picnic on a big scale. Four hundred miles from home.

Bokman produced his concertina, Louis played the flute, Oom Willem got out his fiddle, and soon all were singing. They sang hymns and carols. They sang the songs they loved—" Sarie Marais," and the others. They danced in the light of the fires, the moon and the lanterns that hung swaying from the tall tips of the wagon whips.

Magdalena Beyers was dressed like a girl in a green silk dress with four flounces and three petticoats—one of green taffeta of a lighter shade, one of white silk and one of white cotton. The dress had a turned-over collar and wide sleeves that fastened with buttons at the wrist. It was also decorated with similar but larger buttons down the front from neck to hem. She wore a little green hat, too, with white streamers as if it was Sunday.

Three things were immediately apparent. That Magdalena Beyers spent much money on clothes, which a woman did only for discreditable reasons unless she was a maid, next that she had taken the very best of her clothes from the kerkklere or church chest and finally that her, Tante Maria's, opinion of this woman had always been correct—a flighty and flirtatious woman who dared to fly in the face of God by ignoring her years.

Magdalena Beyers looked at Louis and found it hard to believe that this big boy could be her son. She saw Tante Maria watching her with her usual disapproval. She went over to her as she sat heavily upon her stool and said, " It is wonderful to still be young enough and thin enough to dance."

" Ja, it must be wonderful to be shameless, Mevrou Magdalena Beyers. For the shameless have no conscience to plague them."

" I have a very fine conscience, Tante Maria. It is often in my mind."

" That is not the place for it," Tante Maria said darkly. She placed her hand on her belly. " This is where the conscience dwells," she said.

Magdalena laughed. " Ja," she said, " that is so if you eat too much. That is where regret for gluttony begins."

An abominable woman, Tante Maria thought, as Magdalena moved away to compliment Oom Willem on his playing.

Oom Willem's playing! Magtig! His fiddle screams like a cat in agony. At Groenplaas he had never played. This instrument had been part of his youth and was associated with his earlier adventures in the North. But Magdalena would praise any man. She was unscrupulous and without honesty. An honest woman of her age, with a grown son, and a widow at that, should be fat. There was virtue in fatness, for the fat were not active enough for wickedness.

Francina was filled with excitement. The night was warm and soft. The shining moon seemed bigger than any she had ever seen before. The men, cleaned up for the party, looked different—more alive and handsome. Flip Beyers more dashing than usual. She had had two glasses of Constantia wine. It was strong and sweet. She was also full of good food—of pork and potatoes and tart. The fires round which they sat illuminated the ring of wagons behind them. Nearer to the wheels the servants were enjoying themselves—feasting, singing, dancing and, as she well knew, withdrawing from the firelight to make love.

Love was in her mind. The food, the wine, the music, the moon, the firelight, the dancing, the smell of sweat and dust, the knowledge of possible danger, the certainty of adventure—all went to excite her further so that when a hand reached out and drew her into the shadow she made no protest, nor did she hang back as she recognized Flip Beyers. He drew her to him, raised her face with his hand and kissed her. She was in his arms, held close, feeling that at last the night was about to fulfil its promise, when Miemie Bokman came upon them.

She flung herself at Flip, scratching his face with her nails. " Beast, beast!" she cried. " Liar, seducer, scoundrel!"

Francina slipped from his arms. If Miemie felt like this about him, let her have him. After all, she was engaged to Barend who, if less exciting than Flip, would make a better husband. All the same, she wondered what would have happened if Miemie had not come. She did not wonder very much. She knew. That Miemie! Well, one day perhaps she would pay her back in her own coin. Still, how was one to know with Miemie? Last month she had been going to

marry Louis. Now she flew at Flip for being unfaithful
to her.

Though it was useless to protest, Johannes Ullman was
much affected by all this debauchery. Dancing was
anathema to him—a device of the devil designed to inflame
the lusts of men. John the Baptist's head would still have
been upon his neck if that girl had not danced before Herod.
Nor did he approve of music in any form, particularly in
the House of God. He was also against hymns because they
were not to be found in the Bible, nor were buttons or braces
mentioned, which was why he and his like wore neither,
keeping up their pants by the grace of God, drawstrings and
little buckles at the back so that a Dopper could always be
recognised from behind by the gap between his shirt and
trousers showing as white as a retreating springbok's rear.
Sybella shocked him too, for she appeared to enjoy the
scene and did not reply to his strictures.

20

THE NEW RECRUITS

HARRY BATES, Fred Carter and Nzobo had no great difficulty in following the Prinsloo trek. In the beginning where there were farms—they became more scattered as they penetrated deeper into the country—people spoke of nothing else. They all knew Oom Willem Prinsloo of Groenplaas and were surprised that such an established farmer should care to risk his all, including his life, in the savage North. They spoke of the hatless girl who rode her grey horse like a man, of Tante Maria, and the great herds of stock that they had with them.

The small dorps and villages they avoided. Grahamstown they gave a wide berth to, terrified of meeting old comrades or saluting an officer by mistake.

Far from having any difficulty, it would have been hard not to hear about the trek that had passed this way. Later, when they were beyond the established roads, the spoor of the wagons was easy to follow. The camp sites were all marked with the ash and charred wood of their fires and the usual scattered debris—bones chewed by the dogs, rags discarded as useless. Here an empty bottle, there a broken cup. There were the chopped stumps of the trees they had felled for burning the bush they had cut to make protective kraals for small stock.

The horsemen travelled much faster than the trek, making twenty or thirty miles a day. Where the trekkers had spent a night they spent an hour, cooking the game they had shot, watering their horses and giving them time to roll in the ash of these old fires.

They did not talk much. They did not have much to say. Certainly nothing new, since they had been soldiers together and had deserted within a few months of each other. Nor had they much in common. Fred Carter saw no romance or beauty in anything. The silence and the vastness of Africa through which they rode oppressed him. He missed the rough comradeship of the bandits. The drinking, the quarrels of the women, the screaming when their men beat them. At times, if it had not been for his great double purpose, he would have regretted ever starting on this adventure.

But as they came to the old camping places he thought of Francina sleeping here. Sometimes he thought he knew the very spoor of her wagon, and that this was where she had sat eating her meal. His nostrils grew wide as he sniffed the air like a hound. He was sure he could smell her. Francina —I'll call her Frankie, he thought.

At other times he looked lovingly at Harry Bates and flung an arm about his shoulders.

" Lord, 'Arry," he'd say, " it's a fine thing to have a pal like you, an old messmate from the Tenth." Then he'd laugh. By God, he thought, it was good to have a thousand guinea friend. He often looked at Harry's little finger with its two joints and ring. He found a little blue glass medicine bottle, very prettily fluted, with a wide mouth, that had been thrown away or lost. He filled it with brandy from his flask. Yet now, as before, the big nigger Nzobo remained the difficulty. He would have to think of some way to kill the Zulu without arousing Harry's suspicions.

For Bates the very things which Carter could not bear were his greatest joy. The wide spaces, the empty horizons, the distant hills, the mountains so sharp against the sky that they looked as if they had been cut out of metal. The silence, too, was wonderful. He rode through it as though it was a new form of air. As though he could breathe it in through his ears. He would pull up his horse to watch a buck gallop away, to listen to the singing of a bird or watch an eagle circling in the upper air. He felt a new life opening up in front of him and responded to Fred's gesture of affection.

" Fred," he said, " I owe you a debt of gratitude."

" A debt, 'Arry? You don't owe me nothing."

" I do, my friend. This was your idea. If you hadn't thought of it . . ."

" Glad you think it's a good idea," Carter said. " But it's pretty bloody dull so far and I'll be glad when we run into them. I ain't used to being alone. I've never been so alone in all my life."

" You've got us."

" Yes, you and a nigger that hates me."

" I don't think he hates you."

" Christ, he hates me. I can feel it. I feel his eyes boring into me back, like a bloody gimlet." He was amazed after he had said it. Let the bloody cat out of the bag now, he thought. If I kill him, Harry'll guess something. However accidental I make it seem. Sometimes, he thought, Harry was very suspicious.

They pressed on hard. Carter eager for company, mad to get near Francina. Bates wanting to meet the Boers and start a new life, and sure that Francina, who had taken such chances to warn him of the dragoons, would be on his side and persuade the old man to accept them. After all, he'd got a bargain in the grey stallion and it wasn't as if three men like them would be a liability. As Fred had said, when he'd brought up the idea, " Coves like us don't grow on trees . . ."

At last they knew they were getting near. They came to

a camp where the ants were still eating the scraps of flesh left on the bones. At the next there were vultures and crows picking in the refuse. At the next the ashes were warm. Now they pressed their horses on. The wagons were not more than ten miles ahead. Soon they saw the dust of the moving herds. Then they saw the laager—a circle of bright blue wagons on the skyline, curled like a snake about a big flat-topped thorn.

" Fire a shot," Harry said.

Fred fired into the air.

The laager burst into life like a disturbed beehive. Even at that distance they could see it. In a few minutes several horsemen were galloping toward them.

They waited, Harry Bates in the centre, flanked by his men with their guns on their thighs.

The Boers pulled up, three lengths away.

" Who are you?" Oom Willem asked.

" You don't know me, Meneer Prinsloo?" Harry Bates swept off his hat. His red hair flamed in the sun.

" The soldier," Oom Willem said. " The soldier with the grey stallion."

" I am he."

" And what do you want?"

" To join your trek. We are good men, well found."

" You are English bandits," Bokman said. " *Ja*, Rooineks. The very men who have driven us from our homes into the wilderness."

Looking over the heads of the Boers toward the laager, Harry saw a rider on a grey horse break away from a group of people and come galloping toward them. He recognised the horse. And the girl. He'd never forget the girl who had come to warn him. He wondered if she would help him now. What effect had the killing of that vermin in front of her had? What, after all, did he know of a young girl's mind?

That hat. The hat with the leopard crown. Bates had come after them. Francina rode past the Boers, driving her horse between that of Bates and the Zulu. Bates noted the officer's saddle, the silver-mounted pistols, the fancy headstall, and began to laugh. Robinson's expensive gear lost to him and here under his eyes in the interior of Africa. Carter saw it too. So that was where Captain Jack's gear had got to. He had wondered about it when he had seen the other saddles. That Frankie was a clever puss. But he'd get it back, and her into the bargain. He'd always fancied saddlery like that.

Francina took Bates's hand, checking the grey that was plunging in a halfhearted effort to fight the strange horses that flanked him.

"You," she said. "You have come here? What is it now? Are you still pursued?"

"We have come to join you, if you will have us."

"Have you? You, to whom I owe my Bloubooi? You, who come mounted with three guns?" She dropped his hand, raised Bloubooi pirouetting on his hind legs, turning him like a dancer, and rode back to Oom Willem.

"Oupa," she said, "these are good men. It is also the Christmas season. I think perhaps the Lord God has sent them to us, and that it would be impious to refuse them."

There was some argument with the other Boers.

Harry suddenly dropped his reins on his horse's neck and stripped off his shirt. "Look, brothers," he said, "and see if I have cause to love the English."

One look at his scarred back was enough. The whole group rode back to the laager together.

"It is a pity," Oom Willem said, "that you missed our Christmas feast."

"Christmas?" Harry said. "Meneer, I had forgotten that."

"Ja, young man. I can see it is time you came to live with civilised Christian people again. But magtig, how can I blame you for living with the brigands since it was I who directed you to them and even gave you a horse to ride into the mountains?"

Bates laughed. "That was a long time ago."

"Time," Oom Willem said, "ja, in time. But life is not so simple. It is in my heart that there are many kinds of time. Look," he said, sweeping the horizon with his arm, "it is thirty years since I was here but it might have been yesterday. I can see no change. Ja," he went on, "Christmas is over. But the feast is not. Much food is left and we are resting here for a few days to praise God and fatten ourselves and our beasts for the trials that lie before us."

"We could do with some good food and rest, Oom Willem," Bates said.

"You shall have both."

It was strange to be among people again. Among women and children. Neither Harry nor Fred could take their eyes off Francina as she tended their wants, pressing food and drink upon them. The children crowded round them, fascinated by the strangers and the big Zulu they had brought with them.

Only one difficulty occurred, when Tante Maria wanted Nzobo to join the servants. Bates rose and bowed to her.

"If he goes, I go with him, for we are brothers. We have fought and lived side by side for several years and are not to be parted. This man, Mevrou," he said, "is a relation of Dingaan, the King."

"The relation of a murderer!" Tante Maria screamed. "It was Dingaan who killed Retief, my brother, the husband of my sister."

"He would also have killed this man, which is why he is with me."

At that Tante Maria gave up and the food continued to be served.

In the afternoon there were other festivities—games, shooting at a mark, foot and horse races. Volleys were fired into the air to welcome the New Year. This was going to be a strange and wonderful year. Upon all this, Ullman turned a jaundiced and sour eye.

Before the sun went down, there was another meal and when it was over the music began. Oom Willem got out his fiddle again, Louis blew some tentative notes on his flute, when the couples who were getting ready to dance were interrupted by a wild scream from Tante Maria.

"Look!" she shouted. "Fire! Fire! And the devils will come later. It is my dream come true."

They looked at the horizon to the east that had been hidden from them by the wagons, and saw it all aflame. As far as one could see, the world was edged with fire. Now they could smell the smoke and in the awestruck silence imagined they heard the distant crackle of the flames. Fire—this was a new terror that might well be the end of them. Each party carried quantities of gunpowder in their wagon.

21

THE BATTLE

At Tante Maria's cry of fire, everyone sprang up. Fire! *Ja*, there was fire. The whole world to the east was aflame. The horizon burned like fat spilled on a stove.

"Come," Oom Willem shouted. "Burn a break back."

Quickly the men—Van der Merwe, Bokman, the Beyers boys, Bates, Nzobo and Carter—ran out and with torches made of grass lit the veld in front of them. Servants with branches controlled the new fires.

Fortunately they had made their laager round Ullman's big thorn tree, where the grass was tramped out or non-existent. Their own road through the veld cut into it, and led on past the camp to the vlei where the animals were watered. Had they camped elsewhere, the grass would have been too long to be safely burned. Here they had the tramped-out camp to work from. All they had to do in lighting the veld against the wind on the eastern side of the road was to see that the fire did not jump it. The boys cut branches and beat out any flame that tried to creep across the trekpad. The fires they lit against the wind burned slowly, deep in the bottom grass. The long grass stems never took but fell and lay like white needles on the black stubble of the burn. As soon as the flames tried to rise they were blown out by the wind so they could only creep. But creep on they did, and as the blackened area beyond the camp increased in size, Willem sent men forward to burn back to the break with the wind behind them. This was dangerous because once they had lit the fire they were caught between the two and had to come on behind it. Had they fallen or been injured, no one could have saved them.

The horses and cattle were driven with the utmost difficulty on to the new burn. Some broke away and fled into the night rather than step on the black, still hot ground. Heaps of cattle dung and game droppings continued to smoulder like red eyes in the darkness. Dead trees glowed in the forced draught of the wind. Buck and smaller animals rushed past the men. Some had been burned and smelled of singed hair. Where an hour ago there had been the peace of Christmas, now was chaos. Beneath the shining moon the sky glowed red. The black figures of the firefighters were silhouetted against it. Children cried. Women called to each other and their children. Terrified cattle bellowed, charged and were beaten back with clapping whips.

But at last it was over. All that could be done had been done. The fire they had lit burned slowly back against the wind toward the fire that was coming toward them, its small flames invisible against the leaping, crackling background of fire that leaped forward, driven by the wind that lashed it on. A wall of flame that leaped into pillars as solitary trees and bushes took fire, flashed upward and died in a shower of scarlet sparks. The flames illuminated their own smoke, lighting the belly of its billows as they rolled over the veld in suffocating clouds. Now there was nothing to do but wait for the dawn.

Harry Bates, his Zulu and Fred Carter lay wrapped in their blankets, their heads on their saddles, against the wheels of the Prinsloo wagon.

Harry was content. They had been accepted by the Boers

and had done good work in fighting the fire. It was he, with
Nzobo at his heels, who had set the second fire burning
down the wind. When it was over, Francina had given them
coffee to drink and had prepared water for them to wash the
smoke and grime from their hands and faces. To-morrow,
she said, she was going to wash all his clothes and mend them.

He lay on his back looking at the stars that were faint in
the moonlight above his head. The great fire had passed
them by. It had come leaping forward till it met their burn
and then, unable to proceed in the centre, had died, living
only on the flanks. There it had passed them by, closed in
behind them to the west and gone rushing on into the
emptiness of Africa.

Harry found himself contented, happier than he had been
since the day he had been arrested, for on that day his life
had ended, the career on which he had set his heart over.
But a new life opened up. No one could take him here. He
would not be flogged or shot or hung on a gibbet for the
crows and kites to peck. The past was gone, the English past.
He was a Boer, a voortrekker. He closed his eyes and slept.

It had been a day of excitement for everyone. They had
eaten the remains of the Christmas feast. Two strange
Englishmen and a big black Kaffir had joined them. They
had almost been consumed by the fire which had raged down
upon them. So all slept deeply, the white men and the
servants, and even the dogs, for they too were full fed and
tired from holding the cattle that had tried to break back
from the burn.

Only one dog was fully awake. Meisie, the bull pup.
Francina had kept her tied because she was afraid she might
be hurt in the uproar of the fire. Now she was uneasy. A
strange smell was borne down to her on the smoking breeze,
and she began to bark. Short, tentative puppy barks, but
deep like all her breed. In a moment the other dogs were

awake. The big Boer hounds rushed out barking and growling among the cattle that had stayed near the wagons. Everyone was awake.

Flip went forward after the dogs, gun in hand. They heard him fire and shout " Kaffirs! The Kaffirs are upon us!" and run back.

" Stand to the wagons," Oom Willem cried. " Stand to and do not fire till they reach the wheels."

Harry Bates, Fred Carter and Nzobo climbed up into the wagon. They cut holes in the sides of the canvas tent with their knives and waited for the attack. They saw the Kaffirs. There seemed to be hundreds of them in the faint light of dawn. But they were poor marks against the black ash of the burnt-out veld. They saw them forming up. Saw the white patches on their oxhide shields. Heard them stamping their feet and rattling their spears against their kerries. Soon they would come. The Kaffirs built up like water about to burst through a dam. More kept coming up from behind. It got lighter. Harry could see their plumed headdresses.

And then, suddenly, with a hissing roar they charged, a black sea of tossing plumes, shields, flashing spears, white eyeballs and grinning teeth.

" *Sah, sah,*" they hissed as they surged up to the wagon wheels. Some leaped up and succeeded in climbing on the top of the tents. Some forced an entry.

Thinking they had taken the Boers unaware and exhausted from fighting the fire, the Zulus became triumphant, shouting exultantly. But it was too soon. For it was only now, as the tide lashed against the defensive walls of the laagered wagons, that the Boers fired. As each man shot, a woman thrust another gun into his hand. The first bullets at close range had gone through several men—the next volley from the old guns, of broken iron potlegs, nails, glass and pebbles, blasted the Zulus back. They hesitated and

broke reluctantly. It had become lighter and the Boers used
their good guns again, picking off the men they thought to
be the leaders.

Falling back till they were out of range, the Kaffirs
reformed.

" They are Zulus," Nzobo said. " *Aaie*, they are my people.
They are the Crows. No others would come again. But
they will come. We will beat them back and they will come
again. And again. Baas, this will be a battle." The whites
of his eyes were red with the lust of war, with pride in being
a Zulu.

For a few moments that seemed an hour there was silence.
The whole universe appeared stilled, waiting for the sun to
rise over the rim of the world. Out of the eastern sea. Out of
Zululand.

Mageba knew a mistake had been made. He had meant to
follow closely behind the fire but the wind had risen and it
had gone too fast for him. And the Boers, by burning back
towards the fire, had ruined any chance of success by
creating such a great area bare of grass. All chance of surprise had now gone but they would still attack and try to
carry the laager by sheer weight of numbers.

The dead lay still, their greased bodies glistening in the
clear early light. The wounded threshed about like fish
fresh caught and flung upon a bank. Like the dying fish,
life was escaping from them, spilling out in red fountains
on to the black burnt grass of the veld.

Here and there were small heaps of dung, grey ash now in
the daylight, burning slowly, sending up their wispy plumes
of pale blue smoke. And over the battlefield came the birds
—small red hawks, black drongo shrikes with neat forked
tails, bee eaters and bluejays bright as rainbows diving for
the insects which fluttered above the burn or lay struggling,
damaged by the fire of the night. A crow dived upon a half-

burned tortoise, rose and dropped it from a height so that its shell broke, and then came down to eat between the laager and the Kaffirs.

" A crow," Nzobo said. " It is a sign." He touched his master's arm. " Kill it, lord. Shoot."

" And waste a shot?"

" It will not be wasted. Those are the Crows. They will take it as a sign."

Harry Bates sighted carefully and fired. The crow, hit by a heavy bullet, burst into a cloud of loose black feathers.

A groan went up from the impi.

Harry turned to Francina who put a newly loaded gun into his hand.

" I think your Kaffir was right," she said. " If they are indeed known as the Crows." She smiled at him, her eyes bright in her powder-blackened face.

They stared out of the torn canvas tent together. Its ragged edge framed a picture bright with sunshine in front of them. None of it was real. It could not be real, Francina felt. Everything was too sharply defined and too small. The grouped Zulus were not as tall as her little fingernail. The dead lay like broken dolls. She could not see those nearest to the wagon where they lay thickest. Only the birds seemed real, natural, as they hovered over the veld, looking for the smaller victims of the fire. She looked at Oom Willem and Tante Maria. Her Oupa stood watching the Kaffirs with his gun ready. Tante Maria was ramming a charge home in one of the old guns. More were leaning ready for use against the far side of the wagon. No one spoke. In all the laager not a voice was heard. The people seemed to feel that peace would last as long as the silence was not broken.

But the Zulus broke it, charging suddenly, wildly, intent on getting home with their short stabbing spears. The guns met them but they pressed on, climbing on to the rampart of their own dead, laying their shields flat upon the bodies and standing upon them to leap upward on to the wagons. Shouting, hissing, crying for death, for blood, for revenge, for the destruction of their homeland.

Below the wagons, the coloured servants, tame Kaffirs and the dogs fought between the spokes of the wheels for their very lives. They fired at the Zulus along the ground. The dogs savaged the legs and feet of those who tried to climb the wagon rampart. The coloured girls screamed and sobbed in terror, while in the centre of the laager the working oxen and horses milled round in terror, sending up clouds of dust that rose like smoke above the camp.

A Zulu somehow got into the Prinsloo wagon without being seen. His assagai was raised, ready to plunge into Harry Bates, the nearest white man to him, when Francina, a newly loaded gun in her hand, fired without raising it to her shoulder, almost blowing him apart. As he went down, the Zulu had struck Meisie the bull pup who had fastened her teeth on to his leg. Cina fell to her knees, sobbing and covering her eyes with her hands.

Nzobo leaped over her and taking the bloody body in both hands flung it back among the Zulus. *Aaie*, never had his master been nearer to death, and it was this little chit of a girl who had saved him. He picked up another gun and went on firing.

Tante Maria continued loading for Oom Willem, but now she was talking. Shouting. She had foreseen all this. Her advice should have been taken. They should have turned back or better still never have come at all. " I knew," she said. " I knew. I saw it all. The fire and the black devils."

Oom Willem, his white mane of hair and beard awry, his eyes flashing, shouted to the Zulus: " Come on and be smitten!" And they came, still swarming, still hissing and screaming defiance—to their deaths in the Boers' fire. A vertical wall of powder smoke surrounded the wagons. It might have been marked off by a plumbline. Through it, as if it was water, the warriors now emerged, singly or in groups, but were unable to remain in touch with each other.

The attack slackened and died. The Zulus retired, halted a moment out of range of the guns, and then, without even looking back, were gone.

Oom Willem passed his hand over his face and fell on his knees. It had been a narrow escape. If God had not been with them not one of them would have remained alive. If they had not laagered. If they had laagered anywhere else in the dry, waist-high grass. If he, Willem Prinsloo, had not told them to bring all the old guns from their homes when they had trekked, and if they had not had them loaded and ready. If the three strangers had not come to reinforce them. There were so many " ifs " that it was obvious that God had taken them into his charge. For this, with bowed head, he thanked the Lord.

Now the damage must be estimated and repaired. How many of his people were hurt? A prayer of thanks must be offered up. The cattle stampeded in the battle collected, though without question the Zulus would have driven many of them off.

This, too, might be a stratagem to draw the Boers away after the cattle and then, with the garrison weakened they might return to the attack again.

Everywhere the people were getting down from the wagons, talking, crying, shouting with anger and relief.

" There are men dead, Oom Willem," Bokman said.

" Dead!"

" Ja, and children motherless. Orphans, for both parents were killed in the last rush of the Kaffirs. The Van der Merwes are dead," he said. " The Kaffirs got into their wagon. Lysbet could no longer help her husband, for she had begun to give birth. That was how we found them, for seeing what had happened, Frikkie and I attacked the Zulus in the wagon and killed them. Magtig," he said, "that is something to see. Dead Kaffirs. Jappie speared. Lysbet cut to pieces with her child half born, and the other children crowded like frightened lambs against the wagon tent. Blood," he said, "blood, man. The blood drips through the wagon bed."

"Enough! Enough!" Tante Maria shouted. "What are you, Bokman, that you can speak like this? Come," she said. "Come, Cina, we will get the children. Orphans! Motherless! That is not so, for now from this instant I am their mother." She glared round her as if someone was about to take the Van der Merwe children from her. She had never thought much of their parents and now regretted her lack of charity but knew herself capable of making good their loss.

The casualties were two white people and three coloured men dead. Two menservants wounded and Eva with an assagai thrust into her buttocks. "Ja," she said, "there I was on my knees praying, with my apron over my head, when it happened."

"It's a good thing you were facing that way," Tante Maria said as she dressed it with turpentine and tar. "Better the bottom than the belly, my girl."

Oom Willem sent Louis off to keep the Zulus in sight. He was to fire in the air and gallop back if they changed direction or showed any signs of returning. Flip and Barend, with some coloured riders, went after the herds. The two Englishmen were posted on one of the wagon tops to watch for danger. All that could be done at this moment was done.

The next thing was to inspan and move before the dead began to rot in the summer heat. But their own dead must be buried. They should lie here where they had died in the Christmas laager beneath Jan Ullman's tree.

The Zulu dead lay piled against the wagons. Sprawled in death, grotesque, like black broken dolls oozing the red sawdust of their blood. They lay as they had fallen under the bullets of the guns. The sea of tossing plumes and waving kilts, of shields and spears that had risen like black spray against the wagons, now lay against the wheels. Here they were thick, a mattress axle-high that thinned out in the distance into odd bodies that lay like rocks in the blackened veld. There were some wounded. These must be killed. The Boers left this to their servants who, safe now, avenged their earlier fears by cracking the skulls of the exhausted men who, weak from loss of blood, expected no other fate. The wounded who could still walk had fallen back with the others when they retreated. Nzobo went with the servants. They were his own people but it was the Zulu custom to kill all those who were beyond quick recovery. If a man was too severely wounded to march, he was killed by his companions, swiftly and without hesitation. As he moved out among the scattered bodies, one of those whom he had thought dead rose on his elbow and hurled his stabbing spear. Nzobo had seen the move. He jumped aside and ran in, his kerrie raised above his head, only to stop at the wounded man's side.

"Mageba," he said. "Mageba, my brother."

"Traitor," Mageba said. "Renegade and coward. Strange that in such a one should flow the blood of Zulu, the father of our race. That such a one should spring from our father's loins and our mother's thighs. That such a one has drunk the milk that once raised heroes."

"It was this or death," Nzobo said. "Was I to remain and be flayed alive before I became meat for the vultures of

the king? Did you want my nose cut off and my lips and my
ears and my eyelids? Did you want me, your brother, thus
maimed and smeared with honey to be spread-eagled beside
an ant's nest?"

"That is the fate of those who touch the women of the
king."

"A woman of the king. He had never touched her.
Three hundred women, all mad with lust, raging in his
kraal."

"It is the law."

"Then I defy the law and the king. The great elephant
who has girls he never touches and destroys those in whose
belly his seed has taken. The king who starves and teases
young men and girls so that he may kill them. Who has
destroyed whole regiments for a whim."

"He is the king."

"And for him you are about to die, my brother. For him
I now must kill Mageba, with whom I played as a child,
with whom I was circumcised, and by whose side I have
fought in battle."

"Kill then, brother. Why delay? For now I have seen
all things. All the fine things in the world. The dances of
the warriors, wars and the blood of war, the maidens against
whom we sharpen the axe as young men and the wives and
cattle that the king has given me. *Aaie*," he said, "all fine
things have I seen and have I done. I have killed men and
made children, and nothing has surprised me till this—the
hour of my death at the hands of a Zulu traitor. Nor does it
matter, since all else is lost."

"Then die!" Nzobo brought the heavy rhinoceros horn
kerrie down upon his brother's head, smashing it as easily as
a child breaks a pumpkin. It came to him then how he had
smashed pumpkins as a child, pretending they were skulls,
and had been chided for spoiling them. He thought: Now

I will never give up this kerrie, for it will remind me of Mageba, the brother whom I loved.

Then he went to where his brother's spear had fallen and picked it up. He spoke to it. " Spear," he said, " now you are mine. Being royal, we know how you were forged in the secret hills and tempered with human blood."

He felt it in his hand. How well he knew it. How often had he seen his brother wipe the blood of battle from its blade before honing it a new razor sharpness. Well, now the biter will be bit, he thought as he drove the wide blade into his brother's belly and gave it a quick cutting turn. Mageba was the first. There were more than a hundred others whose bellies must be opened up so that their spirits could escape. This was his duty as a Zulu.

The double grave for the Van der Merwes and their baby was dug. These were the first of their dead. Tante Maria stood with the orphans beside her, the youngest child in her arms.

Oom Willem had told the boys to dig deep, for there were no stones here to pile upon the bodies and keep them safe from the wild beasts that dug out the corpses that were not protected, sometimes even digging in from the sides to get at them if they could not get in from the top. Not that there were such dangers here, for there was enough Zulu carrion to feed a multitude of beasts.

So surrounded by their children and their friends, the Van der Merwes were laid to rest, the couple and their half-born baby that had died under a spear before it was quite alive. Oom Willem said such words of the funeral service as he could remember and then he said, " Brothers, these are our first dead, and though after their skin worms shall destroy their bodies, yet in their flesh they shall see God. They shall see for themselves and their eyes shall behold

Him and not another. And when we die they will be there to welcome us, for they are part of us, of our bodies, and our trek. Many will pass this way, for we are making a trek road. The dead will not be long alone nor ever forgotten. This ancient tree is the landmark of a battle—that of the Christmas Laager—for so men will speak of it, and if the Lord had not been on our side the Zulus would have swallowed us up quickly. " Ja," Oom Willem said, " we got not this victory by our own sword neither was it our arm that saved us. It was the Lord that covered our heads and made us to stand in the day of battle. Praise ye the Lord."

" Praise ye the Lord," the people echoed.

And already while they stood about the grave as the boys shovelled in the dry red soil, the shadows of the circling vultures passed over them, sailing on tireless wings, waiting for the departure of the white men so that their feast upon the black dead could begin. The flies were thick, too. There were always flies, but now they were like those that plagued the Egyptians, as thick as fur upon their faces. Where had they come from? How had they knowledge of those piled heaps of dead?

At last the whips clapped and the wagons moved, crushing some Zulu bodies beneath their wheels. They left in a line, one behind another, with the Boers riding on the flanks.

22

IVORY

THE MEMORY of the battle remained with all. It was covered
up—hidden by the bragging of some and the silence of
others. But death had come to the trek—violent death.
The hand of God had been the shield of most but a Kaffir
spear or two had somehow slipped between His fingers and
some had perished. This thought was constantly in Cina's
mind as she sat on the wagon bed dangling her legs over its
tail, as she walked beside the great creaking wheels, as she
rode her horse over the veld. Why some and not others?
Why was she not dead? Why was it not me? Why the
parents of innocent children? Why, out of all the people,
had the Van der Merwes been taken? Why had her own
parents been killed? This was her second experience of
war. The first she lived again in her mind. The shots, the
screams. Her father's shout: " Ride, Ouma, ride! I can
hold them for another minute." In a way she had been
worse off than the Van der Merwe children, for they still
had each other. How alone she had been! How alone she
still was. Perhaps girls were always alone until they bore
a child to keep them company. For a child was a part of
yourself to whom you could speak from your heart, without
being considered mad. That was what Tante Maria said
of her when, out of loneliness she talked to the animals. She
said people will think you are mad, if they hear you. What
people, Ouma? For there were no people, only Ouma and

the servants and the mountains and the clouds in the sky were here.

So they all rode on. Each with his own thoughts and memories and hopes. The young men, now that it was over, hoped for more fights and told Miemie how they would defend her—as she sat on a stool, her long lashes lying against her cheeks, looking down at her hands which she held folded on her lap. The older men took more precautions than ever. The women prayed that the trek would be spared more death. The pregnant women, feeling life move beneath their hearts, said nothing, but when they met looked into each other's eyes for comfort, and it was to them that Sybella confided her fears—that she, too, was again with child and this would not have frightened her except that she thought her husband might leave the trek and go off on his own once more.

" He has been strange since he shot a big dog baboon four years ago," she said. " I told him not to, for what is the loss of a few mealies when set against the bringing of bad luck down upon your head? It is ill luck to kill a baboon, for no man knows when he does so how near he comes to murder. Allewêreld," she said, " how this one screamed. Like a man. He fell with his hand clasped to his heart. ' You have done an ill deed,' I said to my man. Before God, it was in my heart even then that we should pay for this, and we have. It is not that I am superstitious. How could I, a good Christian woman, be superstitious? But since that day nothing has gone right and we, who were once comfortably settled people, now wander like fleas over the back of a dog, having neither purpose nor hope in our lives. He joined this trek because I persuaded him to, but his heart is not in it." She covered her face with her hands and wept.

The women understood, for it was not an easy thing

for a woman to bear a child alone in such times of danger.

But apart from the secret thoughts of the company, life was uneventful—a routine of daily treks. Five miles, ten miles, according to the condition of the stock and the grazing. When the grass was sweet and good they would go slowly and even stop for a day or two. When it was bad or the water short they would push on. Some of the men with their coloured after-riders were always away reconnoitring the flanks, protecting the rear, hunting meat, or searching for a new outspan or camping place. These activities went on around the wagons, out of sight of them, as they rolled on massively, like heavily laden ships over the uneven grassy waves of the veld. Between them and the flanking screen of mounted men were the herds, each drifting forward in its own cloud of dust. About the wagons were other mounted Boers, children and women walking for exercise, coloured and tame Kaffir servants, dogs, Tante Maria's pigs, Cina's two rams and sometimes her goose—when the wagons were delayed by heavy going and she put it down so that it could graze a little.

So day followed day and each was lost in the immense boredom of this stolid progress, this routine of inspanning, outspanning, fire lighting, camping, making defensive laagers against attacks that never came—as if a wall of thorns and canvas could keep out the thoughts that seeped into each mind out of the starlit nights. Hope and fear balanced each other very neatly, cancelling themselves out into a simple anxiety which manifested itself in sudden acts of extra kindness or equally sudden violence, a curse at a dog or a blow to a servant.

These people were not trek Boers, not homeless wanderers as accustomed to living in their wagons as Arabs were to their tents. These were solid home-loving burghers on trek—something quite different—people looking for new homes and a new life. A new life. They were having new deaths too, and all but the boldest wished for the journey's end. They had severed their roots and could only long for the day when they could sink new ones into some safe and fertile valley. Some place where the grass was good and water plentiful. Here they would start again, build the houses that would one day, as their numbers increased, become a village. Build a church to the glory of God and a courthouse from which to administer His justice. They would make gardens and plant fruit trees. And their seed and that of their servants and stock would replenish the earth. All this was in their hearts as they sat listening to their great Bibles that were read each evening. It was in the hearts of the men as they hunted or herded cattle, in the hearts of the women as they sewed and cooked. It was for this that they prayed to the Lord their God. This was in their souls, but with their bodies they enjoyed such pleasures of the flesh as lay to hand. They made love, they courted. They hunted, they ate with gusto the game they shot. The girls made sheep's eyes at the young men. The women exchanged recipes too complicated to make as if they were at home, as the children played about their feet. For life goes on even in fear and boredom as long as there is hope, and this they had in abundance. Faith and hope were not their lack.

Before them security fluttered like a thick-kneed plover simulating a wound to draw its pursuers from its nest. The security of a home, of a hearth. When they hollowed out an ant heap to use as an oven to bake their bread, they thought of it—of the time when, day after day, they would cook in their own houses, when over their heads they would have a roof of solid thatch instead of the canvas of their wagon tents.

Yet, despite all the hardships and discomforts she endured, Tante Maria was happier with her adopted children than she had been for many years. She even found it hard to be sorry for their parents. Their troubles were now over—safe in heaven, among the blessed, knowing that their children were in good hands, there was surely no need to grieve any further about them. What they had now was what every good Christian hoped to have one day. She herself could ask for nothing better than to sit in heaven, which she pictured as some kind of vast sitting-room upholstered with clouds, listening to soft music and drinking cups of coffee without end. Though naturally, being a woman of good sense, she would not choose a Kaffir spear as the best way out of this world and into the next.

She comforted the children with her visions of bliss and they, confident that nothing as big as this woman who had taken them to her bosom could ever be destroyed or disappear, recovered their natural gaiety and revolved round her like tops, spinning with the games and mischief of their age.

Francina slept in the Van der Merwes' wagon with the children. It now rolled beside Tante Maria's by day and lay next to it at night. Tante Maria had wanted the children in her bed, but had heard Oom Willem who, not knowing she was near, tell a story about a fat sow that always overlaid her piglets, and decided against it. Not that there was any danger of her squashing a child but if one woke screaming with a nightmare she knew what her brother-in-law would say. This madman that everyone else had been deluded into respecting was utterly without sensitivity or feeling.

Lying with the children beside her, Cina often stared up at the dark patches of the canvas where the spear holes had been neatly repaired. It was strange to think that wagons, like men, should bear the scars of battle on their skins. That perhaps in the distant future people, seeing the patches, would be reminded of the Christmas Day battle and tell the tale. Then she would fall asleep with the children heaped like puppies against her, their warmth confused in her dreams with that of the man who would one day take their place, and of the babies that would be born to her.

Half child, half woman, wild, tender, her love ready as a bud to burst into flower with the first hot rays of the sun, Cina waited, her dreams by night more real than the thoughts by day, for time to pass—only time—for time she knew was all that stood between her and womanhood. Once it had almost happened. The thinness of the veil had been apparent. She had glimpsed the full richness of the land beyond.

In her sleep she put an arm around the boy who lay next to her and pulled him to her, his face against her breasts. She never knew that Fred Carter was watching her. That he had got up from his blanket for this purpose. He was glad she was sleeping with the children. Children slept as heavily as drunkards and he was afraid of the old woman. One day he would have this girl. In his mind he already possessed her. The back of the wagon tent had not been securely fastened down. The moonlight lit Cina's face. Her lips were parted in a near smile, the long coil of her hair lay like a silver snake on the jackal skin kaross on which she slept. He wondered if he could touch her. If she would scream. He put his hand into the wagon. This was the nearest he had ever come to her. He wondered if she was like other women. If now, when it was safe in the silence of the night, she might not welcome him. Women were like that. Their virtue a variable, dependent upon security. He had just moved his foot to come closer when something gripped his leg. He had forgotten her dogs.

Luckily they did not bark. When he drew back the dog
let go. By God, he thought, if I ever get a chance I'll kill
those bastards. But for the dogs he might have had her.
Now it was only the dogs which had prevented the fruition
of his hopes. The girl would have given in rather than
create a scandal. Women always did and once they had
done so they did it every time. The first time was the only
difficulty. He shrank back to his blankets with the dogs
standing side by side staring at him as his body merged
back into the shadows. Fred Carter moved like the accomplished thief that he was—a creature of the night, returning
to its lair. Angry at being thwarted, he cursed beneath his
breath, his lust now mixed with rage.

Oom Willem Prinsloo took some days to get over his
distress after the battle, for he blamed the death of the Van
der Merwes on himself. He was the leader. Therefore the
blame was his. Then after four days he realised that things
might have been much worse. The Zulus might have
overrun them—indeed they nearly had. And if blame was
his due, so too was praise for good judgment, and it was
only his good judgment that had saved the whole trek from
disaster, from death, and worse than death for the girls and
women. Moreover, all was not bad. With the children to
look after, Tante Maria—again he wondered how his
brother, so sensible in other ways, had come to marry her—
was less infuriating. Then there was Magdalena. He liked
to watch her, talk to her, and see her big dark eyes light
up as if a fire had been kindled behind them by his tales.
It was hard to believe she had an almost grown-up son. If
I was younger, he thought, I might propose marriage to her.
And, oddly enough, he felt himself growing younger every
day. The hard life, the sparse food—a diet composed almost
wholly of meat and bread—agreed with him, and so, in a

quiet unassuming way without being serious about it, he courted Magdalena Beyers; partly because he liked her looks and her company, and partly to annoy the old sow, as he called his sister-in-law in his mind. But he was glad Maria had the children. That once again there was young life about his wagon and small hands to grasp at his moleskin trousers with shouts of " Oupa! Oupa! " as he passed them on his horse.

Ullman now did most of the hunting. He was a good hunter, a veritable Nimrod who lived only for the chase. Each day he rode out with a couple of boys to shoot meat, and seldom returned empty-handed. So when one night neither he nor his servants returned, there was some consternation in the camp. His wife, wringing her hands, saw herself a widow, and pregnant at that, dependent upon the charity of people who had so little themselves that they could ill afford to give anything away. Oom Willem saw the trek deprived of three guns and a good hunter. So all through the night each hour signal shots were fired, one after the other, so that if the party were lost they would know in which direction to come. In the morning they remained laagered while Flip Beyers, with a horse boy, went out to seek news.

They had ridden west for a couple of hours when they saw the smoke of a fire and approached it carefully. There was no knowing what a fire might signify or who had kindled it. He found that Ullman had camped here and saw why. He had been following a herd of elephants, some of them very big from the diameter of their spoor, and had slept beside the trail. Flip decided to follow Ullman and the elephants. He could not be far away.

When hunting, Ullman always made one of his boys

carry his four-pounder. There was always the possibility of coming across elephants and a heavy gun was the only way of killing rhinoceros or even buffalo with certainty. Ullman was not one to take unnecessary risks and his love of sport never made him reckless. But elephants were his passion and when he came across fresh spoor he had forgotten everything else—his wife and children, his companions with the wagons who needed meat. Without another thought, he followed the elephants. He was riding into the wind. There was no need for precautions yet, and he was able to canter his horse along the wide path the elephants had trampled through the grass. Here and there a limb had been torn from a tree. There were chunks of chewed up branches that had been spat out in great skeins of fibre. There were droppings bigger than the balls that children played with, droppings as big as the head of a child. When he touched them they were still warm and moist. Now he must proceed with more caution. The elephants were not hurrying. The spoor and the droppings showed that they were drifting, feeding slowly, standing a while and moving on. There was a dip in the ground ahead of him. It looked as if there might be water and trees there—the kind of place where elephants would like to rest and bathe in the heat of midday.

Leaving his horse with his boys, Ullman crept up to the top of the ridge and looked down. He had been right. There was a small stream that ended in a vlei. There were some big trees. Giant wild figs and ancient thorns. Standing in their shade were about twenty elephants in groups or alone. There were six bulls. Two of them with magnificent tusks. He watched them for a while as they brushed the flies from their backs with switches of small branches they tore from the trees, as they blew dust over their backs, as they stood with entwined trunks, holding them in affection as men might hold hands. He saw young elephants butting each other in play and younger ones drinking from their mothers whose teats were situated between their forelegs, as were the breasts of women between their arms.

As he watched, he made his plan. He would wait here. The boys would ride round the marsh and approach it downwind, shouting and firing their guns, The elephants would bolt over the ridge and past him on to the plain he had just crossed and here he could hunt them from his horse. Galloping up to the biggest tusker, dismounting, shooting it in the knee, which would hold it pinned till he came back to finish it off, and going after another. In this way a single man, if well-mounted, might disable half a dozen bulls in an hour. For an elephant, unlike all other animals, could not run on three legs, could not even move.

The boys rode off, one to the left and one to the right. Ullman waited, hidden in a small cleft between some rocks, beside his horse with his arm around its neck. The sun seemed to be standing still. What were those damned boys doing? Had they made a mess of it? Suddenly his fears left him. There were the shots. He heard the boys shouting. A few minutes later the stampeding elephants began to come. They came at a slow run, trumpeting, with their trunks curled in the air. He let them pass. When they were all in the open he rode round the biggest bull, dismounted and, resting his gun on the saddle of his horse, shot him in the near knee. The elephant which had stood still to look at him screamed with pain and rage as it fell and then raised itself again, standing on three legs, holding the fourth bent at the knee as it explored the wound with its trunk. This was enough for Ullman. That one would never move again. And he galloped after the herd. The second bull, even bigger than the first, charged him twice but each time he was able to mount and gallop away. Then it, too, stood as if to take stock of things, and he shot it as he had done the other in the knee, for this was the classic Boer elephant hunter's shot. The herd was not out of sight. But he was pleased with himself. The tusks all looked as if they would go over a hundred pounds apiece, and ivory at the coast was worth ten shillings a pound. His boys now joined him and they all sat their sweating horses and watched the furious elephant in front of them. Mad with pain and rage, trumpeting, screaming, its little yellow eyes blazed with fury as it strove to reach them with the immense serrated coils of its trunk.

The bolder of the two coloured boys gave his horse's reins to his friend and danced about in front of the wounded beast, teasing it, picking up small pebbles and throwing them into its face while the mounted men almost fell from their horses with laughter at the antics of the wounded beast.

A mile away, but clearly visible, the other elephant stood, shrilling out its loneliness and anger.

So busy were the hunters with their game that they were unaware of Flip's approach till his horse neighed its greeting and defiance to the other stallions.

" So," he said, " you are off elephant hunting."

" Ja, Flip. I can never resist an elephant. With some men it is drink or meisies, but drink and women mean nothing to me."

" We thought you might be in trouble, so the Oubaas sent me to see."

" Trouble? I am in no trouble. Just look at those tusks, and the other "—he nodded his head towards it—" is nearly as big," he said. " Four hundred pounds of ivory at ten shillings a pound."

" Ja, Meneer," Flip said. " That is the price a thousand miles away. But if you could sell it here to-day in this instant, what could you buy?" He looked out over the empty veld and laughed. "Meneer," he said, "gold is no good here. You cannot eat or drink it, and ivory is not even gold." With that, he turned his horse and, followed by his after-rider, left Ullman, whom he felt was mad. For who but a madman would bother with hunting elephants on a trek like this? Who would carry the tusks? Who would throw out food, furniture, tools or other necessities that filled the wagons to make room for something so utterly useless?

No one would profit from his idiocy except the vultures which already approached in great circles from every side. Flip hated aasvoels. Last month it had been the dead Zulus. To-day dead elephants. To-morrow? Who knew what they would be eating to-morrow?

23

THE CHIEF

FLIP HAD not been the only one to see the vultures. He was hardly out of sight when the first Kaffirs appeared—four men carrying spears, and naked but for small aprons of leather cut into strings. Ullman signalled to them by raising his gun. They came closer. He handed his gun to the nearest boy and came forward unarmed. He had not thought of Kaffirs. He had not thought of how he would cut out the tusks—he had no axe with him—or how he would transport them when he had them clear of the great skulls to which they were attached. All he had thought of was the elephants, from the moment he had seen their sign till Flip had, in all but so many words, called him a fool.

The Kaffirs stood about him, neither menacing nor friendly. He did not seem to interest them. It was the elephants they looked at. The tons of living meat that stood enraged on three legs, impotent before them. The tallest Kaffir, who appeared to be the leader, unslung a buck's horn from his shoulder and blew a series of long blasts. Then he and his companions sat down to wait.

Soon more Kaffirs came. First singly, then in pairs and small groups, all of them armed with spears, and finally women and children by the score accompanied by their starving greyhound-like curs. All Africa seemed to be surrounding the wounded beast in a black ring that pressed

245

ever closer. The inside of the ring was prickly with the spears of the men, the outside a howling, yelling, seething mass of women hungry for meat—of children screaming with excitement and dogs, which, unable to bark, were whimpering, howling and making curious sounds that almost resembled a woman weeping.

Ullman was outside the ring, the only alternative to being within it. He stood outside with his boys and the horses. This was not what he had imagined the end of his hunt would be. Moreover, he was both hungry and thirsty. He could catch up the trek with a four-hour ride. It was in his mind to do so. But he could not leave his prey. My elephants, he thought, though they were no longer his in actual fact.

Then suddenly, as he watched, the picture changed. A hush fell over the seething crowd—a kind of sigh rose from them as a couple of hundred right arms were raised. The spear blades flashed as they were flung into the elephant's body. They stuck there like wasp stings in the arm of a man. The screams of the elephant were redoubled as it tore out the assagais that it could reach with its trunk. More assagais were flung. Those that could be safely recovered from its body or the ground were picked up and thrown again. The elephant was red with the blood that poured from its hundred wounds.

The crowd, which had fallen back, now surged forward. One man with a sword severed the elephant's trunk with a single blow. Helpless now, except for the sideways action of its tusks, losing blood by gallons a minute, the great beast fell on its good knee, tottered an instant and rolled over on its side. This was the signal. Like a pack of black hounds breaking up a kill, the Kaffirs were upon it. All over it, men, women and children. Cutting it up, ripping out its mountain of heaving guts while it still lived. This was the meat—hot, red and bloody—that they craved. They dived into the cavity of its belly to cut out the fat round its kidneys. They stripped great sheets of skin from the elephant's back and, using them as platters, piled the dripping meat upon them and handed them to their women who bore them back upon their heads to the village.

Mounting their horses, Ullman and his boys went after the girls and women, following in their bloody spoor. Before long they picked up a little native path a foot wide which led in a roundabout manner to a slight rise which was covered with very large rocks, some of them as big as a house. The spaces between them had been closed with high walls of stone, mortared with dagga. As they got nearer, the track widened as others coming from all directions joined it, converging on the gate that was now open. It consisted of large trees sunk in pairs to make gateposts that could be closed by heavy slip rails being pushed between them.

Inside, the huts were built against the rock that formed the outer wall, but in the centre of the village there was a large hut surrounded by a kraal of huge weathered tusks that were embedded like posts into the bare red soil. This enclosure was entered through an arch of two tusks that towered above the other giants, none of which showed less than five feet of ivory above the ground.

They stood and stared. Ullman and his boys were alone. The women with their burdens of flesh, their children and dogs, had all gone to their own huts. The long chain that had marched from the dead elephant was now scattered like a string of beads that has broken.

Not only had Ullman never seen a village like this, he had never even heard of one that was so well organised or strongly defended. But he knew enough to seek out nobody. So, tying the horses' reins to the ivory fence, he and his boys sat with their backs to it to await events. Everywhere, he knew, hidden eyes were peeping at them, watching them to see if they were uneasy or afraid. He was afraid but he showed nothing and, lighting his pipe, passed his pouch to the boys.

They had smoked two pipes before anything happened; then, hearing something, he looked round to find six maidens approaching bearing food of various kinds. Kaffir pots of water, of beer, of *mas*, the thick milk curd which is a favourite dish of the cattle-owning tribes. There were also roasted mealie ears and chunks of half-cooked elephant.

The girls were sleek, fat and shining with oil. They had put on their finest bead aprons and armlets to do these strange visitors honour. This was a good sign, and no sooner had they put their dishes on the ground with smiles and a flash of white teeth than the hunters fell upon the food.

The next move, Ullman knew, would be the arrival of some elder or captain who would lead him to the chief. This might happen in an hour or they might make him wait a day or more. Meanwhile, he worried about watering the horses and grazing them. They were not off-saddled and stood dejectedly, with lowered heads, flicked their long tails half-heartedly at the flies which swarmed over everything. The unfinished meat of the meal was covered with a black fur of flies. So were their own arms and faces as they sat, unable to sleep because of them, waiting for the summons that must come sooner or later.

Two hours had passed before an old man appeared in front of them and made signs for Ullman to follow as he turned away towards the entrance of the royal kraal. Leaving one boy with the horses, Ullman told the other to come with him as, being a tame Kaffir, he could make himself understood by most tribes.

The chief sat on a low carved stool. He was dressed in a

kilt of monkey tails. Behind him stood two young warriors armed with spears and kerries and the tall man who had blown the buck trumpet.

For a few moments they all stared at one another. Then the king spoke and Ullman's Kaffir translated.

"The great King Endula says: 'Welcome, white man.' He says the tusks of the elephants you slew will soon be brought in—to-morrow or the day after. He says that he has many elephant teeth as you can see "—he waved his hand at the kraal posts—" though these are nothing compared to those he has stored away, and wishes to trade for lead and powder. He has guns but their bellies are empty. But you with a wagon could transport the ivory to the coast and come back with all that is needed in his kingdom. He says he will make you rich. That he will send guides with you."

Ullman said; "Ask him how much ivory he has."

The Kaffir turned back to the king.

When they had done talking, he spoke to his master. "The king says he has many wagonloads of ivory stored in huts. The tusks in the kraal are very old, being put there by his father's father. He says he and his people have always been elephant hunters, living for a great part on their meat and never killing cattle except for sacrifice."

Ullman smiled. This was what he had been looking for. It must have been meant. God had sent him this way so that he should have this chance to get on his feet again.

"I will go and return with my wagon," he said

The king said a new hut would be put at his disposal as it was too late in the day to leave now, and that his horses had been taken to water and were grazing, so that they would be strong and ready for the journey.

As he slept that night in the new hut, on a mat of clean

woven reeds, Ullman dreamed of fortune, of the new farm
he would buy and how he would stock it with the finest
beasts. Of how, instead of going north with a pack of madmen, he would return in triumph to his own district and
show them what could be accomplished by a man who
combined courage with intelligence. This would teach
those fools who had despised him because his religious
principles forbade him to wear buttons. Ja, he would show
them what a buttonless man could do if he was bold and
resolute. Of course his wife would not like it. But she never
liked what he did. She had not wanted to leave the farm.
She had wept when they parted from Potgeiter's trek and
their old friends. Now she would cry again when they left
their new ones. She acted as if friends were everything.
As if his company and that of her children were not
enough. As if he was not always acting as he was directed
by God to act. And who was she to spit in the face of
Providence?

Leaving at dawn, he rode into the rising sun, knowing
that he was bound to cut across the spoor of the trek as
long as he did not get too far ahead of it. But before he
reached the spoor, he saw the long low clouds of dust raised
by the moving column of cattle and cantered towards
them.

Ullman was somewhat surprised at his reception. Apart
from his wife and children, who had thought themselves
widowed and orphaned, no one seemed very glad to see him.
He had caused them some anxiety and delay and they had
had to kill a steer since he had not returned with the
expected meat for supper. His story of hunting elephants
was believed but regarded as a somewhat childish escapade
considering the seriousness of their position. They were a
people on the move. They were Israelites escaping the

Egyptians. Here they were crossing a great Red Sea of earth and grass into a promised land of freedom, and he ran off like a child to play by himself.

When he told his wife of his plan to become the trader of a Kaffir chief, she broke down.

"No," she said. "No! You shall not do it. You shall not kill my children, my sons and the child within my womb. For this is death. Only a month ago we were all but overrun by naked savages, and now you place yourself alone and helpless in their hands."

"It is God's will, Sybella," he said, "and I trust the king."

"Allewêreld," she said, "you trust. I trusted too. Before God I trusted my life and that of my unborn children to you when we married—to a man who trusts a snake, a man who would put out his hand to touch a cobra, a man who, seeing a puff adder at his feet, says: 'This is nothing. It is only a worm.'"

Her husband said: "Scream as much as you like. We are going. I am off now to tell Willem Prinsloo of my decision. And let me tell you, woman—we shall be better off alone than under the direction of that old man, a fanatic and a visionary. I am practical. I am even doing what you wanted. You were against trekking. Very well, I say you were right. We will go back. But first I must make my fortune. I cannot go back empty-handed. I should be ashamed."

Giving his horse to a boy, he climbed into his wagon to change his clothes. He wanted to look his best, both as he rode away from these fools and when he returned to the kraal of the king. The Kaffirs were much impressed by clothes. It took him half an hour to dress. He put on a blue nankeen jacket with a red stripe, buff-coloured trousers, a red waistcoat, a black silk stock and a tall beaver hat. On his bare feet he wore half-Wellingtons. Never had he looked better—not even when he had gone courting.

Now to find Oom Willem and tell him his plan to leave the trek. But the story had preceded him.

"What's all this I hear?" the old man roared, getting up from his stool.

"I do not know what you have heard, Oom Willem," Ullman said, "but I have made certain plans and have come to inform you of their nature. This trek and all treks are mad. I was mad to have been talked into leaving my home. So I am about to give up and return with my family to the Cape. However, since I refuse to go empty-handed, I have made a pact with a native chief to trade his ivory, trekking it to the coast and bringing back such goods as he needs."

"Goods . . . goods . . ." Oom Willem shouted. "I know the goods. Lead and powder, axes, six-inch nails that can be hammered into spears, iron bars and chains. Those are the goods Kaffirs want. Ammunition, iron that they can weld and beat into weapons. Chains to fasten the slaves they capture."

"I do not think . . ." Ullman began.

"Ja, that is it. You do not think. Why . . ." Oom Willem said, "I even know this chief of yours. I was here before you could walk. I know this kraal of ancient tusks. Your chief was a baby then. His father, Mamba, ruled. A wicked man, allied to the slavers of the coast. He also hunted elephants. That is the only true thing you were told. And you trust him with your life and that of your wife and children!"

"He needs a trader. He said he would send guides with me. A man is safer as a trader alone than in such a company as this."

Oom Willem sat down and fingered the pages of the Bible open in front of him. " I have been seeking counsel," he said. " I have prayed that God should give you sense. Not much, for that would be too difficult even for the Lord Almighty. But just a little sense. Magtig "—he raised his voice into a shout—" if I had enough men to hold you prisoner I should do it."

" It is you who are mad, Oom Willem," Ullman said. " You with your promised land, your dreams—you who see yourself a Moses leading the people out of Egypt. It is you who are the false prophet and it is I, Johannes Frederick Ullman, who am wise, wise enough to leave your band before it is too late."

Sybella now came up to the group with her children clinging to her skirt. " Stop him," she cried. " Stop him before he leads us to our death. Stop him, Tante Maria. Stop him, Oom Willem. Stop him for the life that kicks its feet in my belly."

" I cannot stop him, woman," Oom Willem said. " A man's life is his own."

" Ja," Tante Maria said, turning her immense bulk towards Ullman and waddling in his direction. " A man's life is his own. But a woman's life is also her own. This woman "—she pushed Sybella behind her—" is more than a life. She is more than the other life within her. She is life itself. She is our hope, like these others who grow big as we travel. This baby is not yours, Meneer. It is ours. It belongs to the trek to the new Africa we will make. Go," she pointed her finger. " Ja," she said, " go if you like, but you go alone, for unless your wife goes of her own free will she and her children remain with us. Go," she said again, " and when you wish to return you will be welcome."

Ullman said: " Sybella, a man's wife must cleave to him."

"Ja, ja," Tante Maria said. "She must cleave to him if there is something to cleave to. But how can a woman cleave to something as slippery as a fish?"

"Tell her to obey me, Oom Willem." Ullman's voice was desperate.

"Why must she obey you when you will not obey me? You asked to join our trek. You agreed to abide by our laws. We are not asking you to leave us. On the contrary, Meneer. In the name of God, of our new land, and the success of our undertaking, I implore you to remain. These are my words. My soft words—the other cheek that I turn. But I only have two cheeks, and if you still want to go, go and be damned! Ja, go and be double damned—you who would trust a Kaffir chief before an elected Boer leader. You without faith in God or Africa. You who think you will be safer alone clinging to the foul blanket of a naked savage than in the company of your fellows. Go, I say. Ja, go. But your wife and your children remain, and if you try to take them by force, by force we shall reply. Ja," he said, "I with my own hand will shoot you down like a dog."

Oom Willem turned to Sybella. "This is the last word I shall speak on this subject for I have been through too much. First thinking your man dead and now finding my trust in him betrayed. Do you wish to go with him or to stay with us?"

For a moment the Ullmans stared at each other. Then Sybella lowered her eyes. "We will stay," she said. "Ja, we will stay, I and my sons and the trek child that is on the way."

To her husband she said: "Johannes, go if you must, but come back. Twice each day we will pray for your safety and return."

Ullman said nothing. He turned away from them and walked towards his wagon.

"Come, Sybella," Tante Maria said. "Come. We will get your clothes and possessions. You will live in the Van der Merwes' wagon with Cina and the children. Magtig," she said, "now we are a trek with a wagonload of orphans and half-orphans."

24

THE MIRAGE

THE TWO GIRLS, Francina and Miemie, stood watching
Ullman's wagon getting smaller and smaller. It was no
bigger than a child's toy and then it was gone. Ullman had
disappeared out of their lives. Only a few weeks ago they
had joined him. Now he had left them, leaving his wife and
children and his cattle, sheep and most of his horses, for his
family would not go with him and the stock were useless to
him. An event of this kind was strange to the two girls, for
they had been brought up in a fixed community, and when
the community had decided to find a leader and trek, the
trek had seemed normal to them. They were still surrounded by their friends, by people they knew, or at least
had heard of as distant neighbours. But the Ullmans were
a family that had broken into their circle, and then broken
out of it again, as if people were of no more importance than
things, as if—and this was a new concept—wives and
children could be discarded like furniture, like chairs and
tables,—to be picked up again later on.

Ullman's going made them more aware of the other
strangers they had with them. The two Englishmen, Harry
and Fred, were also mysteries. Men of whom one knew
nothing—runaway soldiers who were said to have been
brigands. Cina of course knew the story—Harry's at least—
since she had been there at its beginning, but had said
nothing of it to anyone, and not even her Oupa or Tante

Maria had heard of all her adventures at the bandits'
camp. But they were always in her mind. She could never
see Harry Bates without turning over the pages in the
picture-book of her mind. Harry riding up on Bloubooi,
then riding off again on the old brown mare; of him striding
down the mountain, of his killing that man, of his house in
the camp, of his coming to join their trek with his friend.
She did not like his friend. He frightened her with his
looks, with the way he stroked her with his eyes. When he
looked at her, his eyes felt like hands on her body. And he
called her " Frankie." She hated that.

" Well, he's gone, Miemie," she said, as the dust which
had lain like a cloud behind Ullman's wagon sank back into
place on the horizon.

" Ja, he has gone."

Cina looked at Miemie. Not that she could see her face,
which was hidden behind the soft leather mask she wore to
protect her complexion. Through the eyeholes she caught
a glimpse of her eyes, and around her ears below the kappie
was a loose strand of her hair. Miemie was dark. Dark-
haired with dark brown eyes the colour of water in a forest
pool. If she had not taken care of her complexion—using
ointments she made from fat and herbs upon it and wearing
a goatskin mask when she went out—her face would have
been dark too—olive-tinted, like an Italian. Her lips were
deep red, almost purple, which made her lovely teeth look
even whiter than they were. Her figure was fuller than
Francina's, her breasts bigger and threatening to be
pendulous as she aged, or so Tante Maria said. Ja, she told
Francina that such breasts as hers, that now point upward
like pears seeking the sun, will hang like gherkins from a
fence before she is thirty. That might well be, but now they
were pretty as rosebuds and a temptation to the hands of
those who saw them. Her waist was small, her hips full and

her walk provocative. Those who were not her friends said no good could come of all this—such manifold charms could only lead to disaster. But they were wrong—Miemie only wanted marriage and having no dowry, for her parents were poor, realised that only by exploiting her beauty would she achieve the security that was her aim. To be secure, she had been more than ready to take such risks that were inevitable on a trek. To be secure she was ready to gamble even with her life.

Cina thought: This girl is pretty. Pretty as a plum on a golden plate. But what went on in her mind? What did she do beyond such household tasks as were possible on the march? What of her heart? The heart that beat behind those pointed pear-shaped breasts? Most of what went on in her mind and heart, Cina knew, was concerned with men. All day Miemie guarded her complexion and wore old clothes, but in the evening when the campfires were lit and the men were eating, Miemie changed. Then there was no kappie. There was no mask. Her dresses were fresh and clean—pink, white or blue linen. Her long hair was parted in the middle and twisted into a knot at the back of her head. No one except Cina wore their hair long and down. It was contrary to all custom. But was there more than this? Was this the way most girls thought and acted? How little she really knew about such things.

" I'm glad the boys stayed," Cina said. " They are nice boys and now we will have a wagonload of children."

" Ja, Cina, a Noah's Ark of children. But there is now one man less," Miemie added, as if Johannes Ullman had been an unmarried man, a free man. But to her all men were mirrors—something to practise in front of, their eyes and reaching hands the testament of her success.

Cina laughed. " A man is a man to you? "

" And why not? A man is a man. Something can always

happen. Their wives can die. Why, as you know, many men have had three wives or more."

"And you would step into the shoes of the dead?"

"Ja, Cina," Miemie flashed back, "ja, I would lie in the bed of the dead if such a man was rich, a man of substance. I would rather have a widower than some poor fumbling boy with his way to make. For you it is different," she said. "You are half a boy in your trousers and long hair. And you are rich, being Oom Willem's heir. But I . . ." She smoothed her dress over her hips and belly. "I have only this to sell." She laughed into Cina's face. "Not that I would tell any of the others what I have told you. To them I am a good and innocent maid, a girl who will make some Boer boy a splendid wife. But they are wrong. If I must marry a Boer he will have to be rich. But I do not want just to be a Boer vrou. I would like to live in a town and to do so I would marry anyone—an Englishman, even a Catholic or a Jew."

"I have never seen a Catholic," Cina said.

"Nor I. But I have heard that they are made as other men, but pray more and have many idols whom they worship as gods. Our people fought them for many years, as you must know, in the Low Countries where we defended our Lord Jesus Christ against the whore of Babylon."

"I have always thought," Cina said, "that Babylon sounded like an interesting place."

"Ja, and so do Sodom and Gomorrah. But we shall never see them." Miemie laughed. "And each day we draw farther away from them or any other town."

The girls linked arms and returned to the wagons which were being inspanned.

Ullman's going had held up the trek. They had stopped to watch him go, hoping he would change his mind or turn back. Now they drove their trek oxen together, calling them by name as they threw the loops of their riems round their long sharp horns. " Kom, Buffel . . . Rooiland . . . Witpens . . . Laksman . . . Donker . . . Geelbek." The oxen responded like dogs and the men pulled them into their place, pair by accustomed pair. The yokes were lifted on to their necks, the strops fastened to the skeys. The voorlooper picked up the leaders' riems. The great whips clapped. " Loop . . . loop. Go . . . go," the drivers cried. The oxen leaned into their yokes. The twisted leather traces tightened into one long strand as solid as a bar of iron and the creaking wheels began to turn.

Ullman was forgotten by everyone except his wife. She had not been able to watch him go, but had sat crying with her white apron over her head and her sons beside her in the kartel of the Van der Merwe wagon.

Anxious now to get away and forget the scene, Cina sent for Bloubooi and rode off to look at the herds of stock. As she rode near them the men turned to look at her for she cut a fine figure and she knew it.

The big blood stallion was at his best. The trek had suited him. His almost white tail and mane floated like banners. The brass on his saddlery, that Cina tended herself, shone like gold. The brass-bound crisscross that went over his face glistened in the sun. The scarlet foxtail that hung from a brass chain joining his throat lash to his nose band swung gaily below his neck.

Cina as usual wore men's moleskin trousers and a short leather jacket over a white linen shirt. Around her waist under her belt she had a scarlet sash made from some of the material the smous had given her. On her head was a wide-brimmed hat. Her hair was tied with a red ribbon and hung down almost to her saddle. In front of her thighs were the silver-mounted pistols in their holsters. They were loaded.

The free stride of the great grey horse, the drumming of his hoofs on the hard ground, the swing of his body as he swerved round a bush, all gave Cina that sense of life, of being one with all living things, that was her joy. The dogs, sensing her pleasure, barked and leaped at each other in play. In the distance she saw Barend and waved to him. He was riding the officer's black charger to whom the saddle she was on belonged. They rode towards each other at a slow canter.

"Well," Barend said, "he has gone."

For a moment Cina, who had been thinking how well he looked on the black, did not know what he meant. Then she said, "Ja, and I hope he is right in his trust of the Kaffirs."

"I do not," Barend said. "For if he is, it will be to their profit and our loss. That he should trade guns and ammunition for Kaffirs is an evil act. For the guns that kill elephants can also be turned against our people."

He drew his horse up beside hers. Their thighs touched. He put his hand on hers. "Ride with me," he said. "Ride with me." In his eyes and the heat of the leg he pressed against her, she read his meaning. He wanted to kiss her, to hold her, to touch her. The hour by the big tree in the forest came back to her. Then she had been ready. But now that he courted her by the wagon every evening when they were laagered, she was less so. Not less ready for love, for she felt her desire running like sap within her, but for Barend she had lost something. Perhaps she had never really had it.

"I will ride with you," she laughed, "if you can catch me." And leaning forward over Bloubooi's neck, gave him his head. For a hundred yards the big black thundered beside her. Then she pulled away and Barend gave up.

A wild girl that sent him mad. Why could he not court

a sensible, quiet, Boer maid? And what sort of wife would she make? He doubted her ability to bake bread, to cure biltong, to cook, to make and repair clothes. She could ride and shoot. She could breed cattle and horses and doctor them when they were sick, as well as a man. But was that what a farmer needed in his wife? He might not need it, but it was this very paradox that inflamed him. This girl's body in her boy's clothes. This woman galloping away from him with the tail of her yellow hair flowing out behind her.

Cina slowed up once she was well clear of Barend and patted the sweating neck of her horse. He tossed his head as if to say: Well, we certainly showed them a clean pair of heels. She laughed and pulled his ears.

The day was becoming hot now. As the sun rose higher in the sky a low haze of heat made the surface of the veld shimmer. In the distance she saw a mirage—a wonderful lake surrounded by trees and piles of rocks that looked like the castles in a book of stories the Englishman had taught her from. She pulled up entranced. This was the best mirage she had ever seen.

What a day it had been! Ullman's going. His wife's sorrow. Barend's ardent approach to her. The wild gallop, and now this. She sighed with happiness as an idea came to her. Half a mile away there was a koppie, a great lump of rock as big as a dozen houses all piled together. On top of it was another rock as big as a single house, and on top of that still a third was balanced. It was the size of a Kaffir hut. Trees and shrubs grew among the rocks of the kop and she was sure she could climb it. That was what she would do. Tie her horse at the foot of the rocks where he would be in the shade and climb to the very top if she could.

She wanted to see what a mirage looked like from above. She had seen them only in the plains. Perhaps she would get a better view—a different view. Perhaps she would see nothing. It might well disappear if looked down upon from above. She rode slowly towards the little sugar loaf of a hill.

How silly Barend was to have said she should not ride about alone. Why, when even he on the black English hunter could not catch her, should he worry? That should teach him. Should show him that she was safe.

She was close to the kop now. It was strange to think that these hills were the solid bone of Africa from which the flesh had been washed away by a thousand thousand rains. That the big rocks that lay upon each other had sunk through the soil that supported them and finally had made this curious structure, and that then the birds and the winds had planted the seeds of plants, grasses and trees upon them so that each was a lovely little world of its own.

Sometimes baboons lived among the crevices and caves of these little hills. Sometimes a leopard or a lion. But she was not afraid of baboons; besides, had there been any she would have heard one bark. They always had a guard watching all approaches. As to lions and leopards, they were too rare to worry about. One could not worry about everything.

She dismounted and tied her horse by his head rope to a twisted tree that grew out of the rock. Bloubooi was in the shade here. She slackened his girths and, telling the dogs to wait beside him, flung herself upwards, clinging to two saplings that she could reach by standing on tiptoe. Above them were more shrubs that gave her hand holds, and after a short scramble on her hands and knees she found herself on the smooth lawnlike grass that covered most of the lowest rock. There were rock rabbits here, the coneys of the Bible, that grazed it down. She found their holes, runways and the crystallised deposits of their urine. If they were here it meant that there were no leopards. For dassies were one of the favourite foods of the tigers, as the Boers called leopards. Cina lay down on the grass to rest and then climbed up the next rock. This one was easy. The last and smallest was the most troublesome as it was smooth and without vegetation. It was also almost too hot to touch where the sun struck it. But at last she got to the top and stood there staring about her. The mirage had disappeared. But she had a wonderful view of the veld. She saw the wagons moving slowly north. Moving into a sea of nothingness and leaving behind them the wake of their spoor—a road that others one day would follow. The North Road which we shall have made, she thought. It is my Oupa's trek that has broken the road. She saw the herds of cattle and horses, the flocks of sheep—all miniatures in the distance. She saw men on horses that were smaller than ants and dismounted people no bigger than the head of a pin.

When she had looked enough she scrambled down. It would be nice to rest for a while on the short grass of the lowest portion of the kop, drink some water from her flask, eat some biltong and then ride slowly back.

It was pleasant lying there on her back. Isolated, away from everything, suspended as it were between the earth and the heavens. Cina lay so still that the dassies had come out to feed quite near to her. A shiny starling, his feathers a metallic blue and green, his eyes orange jewels, sat perched on a twig above her head, looking down at her. How beautiful he was—sleek, clean, brilliant, vibrantly alive. Neither she nor the trek passing in the distance meant anything to him or the dassies. They had lived here since time began.

Cina loved to dream about the animals. Of how the ones

she saw were descended from others who had lived in the same place for hundreds of years. All exactly alike, all living the same lives so that one might almost say that they lived for ever. Just as a river ran for ever, though the water changed each instant. Men, too, were the same, following each other. But men changed their ways, their clothes, their habits. This trek was a change. It was a migration like that of birds or the springbok, only there would be no return. It was final.

Fred Carter had been detailed to take Ullman's place as the chief hunter of meat. He was a good hunter and horseman. He had no stock to care for and it had seemed a natural choice. Hunting suited his temperament. The search, the stalk, the kill. The Boers bored him with their heaviness, their absurd interest in their livestock, with their religion that they took so seriously. Only the girl excited him. Sometimes he wondered why she did. Perhaps it was because he had never seen her like. So wild, so free. So girlish despite her clothes. He was a man who hated to see things free. Freedom should be his alone. The liberty of others seemed to impinge upon his own. The free should be trapped, caged, broken, tamed or killed. As a rough rider, breaking horses in the Dragoons, he had been unnecessarily harsh and brutal. To pull himself up he had to pull others down.

He had shot a fine eland bull, pig-fat, that he had ridden to a standstill and had killed like a steer as it stood staring at him with soft brown eyes. With his boys he had delivered it to the wagons, and changing horses had ridden out again, alone. He had a compulsion to be alone now, away from the stupid Boers. Away from Harry who was now as bad as they were. It looked as if virtue might be contagious. He laughed at the idea. When he was in camp or with others he could not think. They all enraged him with their smugness. And he had to think now. He had to figure out a way to deal with Harry and his boy. That was the trouble. It always had been. How did one murder two men and make it appear to be an accident?

He pulled up his horse, lit his pipe and stared about him. This bloody country bored him too. A country full of nothing. Long waving grass, odd trees, patches of bush and big rock outcrops, all empty of life except for the game that roamed in great herds, patching the veld with shadow when you did not need meat and hard to find when you did. Suddenly he saw something. Shading his eyes with his hands under the brim of his hat, he looked more closely. Something . . . By God, it was the girl, Frankie! She was climbing down from the big outcrop he had been looking at. He could not take his eyes off her. Now he could catch her alone. She would have to talk to him. They would ride back to camp together. Then he saw that she was not coming down. She had settled herself with her back against the rock and was drinking from her flask. This was even better. He would join her up there. Looking carefully, he saw where she had tied her horse. The dogs would be beside it. He rode towards the koppie but not directly. He would approach it from the far side. He did not want her horse to neigh or her dogs to bark. How he wished he could kill those dogs. With her it was the dogs. He still felt the grip of those teeth on his leg. He had not been bitten, only held, but held in the grip of a vice. The girl and her dogs. Harry and his damn' Zulu. There was always something that stood between him and his desire.

25

A GIRL ALONE

CARTER HAD no difficulty in scrambling up the far side of the koppie. No one had seen him. Neither the dogs nor the horse had picked up his scent. He made no sound in his bare feet—he had left his shoes by the horse—disturbed no loose stone. He came up like a leopard, stealing from shadow to shadow. Once up, he paused to get his breath and then crept forward to peer through the bushes that grew clustered about the base of the second rock which rose above him.

There she lay, half asleep in the sun, her wide belt unbuckled, her red sash loose, her shirt open so that he could see her breasts. She lay like a child, knowing herself alone, safe, inviolate, utterly unobserved—and because of this infinitely appealing. Standing as if frozen, Carter watched her breasts rise and fall as she breathed. His heart beat faster. She was even more beautiful than he had thought, for never before had he been able to look at her so long or so closely.

Francina was staring up at the blue cloudless sky with half-closed eyes. She saw the shiny starling fly off. Why had it flown? A moment ago it had been preening its metallic feathers. She looked for the dassies. They, too, had gone. Then she felt she was being watched. There was something here. A lioness with cubs with a lair in the rocks perhaps, or a leopard. While these thoughts passed through her mind, she lay quite still. As long as she lay still nothing was likely to attack her. Then she heard something. A twig cracked. She raised herself on her elbow and looked at the bushes beside her. Someone was there. A man. She would not have believed it possible for a man to have got so close to her without her knowing, without feeling his presence.

Seeing that she had seen him, Carter came forward.

" You," Cina said. " What are you doing here? "

" I saw you, Frankie. I thought I'd come up. I thought we could have a little talk and ride back together."

" Do you always creep up to talk to people who are asleep in your bare feet, Meneer? " She had buckled her belt and was buttoning up her shirt. " And I do not like being called ' Frankie.' "

Carter felt his temper rising. There was no need for her to talk to him like this. He wanted to undo her belt again, to put his hands inside the linen shirt and feel the soft silken warmth of her body.

She was pulling her red sash tight.

" I meant no harm," he said. " I just wanted to talk to you. You always avoid me."

" Perhaps I do not want to talk to you, Meneer."

" Fred's the name," he said. " Why won't you be friends and call me Fred? We could be good friends, you and I. You are so beautiful, Frankie."

He came closer.

Cina looking down, saw his bare feet, encrusted with dirt, the big toes widely separated from the others. She watched the feet moving towards her. His hand touched her bare arm. Like a wild creature, she sprang back. The hand closed on her and held her. With a scream of rage she struck out.

Carter's head was rocked back by the blow. She had hit

him. Never in his life had he been hit by a woman, though he had hit many. He felt his control leaving him. He felt loose, free, like a horse when the harness is slipped from its back. The blow had brought up all the evil and lust that had lain half dormant in his heart. With his left hand he tore open her shirt. With his right leg he tripped her.

But Francina was a strong girl and angry. Bringing up both her legs like a fighting cat on its back she kicked him in the belly, lifting him clear off the ground, and sprang up with a stone in her hand.

Hearing the disturbance and her cries, the dogs twenty feet below her were barking insanely and leaping at the wall of rock on which their claws could get no purchase. One of them got part of the way up and fell on Bloubooi's head. This was too much for the horse, who plunging backwards pulled his head rope loose and set off at a gallop for the wagons that were his home.

Bates, coming back from one of the herds, saw him, heard the furious barking of the dogs and turned his horse towards the koppie. Never in his life had he ridden harder. Throwing his reins over his horse's head so that it would stand, he climbed the rock only aware that something terrible was going on. Cina was in danger and he must save her.

He was only just in time. Strong as Cina was, Fred Carter was stronger. Inflamed with fury, he was immune to her blows and the savage scratches she had scraped along his face or the bleeding forearm from which she had torn chunks of flesh with her teeth.

In the fight Cina, too, had gone mad. She would die before this man took her. She would kill him or die herself. In her swollen mouth she tasted blood from her lips cut open where Carter had struck her, and from the flesh she had torn from his forearm, and spat in disgust. But she felt herself weakening. Even a strong veld-reared girl was no match for a man in his prime. All she could do now was hold him off. To damage him. To strike, scratch, kick, and bite. If his face came near hers again she was going to take off his nose or his lips. Once she almost had as he tried to kiss her. Her teeth had snapped in his face like those of a dog as he drew back.

When Bates reached them, Cina's shirt was off—hanging by one sleeve, her trousers were slipping off her hips as Carter dragged at the belt. Her mane of hair swung loose in a cloud about her bloody face as she spat with rage into the face of the man who held her.

With a shout, Bates threw himself on Carter, seizing his neck from the back and cutting his wind with his fingers around his throat.

Carter flung him off and turned on him. " You! " he shouted. " What the hell are you doing here, you interfering bastard? " He struck him a terrific blow that caught him on the point of the jaw and knocked him on to one knee. Carter raised his foot to kick him in the belly. Now was his chance. Kill him now. Cut off his finger. Carry off the girl. I've got him alone at last, he thought. Got the girl alone. Your luck's in, Freddie boy. Your luck's in. But he had forgotten Francina. Before he could send home his kick, while his right foot was still in the air, she hit him from behind. Harry sprang up and drove his right fist into his face, flattening his pudgy nose. He followed with a left into his eye and jumped back as Carter's great gorilla arms came out to grasp him. If they ever got hold of him he knew they would crush the life out of him—smash his ribs, driving their needle points into his lungs.

" You'll never get away," Carter said. " No, by God! It's dead you are and your finger pickled and the girl in me bed, and all before you can say ' Jack Robinson.' " He laughed wildly. It was the laugh of a maniac. All humanity had left him. He jumped forward like a great albino spider. Blood dripped from his nose, one of his eyes was almost closed. A white soapy foam of spittle dribbled from his mouth. On his cheeks were the stripes torn by Cina's nails. His strong hands opened and closed spasmodically. He was no longer a man but a savage apelike creature mad with fury. Harry avoided his next rush, sidestepping it. Carter turned and attacked again. He came with his head down like a charging bull, his arms swinging.

Harry met his rush with an uppercut which, though it jolted his arm, appeared to have no effect. Carter was berserk, beyond feeling pain. The great arms closed about his waist, one hand reached up over his back for his neck. This was another of Crusher Carter's tricks. Holding a man with his left arm against his body he would bring his right hand up to his opponent's chin and with a sudden pull and thrust break his back as easily as a boy smashes a stick across his knee.

He's got me, Harry thought. I should have kept farther away from him. The girl. What would happen to the girl now? He saw himself, probably not dead—just helpless with a broken back—watching what Carter did to the girl. He tried to drive his knee into Carter's groin but he was held too tight. Any moment now it would come. Carter had the grip on his chin and waist.

Carter was savouring his triumph. He loved to kill. This was his moment of power, of exultation. A quick jerk now, something no stronger than would be required to wring a cockerel's neck, and friend Harry would go limp, slack in his arms—still alive but finished—a sack that had once been a man. His mind was calmer now. He was thinking of how to escape with the girl and the finger. He would not wait for Harry to die to cut it off. That might take some time. Days even, sometimes. But he'd tell him who it was for and why, and leave him for the vultures. He'd get some of his own back that way, as he thought of him dying slowly, growing weaker and weaker. Then the girl. He wondered why he had not used his full strength on the girl and taken her at once, and then he realised that he had enjoyed the struggle with her. But now he would do it. A ripple ran through the muscles of his arm. Smash Harry's back and take the girl in front of his eyes. That would teach him to act the hero.

Cina had stood watching the fight, appalled. These men, whom she had seen so often on the trek, had even met at home before they set out, had turned into wild beasts. Into savage males, into bulls, stallions, fighting for a female— for her. In spite of her fear and horror, her heart beat faster. Her breath rose and fell, her nostrils dilated. It was for her. There was no fight left in her now. She would belong to the victor. To the good Harry or the bad Fred. It was like something out of a fairy tale. Something she would never have believed. Though she hated Fred, she knew that if he won she would be his. She would not fight any more or run away. Some terrible female instinct dominated her. Good and bad, happy or unhappy, were words without meaning. They carried no thought, no associated idea. Only man was in her mind. Only the victor. The loser, though the fight was not yet over, did not exist.

She came closer then, heard the sobbing gasp of their breath, saw the corded muscles twisting like great snakes beneath their skin. Smelled their blood and sweat. Looked into their unseeing eyes. The glowing eyes of fighting dogs, of gamecocks. And suddenly she saw them change. She saw Harry's grey eyes cloud and darken. She saw the triumph burning in Carter's pupils. She saw the grip he had on Harry's chin. Harry, who had tried to save her,

was going to be killed before her eyes. Now she became a
mother. Harry, the weaker man, her baby. Someone she
must save from death. Stooping, she picked up a stone and
brought it crashing down on Carter's head. He tottered,
swaying for a moment, and fell at her feet.

Bates stood staring at the girl. How beautiful she was!
Her eyes met his. They seemed to be looking into each
other's hearts. In her he saw all beauty, all life. He saw
what she had in her to give—love that would flow from the
spring of her heart in an endless stream, bathing all about
her. Her husband, her children, her servants. This was
only a girl, a flower that would soon ripen into fruit of
womanhood. There was strength here as well as beauty.
It was her strength that had saved his life.

" You are safe? " he asked. " I was in time? "

The spell was broken. She dropped her eyes and tried
to cover her breasts with the remnants of her shirt. Like
Eve she had become ashamed of her nakedness. Like Eve
the fruit of knowledge had once again been within her grasp.
A brilliant blush swept over her face. This man who stood
in front of her, still breathing hard from the fight, had saved
her. Saved her from what? She felt the strength of her
attacker again as she struggled in his arms. She smelled the
savage male reek of his sweat, of his hair and his clothes.
She tasted his blood in her mouth. She felt his hands on her
belly as he tore at her belt. Man again merged into man,
good into bad, bad into good. There was only woman and
man in this lonely world of isolated rock and sky. She
belonged to the victor and surely he would take his spoils,
the willing fruits of victory. The girl in her was at once
desirous and afraid. The woman knew that she would be
considered blameless. Force had been used. Her condition
proved it. Spiritually it had already happened. The man
lying at their feet would be blamed. She moved into

Harry Bates's arms. They closed around her, holding her safe. But he did not hold her as a woman, pressing her to him, his body arched over hers like a bow as he bent her back and into him. He held her tenderly as a man holds a child and then, spitting on his handkerchief, began to clean her face.

26

THE PRISONER

THESE EVENTS which had turned the camp upside down had had small effect on Tante Maria. She was upset when things went right. When nothing happened. That was the time to look out. On a fine day with a full belly, when the birds were singing in the trees and the cat was purring at your feet. That was when the blow fell. Many times had she seen it happen. It was on just such a day that the Kaffirs had overrun the farm and she had seen her family butchered before her eyes.

Now that this blow had fallen there was much to do. Of course the poor child had been raped. She had always known it would come to this sooner or later. Riding about alone like that in tight men's trousers that showed her shape to all and sundry. Ja, to every Tom, Dick and Harry, as the English said, so that they lusted after her with their eyes and hands. For a man's hands were like dogs that followed on the spoor of his eyes.

But in spite of what people said it was better to be raped and alive than dead a virgin. But how did one tell girls this? It was accepted that to be ravished was worse than death. How did one explain that it came to all girls anyway, and that one man was not much worse or much better than another? She began to tremble with laughter. It was a long time since she had been ravished and how she had enjoyed it! What a ravisher her Jan had been! What a

man! Tears flowed softly down each side of her nose. She
caught them with her tongue. Salt tears. Why should they
be salt? Why, if one was sad, should one produce salt out
of one's eyes? Sometimes tears came into the eyes of a
wounded buck. She wondered if they were salt too. Magtig,
that girl. What a fury she had gone into when she had tried
to comfort her. When she had said: "Ag sis, to be raped
is not the end. After all there has to be a first man and
though he is a brigand he is not a savage monster." In a
way, though she dared not say so, she had some sympathy
for Carter. The girl must have led him on.

"He did not, I say," Francina shouted. "Nee. Nee. I
was not raped. I am as I always was."

"What stupidity," she said, "and why lie to an old
woman like me? As if I would be shocked."

How much better, more girlish it would have been to
have wept in her Ouma's arms than fly into a tantrum.
Still, as everyone knew, there was no understanding girls of
that age. Like heifers or fillies before they were served,
they were unreliable in their moods and intractable to deal
with.

She looked at the girl as she sat on the bed at the back of
the wagon, kicking her heels against the tailboard. Now,
when it was too late, she wore a pink cotton dress. Her hair
was up and braided. To-day she looked like what she was—
a respectable farmer's daughter. But it would not last. The
boy inside her would break out again. She would soon put
on her trousers, jump on to her horse and gallop away, with
loose flying hair once more. And this time—now that she
had lost her virginity—she might seek out a man. That
was the way it was with girls. They were afraid of that
first time. So it was really only pain and the strangeness of
it that stood between them and dishonour. But once it
was over and they had time to think and remember, they

changed. They wondered exactly what happened and how it had been done. There were details they could not remember, so the thoughts grew in their minds till curiosity overcame their scruples.

Francina stared with hot angry eyes at her grandmother. What a horrible old woman. What dirty thoughts she had in her head. She knew they were there. She knew she was thinking them now. That she was seeing her lying naked under that brigand, and enjoying the picture. Were the old always like that? Seeing nothing but evil wherever they looked?

And Harry. How furious she had been with him. Cleaning her face with spit as if she had been a little child instead of a woman worked up to a fury of desire. How she had clung to him. How she had thrust herself against him, and all he had done was to clean her face and pat her behind. She smiled softly. How wonderful he was.

Barend came up and put his hand on her bare leg. She pulled it back. She was in no mood to be touched by a man.

" Well," he said. He did not know what to say next. He loved this girl. She was going to marry him. It was all arranged. He wanted her more than ever now. What had happened was not her fault. She could not be blamed, but it had happened and there was no need for her to draw back from him like that, particularly since they had so nearly made love once. He hated Carter. The man ought to be shot, but because of this, because he was going to be punished, he was not jealous of him. He had ceased to exist in his mind. Only the act existed—the act that had roused his own desire, sending the blood pouring through him, the love Carter had made to the girl who now sat staring at him with her long legs curled under her body.

He said: " Well," again. How did one go on? He could

not say: How are you? How do you feel? What was it like to be raped on the top of a little hill like that? But these things were in his mind. The picture of it was in his mind. He saw her clothes torn and rumpled, felt the softness of her thighs as he watched the struggle she had made in Carter's arms before he mastered her.

Francina looked into his eyes, then sliding her bare legs out from the folds of her pink frock she slipped to the ground. "We will have coffee," she said.

"Ja," Barend said. "There is nothing like a cup of coffee." Of course the coffee, except for small special hoards for great occasions, had long since been used up. But the mixture of ground wheat and acorns they used now was still called coffee. What else, after all, could they call it?

One of the Cape girls brought the brew, setting it on a box that served as a table standing beside one of the big rear wheels of the wagon.

Barend stared at the yellow wheel—at the spokes running into the hub, at the red dust that almost masked the shabby paint. His eyes went down to the girl's bare feet, to her legs and then back to the yellow wheel hub out of which the spokes sprang like the legs of a yellow spider. The hub was the heart, the centre of the wheel—its life as it were. The life of the wagon, of movement. And it was pierced by an axle and held by the linchpin. Somehow in this moment Barend saw the relationship between men and women, male and female. They were the axle and the hub of life that kept it moving on as if it were a wagon—over the veld of time—over the years. None of this, neither the thought nor the feeling, was quite clear to him, but he was oppressed by them, wrapped as it were in a blanket of ideas that choked him, making it hard for him to breathe, and he breathed loudly as if he had been running. The girl stood before him with one foot raised on its toes, the heel touching the ankle of the other leg. He looked at her high instep, at the fine bone, at the blue veins of her feet, at the calves that swept upwards, disappearing into the pink hem of her dress, and reached out for her waist to hold her.

Quick as a buck, she jumped away, laughing at him. Then she came back, with downcast eyes. " Let us drink our coffee," she said.

" Then you will walk with me? "

" Ja, I will walk."

It would be better to walk, she thought. They would walk. Then she could say: You will eat with us, and he would agree. Then when night had fallen. . . . Then she would see. She laughed. But she would not marry him. No, never. Not while Harry Bates was still alive.

Barend thought it was curious that a girl who had been through so much a few hours ago could laugh like this. But he made no pretence of understanding women and this girl was more difficult than most. Much harder to understand than Miemie, who at that moment walked past them swaying her hips and walking on the balls of her bare feet.

Harry Bates stared at his prisoner. Carter was chained to a heavy ox yoke. The chain went round his waist and was padlocked. What a fool he had been. What a stupid thing to do. And now here he was chained like a baboon to a pole. While they, the old man and the others, were deciding what to do with him. What did one do in a case like this, he wondered?

Carter must have been wondering too. " What'll they do to me, 'Arry? " he said. " What'll those bloody Dutchmen do, d'ye think? "

" I don't know. But why did you do it? What happened? "

" I was insane, Harry. Insane for the girl and then there

she was. And us alone and the bloody dogs for once couldn't get to us." Why was there so often something that stood between him and his heart's desire? The dogs that would never let him near the girl, even to talk to her, growling as if they knew what was in his mind, as if they could smell the leaping of his blood. And that God-damned buck nigger that never left Harry's side. If it wasn't for him, he thought, I'd have had him dead and the pinkie finger pickled in me saddlebag. Aye, he thought, and then I'd be riding hell for leather with the girl held in me arms. This was his fantasy. He saw no other difficulty—only the dogs and the Zulu stood between his having his will with Francina and collecting the thousand pound reward that had been promised him for killing Harry Bates.

Bates was astonished that he did not hate this man. He had hated him while he fought him. He knew Carter would have killed him and now he tried to come the old comrade over him—the old Dragoon. But he was a bad 'un. Bad all through. There were bad men, evil men, as there were bad horses, wicked horses, killers. Slowly, he was learning about evil. It had not been easy. For a long time he had thought there must be reason for things. Now he knew that often there was no reason for hate. That there need be none, that some men got pleasure out of inflicting pain. He had seen it when he was flogged. He had learned more among the brigands. How odd that but for this man he would never have known love. Without Carter he would never have held Francina in his arms. Once she had saved his life. Now they had saved each other. So there was a bond between them that could never break. He thought of her struggling, almost naked in her torn clothes, fighting Carter off, her breath coming in sobbing gasps. He still felt the skin on her back against his arms as he held her to him. He still felt her breasts—full and softly firm—bare against his chest. As he had covered her with his coat he had held them. Unable to resist the temptation, he had cupped them in his hands. That was when he should have kissed her, have taken her, for she was his. But he had not been able to, and now she hated him. He was sure she hated him. For he had seen her naked and left her. She had said: " I am a woman," and he had treated her as a child. But how could he explain that he could not do this thing? Not in this way. Oom Willem had taken him in. He had allowed him to become one of the trek. Was he to betray that trust, was he to be as bad as Carter? He knew, too, that she, feeling Carter would be blamed, could not understand his reluctance. Honour was one thing to a man and another to a woman, and now she had turned from love to hate. From pride to shame. She would have been proud to show her nakedness to her lover—she was ashamed that the man who had seen it had spurned her gift.

The sun was low in the sky, painting this wild and empty world in a roseate light. Pink, mauve, lilac. The long shadows were indigo and Prussian blue. In the distance the hills were ultramarine. The sparse trees threw shadows a hundred yards long. The grass tufts stood up blood-red out of the blackness of their shadow.

Into this unearthly beauty Harry saw Cina and Barend walk together. This was the man she was going to marry. The man in whose arms she was going to lie, whose sons she would bear in this new land of the North.

The girl seemed to float, so easily did she move. Her pink dress glowed, her hair shone like sovereign gold. It was only this morning that he had held her, that she had offered herself to him and he had let her go. Only this morning that the man he now guarded had fought to master her.

Carter's curses broke into his thoughts, smashing the lovely silence as if it were a fragile vase.

"The bloody bastard," he said. "Look at him with that little dancing bitch. And I could have had her. Christ," he said, "if it hadn't been for your bloody interference. You . . . You . . ." he shouted. "I should 'ave killed you long ago." It occurred to him now when it was too late that he should have got one of his brigand friends to deal with the nigger. It would only have cost him a quid or two. Then he regretted what he had said, pretended he had not said it. "Let me go, chum. Let me go, for old times' sake." For an instant Harry Bates looked at him. Then he hit him in the face. Never before in his life had he struck a helpless man. Then he sat with his gun across his knees and his head sunk in his hands.

It was dark when Willem Prinsloo left the laagered wagons. He had to be alone. This thing that had happened, this decision that had been thrust upon him, was more than he could bear. His granddaughter, the only thing left him in the world to love, had been set upon by this English brigand and but for the coming of the other Englishman would have been raped. Perhaps she had been raped, as that fat cow said. Though the girl denied it and certainly she was the one to know. Maria had suggested finding out. "After all, there are visible signs," she said. "Why should I not . . ."

"No," he'd shouted. "No! We will take her word."

So it was on the girl's word alone that Carter must be judged. Her word was that she had been attacked but had not been raped. He thanked God for it, because had it been otherwise he would have had to kill this man.

An eye for an eye, a tooth for a tooth—that was God's law. For three hours he had thumbed through the big leatherbound Bible by the light of a flickering candle. Now he was out on the veld seeking wisdom, hoping for counsel from the stars that shone in the dark velvet sky above him.

At the wagons, still chained to the heavy yoke, Carter waited for the dawn. What would he have to say when they came to judge him?

The old man walked on. He was unarmed. He had come out to seek wisdom from the Lord. One did not come to God gun in hand. He looked up at the stars again. He looked at the Milky Way, spread like a torn and speckled mat over the heavens. How many men had sought the silent stars for counsel? How many thousands, over how many years? These were the stars that the Israelites had looked up and seen. This was the firmament that had covered Moses like a cloak. These were the stars that had looked down upon our Lord Jesus in the wilderness in the forty nights he had spent fasting alone.

A hunting jackal called. In the distance a lion roared. In his mind Oom Willem saw it, with its head down and near the ground, its belly contracting as it sent its great coughs echoing across the plain. A hyena laughed. Where there were lions there were hyenas, who lived upon their leavings and, finally, when age robbed them of their teeth and strength, fell upon the lions themselves and consumed them.

But Oom Willem was unafraid. To-night no lion or tiger would stalk him. No snake strike him. For he was walking in the company of the Lord. It was coming now. Carter was a hyena. He must not be killed. He must be cast out. But first his teeth must be drawn, for only a fool would trust a hyena.

27

THE VERDICT

Oom Willem looked at the assembled people. All were there—men, women and children—and all were dressed as if it were Sunday. The klerekiste or church chests had been opened. The women wore their best pleated kappies; some of the men wore top hats and frock coats, which among the younger were heirlooms inherited from others who had also worn them upon all serious occasions. Each carried his gun and wore a bandolier. Tante Maria was surrounded by her adopted brood whose faces shone from scrubbing. The girls could hardly blink their eyes, so tightly had their hair been braided back.

The prisoner stood with his back to the crowd between the elder Beyers brothers. The trek chain was still around his waist and hung like an immense clinking tail behind him. There was no chance of his running away. Besides, where could he run? In this vast emptiness there was only the trek and, if it could be found, a native village such as the one Ullman had gone to where a white man, unarmed and alone, was not likely to be well received.

Oom Willem stood like an Old Testament prophet— silent. His head was lowered, his eyes closed in prayer. He held his beaver hat against his chest.

The people in front of him prayed also—but they prayed less for justice than for safety for themselves and their loved ones.

At last, after minutes that had seemed like hours, Oom

Wiliem looked up, clapped his hat on to his head, and said:
" Burghers, friends. On this trek we have suffered much.
We have left our dead behind us. We have been cold and
hungry. We have suffered from thirst. But we have upheld
each other. The strong helping the weak. The weak helping
the weaker. That is as it should be, for a trek is like a family,
between whom there must be the bonds of love and faith.
Ja, we have suffered and have overcome our suffering.
The hand of the Lord has upheld us and we have never
faltered in our purpose—to create a republic that will be a
glory to God and a comfort to all free men. A republic of
brothers that will be a beacon of light in a sea of pagan
darkness. Then we took unto our company two strangers,
gathering them to us like good Samaritans—two men of a
different race, men who told us that they had fled the
English oppressor and would join us, live with us, fight with
us and become good Boers when we came to the land of
Canaan and settled down at last."

He paused and looked at the people before him—at the
multitude. For that was how he saw it. Not just this handful
of bearded men, of boys, women, children and their servants
—white and black—but the multitude that would spring
from their loins and wombs—the nation that they and their
sons would build in the promised land.

" And what happened? " he went on, raising his voice.
" Ja, what happened? " he asked them. " You all know
what happened, but I will tell you again. One of our girls,
a young maiden—my Francina—went out alone and was
set upon by one of the men we had taken into our trek, a
viper that we had nourished in our bosom. Ja," he said,
" this man, this animal, this hyena—for surely we cannot
call such a creature a man—flung himself upon the maid
and ravished her, stripping the clothes from her body and
flinging her down upon the ground. I am sure that this is

the truth. But Francina denies it. She says he attempted to ravish her but failed owing to the arrival of the other Englishman who, seeing her horse running riderless, galloped to her rescue. But since in the Bible it states very clearly that to look with lust upon a married woman is to commit adultery with her, I say that to strip the clothes from a maid when she is alone on the veld is to rape her. And here I have authority—this case is also dealt with, for it is said that: If a man find a betrothed damsel—and Francina is betrothed—in the field—or on a koppie—and the man force her, and lie with her; then the man only that lay with her shall die. But unto the damsel thou shalt do nothing; there is in the damsel no sin worthy of death. . . . For he found her in the field, and the betrothed damsel cried, and there was none to save her. This, my brothers, is the word of God from the Book of Deuteronomy, Chapter 22, verses 25, 26 and 27."

Again he was silent.

All eyes turned to Francina who, in her pink cotton dress and kappie, stared back at them unblushing and unmoved. What fools they were. Surely they must know that if a girl was raped it would show. Not only would the blood of her virginity be spilled but her eyes and her manner would be changed. Even the appearance of an animal was changed. A filly or a heifer looked different afterwards. Ja, she thought, had he done it I would be different. I would be a woman now with full knowledge—fuller than that of most wives, since it would have been against my will. And if the other had done it, as I wished him to, I should also be different, but in another way. Not angry, but queen-proud that I was his woman, flesh of his flesh. Her eyes brightened at the memories of yesterday. Her muscles quivered under her dress as she fought off Carter once again. Her body became limp and soft as she thought of herself in Harry's arms. She did not hate Carter. He had not hurt her seriously. Even his intent did not disturb her. That was as it should be. Any female should be able to send a male insane. How often had she seen it with a cow, a mare or a bitch in season. The males served them, making them pregnant, or they were restrained by force, or they were cut, or killed if unfit for breeding. Only the best males survived.

She did not see the crowd. She saw the tossing crests of the stallions, the horns of the bulls, the rams and the goats, understanding their desire. She began to laugh. Tears came into her eyes. She could not stop laughing. It was all so funny.

Tante Maria picked her up as if she was a child and carried her away. The people opened up before the old woman like water to the bow of a ship.

" She's hysterical," Magdalena Beyers said. " And why not? Who would not be after what she had suffered? "

" Why not, indeed? " those near her echoed, quite convinced now that Carter's attack had reached its vile conclusion.

Oom Willem began again: " I have thought of all punishments. Ja, even of death, for here beyond the law we must make our own. But the girl is not dead and denies his act, so Carter will not die, much as I would like to shoot him as I would shoot a dog that has suddenly gone mad. But, as all men know, good dogs can go mad, while this man is all evil, a brigand and a rapist. Ja," he went on, " all last night I sought guidance. I prayed to the Lord our God. I walked under the stars looking up as our Lord must have done when He was alone in the wilderness. And this is the punishment which has been revealed to me: Because this man has committed a sin against the flesh of a girl so must his flesh suffer."

"No!" Carter shouted. "No! No! You cannot cut a man like a bull."

Oom Willem took no notice of his outburst. "Ja," he said. "He must suffer. He will be tied, spread-eagled to the rear wheel of my wagon and then receive six strokes of the sjambok given diagonally—three from each side. Then he will be set loose and turned away from us to live or die alone as the Lord wills. For then his life will be in the hands of the Lord. Should he try to return, he will be shot."

"Do you all agree?" he asked. His head turned slowly as his eyes searched the crowd.

"Ja," they shouted. "We agree." Though some added: "Let us shoot him at once and be done with it."

Oom Willem raised his hand for silence. "I would shoot him if he had killed one of our number, but since he has not killed, to kill him would be murder. In this way he may die. Even with the small amount of food and water we give him, he may die. There are lions in the veld, snakes, elephants, buffalo. Ja, even for an armed and mounted man the dangers are manifold. Therefore I say, if he lives it will be the Will of God and a sign to him to change his ways. Now take him."

Flip and Barend Beyers took Carter's arms. Louis marched behind carrying the trek-chain tail.

Carter was cursing. Foaming spittle dripped from his lips. "Whip me," he shouted. "Flog me like a thieving Kaffir, and then turn me loose to die? Are these the acts of Christian men?"

Louis kicked him from behind and he would have fallen if the boy had not jerked him up by the chain he held. Five minutes later he was tied—crucified—his arms and legs apart, to the great yellow wheel of Willem's wagon. His wrists and ankles were lashed tight with riems to the felloes passing over the iron tyres that glistened like bands of silver in the morning sun.

Who was to beat him? All thought he should be flogged. All were eager to see this justice done, but no one there had ever raised a hand to a white man.

Oom Willem, towering above them all, strode through them with a long sea-cow-hide sjambok in his hand. It was a full inch thick and bound with bands of plaited copper wire every twelve inches of its length. He stared the people down. No one could face those blazing blue eyes.

"I would do it myself. I am not too old," he said. Suddenly he saw Nzobo standing behind Bates. The Zulu was as tall as he. Alone his eyes had not fallen. Aie, this old man was a chief. When he was older his own master would become such a one in his turn. A chief, a leader, a king.

"Come here, you," Oom Willem said. He handed him the whip. It was six feet long. It bent of its own weight. "Give it to Baas Beyers. Take it, Barend. You are to marry her. To avenge her is your duty."

Nzobo took the sjambok but looked at the others. Did they approve of this? There was no dissent. He looked at Bates. He said: "Go on. It is justice."

"By God, you'll die for this," Carter shouted. "You and that bloody Kaffir and others too. By God and by Jesus, you'll pay, you bloody Boers. The lot of you."

Oom Willem led Barend into position. He said: "You understand? Three cuts. I will count. And then"—he pointed—"you will stand here and give three more."

Barend stripped off his shirt. Beneath his skin his muscles rippled like snakes. He kicked off his veldschoens and stood with his knees a little bent, flexing the whip while he waited for the word. This would resolve his problems of love and of hate. This was justice. It was happiness.

Everyone held their breath.

" One . . ." Oom Willem said.

The sjambok went up. The polished copper wire bands shone in the sunlight. It came down.

Carter gasped with pain. He would have collapsed if he had not been held by the wrists, as the blood sprang through the broken skin of his back.

" Two . . ." Oom Willem said.

Again the whip rose and fell, leaving a bloody strip six inches below the first.

" Three! "

The third blow fell. Carter was screaming now.

Barend stared at the dripping back in front of him. Blood-red from shoulders down to trouser top. Flies buzzed about the wounds.

Nzobo stared entranced. This man had tried to kill his master. He wished he could flog him till he died. He wished, instead of six it was sixty strokes, and that he had been allowed to give them. Then, with such a splendid whip in his hands, he would have cut him in half, laid his ribs bare and spilled out his kidneys in the dust. Dazed by his thoughts, he stood as if his bare gnarled toes were nailed to the ground. The whites of his eyes were red-veined, his lips drawn back in a savage grin. He stared, but saw nothing, through his glazed eyes, only the hated back in front of him. He felt nothing but the weight of his hate and envy of Barend Beyers for the whip in his hand.

" Come," Oom Willem said.

But Barend did not move.

The old man took him by the shoulder and placed him on the other side of the sagging body. Then he realised what he must do and woke from his bloody trance. Only he and the big Zulu seemed really to understand this thing.

" Four . . ." Oom Willem said.

The first diagonal of the second series was cut.

" Five . . ."

Now two squares of flesh were outlined by the broken skin.

" Six! "

Two more squares were cut.

" Turn him loose," Oom Willem said.

Flip, drawing his hunting knife from its sheath, severed the riems that held him. Carter fell in a heap on the dust below the wheel. He did not look like a man but a bloody sack.

Nzobo took the whip from Barend and drew it through his hands. Then he looked at his hands and he wiped them on his trousers.

The chickens, which had been driven from their accustomed place around the back of the wagon, returned to look for scraps.

" Throw water over him," Oom Willem said.

A bucket was emptied over Carter. He twitched like a dog dreaming in its sleep. His legs jerked as if he was running and he came to, spitting and snarling with fury.

" Bloody bastards," he said. " You thought I'd die of it, but it'll take more than that to kill Freddie Carter. A hell of a lot more. And I'll tell you this. Even if you turn me loose like this in the wilds, I'll still not die and it won't be the Lord Who will save me but all the devils from hell."

The Boers fell back before this blasphemy. Surely God would strike him dead at their feet. But God did not strike him. Instead, Carter hauled himself up by the spokes of the wheel and turned to face them like a hyena brought to bay.

" I curse you all in the devil's name. You, Harry, and your nigger shadow. Frankie, the little teasing bitch.

Barend, the lout that she'll betray one day. Willem, the false prophet, and all—all men, women and children I curse in Satan's name. And the cattle, the horses, the sheep, the goats, the dogs, the very chickens do I curse and wish all evil down upon them." Carter's pale eyes flamed. Spittle dripped from the corners of his mouth. He looked like a white cornered rat, turning on its pursuers. "You'll see," he said. "You'll see. You'll live to regret this day, the whole bloody lot of you."

Flip turned to Oom Willem and said: "Perhaps he is right. Perhaps the devil always looks after his own and we should make an end of him?"

"Ja," Oom Willem said. "But who will do it? Will you? Will I? Jong," he said, "that is something to remember. If a man is to be killed, someone must do it."

He took the cow-horn trumpet from his back and blew upon it. This was the signal to trek.

"Trek . . . trek . . . bring in the beasts. Inspan and trek . . . we have delayed enough."

Carter's leather-covered water bottle was filled. He was given a small bag of rusks and another of biltong. His knife had been taken from his belt. He had no gun. He sat on an ant heap surrounded by flies and watched the wagons prepare to move. Watched the oxen being tied in pairs to their yokes. Listened to the shouts of the drivers and voorloopers, to the barking of the dogs, to the cries of the children and the rifle claps of the great giraffe-hide whips.

There was the dust of the moving herds. There were the great wheels moving. This thing—for a trek was a thing— that he had been a part of was leaving him. Sloughing him off. It had used him, broken him, discarded him. What those fools didn't know was that he was more than a man, he was an entity. How could they guess that he had absorbed the pain into himself and dissolved into a hatred so fierce that he felt no hurt and was completely unafraid?

Only when the trek was well on its way, winding over the veld like a great snake, did Oom Willem think of Francina. How was she? Where was she?

He rode over to the wagon where Francina slept with the children. She was not there. He sought Tante Maria.

" Francina," he shouted, " where is Francina? "

" She's here, Willem. She must have been here all the time."

All the time . . . all the time . . . lying hidden behind the canvas within a foot of Carter's head as they flogged him.

28

CARTER'S CURSE

TANTE MARIA had taken Francina back to the Van der Merwe wagon where she slept with the orphaned children. She had left her still laughing and crying among the pillows and blankets of the kartel.

Cina knew this was going to be too much for her. At any moment one of the children would come crawling back like a little animal to sleep. They popped in and out of the wagon all day long. She could not stand the sight of one of them now, nor answer another question—Why this? Why that? Why are you sad? Why do you laugh and cry at the same time? Have you a pain in the belly? What will they do to the wicked Englishman who raped you? Why? When? What? It was always the same, and stories of what they had done, seen, overheard, expected, hoped, wanted. She would hold no more filthy rag dolls, kiss no more milky faces. No. Not now. Not to-day. And as soon as she felt it safe to do so she slipped away—back to her old bed. To be safe from interruption, she pulled down and fastened the canvas flap that closed the rear of the wagon, and lay on her belly muffling her sobs against her forearms.

She had noticed nothing till she had heard her Oupa say: " One " in a loud voice. One what? Then the blow of the whip had come, sickening her as it thudded against flesh. Then the groan and the slumping of a body which shook the wagon. Carter, Carter. They were flogging Fred

Carter for what he had done to her. But he had not done it. Why would no one believe her? If she had had the strength she would have run out to stop them. But her strength was gone. She lay still, like water, like a pool over which the swift wind of her passions blew in a tempest of fear, hate, love, desire and regret, but was unable to move her. Harry, Carter, Barend, Flip, all merged, fading into each other till at last only Harry remained—only Harry and her desire.

The voice went on counting. The blows continued to fall. She felt sick. Bile came up, sour and bitter, into her throat, into her mouth. She was sweating, trembling. She felt cold, so cold that her teeth chattered. She felt sick, ready to vomit. What a fool she had been to come here. At each blow, Carter's body was driven against the wheel, and lying within the wagon she felt its impact. Four . . . five . . . six, and then she heard Oom Willem say: " Cut him down," and it was ended. She almost fainted. It was as if she had helped Carter sustain the whipping and that now, her strength was spent. It was in this state, half conscious and utterly distraught, that she heard Carter curse them all. Barend, who had flogged him. Harry, who had betrayed him. Oom Willem, who had condemned him. Herself, Francina, who by her teasing had driven him to this act. One and all he cursed them. He cursed the trek and everyone in it, every beast, calling all evil up from hell to strike them down. There was something terrible in the sound of his voice. This man, who should have been broken, was not broken. He was only hurt. Hurt to the point of death perhaps, but somehow she felt that even if he died the evil he had wished upon them would not be ended. Only now did she know what she had escaped, or why she had struggled so hard. With another man she might have given in, for she was ripe for love, but her instinct had forced her to battle to the end, to battle till Harry had come to save her. With Harry Bates's name on her lips and the picture of him in her mind, she fell into an exhausted sleep that was almost a coma. She never knew that the wagons had moved and was surprised to find herself in a new outspan when she woke in the late afternoon. She saw Harry but he avoided her—as if he did not want to see her. Perhaps he was disgusted with her, upset that she had flung herself, half naked, into his arms. Or did he think her ugly? Both thoughts upset her. How could she change his opinion?

The Beyers men came up to the cooking fire. She tormented Barend by flirting with his brothers. Flip responded to her teasing, chasing her, pretending to catch her in his arms, and then allowing her to elude his grasp.

From a distance, Harry Bates watched them at play. He knew that she knew he watched, and he was puzzled by her behaviour. It was as if she tried to pretend that everything was as usual—that nothing had happened. That no great events separated the present from the immediate past. In his heart he was much upset. He could not help thinking of what would have happened to Cina had he not arrived in time. Of all the trek he alone knew that he had come in time, but no one believed him. Naturally, a man in his position would have to lie, just as the girl did, in her support. Then there was his discovery of Fred Carter's true nature. He had always known him to be bad but had put it behind him, trying to believe the best of this man who had once been his comrade—this other Englishman, the dragoon who had disgraced both his country and his regiment. And then, finally, there was the curse. Nonsense, of course. But the words left an unpleasant memory. And he was not the only one who felt it. Even the children were subdued. Something evil had been let loose upon the veld, a shadow like that of some great evil bird had come between them and the sun of their hopes, obscuring its brightness.

For ten days more they trekked on and then, because they were losing stock, several horses had died and the cattle, covered with ticks, were listless and thin in spite of the good grass, Oom Willem decided to halt and rest for a week. It might be even longer, as Sybella Ullman was beginning her pains and this seemed to be a fair place for the baby to be born. There was water here in plenty, large pans and pools much frequented by wild fowl and game. There were beautiful trees here with fine foliage and a lovely yellow bark which came off like the bloom of a grape when rubbed, leaving the trunk a smooth and shiny green beneath. Some had been broken down by elephants who seemed to relish them for food. So for the woman to bear her child and the cattle and horses to rest and fatten on the buffalo grass that grew beneath the trees, there could be no better place, which was why Oom Willem had called a halt. These were not the only reasons, though they were the ones he gave.

In actual fact, Oom Willem was lost. Since they were going north, to be lost was not serious, but it worried the old man. Up till now every landmark had been familiar. But somewhere in the last week he had erred. He had gone too far to the east or west.

Tante Maria profited by the long halt to bring the trek into shape, marshalling the women to see that they laundered and repaired their clothes. Her adopted children were scrubbed till they shone from head to foot. How lucky it was that she had made so much soap. The boys' hair was cut, all toe- and finger-nails were seen to. An inventory of such preserved food as was left to them was made. The servants who had grown slack on the trek were chased and disciplined. All the domestic livestock was counted and doctored. Two baby boars were killed, others were castrated, for in the months that had passed her herd had increased, and moreover the character of her pigs had changed. They followed her wagon like dogs and with the dogs. She looked longingly at Francina's rams but dared not touch them. Not that she wanted to so much now, as they would be tough, but their fat tails were a temptation. And all the while she watched Sybella. She would not let Willem move till the child was born. And then on the seventh day Miemie came to call her.

" Her time has come," the girl cried, her eyes bright with excitement.

" Ja," Tante Maria said, slapping her face, " and yours will come too one day, my cheeky little meisie and then you will not be laughing."

Followed by the girl and Francina, she set out for the wagon where she found Sybella kneeling on a great ox skin, gripping the wheel with her hands. The maidservants had rigged up a kind of screen made of skins set on poles between forked sticks to give her a measure of privacy. A fire had been made, water was heating and there were clean cloths laid out upon an upturned box.

The birth had gone well and there was great rejoicing, for this was the first child to be born, and a boy at that. His mother called him Willem François. And then suddenly, things which up to now had gone well changed. More horses died, cattle by the dozen and sheep by the hundred. It was as if the trek's luck had flown like a bird from its perch or, as some said, that Carter's curse had descended upon them.

It was only after it was discovered that there was a poisonous herb in the veld here that a forced trek was made to higher ground. Some of the sick stock picked up but it was too late for others. And the great herds and flocks with which they had set off from the Colony were only a memory now, their bones landmarks of disaster upon their path. The defection of Ullman and the rape of Francina had been bad, had been disappointments—failures in the smooth running of their little travelling republic—but this was a capital loss. It was irreplaceable. It would take several settled years to breed up the stock again. All the English horses had died and so had a number of others. Nearly all the mares in foal or in milk with foals at foot were dead. Most of the entire horses needed for hunting and defence were left, but they were, as it were, the interest on the herd; the capital was the breeding mares. With the cattle it was the same, the bulls and oxen had proved relatively immune and some of those that had sickened had even recovered before the move to the hills, but many in-calf cows and heifers had died. In addition to the animals, many of the people became sick of fever, their teeth chattering with cold one minute while an hour later they were casting off their clothes, so unbearably hot had they become. None died but few were well, and the eyes of the children were big pools of blue or grey or brown deeply sunk into their yellow faces.

Francina had become almost ill herself, though not with fever, in her anxiety about Bloubooi. Every day she led him to graze on the end of a riem, choosing only the best grass and keeping him away from any herbage which looked unfamiliar. Oom Willem, depressed by the anxiety of everyone and nagged at by his sister-in-law, decided, after several hours of prayer, to set up a strong laager where they were now and, taking a single wagon, spend a few days looking for some landmark that he remembered. It was the business with Francina and Ullman that had put him out. Since nothing changed here, since thirty years was no more than a day in this ancient land, he would have no difficulty in finding what he sought. But his difficulties began with Tante Maria. "Trek off with you into the bush alone? . . . Now I know you are crazy. What of Francina and the children? What of Mevrou Ullman and her baby? Who will command when you go? How do you know you will find what you seek?"

The questions poured out of her like water out of a barrel with the bung knocked out.

Oom Willem stared at the horizon while he waited for her to end, to empty herself. When she had done he said: "Ja, perhaps you are right. You are too old, too fat and heavy. Yes, indeed it will lighten the load a lot if you remain and Cina and I go alone with a few boys."

She turned away from him and going to the wagon began to pack. No man could say things like that to her. Fat. She was not fat. Heavy yes, but it was all bone and muscle. She filled the chest with clothes and sat upon it. The lid sank into place beneath her weight as she leaned over to slip the hasp on to the staple and fastened it in place with the little wooden rod that hung from a leather lace beside it.

Now that her decision was made, she became very active. She shouted to Francina: "Where are those girls?" She called the girls. When they came, she said: "The Oubaas and I are going to look for the path to the north. So pack up and make haste. We cannot sit about for ever on the veld like flies on meat. The holiday is over."

A day later, leaving Barend in charge of the laager, Oom Willem's wagon pulled out. Now he knew what he was looking for. It had come back to him as he prayed. He was looking for a big cream of tartar tree, a giant baobab that towered over the bush, turning all other trees that grew about it into shrubs and dwarfing a man to the size of an ant. It was not that he had ever forgotten the tree, simply that he had thought to find it farther on.

"A tree?" Tante Maria said. "A tree that was here thirty years ago must still be here? In spite of storms and fires? It is to things like this that madmen pin their faith. So our fate now depends upon a vegetable, for what else is a tree?"

"Silence," Oom Willem shouted. "These cream of tartars live for ever. They will not even burn."

"Trees that live for ever and do not burn—Ja, that is something that I wish to see. But if you want to know what I think, I will tell you." She stood with her hands on her hips.

"I do not wish to know."

"Nevertheless I will tell you. We have been cursed. The evil eye of the rapist Carter is upon us. You should have shot him out of hand before he had time to think. Did he not curse us all? Curse the livestock, the very trek itself? Did he not . . ."

"Shut your mouth, fool woman. Do you not believe in the protection of God? Do you think we should have come so far with so little harm had we not been sheltered by His hand?"

"Ja, Willem, but what has happened to God's hand now?"

"Have you no faith? No understanding? Certain things are sent to try us, to see if we are worthy."

"Willem," Tante Maria said, "I would sooner believe in the devil and the curse of the Englishman, for it is not in my heart to think that God would kill a half-born child and its parents to test our faith. Nee, nee, it is the devil with his horns and three-pronged tail that is among us."

Tante Maria lowered her bulk on to a bench and

covered her face with her apron to hide her tears. Here, alone with Oom Willem, Francina and their servants, she was not afraid to weep. Her big body quivered like a jelly. It was wonderful to be able to show weakness—not to have to lead, to command, to comfort, to scold, to advise. Wonderful to unbend and slacken the spring of her will. To be able to speak the truth, to tell that Willem what she really thought of him in a loud voice instead of having to reassure the others about his qualities of leadership. She pulled the apron from her face.

"It was the devil that drove us from our homes," she said. "Ja," she pointed at Francina who was picking ticks off her horse. "Ja, and the devil is in that horse. Was it not brought to us by an Englishman? Did it not seduce Francina with its beauty and bring the soldiers on to our backs so that we had to flee? The devil is in that horse, I say, for it is he who turned my little girl into a wild half-boy. He who has blighted all our lives."

All the hatred, all the jealousy she felt for Bloubooi rose into her voice. Picking up a great stick she advanced towards the horse.

Francina seeing what was in her mind, pulled a pistol from the holster of the saddle that was set on a stump beside her.

"Come no nearer," she said, "or I will shoot. Touch him now or ever and I will kill you. Ja," she said, "you or any other, for he is my heart."

Tante Maria shrank back. So it had come to this. To be threatened by this slip of a girl, the child whose life she had saved, and whom she had brought up. The stick fell from her hand.

"Now indeed I know it is true that we have been cursed, for I have felt the hot breath of the devil upon my face as I looked into the barrel of a pistol pointed by my child."

Francina put the pistol back into the holster.

"The devil is certainly here," she said, "when a good woman like you, Ouma, is inspired to turn upon a dumb beast that is our friend."

"You and your animal friends. Your horses, your dogs, your sheep, your goose."

"They also are God's creatures and were taken into the Ark by Noah."

"Ja, but so were lions and tigers and snakes. Sometimes it is in my heart to think that Noah was as mad as your Oupa."

"Blaspheme not, Maria." Willem had returned to the group in time to hear her words. As he stood looking at them, at the wagon and the little camp they had made, his eyes suddenly went quite blank.

"What is it, Oupa?" Francina cried, and ran towards him.

The old man swayed. She caught him as he fell.

"He is sick, Ouma. Oupa is sick."

"Ja, my child. It is the curse. It is as I said. By now you should know that I am always right."

She called the servants and they carried the old man into the wagon.

Tante Maria began to search for some roots she carried in the medicine box. She was not unhappy. This was her function—to advise the healthy and heal the sick, and once again she had been proved right.

29

THE STORM

WITH OOM WILLEM too sick to move, new plans had to be made. A strong *skerm*—enclosure—was built for the oxen and horses. Trees were cut and dragged into a circle, their thorn-armed branches outwards. Hendrik was sent to hunt meat. There were plenty of buck: kudu, rooibok, duiker and steenbok abounded.

This was a pretty place, almost flat but broken up by big, nearly circular patches of bush. Between them the grass was good—rooigras and finger grass in the open with buffelgras under the shade of the big isolated trees.

The camp assumed the settled look which was usual when the Boers stayed more than a single night in one spot. Radiating from the wagon were little paths leading to the various places that they used—the main track to the water, a small pan five hundred yards away. A path to the hollowed-out ant heap where Tante Maria baked her bread. Another to the tree where the salt-meat strips hung from the branches. It kept badly in the heat and something had to be shot each day. There were private paths used for private purposes. There were old game paths that had been there since time began.

Francina was not unhappy. She took care of her horse and supervised the grazing and watering of the draught oxen. She cleaned her saddlery and practised shooting with both gun and pistols. All thoughts of a settled life and home had left her. Indeed by now the various parts of any camp had come to be regarded by the younger Boers as if they were parts of a house. The tree, festooned with pots near which the cooking was done, became the kombuis or kitchen. Something being in the kitchen simply meant that it was hanging on a tree near the fire. The wagon itself was the house or home.

Tante Maria's remedies were doing Oom Willem good and there seemed little doubt that another day would see him well enough to move back to the main laager. He was satisfied, or said he was, that though he had not found the tree he sought, this was the right direction and they would soon come upon it. He recognised this country.

" Ja," he said to Tante Maria who had climbed up the steps into the wagon to sit with him, " we approach the promised land to which I must lead my people. That is why I must not die."

" To be a little sick is not to die."

" No, Maria, it is not to die, but in my fever I have seen visions. I know what I must do. The village we must build. The church to the glory of God. All this has been shown to me very clearly and in bright colours. Also, and this will prove to you how far I went down the valley of death, how nearly I approached the pearly gates of Heaven. I thought well of you. I thought perhaps I had been unjust in my thoughts about you. It was as if the Lord God said: ' Willem, she is an old cow it is true, but she is a good old cow, and once was a beautiful heifer, which is why your deceased brother, who is now farming up here, married her, and you must try to see her with his eyes.' "

Before Tante Maria could reply, Francina ran up to the back of the wagon.

" There is a great storm coming. To the east the sky is suddenly as black as ink. Come . . . look . . ."

Tante Maria peered round the side of the wagon.

" Magtig," she said. " It is like night. Like blood."

This was because in front of the black rolling storm clouds was a billow of red dust driven by the wind. Oom Willem raised himself on his elbow but could see nothing since the sky behind the wagon was still a clear blue, and fell back. Because there was nothing he could do and he escaped back into his illness. Let Maria see to things. It was she who was always telling him he did things wrong. Let her now do them right. He watched her lumber out of the wagon backwards down the creaking steps. First her great backside—as big as a Flemish mare's—was thrust out. Her hands grasped the framework of tent. Her feet felt for the steps. He could not see her face, hidden beneath her black kappie, till she stood up.

She said: " Do not worry, Willem, I will see to everything." Then she turned and shouted her instructions.

" Get the cattle into the kraal, make fast all the cook pots, the buckets, plates, cups. Kom maak gou. Hurry before the storm is upon us. Rig tarpaulins against the wagon wheels to give cover to the dogs, people and gear."

This was a race with the storm. Francina, riding bareback, drove in the oxen at a gallop with her dogs barking behind them. Hendrik and a tame Kaffir were lashing heavy oiled canvas buck sails to the wagon wheels and dragging bedding, trek gear, boxes and camp furniture under the wagon bed. The girls, screaming with fright and giggling with excitement, were clattering pots and pans. The tame rams bleated. The goose screamed. Salome brayed. And all the while the storm came up on the wind like a black red-bordered cloak that was being drawn over the world, closing it in as if it were a box with a lid of wind and hail.

First came the dust—a red cloud borne up on a savage

wind, carrying with it all the trash it had collected—leaves, small branches torn from the trees, dry grass. Birds, too, unable to resist, were borne along, riding the storm with futile tiny wings till they were dashed into a tree or flung upon the ground. Following the dust came darkness and the hail. The stones, some of them the size of a pigeon's egg, beat everything before them, stripping the leaves and even the bark from the trees that lay down before their icy whips. One struck the goose as it sat beside the wagon and killed it.

The wagon shook with the force of the gusts. The wet canvas, tight as a drum, vibrated to the blows of the hail-stones with a kind of savage hum. The hail passed on over them and the rain came in a deluge. Then it, too, slowed up. It still rained hard but one could see through it for a few yards. Then the thunder and lightning began, peal after peal, with the lightning so close that Francina heard it crackle, saw a tree struck with more lightning springing upwards from the ground to join that which came down from the heavens.

She was frightened. She had never got used to the storms in the north.

" The curse," Tante Maria said, " the curse."

Francina laughed at her. " What a thing to believe—that a man like Freddie Carter could cause a storm like this."

Her Ouma flashed back at her: " That you even mention his name is beyond my understanding. The man who . . . have you no shame? "

Now the lions began. They had heard one or two in the distance before, but these were nearby.

" Magtig," Tante Maria said. " This is all we need—lions! "

" Carter sent them, Ouma," Francina said. " They are

part of the curse." She believed it, too, in a way and
mockery was her only answer to her fears.

The roars had brought Oom Willem out of his doze.
"Ja," he said, "they like to hunt in the storm. It is their
nature. The game is wet and cold, standing with lowered
heads and tucked-in tails, waiting to be slaughtered.
To-night they will not run."

In the old man's mind all the lion lore he knew had
sprung up. Once again he saw the hunts he had made in
this very country. Saw all the lions he had killed in his life
as his mind passed out of the door of the present back into
the past.

Tante Maria prayed in a desultory manner. Storms
always made her nervous. There were seldom storms in
the Colony, and since they were clearly an indication of
the wrath of God, God was clearly in a worse temper up
here than He was farther south, which did not surprise her.
For she saw God as a very large man dressed in white robes
with a long white beard and hair, a man who looked rather
like Oom Willem, but very much bigger and differently
attired. The nearest she came to her concept of the Almighty
was Oom Willem dressed in his nightshirt sitting on a pile
of newly shorn fleeces in the blazing sunlight, but with
everything much enlarged—so big that Oom Willem's
nose was the size of a man and his eyes as big as the half-tubs
in which the girls did laundry when there was no stream.
The light was brighter even than sunlight, and the fleeces
stretched in cumulus clouds as far as the eye could see.
Thus, Oom Willem, much enlarged, became God, and
Oom Willem as he was in actuality a miniature and feckless
image of the Creator with whom it seemed to her he sometimes confused himself.

Francina's mind was occupied with neither God nor
lions. She was thinking of men, weaving a design of mascu-

linity, hoping that out of her confused thoughts of the
smous, of Harry, of Barend, Flip, Louis and Fred Carter,
some kind of image she could understand would become
apparent. She knew, and it had been proved to her beyond
question, what men wanted of women. But why was their
approach so different? Why did Harry avoid her? Why
had he rejected her nakedness when Carter had stripped
her clothes from her? And Barend. Barend who was neither
one thing nor the other, a man who could not keep his
hands off her; then, overcome with scruples at the emotions
he aroused, changing his tune completely. Or had he not
changed? Was it only an accident that had saved her by
the great yellowwood? Only luck that had made her
gallop away from him and into the arms of Fred Carter?
Suppose she had not run away? Suppose I had waited, she
thought, would he have done it? She knew herself to be
willing now. It, as she called it in her mind, had so often
nearly happened that now she could hardly wait. But it
must be with Harry. Her cheeks burned, in spite of the
cold air, at the thought of him. She felt his hands again on
her bare flanks as he took her in his arms. She felt her
breasts harden as they had done that day when they were
pressed against his chest. She knew she had power over
men. The thought elated her. All women who were not
ugly, and as long as they were not ugly, had it, if they dared
to use it. Miemie had it. And what was it? This she had
not thought of before. No more than this power to give or
to withhold. A pretty girl was like a food that men could
not resist. Her young beauty set them dribbling, slavering
like hounds.

Her Ouma lit the candle in the lantern and got out the
Bible to read aloud. She was reading it through from cover
to cover again. The rain had almost stopped, the thunder
was more distant and the lightning much paler and less

menacing. The lions still roared but they, too, seemed farther away.

Soon after a meal of biltong, rusks and water—cooking had been impossible—the women lay down to sleep beside the old man on the bed.

Hendrik's shouts woke her. " A lion," he was shouting, " there's a lion in the kraal." Under the wagon they could hear the maids screaming.

" Leeue! Leeue! a lion that will eat us all! "

The dogs were barking savagely.

Tante Maria struck her flint and steel and blew up the tinder. Then with a spill she lit the candle in the stable lantern and hung it up again. The soft light showed up the interior of the wagon. The loaded guns in their rack. The powder horns. The bullet pouches. The clothes. The tin beakers from which they drank. The chests in which they kept their clothes. The barrels of meal, of powder. The coffin that was being used as a table. It showed Oom Willem, deep in the heavy sleep of convalescence, and Tante Maria, her sparse hair twisted into two stiff plaits tied with broken voorslae—whiplashes that were too short to be of practical use and too long to throw away. She slept in her striped blue-and-red petticoat with a man's linen shirt hanging loosely over her enormous hips.

Francina sat up in her white flannel nightdress. The neck came up to her ears, the sleeves down to her wrists, and the hem dragged on the ground if she did not hold it up.

Hendrik was still shouting and throwing more wood on to the fire that he had made when the rain stopped. But the wood was wet and did not burn up. From the kraal came the bellowing of the oxen and the growling roars of a lion.

Tante Maria grunted as she pulled on her shoes.

"What are you going to do?" Francina asked. "What can we do with Oupa sick?"

"Do? What can we do but kill the lion? Give me the gun." She pointed to the six-bore that was always kept loaded with slugs.

"And I, what shall I take, Ouma?"

"The lantern. I must have light. And you can put on a belt and pull up that nightdress of yours. Fortunately you are shameless and so will not mind showing your legs. No nice girl would do this even in the dark with no one there to see."

"I'll take my pistols," Francina said. "If we are going to hunt lions in the night I want to do it with more than a lantern in my hand."

"Well, be careful," Tante Maria said. "Those pistols are dangerous weapons."

She backed out of the wagon. Francina handed her the gun, the powder horn and a bandolier full of slugs packed in greased buckskin bags. Then she gave her the lantern and climbed out herself. Her fair hair hung in a long single plait below the belt she had put on. Into the belt she had stuck her silver-mounted pistols, one on either side, like a pirate. Her nightdress billowed out over the belt in a sort of blouse where she had pulled it up to free her legs. She had put on her veldschoens to save her feet from thorns.

"Kom," Tante Maria said, "pick up the lantern."

She told the girls to tie the dogs. "We do not want them killed," she said.

Francina led the way. The oxen were milling about, lowing with fear. The lion was growling as he ate. They could hear him tearing at the meat and crunching the bones. Hendrik sprang up and ran to them.

"You must not go in there. It is death. Only a man

could go. But, man as I am, I cannot go. I am not man enough."

Tante Maria pushed him aside. "This is for white people," she said.

"Ja," he said, "all white people are crazy."

Tante Maria patted his shoulder and said: "Perhaps you are right. But what can we do about it? Now, my friend, come with us and open the gate of the kraal."

"You are going in, you and the nooi? That young meisie is going in with a ravening beast? Magtig," he said, "hark to him growl." He covered his ears with his hands.

Tante Maria gave him a push. "The gate," she said.

The gate consisted of six slip poles threaded between two pairs of uprights. Usually, this being the weakest part of the kraal, the gate was protected by a fire that was lit after the cattle had been put in. To-night, when it had been most needed, it had not been done, the rain had made it impossible.

"Stay here," Tante Maria said to Hendrik. "Crouch to the side of the gate against the thorns, and the lion, even if he comes out, will pass you by."

"How do you know what is in the heart of the lion?" Hendrik asked.

"I know," Tante Maria said, "and I know that it is in your heart to bolt if the lion comes, and I know that if you run he will kill you. So do what you are told.

"Now, Cina," she turned to the girl, "you go in first with your lantern. Go as near to the lion as you can. Go till the light shines upon him clearly—you will see his eyes shining like candles—and then put the lantern down. Put it down carefully and draw back."

"And the lion, Ouma, what will the lion do?"

"He will growl," Tante Maria said, "and lash his tail, but he will not leave his kill."

" How do you know? Are you sure? "

" I know because I have done this before. With my husband, Groot Jan, your Oupa, your real Oupa, and then it was I who carried the lantern."

But in her heart Tante Maria was not so sure. A young moon appeared between the clouds and she could see down into the kraal which had been placed on low ground nearer to the water. There were the oxen bunched up on the far side. That meant that the lion was on this side. She could see the black mass of the oxen and the white markings of their bodies that stood out like curiously cut sheets of paper. As she got nearer she thought she could distinguish the lion crouched over the ox he was eating. She could smell the lion and the blood of the ox and the half-digested grass in its belly which the lion had ripped out before he began to feed. Hendrik drew out the bars of the gate. The moon was covered again.

Francina, pulling herself together, went into the kraal. Only her anger gave her courage. The span of oxen were her friends, she could go up to any of them as they lay chewing their cud without their getting up. She splashed through the churned mud of the kraal. The light of the lantern threw a faint yellow circle about her. She went towards the noises of the crunching growl and then suddenly she stopped. On the edge of the circle she saw the lion's eyes blazing a green fire, blazing as if they were lamps. But this was not near enough. She went closer. Now she could see him crouched over the ox he had killed. A red ox with two white forelegs and a half-white face. Bloem, one of her favourites. The lion stood up, looking very tall, his great feet on the barrel of the ox, still staring at her, motionless but for the lashing of his tail. She stooped down, smoothed the mud with her hand to set the lantern level, and drew back.

Tante Maria had been following behind her. She saw the old woman raise her gun. She drew her pistols and stood with one in each hand. Here was something she would never forget—the lion standing, lashing his tail, half in and half out of the lanternlight. Her Ouma with her gun raised, silhouetted against the cone of light that came from the muddy kraal where water still shone in the deep hoofmarks of the cattle. Then the gun went off. Tante Maria, rocked back by the heavy charge, fell into the mud, splashing it up into the air. The lion fell dead upon the ox it had killed, its head almost blown off. Francina dropped her pistols and clapped her hands to her face in excited horror, only realising what she had done when she tasted the mud upon her lips.

30

THE DELUGE

WHEN FRANCINA woke and looked out through the tent
of the wagon, she thought that she was still asleep and
dreaming. It was scarcely dawn, but the world she had left
yesterday in which, after the storm and the lion hunt, she
had gone to sleep had disappeared. The dawn sky was
pearl-grey tinged with pink; so was the veld which reflected
it like a mirror, blotched with the dark patches of bush and
trees that stood out of the water. Opening the tent wider
she put out her head and almost bumped it into the nose
of an ox. All the oxen stood round the wagon beside the
horses which had been tied to the wheels for the night. As
she climbed out the cattle turned towards her. They were
glad to see her. When the kraal had been flooded they had
found a gap washed out by the first rush of water and had
made their way to the wagon that stood on the higher
ground—the wagon and people, their security. Bloubooi
neighed his welcome. The dogs fawned on Francina, putting their feet on her shoulders, pressing their noses into
her body and licking her face.

Looking down she saw the body of her goose. What a
long way he had come to die. Their camping place was an
island, the only raised ground for as far as she could see,
though it stood only five feet above the water. Not only had
their oxen found safety there but many wild animals as
well. She saw a herd of twenty rooibok and three kudu—

two cows and a bull—all staring at her. There were two
hyenas sitting on their haunches. There was a tiger in the
fork of a tree and snakes everywhere. So this was why the
dogs had whimpered in terror. This was a phenomenon,
an Act of God, an amalgamation of the Garden of Eden,
when all His creatures had lived in amity, and the Ark in
which they had been saved from the flood. For once, for a
few hours, the lions and the lambs, astonished at the collapse
of their world, at the destruction of their environment,
would lie down together as predicted in Holy Writ. Ja,
they would lie till hunger overcame their fear. In the
meantime there was no danger. The water seemed to be
falling as she went to rouse her Ouma and the servants.
She kicked at the tarpaulin that had been rigged round
the wheels.

"Hendrik," she called. She called the girls. Like all
their kind they could sleep through anything. Her shouts
woke Tante Maria who pushed her head out of the wagon,
crying: "What's going on? What is all this noise about?"
Then she said: "Allewêreld! The water!"

"Ja, Ouma, the water!" Francina said. "It must
have come down hard in the mountains to flood us out like
this."

Tante Maria came down from the wagon and looked
about her. She saw the kraal—a semicircle of bush that
was almost submerged.

"My lion!" she shouted. "Kom Hendrik, Klaas, bring
riems." And before Francina realised what she was doing,
she was wading after her grandmother and the boys, the
dogs swimming and splashing beside her. "The skin,"
Tante Maria was bellowing. "If I don't get my lion skin
who will believe I shot him? Men are such liars themselves
that they never believe the truth. Ja, magtig, it is not
every woman who shoots a lion in her fiftieth year."

"It may have been washed away," Francina said hopefully. "It may have floated through the gap the oxen escaped by."

"Ja, it may have, but also it may not. That is what we are going to see."

How Oom Willem would have laughed, Francina thought, to watch Ouma splashing through the water, leaving a wake like a sea-cow.

"There he is," Tante Maria shouted. "There's my lion stuck in the thorns. Bring the riems. Make them fast to his legs."

They tied the riems above the lion's hocks and towed him back through the water with the dogs barking and worrying him as though he were still alive, and Francina laughed so much that she did not pay attention to what she was doing and almost fell down.

When they got to the wagon the coloured girls were in each other's arms, screaming hysterically: "Die slange . . . die slange. . . . The snakes, the snakes! There are snakes everywhere."

Tante Maria banged their heads together. "Make coffee for us while we skin my lion," she said. "Snakes indeed! What are a few snakes when there is a lion to skin?"

Francina climbed into the wagon to change her clothes. Oom Willem was sitting up.

"Now we can go. I am better," he said. "I woke up when you had all gone and I am better."

"Ja, you look better. But when we go is something else. We are flooded out."

"I can see, child, I am not blind. But is it not lucky we camped on a rise? That our oxen are safe, and that now we shall not be short of water?"

"No, Oupa," Francina said, looking out at the enormous

lake that surrounded them. "That, at any rate, is true: we shall not be short of water."

Tante Maria joined them.

"Well, Willem," she said. "What will come next? We have been spoiled by the Egyptians, smitten by the Nubians, plagued by death and disease, burned up by fire, and now we sit in the midst of nowhere upon an ark of mud."

Oom Willem said: "God has watched over us in all these trials, there has been little real disaster."

"Are my fatherless orphans no disaster?"

"Magtig, woman, people die at all times and in all places."

"Ja, but in bed, in comfort, like respectable burghers, not on the floor of their wagons with spears in their bellies!"

Francina said: "That was at home. I do not think up here many men will die in their beds because there are no beds or homes."

To her this was all adventure. Danger excited but did not frighten her.

Tante Maria turned to Oom Willem again. "Perhaps you are right, Willem, the Lord has watched over us. It was the Lord that sent me to you. That I know, for without His comfort I could never have stood a man like you who are little more than a beast clothed in human form. Ja, a wolf who would have devoured your deceased brother's lamb. Yet, I have stood it because I am a good Christian woman and have protected you time and time again, saving you from illness and even slaying the lions that attacked your cattle upon occasion."

"Lions!" Oom Willem said. "You are mad!"

"Mad, am I? Mad? Klaas, bring the lion to the old baas, who says I lie."

The men, assisted by the girls who, now that it was fully

light and the lion dead, were very brave, dragged the beast
over for the baas's inspection.

"See," Tante Maria said. "It is a lion and it is dead. I
killed it with the aid of my little girl while you slept, snoring
like a drunkard."

"I was sick," Oom Willem said.

"You slept," she said. "And I, braving death with this
infant carrying the lantern, slew the lion in the cattle
kraal, as St. George of the English slew the dragon.
Magtig," she said, "you never saw such a lion; fire blazed
from his eyes and smoke billowed in strong jets from his
nostrils."

"What was he doing?"

"He was killing all the oxen in the kraal. He was eating
one when . . ."

"Bloem," Francina interrupted. "He has killed Bloem."

Tante Maria spat on the ground and rubbed out the
spittle with her foot. She turned to Hendrik and said: "I
hope you noticed that. When a lady spits, she rubs it out.
Just see that you do the same, and when you blow your nose,
too. You, also, you grinning little girls. How quickly you
come when you can drag dead lions about and rub yourselves against the men you are helping. How slowly, when
no men are about. Ag," she said. "You disgust me, you
are so natural."

The girls held each other and screamed with laughter.

"Make more coffee," Tante Maria said. "Get busy with
something or I'll take a whip to you."

"Ja, ja," the girls said, and still giggling stirred up the
fire and put on more wood from the little heap that had
been kept dry beneath the wagon.

With Oom Willem directing operations from his bed,
the boys began to skin the lion. First, setting it on its back,
they cut down its breast and belly. Then they slit inside its

legs and neck, and while Klaas pulled at the skin Hendrik cut the white membrane that held it to the flesh, slowly driving his hands and knife around the body, working first on one side and then on the other. The tail was skinned, the claws were cut from the feet so that they would remain attached to the skin. Hendrik held up the tuft and felt for the thorn that ends a lion's tail, concealed in the long hairs. It was believed that with this thorn he lashed himself into rage.

Tante Maria, puffing with pride, watched every move. "Be careful, Hendrik, do not cut the skin." To Willem she said: "Is that not a very fine lion?"

"Ja," he said, "it is. But it is a pity you shot off his head."

"Ja, ja," she said. "You would say that. You would have liked him to eat me, as the early Christian martyrs were consumed in the arenas of Rome. Ja," she said, "never was there such a dog in the manger as you. If you cannot have me yourself, you would throw me to the lions. Am I not your deceased brother's wife and therefore forbidden to you in marriage? And what cause have I given you to think that I would live in sin with such a man as you? I do not say that, terrible as you are, had you not been my deceased husband's brother I might not have permitted your attention, but . . ."

"My attentions!" Oom Willem leaped from his bed. "My attentions, you old cow. . . ." He stopped and said, looking round him: "I am well. I am up." He gave Tante Maria a slap on her rump. "Maria," he said, "I take back what I have said about you. You are a fine woman and a great hunter of lions, but you suffer from certain delusions which are not unusual in women of your age."

"My age?"

" Ja," he said. " And also of all other ages. All women of all ages have delusions."

Francina and her grandmother looked at each other. Tante Maria said: " Men! " and spat again.

Oom Willem bent over the lion. The skin was free now.

" Peg it out," he said, " and rub it well with salt, particularly round the edges."

Leaning on his stick, Oom Willem walked round the wagon. The buck and hyenas were still there, but the water was dropping fast. They would not be here long. He went back to get his gun.

" What are you going to do, Oupa? " Francina said.

" Shoot a kudu cow," he said, " before they run away."

" You cannot, Oupa, you cannot do that! "

" And why not? We need the meat."

" We have meat. The lion did not eat much of the ox he killed." She could not trust herself to use his name, for fear of crying.

" Nevertheless," Oom Willem said, " I shall shoot the kudu." He moved slowly with Francina behind him. The buck stood staring at him with great, soft brown eyes. They were less than thirty yards away but still afraid to plunge into the water. Oom Willem rested his gun in the fork of a tree. As he fired, Francina pushed his shoulder with her hand. All the buck plunged into the water which did not now reach much above their knees.

" Why did you do that, Cina? "

" Oupa, this is the Ark. God put it here for us all—both man and beast. Ja, he said, ' Even for the wolves and the tigers which are also His creatures.' "

" You are a good girl," Oom Willem said, " good, but strange."

They stood together watching the kudu plunge through

the water and get on to a ridge where it was only a few
inches deep. Here in the bush some wild dogs had managed
to survive, by climbing on to the lower branches that were
above the water level. With a screaming bark the pack of
six flung themselves at the cow which Oom Willem had been
going to shoot, drove it into the deeper water and killed it
there. The other buck and the kudu and rooibok fled
through the water till they were out of sight.

"Shoot them, Oupa, shoot them," Francina cried.

"It is too far," Oom Willem said. "But certainly the
ways of God are strange."

Francina, unable to watch any more, turned back
towards the wagon. She could not get the scene out of her
mind. The buck's big soft eyes and great grey twitching
ears. Its wet nose shining like patent leather as it sniffed
their scent. Then the wild dogs, a slavering, screaming
pack, and the kudu's almost sheeplike bleat as they splashed
round her and pulled her down.

At the wagon she drank coffee and ate two hard-boiled
eggs and rusks. Then she lay down to rest. But rest did not
come easily. Too much had happened. Her mind was too
full. This was where she had lain when they had flogged
Carter. What had been in his mind? What had he felt?
What had he wanted with her? That she knew, but how?
And what would it have been like for her? What exactly
was it that she had escaped at the hands of this man, and
whom, eventually, would she marry? Harry Bates was the
man she wanted, but he seemed to avoid her. Tears came
into her eyes; she cried softly for a few moments and then
she slept.

31

THE BROTHERS

WITH OOM WILLEM away, life at the laager had lost its driving force. For each individual, someone in the Prinsloo wagon had been the fulcrum that enabled them to lift themselves out of boredom or fear. Oom Willem was their prophet, their Moses, leading them out of the wilderness. Tante Maria was the comfort of the women. Nothing, they felt, could go really wrong with so fat and powerful a female in charge of their health and comfort. It was the joy of the men to watch Francina in her beauty and freedom. Some loved her—Harry, Barend, Flip, and Louis with a boy's love. The older men watched her and wished themselves younger and unmarried. Miemie missed her friend and rival. They missed the braying of Salome, the bleating of the tame rams and the screaming of the goose. They missed Bloubooi, the finest horse that any of them had ever seen. All that was left were Tante Maria's adopted children and her pigs, both in the grudging charge of Magdalena Beyers.

But the rest was doing everybody good and there were the sick stock to watch over and see to. Young bulls to be cut and branded, an ox here and there with an ingrowing horn— one that went forward instead of backward and was penetrating his skull near the eye or cheek—to be thrown and have the point sawn off. There were the usual endless repairs to wagons and trek gear and shoes—Magtig, how fast the shoes wore out! There were young oxen and horses to be broken to yoke and saddle. Game had to be shot for meat, the country reconnoitred for Kaffirs and the discipline of the laager maintained.

Harry Bates liked the Beyers brothers and spent much time at their wagon. He was with them when the great storm broke. It was dry at the laager. The lightning sizzled and crackled around them as the thunder rolled but the rain went on and broke on the range of hills that Oom Willem had crossed.

" They are in the midst of that," Harry said.

" Ja, that is so, but Oom Willem will know what to do."

Nevertheless, leaving Bates in charge, Barend and Flip rode north next day and came back with the news that the country on the far side of the hills was under water.

" Man," Barend said, " it must have been a cloudburst. Never have I seen the like."

Flip said: " To-morrow we will go again, for the water will have run down. But it could be bad. If the wagon was caught in a dry sluit and the water came down the way it sometimes does, in a wall ten feet high, what could they do but drown? "

" Water and fire are hard to fight," Barend said. " They are both the friends and enemies of man."

It was terrible to think of Francina alone fighting for her life in the flood. Harry put some faith in the horse. If anything would get her out it would be Bloubooi. Still . . .

" We will offer up a prayer for them to-night," Barend said. " And to-morrow we will go again."

Harry said: " I wish I could go with you."

" You must stay here. For though you are English you are the best man. One with the habit of obedience and command." He laughed and said, " That is something that few Boers have. With us all men are generals."

The two men were drawn together by a bond of friendship that had sprung up between them for no clear reason, unless a certain physical resemblance was the explanation. They were much the same height and build and their features were similar. Only Harry's red hair differentiated them. That he was the older scarcely showed except at close quarters.

Next day when the brothers rode off, Harry Bates and Louis accompanied them for a couple of miles, and then sat their horses watching them disappear, hidden by folds in the ground, into the veld, saw them reappear again and then sink finally into the bush that clothed the hills.

The brothers followed the spoor as they had yesterday, reached the hills about midday and then rode along the higher ground where the water had receded, seeing no sign of the wagon, off-saddled by some big trees to rest. Flip climbed one of them to see if he could see anything.

" I see smoke," he shouted, pointing.

" That must be them," Barend said. " But first let us fire three shots into the air to make sure."

They let off their guns and Barend reloaded and fired again. A few minutes later they heard three answering shots.

Now they rode straight, taking the country as it came. The going was very slippery, the red soil shining like grease in the sunshine. Twice they had to swim their horses across wide areas they could not go round. But the horses knew their work, and the men, putting their powder horns into their hats and holding their guns as high as possible, slipped from their saddles and held on to their horses' manes. Each time, once out of the water, they fired their flintlocks and reloaded them, partly as a signal and partly to make sure that they were dry and in order, and each time, before they had time to reload, an answering shot came back. Each time it was nearer. Then they saw the wagon and the oxen on a little rise silhouetted against the sky. They saw Francina. They saw Oom Willem and Tante Maria standing together, and their servants waving their hats. So all was well. They rode towards them slowly, the horses picking their way, slipping and recovering.

Francina ran to meet them. Barend swept her up on to his horse.

"Oupa was sick, but he is better now," Francina said. "It was our Ouma who cured him with her story of the lion she shot."

Barend looked into her laughing eyes as she turned her face up to his.

"Ja," she said, nodding. "It is true we killed a lion, she and I. I led her to the kraal with a lantern. He had killed Bloem. You remember Bloem?"

"Of course," he said. By now the Boers knew most of each others' oxen, all by sight and many by name.

"Well, well," Tante Maria shouted, coming up to them. "The rescuers have come, but too late. Look," she said, "look at the lion that I have shot. Look at his skin pegged out as big as a giraffe."

The brothers slid down from their horses.

"Coffee," Tante Maria shouted.

"It is here," the girls said, bringing it and setting it on a folding table. "We saw the baases coming and made coffee, because that has always been your order. 'If you see a baas on a horse in the distance, make coffee at once.' Ja," they said, "that is what must be done in a good Christian home."

"You'll get a good Christian slap," Tante Maria said, "if you don't behave. Just because you see men again and feel safer with them about."

"That is so," the girls said, clinging to each other and

giggling. "With men one is safe in one way, though sometimes not in another."

"Who shot the lion in the night?" Tante Maria shouted. "A man?"

"Nee, nee. It was you. It was you and the nooi."

"Then go, leave us."

They scuttled away to the front of the wagon and the cooking fire, where Hendrik was extracting the teeth from what was left of the lion's skull. He put it down and came to get the horses.

"Well, Oom Willem," Barend said. "How goes it?"

"I was a little sick," Oom Willem said, "but it was nothing, and now I am well again."

Francina was pouring coffee. "That is a fine waistcoat," she said to Flip.

"Ja," he said. "I put it on for you."

She laughed. "And also for Miemie, so that you would look gay and gallant as you rode off, with a fine spotted calfskin waistcoat and feather in your hat."

He laughed back at her and put his arm about her waist.

"You'll make me spill my coffee," she said.

"I want to kiss you, Cina." His lips were near her ear. What pretty ears she had! And her hair, as long and beautiful as a horse's tail.

"This is no place to say such things, Meneer," she said, "much less do them. And you forget I am to marry your brother and you are to be godfather to our firstborn." She looked toward Barend who was still talking to Oom Willem.

"Then there is a place?"

"Perhaps there are places, Flip. Who knows? The world is a big place."

Flip left her and went to join Tante Maria at the lion skin.

"It is a big skin."

"It is a beautiful skin," Tante Maria said. "Ja, you

never saw such a lovely lion. The colour of butter, and the size of a giraffe."

"Ja," Flip said, "but that is on the other side." The skin was flesh side up.

"You wait, jong, and you will see. The whole world shall see my lion."

"And what are your plans, Oom Willem?" Barend said.

"That you stay the night with us and ride back to-morrow. Then break up the laager and lead the people here."

"And after that?"

"Then we will go on, for though I was held up by my sickness and the rain, I know where we are. It will not be long before we come to the land of Canaan. No," he said, "thanks be to the Lord, it will not be long before we rest. I see it," he said, "the little dorp we will build, the wagons and the Hartebeeste houses. Later the real houses and a church to the glory of God. Twenty feet wide and fifty long, with loopholed windows in case of war—white within and without. Is that how you see it, Barend? And the houses each with a garden, and fruit trees and flowers?"

"Ja, Oupa," Barend said, "ja, that is exactly as I see it." He hoped it would all come true, that this was not an old man's dream.

Oom Willem drew him away, his hand upon his arm. "There is something I must tell you."

"Ja?"

"All is not as well as I have said, but I do not wish to frighten the women. I feel that my time is coming. That perhaps, as I told you in the beginning on the farm before we started, I was too old."

"You have brought us thus far safely, Oom Willem."

"That is so, and we are nearly there, but if anything happens to me you will lead them?"

" I will lead them if they elect me."

" They will elect you. That is why I must explain." Oom Willem sat on a fallen tree.

" What is there to explain? If, and God forbid, you are unable to lead this trek . . ."

" If I die."

" All right then, if you die, I will lead if the people are willing. What else is there to say?"

" That you see what this is, Barend Beyers. That you understand that this is a holy thing. We go to make a new land, to found a new people in the name of God and with God's help." He paused, his blue eyes much paler since his illness, searched the bush as if he sought something. Then he went on, " You must remember we are alone, us Boers, now. The English are behind us. They ruled us but we never belonged to them. Our people, our fathers, have been long cut off from their lands over the sea—the Low Countries, Germany, France. Thus we are alone. The smallest people in the world, and of those people you and I are in the front. The voorloopers of our race. The voor-trekkers who drive our tented wagons into the black womb of Africa, who risk all, our lives, the lives of our women and children, our wealth of stock, to do this thing. To found a nation." He paused again and said, " That is what you must know. For to do this you must be more than a skilled hunter, and a farmer who knows the veld and its ways. You must be a lover—a lover of our land. You must have faith, for so great a project is only possible with the help of God.

" Ja," he went on, " we enter into a strange and dangerous territory, but we go with a firm reliance on our all-seeing and merciful God. We go without fear, like children who hold their father's hand."

This was a new Oom Willem. Barend felt the weight of

his cloak upon his shoulders. If he died he would try to be worthy of him. He saw that what had at first seemed to be only a great adventure and a desire for change was more than this.

The old man got up. " Pehaps, after all, I shall accomplish the task myself," he said. " But now, should anything happen to me, I shall die in peace. My message, and the deep feelings of my heart, have been passed on. I lack sons. I have only Cina, but when you marry her you will be my son. Come," he said, getting up. " Let us go back. I smell meat cooking." He laughed. " Our dinner was the lion's breakfast that he had no time to finish."

The young men slept at the wagon and in the morning Barend rode off, leaving Flip in charge.

" I would not be happy, Oom Willem," he said, " if I left you alone here. In two days I shall be back with the others."

Two days, Francina thought, as she kissed him good-bye. Was it a wise thing to leave Flip alone with her for the two whole days? But it would be fun to have him. It had been dull alone after the company of the trek.

The breakup of the laager did not take long. All were rested and ready to move, and following Barend's horse the inspanned wagons unrolled like a ribbon from the reel of the camp. They crossed the dry plain and went through the hills into the lush steaming bush where the heavy rains had fallen. Now there would be no more difficulty, and leaving them to follow the spoor of his horse, Barend left the wagons in charge of Harry and rode on.

The flood had run down fast. The water had not stood long enough to rot the grass which, flattened by the tempest, had now sprung up with renewed vigour. Shrubs had burst into flower, birds twittered in the trees, white marsh lilies perfumed the air that was alive with insects. The world of the veld was drunk with a surfeit of water. For once it was without danger or grimness. The pans were full to overflowing, the game unwary, as if at a time like this after so long a drought all danger was unthinkable. This was Africa at its best. Its most beautiful, like a woman veiled, half seen but promising all things to those who served her well. This was Africa in the most seductive and the rarest of her moods.

Barend rode along, savouring the afternoon. Trash marking the height of the flood water was piled against the trees, held tightly interwoven in the thorn scrub. The spoor of the animals that had passed here was as clear as the writing in a book to a hunter. The slate had been wiped clean for these new words. Kudu, rooibok, two tiny steenbok, a solitary wildebeest, a tiger, hyenas, had all crossed the line he was taking. He stopped to fill his pipe. As he was about to strike the flint he heard voices. A girl's voice and a man's.

Francina and my brother, he thought. What were they doing here? Dropping the reins over his horse's head and putting the unlit pipe into his pocket, he slipped into the bush. The horse would stand indefinitely. I'm spying, he thought, spying on the two I love best. But he went on, unable to stop himself. He had to know. The suspicions he had had returned more strongly than ever. Cina and Harry Bates, Cina and his brother, Cina and that man on the koppie—Carter.

Had he raped her or had she been willing? What kind of a girl did he love? For it was love, at least love of a kind, for the more he suspected her the more wild for her he became. That others should have had her was intolerable. If they had? He knew how nearly she had given herself to him. Perhaps it was he who had aroused her for others. Perhaps it was all his fault. With this in mind, he stalked the voices but tried not to think of them as people, as individuals. He made himself throw his mind back into the past, into the farm at home, for probably with men, as with animals, thinking of them would frighten them away. With wild beasts he knew this to be true, which was why the hunter, who concentrated his mind on the game he sought, seldom saw as much as others who, unthinking, stumbled over buck after buck as they stood or slept unaware of his approach.

At last, screened by a bush, he saw them, and could hear what they said, for they were upwind. Francina looked beautiful as she stood with Flip beneath a big maroola tree. The sunlight that pierced the leaves flecked her with gold. Flip stood in front of her, stopping her, forcing her back against the smooth trunk of the tree.

" No," she said, laughing. " No, I will not."

He said: " You have with others. Why not with me?" He put his arms about her. He had hold of her hair near the head and raised her face to kiss it. Barend's hand tightened on the gun he held.

Francina pushed Flip back. " Don't try to force me," she said. " A word and the dogs will tear you in pieces."

" But last night you let me kiss you and you promised."

She laughed out loud. " Ja, ja, that was last night. A maid can change her mind, and just as yes then could mean no now, so no now may mean yes at another time."

" You send me mad," Barend heard his brother say. His brother whom, up to this moment he had loved so much. Of course, she had flirted with him before. He had watched her teasing him, but he'd had no idea that it was more than play with either of them.

" I'm going back," Francina said. " Do not come with me. Come later," she said, " and from over there." She pointed in another direction. How skilled in deception she was. How terrible it was to love a girl like this. How terrible to hate one's brother.

He went back slowly to his horse and waited for the

wagons to catch up. He would say nothing. What was there to say? When Flip had tried to kiss her she had pushed him away and threatened him with her dogs. But there had been something. After all he knew the girl and what she could do. He knew his reckless brother, too. Flip, Flip, he thought, how could you do this to me? And Francina—had she forgotten that she had promised to marry him?

But he would say nothing. He would act as if everything was well. Yes, he thought, as he led the column of creaking wagons up to Oom Willem's camp and Cina ran to greet him, springing up into his arms as he still sat his horse, with one foot on top of his in the stirrup, I will show nothing. I will play Samson to her Delilah. But I am better off than he, because he did not suspect her. Then, as he held her to him, kissing her eager lips, he wondered if Samson had loved Delilah as he loved Cina. If, when he kissed her, she tore the bowels out of his body with the softness of her mouth and the supple warmth of the body she pressed against him. It was not Cina's fault, it could not be. It was his brother who had led her astray.

32

MAROONED

CARTER STAGGERED away from the laager without looking back. Trembling with weakness, with pain and fury, he drove himself on, supported by the staff of his hate. What fools they were to half do the job—to go off at half cock. Should have shot me, he thought, or given me a proper hiding with a cat. Forty strokes less one, that was the army ration. Six cuts with a sjambok, what was that? Just enough to enrage a man not enough to break him.

Cowards, too. The God-damned cowards. Afraid to kill me, they was, he thought. Those Boer bastards. So they just turn me out to die. Afraid to do the job themselves so they leave it to God. But it takes more than that by a long chalk to kill little Freddie Carter. In the hands of God. Ja, my fine kerels, he thought, you'll be needing God yourselves before I'm through. That old fool Willem, Harry the traitor who had betrayed him. My God, he thought, five minutes more and I'd have 'ad 'er, the teasing little bitch. He hated Francina now. It was all her fault. But, by God, it had been a near thing. I should have dropped the girl and killed him at once. He wondered why he hadn't used his knife. " Because I 'ates 'im too much," he said aloud, " because I wants to break 'im with my two 'ands—to smash him." He gave a sort of laugh, a horrible sound. They didn't know, those Boers, how tough he was. " No one can 'urt me," he said, " no bloody soul can 'urt Freddie Carter. You got to kill 'im. Marooned. That's what Sailor Jack would have called it. Marooned in a bloody desert!" He began to laugh wildly.

Now that he was out of sight, he sat down on an old ant heap to think things out. What had he lost? What had he got? No horse, no gun, no hunting knife. No weapon of any kind, and nothing to make one with. He must find something, pick up stones, make a sling. He'd used a sling as a kid.

They had given him a blanket, a tinderbox, a water bottle full of water and a small bag of biltong so he wouldn't starve for a day or two, and a little folding knife. But it was certainly a shame he had no gun, he thought, looking at the game that dotted the veld. Laughing at me too, he thought, laughing as if they know I can't touch them. These animals had never been shot at but still they seemed to know.

This was open rolling country. Parklike, dotted with splendid thick-foliaged trees. Under each, in the black pool of its shade, stood wildebeest cows with their young, almost chestnut-coloured calves, with yearlings, miniatures of their parents; or bulls alone, each with a tree to himself, each snorting defiance. The grass was short, cropped like a lawn by the thousands of head of animals that had pastured on it.

To his left there was some light bush and open scrub. Here a herd of zebras, almost invisible in the brilliant sunshine, their bodies fragmented by the black stripes of their hides, stood staring at him, their ears cocked in curiosity. Wildebeest and zebra often ran together—protecting each other, for the zebra's ears were sharper than those of the wildebeest, and wildebeest sight keener than that of zebra. So they all stood, the animals and the man, looking at each other, the man quite helpless against them.

This world Carter was looking at was the ancient world of

the past. An Eden in which he was the first man. Ten thousand years ago it had been like this. In all that time there had been no change here. But he saw no beauty in it, no mystery, he was only filled with rage and an ever-increasing lust to kill. How dare these stupid animals face him. They should be running away. By God, if I had a gun I'd shoot them, he thought. And he would have, as he had before now, killing for its own sake. Killing far more than could be used, just as in the old days when he had robbed he had destroyed what he could not take. Suddenly the animals ceased to look at him and all turned to face one way. He turned, too, and there, walking out of the scrub, came a pair of lions. Nothing ran away. The zebra and wildebeest merely watched them. They knew that the lions were full fed. There would be no more danger till night fell.

Carter stood frozen. Lions. He had not really thought about them and that rather changed the picture. The Boers had mentioned them as among the hazards he must face. He knew they thought that if God considered him guilty the lions would eat him. Death by lions, his at any rate, being an Act of God. But he had kept them out of his mind. The lions went by him without a look, padding past like great tawny cats. First a heavily maned male and then the lioness, her great muscles moving under the loose skin of her shoulders. They were not more than fifty yards away.

When they had gone, Carter sat down, took a drink of water and shredded some biltong with his little knife. He knew he must hoard his food. He was going to have to eat anything he found, but they would have to be small things that he could catch and kill with his hands. Toward evening he found a waterhole and drank. The water was foul, tasting of the game that had stood in it, but it was water and his bottle was empty. He spent the night in the fork of a tree, strapping himself into it with his belt, belly foremost, with his arms about it. He could not lean against it with his sore back.

Next day, having drunk again and filled his bottle, he continued his march to the east. His aim was Portuguese territory and the sea. Later, as he sat resting, he saw a mouse disappear under a flat stone. Lifting it, he found her nest. He killed her and her six young. Then, collecting some of the dry game dung that lay about, he made a little fire, grilled them and ate them whole. Later in the day he ate some large green caterpillars. He had seen the Kaffirs eat them.

And so it went, a blur of staggering, starving days and bitter nights strapped to a tree in the cocoon of his blanket. Then he began to follow the vultures and wait with the hyenas for the lions to leave their kill, striving to cut off a chunk of meat before the scavengers drove him off. Then he found a weapon—the leg bone of a giraffe. With this club he laid about him, driving back the snarling carrion eaters till he had taken what he needed. Once they almost had him, two hyenas coming at him at once, one from either side. He evaded them by jumping over their heads, their jaws snapping like steel traps beneath him. Now, though in rags, he was living better. His back had healed. He was tougher, hardier, and more savage than he had ever been. More filled with hatred for every living thing. His beard had grown, his hair was wild and matted, his face and body plastered with sweat and dried blood, for now he hardly bothered even to sear his meat, but ate it almost raw. Fred Carter had ceased to be a man. He had become something lower and more dangerous than any beast, more cunning. Each dawn he searched the sky for vultures circling a kill. Each dawn he saw them somewhere.

To-day was no different from the previous day, except that

he was more hungry. The kill must be near, he thought, as he watched a vulture perch with great flapping wings on a dead tree. It sat hunched, its bare, white-frilled neck sunk between the shoulders of its wings as it stared downward. More vultures came, their black shadows passing swiftly like animals across the bare red earth. He saw several of his colleagues—the hyenas—arrive and gripped his long bone club. What a feast he would make for the vultures and hyenas if ever they got him down. How quickly they would finish him off, leaving nothing but the skull and shreds of his cracked bones for the ants. Two pied crows flew down. They had not paused to perch and flew up again screaming with anger. The lion must still be there, or nearby, watching over his kill. The one thing no lion could bear was the fouling of his meat by birds. Hyenas and jackals he might tolerate, but no birds.

Carter never went too near till the vultures were down and eating. They drove the hyenas off and before he had his weapon he had had to wait till they had finished too. Now he cleared off the birds as if they were sparrows, generally killing one or two and throwing their stinking bodies out for the hyenas to sniff at while he snatched his meat.

Then, as he waited hidden in the bush, he heard men shouting and the clap of a whip. The vultures rose and began to circle again. He crouched lower. Who could it be? Boers? Kaffirs? It sounded like neither. Carefully, he crept forward to the end of the clearing. There was no danger from a lion now. There was the kill, a zebra, disembowelled and half eaten. Beyond it were a line of marching men. A line of Kaffirs, but moving oddly. Now he saw them clearly. They were fastened together. Slaves. And marching beside them were other Kaffirs carrying guns and whips, and a white man. Well, not white, but not black either. This was the kind of man he sought. Portuguese half-caste slaver, a man of his own kind. He stepped out into the open and hailed him.

" Hi," he shouted. " Hi, there!"

The slaves came to a shuffling halt. The men, both white and black, turned towards him with raised guns.

Carter held up both his hands, the left empty, in the right his bone club, and walked on towards them. He was a fearless man. When he was ten yards away from the leader he stopped, lowered his arms and stood still with his hands on the top of the leg bone.

The leader was dressed in brown moleskin trousers. Over them he wore a dirty linen shirt with a wide belt to which was hung a long straight sword. He had on a wide-brimmed straw hat in the brim of which were stuck ostrich feathers arranged like a wreath. In his hand he held a gun. Over his left wrist, hanging by a leather thong, was a heavy whip. His ivory-coloured face was pitted with smallpox, his dark eyes glittered like those of a rat. The face was ratlike, the nose sharp, both the forehead and chin receding, so that it came to a point like the mask of a rat or fox.

Carter was glad to see there were young women among the slaves. They were fastened to each other in pairs by forked trees which rested upon their shoulders and held their necks imprisoned by a small metal rod that ran through holes drilled in the branches of the Y and was padlocked. In one it came from the back, in the other from the front, alternately, and the trunks of the trees were half checked into each other, pegged and bound with hide. Carter saw at once how practical this system was. The raiders, when they set out, had nothing to carry, no chains or manacles, just the little iron rods and padlocks. The trees could be cut anywhere. Every slave carried a tusk, the girls and women the smaller ones, some no bigger than the arm of a man. Here

was a wonderful system. Not only was this transport free
but it could be sold at a high price when the journey was
over.

All this Carter saw at once, taking it in in a flash, calculating the value of the ivory and the slaves, deducting the
expenses in food for the party, the rations and the wages to
be paid to guards and catchers. There was money here and
sport. The thought of slave raids, of killing men, of burning,
looting and enslaving whole villages, made his eyes glitter.

He licked his lips. This looked as if it would suit him.
Even the half-caste staring at him looked like a man after
his own heart—evil, savage and easy to understand. He felt
that he had come home at last. That given a trip or two to
learn the business, he would take over and show these half-
caste niggers what a dragoon, a trained soldier, could do.

But he said nothing, and nothing showed in his face
except for his eyes. He stood as still as if he was carved, as
silent as if he were dead, only his fingers moved as they
caressed the polished knob of the leg bone under his clasped
hands. Coming closer, the leader of the band stared at
Carter in astonishment. A white man alone, half naked, half
starved, and apparently unarmed except for a big bone club.

"Don Alfonso João da Sousa y Madrigo," he said,
making a leg and sweeping off his hat.

Don like hell, Carter thought. Joe Sousa, that's what I'll
call you. He took his club in his left hand and held out his
right.

"I am Frederick Carter, the Earl of Sussex, Lieutenant
Colonel commanding the 10th Dragoons," he said, "and at
your service, Senhor," he bowed. Then, looking up at his
rescuer he said, "My hentourage 'as got itself mislaid as it
were, but things like that don't worry Freddie Carter. You
can't 'urt 'im, you got to kill 'im."

"Si, Senhor," da Sousa said.

"*Si, si, Senhor*," Carter said. "Shall we go now?"

He walked over to the coffle, stared at one of the girls a moment and then pointed in the direction they had been going. The whips cracked again and they were off, shuffling along, the yellowish tusks swaying as the slaves walked, trying to support them with one hand while they eased the wooden forks that galled their necks with the other.

There were a hundred-odd slaves, each carrying an average of twenty pounds of ivory. Two thousand pounds of ivory at ten shillings a pound, and the slaves would fetch at least half as much again. But it would be better not to work them so hard and give them more food. Fat and ripe they'd fetch more, like any other form of livestock. Carter wondered if any of the party spoke English or the Taal dialect. A proposition that might please everyone concerned had come into his mind.

After marching along a well-worn path through the bush, they came to a small clearing near some rocks where there was a spring. Here there was another half-caste, even more villainous looking than the first; a dozen armed Kaffirs and a group of slaves seemed to be waiting for them. Three-legged iron pots were cooking over several fires, and there was a kind of kraal made of upright tree trunks sunk into the ground with thorns pulled in between them in which the slaves could be confined for the night. Carter's presence inspired astonishment.

"Well," he said. "Anyone 'ere speak English?"

To his great joy the half-caste said: "My name is Tomaso —Tomaso Romero—and I do."

"Good," Carter said, and he told them his tale—his version of it, of how this girl had said he had taken her, which was a lie, for he was a man of honour to whom a virgin was sacred, and how they had beaten him and thrown him out to die. He told them he was a soldier, and pulling da Sousa's sword from its sheath he went through his exercises, his legs apart as if gripping a horse. Cut. Thrust. Guard. The sword whistled through the air like a cavalry sabre. He handed it back to its owner.

" Now," he said, " I'll join you, and I'll give you the benefit of my soldiering. But I'll do more," he said. "I'll give you gold. Bag after bag of gold, golden sovereigns like the pebbles on a bloody beach."

" Gold," they said, " gold? *Ouro. Muito ouro?*"

" *Si*," he said. " *Muito, muito.* Golden sovereigns by the bloody bucketful."

" Where?" Tomaso said.

" Give me a drink," Carter said, " and I'll tell you."

"*Vinho*," Tomaso shouted. " Bring *vinho* and food, too."

When he had gulped the wine and eaten half a loaf of stale bread, Carter said: " Well, here goes. Now, the Boers when they left the Colony, sold a lot of stock. They sold their farms and they put their gold into little leather bags in their wagons. So there's the gold." He pointed vaguely behind him towards the sinking sun. " And 'ere's what we'll do. We will go to them and say we know what they are seeking and will guide 'em to it."

" You will go back?" Tomaso said.

" No, not I. You will go. You will stay with them as a guide and lead them into the ambush that Senhor da Sousa and I will prepare."

" But who will ambush them?"

" Kaffirs," he said. " Have you no Kaffir hunters? How do you get this ivory?"

" Mapela," da Sousa said, when this had been translated to him. "*Si, si*, it will be easy. There is nothing he would like better. He hates white men and there would be good loot. Guns, powder, and lead and iron. All that has ever held him back is the want of a leader. He does not care for fighting himself, and does not know the white man's ways."

" I will lead them," Carter said.

" *Si*, you are a soldier, that is your business. Tomaso will guide them into the trap."

" And these?" Tomaso pointed to the kraal where the slaves were being fed by the Kaffir guards.

" The askaris can take them on to the coast," da Sousa said. " It is only ten days' march away. This is too good a chance to miss. Gold," he said, rubbing his hands together. " Gold in bags."

" There is only one thing," Carter said. " The girl, she must not be hurt. I want her."

" And the money. I suppose you want your share of that?" Tomaso said, translating da Sousa's words.

" No," Carter said, " only the girl and to become one of you and share in your work. The gold is my gift. A token of my good will."

Da Sousa took his hand. " *Amigo*," he said, " *amigo*," his eyes bright with tears. What a man this was. God and the Blessed Virgin had certainly had a hand in this. With gold like this, much larger expeditions could be arranged and more slaves taken, each one a soul to be saved when landed in Brazil.

33

THE VISITORS

IT WAS a relief to Oom Willem to have the trek assembled again. He felt better at once, with the flattery of Magdalena Beyers, and the shouting of Maria's adopted children about him. This was the way things should be. And thus encouraged he had few doubts in his mind. They were almost there. Two or three months more would see them home, though home was nothing yet—just a place remembered from the past. Just some low hills and a fair valley with a little river running down it fed from the springs above. But this was Canaan—the land that flowed with milk and honey.

The wagons and the stock moved on slowly, sometimes only moving one skof of three miles a day. There was no cause for haste and the progress was regular till they came to closer country when Oom Willem halted, sending Barend and Flip out to reconnoitre and once again the other men profited from the delay to fix their gear while the women laundered and mended their own and their families' clothes. So that before long the wagons were gay with the white and coloured flags of the washing as the dresses and underclothes, strung out on the halliards to dry, moved in a sudden breeze. Ovens were prepared for baking bread, and folding tables and rusbanks set out for meals as if it was really a picnic.

This was the camp that Barend and Flip left when they

rode out together to find the next place to laager. Flip was very gay in his usual manner.

"Man," Flip said, patting his horse's neck and looking at his brother, "why so serious?"

Why so serious, Barend thought. Because I hate you whom I used to love above all others. Because I have been betrayed and my heart is broken. He said, "These are serious times. The old man is ill. If he dies the leadership will fall to us."

"They will elect you, Barend, you who are so solemn that you might be the father of ten children," Flip laughed loudly.

"So you can joke about marriage, Flip?"

"Why not? I love the girls but marriage is not for me. Not yet, at any rate. A married man is like a hobbled horse. When he lifts his head to see he must stand on three legs and cannot move, and when he stands on all four legs he cannot see."

The brothers rode on in silence. The only sound was the thud of their horses' hoofs and the creak of their saddlery. They saw no game. They heard no birds.

"It is too quiet," Barend said.

"Ja, it is quiet."

"Look to your gun, Flip," Barend said, examining his own. "There is something here I do not like."

"You are always imagining things."

Ja, like seeing my Cina in your arms, your hand on the thick tail of her hair, Barend thought. He said, "Sometimes I feel danger."

"Well, I feel nothing."

Barend said: "From here we will ride separately, two hundred yards apart." He turned away from his brother. "But go carefully," he added.

Flip laughed again. Old Barend was always the same.

No wonder Cina was ready for a frolic. How pretty she was, how soft and warm to touch. How sweet the smell of her hair. He wondered how much that Carter had had of her. That was something no one would ever know except Cina, and Carter, who must be dead by now, and perhaps Harry Bates who had saved her, if he *had* saved her. A dangerous man, Carter.

This was strange country they were going through. A series of small hills and valleys. The valleys ran into each other with a certain amount of fall. The flood had washed out their centre, making a kind of road that it would be easy for the wagons to follow.

Barend pulled his horse into the shadow of a rock and was watching his brother ride forward on his left. Once again he wondered at his reckless confidence. Flip never believed anything could go wrong. He never thought of anyone but himself or his own desires. A wave of hatred ran over him as he thought of Cina again and saw her lying limp in his brother's arms. This was the chance he had been waiting for. Now he could kill him. Shoot him in the back and be done with him once and for all. The lips that had kissed her and the hands that had touched her body would be for ever stilled. His brother whom he had loved so much, and now hated the more for it, could lie out there in the bush and rot. Lie there and be eaten by the vultures and hyenas. Murder. Fratricide. These were but words. This time Abel would kill Cain. God and right were upon his side. He raised his gun to slay the fornicator, for surely he was that in wish if not in actual fact. As he looked along his sights he saw something move in the bush behind his brother. A Kaffir, by God. A Kaffir was creeping up upon him. Well, let him. Let him do the work he had been about to do and blame it upon the Kaffirs. For that had been his plan, to gallop back and say Flip had been shot by

Kaffirs. This was a judgment. God had sent the Kaffir to do his work, to save him from the sin of fratricide. He praised the wisdom of God and lowered his gun. Then he raised it again.

Flip had ridden happily away from his brother. Old Barend was in a bad mood to-day. There seemed to be plenty of grass and firewood. Water stood in pools everywhere so that a good place to laager would be easy to find once they got through the hills and into the open. Everything was going very well. He was happy. It was a lovely day. His horse was fresh under him. He heard the call of a partridge and another answered it. How odd. This was the first bird they had heard. Then there was a shot and a cry. He turned in his saddle, bringing up his gun. A naked, knob-nosed Kaffir lay writhing, with his assagai still in his hand, within a yard of his horse's quarters. He saw more Kaffirs running towards him. Barend had seen the Kaffir and had shot him. Barend had saved his life. He drove his single spur into his horse, laid his body against its neck and galloped back to where he could see his brother sitting his horse, the reins lying upon its withers, his gun raised to cover him. As he came level Barend turned and side by side, stirrup to stirrup, they galloped for the laager. As they came near, Barend fired a warning shot. They had been seen and within minutes the camp had changed its aspect. Cattle and horses were being driven in, spare guns prepared. Men and boys were saddling up ready to ride out if that was required of them.

Into this activity the young men rode their sweating horses, pulling them up on to their haunches at the chair where Oom Willem sat directing the operations.

" What is it, kerels? he asked. " Why the shot and the haste?" He stood up and put his hand on the sweating neck of Barend's bay horse.

" Kaffirs, Oom Willem," Flip said. " One tried to assagai me and Barend shot him. Ja," he said," my brother has saved my life."

They became aware of the two strangers standing near the old man, a half-caste and a Kaffir armed with a good gun.

" You see, Senhor," the half-caste said, " it would be best if you took my advice and used my services as a guide. I know these parts and can lead you clear of the savages into the very heaven that you seek."

These two young men must have run into the warriors collecting for the ambush who, their spears thirsting for blood, had been unable to resist the temptation to kill a man alone—they could not have seen the other. Someone must certainly pay for this, for now that he had seen the Boers and their piled riches he was not going to give up. No, no, he thought, all this is ours. And the girl? Well, he understood Carter's desire for the girl. But men tired of girls as they did of a single sort of food if served up day after day, and when he had done with her he, Tomaso, was quite prepared to take his leavings, and even to pay for them.

" Who are these men?" Barend swung his horse towards Tomaso and the Kaffir.

" They came after you left," Oom Willem said, " with an offer to guide us . . ."

" They came on foot? From where? And why should they guide us? How can they, since we do not even know ourselves where we are going?" Barend did not like the look of the visitors, a villainous-looking half-caste Portuguese and a Kaffir, arrogant in his gun and his security.

" They are elephant hunters," Oom Willem said. " They have lost their horses with horse sickness and wish to buy others from us. For this they will lead us to the valley that we seek. They know it well."

Tomaso broke in. He did not like this young man who

appeared to mistrust him. Why should anyone not trust him, he wondered, opening his eyes wide in what he considered an expression of childlike innocence. "Often, Senhor," he said, "when we are hunting the giant pachyderm I have said: 'Ah, if we were farmers and not hunters this is where we would dwell. Water in plenty, deep black soil as rich as velvet, game in countless thousands, trees for shade and fruit, birds singing upon the flowering bushes.' Senhor," he said, "this is . . ."

"Senhor," Barend broke in in the Taal, "I do not understand a word."

Harry Bates, who had been interpreting Tomaso's English, said: "He is describing heaven."

Francina, who stood beside him, laughed.

Oom Willem said: "And the Kaffirs?"

"Ja," Barend said, "I saw about twenty,"

"There may have been more hidden, jong."

"Ja," Barend said. "I could not see what kind they were."

"Knob-noses," Flip said. "As he fell beneath your bullet I saw his face." These were Kaffirs who cut their noses so that they grew into knobs, that they might terrify their opponents with their looks.

Tomaso breathed a sigh of relief. Then it was not his people. Just a band of wandering Knob-noses. But he did not like the way the older of these two young men was looking at him. He does not trust me, he thought, he will give me trouble.

The brothers went to their wagon. Their stepmother gave them food and coffee. Barend was silent, listening to his brother tell the tale. How nearly he had killed him to stop his tampering with Cina. But this would do it too. How strange that to kill a man or save his life should amount to the same thing.

"I do not trust that half-caste," Barend said suddenly and, banging down the tin beaker from which he was drinking, got up and strode off. He found Oom Willem sitting asleep on a bench with his back to the wheel of his wagon. Cina, in her boys' clothes, was keeping the flies off him with a whisk made from the tail of a wildebeest.

She looked up, smiled, and held her finger to her lips. Her long horse tail of hair swung as she turned her head. Barend longed to take it in his hand, to hold it close to her head as he kissed her. For a moment his blood boiled at the thought of Flip having done just that. Then he calmed himself again and thought: All that is over now.

Francina led him to one side. "He must rest," she said. "All this has excited him. The Kaffirs again, and that man."

"That's it," Barend said. "That is why I am here. I am taking another horse and going out again. I do not trust this Tomaso. If I am not to disturb him you must tell him when he wakes. Tell him to stay here in laager till I get back."

"How long will you be?"

"Two days . . . three days. How do I know? But stay here in laager."

"Oh Barend," she said, standing on tiptoe to kiss him. "Barend, be careful." He swept her up from the ground and held her to him.

"My brother is a good man," he said, as he put her down. "Flip will take care of you."

"And you, who will care for you?"

"God," he said. "The Lord God."

With that he kissed her again and left her. A little later she saw him riding off alone.

Oom Willem woke slowly. As he had rested it had become clear to him that this man—this Portuguese—had been sent by God to guide them. That was the only possible explanation of his coming. How else in the middle of the wilderness like this should a man arrive who knew the whereabouts of the hills he was seeking. The hills that he called the Hills of the Hunter. That he knew them, and the road to them, was beyond all doubt since he had described them to perfection. The five hills, the valleys, the little river, the springs, even the great rock outcrop rubbed smooth by elephants. And what was more, they must move as soon as possible while he was still well enough to direct them. They must get there before he died. He had felt the wind made by the wings of death upon his face and would not live much longer.

If I die, he thought, it must be there. It must be after we have arrived so that my bones will lie in the graveyard we shall make. Mine must be the first, and I will not be buried in a hole beneath a tree along the road. He even thought with some pleasure of his coffin that was in the wagon packed with seeds, carpenters' tools, bars of lead, spare flints and other necessities that were held in reserve.

He opened his eyes wide and stretched.

" Oupa," Francina said, " are you awake?"

" Ja, my child."

" Then I have news. Barend told me to tell you to wait here till his return."

" Where has he gone?"

" Gone to spy out the land. He is not content with . . ." She let her eyes rest on the guide and the Kaffir who sat on the ground by a tree.

" Content!" Oom Willem boomed. " God sends us a sign and a guide and he is not content?"

" We will wait, Oupa?"

" Ja, we will wait, but not for ever." His rage seemed to choke him. " The young whippersnapper!" He put his hand to his throat and fell from his seat.

"Help, come quickly!" Francina shouted. "Oupa is down."

Several people came running and in a few minutes the old man was lying quietly on the kartel in his wagon, while Tante Maria shouted: Do this, Do that, as she prepared her medicines once more. She was bent over a pot, stirring it with an iron spoon, when Magdalena Beyers touched her shoulder.

"It is time I took a hand," she said. "You have nearly killed him already with your nursing."

"What did you say?" Tante Maria stood up waving her iron ladle above her head.

"I said you had nearly killed him with your poisons and purges. The old man is empty," she said, "exhausted. His bowels are only filled with water."

"You . . ." Tante Maria said, "is it seemly that you, an unrelated widow, running loose like a bridleless horse, should discuss the contents of our great leader's bowels?"

"That is why. Because I wish him to continue to lead and not lie in that splendid coffin you polish to such perfection with your great behind as you sit upon it every day."

"You wish to marry him," Tante Maria screamed. "Ja, shameless as the daughter of a horse leech, you stand on the street corners offering yourself to all comers."

"It is an idea," Magdalena said. "Ja, that would be an idea, to marry him and save him from you. But in the meantime I have brought him some medicine which he will take."

"He won't take any more medicine. That's why he is not better. Whatever I make he throws in my face."

"He will take mine," Magdalena said. She went up to the back of the wagon with Tante Maria wobbling behind her. "This I wish to see," she said. "Ja magtig, if he will take medicine from a stranger rather than his beloved sister . . ."

" Oom Willem," Magdalena said.

" Ja, what is it?" The old man raised himself on his elbow. It always did him good to see her. Young, fresh, with her soft voice and eyes. Young, ja. What was thirty years? A girl.

" It is medicine," she said.

" Medicine? I have taken all the medicine I will swallow. I am weak with medicine.

She held up the tin cup to him. " Drink this, Oom Willem, it is different."

He drank it, screwing up his face. " Magtig, it is bitter. What is it?"

" It is a decoction of Peruvian bark that I bought from the smous." She turned back to Tante Maria. " You refused to buy it. You said you had everything you needed, but you did not know the North and the fevers that are bred here."

" Nor did he. That Jew was never in the North."

" No, but he knew of hunters who had been and of this sickness and its cure."

" We have still to see if it cures," Tante Maria said darkly. " It might well kill the poor old man."

On the other side of the wagon Francina had come upon Flip, and stood beside him.

" Well," she said, looking up into his eyes, " do you not love me any longer?" She laughed.

" Love you," he said. " You drive me crazy. But my brother saved my life. You are his."

" His?" Francina said. " I belong to no man. I may marry Barend or I may not."

" He thinks . . ."

" I know what he thinks," Francina said, " but I do not know what I think. One day it is one thing and the next day it is another."

34

THE OLD WOMAN

BAREND LIT no fires. He had seen no sign of lions and preferred to chance the danger from them rather than give his whereabouts away to any prowling Kaffir. He rode carefully through the bush, watching every open space for movement before he ventured out of the cover in which he was hidden. The first day he found nothing suspicious. He slept rolled in his blanket with his head on his saddle and his gun beside him. His horse was tied to the tree under which he lay looking up at the stars through the twisted branches of the old thorn tree above him. He thought of Francina, his bride-to-be, of his brother Flip, and how he had so nearly shot him. How far had she allowed him or any other man to go? Again doubts swept over him. Suppose she lied. Suppose that the Englishman Carter had really mastered her, and the other Englishman, Harry? What of him?

Then there was Oom Willem. Did he really know where they were, or was he lost? Confident enough when he spoke, but sometimes when he thought no one could observe him the old man looked puzzled. He seemed to have lost his inspiration. The prophet was changing into a tired old man. He is sick, both in mind and body, Barend thought. That's why he spoke to me. Why he had said, " If anything happens to me you must lead them." Thus had Elijah spoken to Elisha and handed him his mantle. Barend had said, "Ja, Oom Willem," and at the time he had not been afraid but now he was afraid. It was a great responsibility. Then he conquered his fear by deciding that these were but night thoughts, and the confidence of all men weakened as darkness fell. As the child needs a candle in its room, so the man, not much braver, consoles himself with thoughts of the sun and the coming day when he knows the appearance of all things will be changed. Yet night remains dangerous. The instincts of the child are rooted in truth, in its fear of the things that prowl on velvet feet, skulking in the shadows, waiting to spring—fears of the lion, the tiger, the night adder, the evil man who, knife in hand, creeps towards his victim. Sleeping quite alone like this it was difficult to control one's fears, one's doubts, one's hates. Everything was magnified by the silence and isolation. But at last he slept and was wakened by the cold that always precedes the dawn. Getting up as the sky in the east began to pearl, he loosened his horse's riem, knee-haltered him and let him graze while he sat with his gun over his knees watching him move from tussock to tussock as he ate.

Barend had a breakfast of biltong, dry bread and water. Then he caught and saddled his horse. Yesterday he had ridden parallel to the spoor of the wagons to see if anyone was following them. To-day he swung round in an arc thinking he would cut round in front of the trek and thus encounter the wagons before night fell. He rode slowly till about midday when the sun was almost directly overhead when, seeing vultures, he stopped. Vultures were always to be watched. If something was dead something else had killed it. What was dead here? It might be no more than a lion's kill—a wildebeest or a zebra—but he had to see. He rode towards the circling birds with the greatest care. Then, seeing the vultures go down to some large object that he could not see clearly, he cantered forward, only to pull up in horror when he came to the remains of a wagon. The wheels had been removed from it and burned to get the iron tyres. The vultures were grouped around the men who lay dead. One was white and half naked. He had been stabbed. Barend drove the birds off. It was Ullman and his servants. The featherbed of which he was so proud had been torn open and the feathers lay scattered like snow over the veld. It had only just happened. The spokes and felloes of the wheels were still smouldering. The vultures had not begun their feast. Ullman, who had thought himself so clever and had left the trek to better himself, had tried to return and been caught and killed. He had not died at once, for he had tried to stem the bleeding of a wound in his throat by stuffing the tail of his shirt into it. There was the spoor of Kaffir sandals everywhere. Barend found a broken assagai shaft. Nothing was left but the wagon body, which lay among the rocks where Ullman must have been caught in camp. The Kaffirs had only stayed long enough to loot his goods and burn the wood away from the metal of the wheels. Only the heat of the fire had deterred the vultures, and the hyenas that were now creeping up. Scattered round were the small useless things that the Kaffirs had left—some broken bottles, fragments of leather and torn papers.

Barend felt he should bury the dead—Ullman at least— but he had no tools. Nor could he alone pile a cairn of stones over the body that would protect it. Besides, how much time could he waste here? He must get back to camp to tell what he had seen and feared. No, once again the dead must bury their dead and, turning his horse, he left Ullman to the hyenas. Looking back he saw them close in. A little breeze lifted the loose white feathers of the mattress and blew them along so that some hung poised on the grass heads, ready to be used by the red and black Kaffir finches, the widow and weaver birds, to line their nests. This was the end of Ullman and his bed. The end of his wagon and his boys, of his hopes, of all that he had been and had possessed. His wife, his sons and his unborn child were with the trek, only these would remember him. To the Kaffirs who had robbed him he was not a person, just another white man whom they had killed.

Leaving this devastation behind him, Barend rode on swiftly but more carefully than ever. Those who had killed Ullman would kill him, too, if they could, and they were not far away. It was only his caution that prevented him from riding into the ambush which he was now convinced was being prepared for the wagons of the trek. Coming from the east instead of the south, he saw the Kaffirs camped behind the trees and rocks of the hillside that dominated a little valley down which, he had no doubt, the guide would have tried to lead them. For this was north of the laager's position and the direction in which they were almost certain to come. Leaving his horse tied to a tree, Barend crept forward, coming close enough to see them clearly and hear them talk. These were the people who had killed Ullman. They were quarrelling over the distribution of the loot. Ullman had evidently escaped from the Kaffirs he had joined or left them on some pretext or another, and had had the bad luck to fall in with these. Never had he seen a worse-looking lot. They were all armed with guns, and good guns at that. He saw the iron tyres of the wagon leaning against a tree. Oxen and horses that he recognised as Ullman's were being grazed under a guard some distance away. Then he saw a white man who looked familiar giving orders. How could this man look familiar? But he was. There was something about him . . . Barend crawled still closer. It was Carter, by God! So Carter had not died. By some devil's ruse he had saved himself and joined up with this savage band. There was something about them too, which was familiar, not that he had ever seen them before, but he had heard talk about the well-armed Kaffirs from the coast who raided the interior for slaves under the command of half-caste Portuguese traders. That was what they were—slavers. And Carter had joined them. It was he who was leading them against the trek, out of revenge. He who had ordered Ullman killed. He who had made them take the iron from the wagon so that the naked knob-nose Kaffirs who roamed here would be blamed. These people needed no iron to forge into assagais.

He crept closer. Carter was what he had always been. There was no change in him except for the worse. His face was harder, more brutal, his body thinner. He was burned almost black with exposure, and his hair bleached white. We should have shot him, Barend thought. Now all he seeks is revenge. It was difficult to think of Cina half naked in his arms. To think that he had been with them in the Christmas laager, fighting on their side and had not learned to love them. Surely it was natural to love those with whom you fought and suffered? Surely this made for brotherhood? And yet his own brother, blood of his blood, bone of his bone, would have betrayed him. There was no understanding the heart of a man.

He watched Fred Carter swaggering about among his men—powerful as ever, his shirt open over his sunburnt chest, a curved Arab dagger in his belt and Ullman's ivory-decorated gun over his arm. The devil certainly took care of his own, for here was a man who had mocked God and survived. No one had thought he would live—withstand the attacks of the wild beasts, find food and water, or survive without shelter or the help of other men. But he had. He had lived till he found these men—also servants of the devil—slavers beyond question and men of his own kidney.

Satisfied, Barend crept back to his horse, led him carefully for some distance and then mounted. He rode hard. Oom Willem must be warned. This was worse than he had imagined. So this was why the guides had come. Oom Willem must learn that Carter, who had sworn a curse against them, was alive and lay waiting, curled like a snake in their path, ready to strike.

When Barend approached the site of the laager, he pulled up. He must have made a mistake. It was not there. Yet this was the place. The more he looked the more certain he was that this was where he had left it. Surely it, too, could not have been so utterly destroyed, leaving nothing, neither despoiled wagons nor tortured dead? Still fearful of surprise he rode on slowly, his gun ready. The wagons had gone. There was their spoor—a dusty track of broken grass and bush that led northward. All that was left of them was the waste of a camp, the ashes of dead fires, broken bones, odd bits of rag and leather that were beyond use or repair, and silence broken only by the endless cooing of the doves. Barend dismounted to let his horse roll in the cold ashes of a fire. There was no grazing left here. As soon as he had smoked a pipe he would saddle up and ride on till he found good grass. Then, after the rest both he and the horse needed, he would pick up the spoor again and follow wagons.

He wondered what could have made Oom Willem move. Why, when he knew that he, Barend, was reconnoitring the country, should he have inspanned and pulled out? He could not believe that any threat of danger would have made him do this. Danger could only be met in one way— by a laager if the danger was wild Kaffirs, and what other danger was there here? So he must have been persuaded to move on. But by whom? There was only one man—the half-caste guide Tomaso. The villainous Portuguese renegade. Never, he thought, had he seen a man with a more untrustworthy or evil face, except perhaps that of Carter as he had last seen him. The two men were now completely connected in his mind. Carter had to be sure that the wagons would pass that way, and Tomaso had been sent to see that they did.

Barend sprang up and knocked out his pipe. This accounted for everything, even the death of Ullman. His suspicions were now a certainty. There was only one thing left to do. To follow the wagons with all speed in the hope that he would catch them up before night fell.

Francina had not been the only one to watch Barend ride off. Tomaso had seen him too. Somehow this young man would cause trouble. He had not actually said anything, but Tomaso felt it in his heart. No good would come of this. There was no knowing what he might find out. But since he could not be stopped now the only possible thing to do was to make the old man move at once. He approached Oom Willem.

" Then, Senhor, to-morrow we go, yes?"

" We must wait for Barend Beyers's return."

" He can follow us," Tomaso said. " The spoor of a trek like this is a road."

" Ja," Oom Willem said. " That is true." And the few miles they would move in two or three days would be as nothing to a mounted man. There was need for speed. They had to reach their destination—before he failed, before the weakness that he felt increased and he passed on into an illness that might well end in death. This was an aspect he had spoken of to no one but Barend, when he had extorted his promise to lead the people if he died. He turned to Tomaso.

" And how far is it in your mind, Senhor, to the hills of which we spoke?"

" Oh, we are near, Senhor. Five days on horseback, ten days on foot, perhaps a month with the wagons. Who can tell time and distance in Africa precisely? So many things can happen. But Senhor, my haste is because I cannot delay too long, much as I wish to help my brother Christians, heretics though you are. In a week you will be well on your way. Once I have guided you through the poort in the hills." He pointed to where Carter was waiting to fall upon them and laughed. " After that, Senhor, you will have no more troubles, everything will be simple."

There were no troubles in heaven if there was such a place for dead heretics, or for that matter in hell. A man burning in hell was beyond trouble too, in a way. The girl, of course, would have her worries. Ah yes, he thought, that Carter would be a worry to a pretty woman, and wondered what the leavings from so dainty a meal would be like when Carter had had enough.

" Tell me about the Hills of the Hunter again, and how you found them," Oom Willem said.

" I found them hunting elephant. It was some years ago," Tomaso counted on his fingers and held up four, " but I have never forgotten their beauty."

He thought of Carter telling him how to describe them to the old fool. " Lay it on," he had said. " Poetic like—like jam on bread for a kid. There are five hills," he had said, " arranged in a half circle like the hands of a man. In the palm there is a sweet marsh and through it runs a little river. In the hills there are springs, and by the fifth hill— the little finger as it were—there is a group of great rocks rubbed as smooth as marble by elephants and other game. Here, also, are slits cut into the stone where the bushmen smoothed and straightened their arrows."

" Senhor," Tomaso went on, " what a pleasure it is to talk to one who has also seen and appreciated these beauties. The five hills, the little streams that spring from the fountains in their bosom and rush like laughing milk down to join the river that bisects the fertile plain below them. Oh," he said, " and the great rocks rubbed smooth as marble by the game, and the slits in the rocks where the bushmen . . ."

" Stop!" Oom Willem said, "stop! I see it all again. How strange that you describe it as I would myself, as I have done time and time again, using my very words. Truly, Senhor," Oom Willem said, " only God can have sent you. We will start to-morrow. Barend can follow on our spoor. Who am I, Willem Prinsloo, to reject a sign from heaven?"

He called Flip who was passing nearby. " Flip, my boy," he said, " we are going to move to-morrow. You will tell the people and see to everything."

" But Barend, Oom Willem, what of him?"

" He will follow. How can he lose the spoor of a trek of so many wagons and so much stock?"

This was true. They would not be deserting him. And he was to lead the trek. He, Flip. At last he was being appreciated.

" Ja," he said. " I will see to all things."

" And this God-sent man," Oom Willem said, pointing to Tomaso, " will guide us."

Flip looked at Tomaso with some distaste. As a God-sent man he left much to be desired, but who was he to question the ways of the Almighty? Everything must be for the best, and perhaps God meant him to lead the trek instead of Barend. Barend might never come back. Then Francina and he would have no obstacles to their love. He was horrified by his thoughts. Barend. Barend who had saved his life!

" Si Senhor." Tomaso smiled into Flip's face. " It will give me much pleasure to lead you. You have no idea," he said, "of the joy in my heart at the pleasure of meeting other white men in this wilderness." He was thinking of the rawhide bags of gold in the wagons, of the guns, powder and lead, of the pots and pans, blankets and other loot that they would sell to the Kaffirs together with the oxen and horses. His face softened into innocence at this beautiful dream of the future when they would all be rich and the splendid raids they would be able to organise with this new capital. The coffles would now number many hundreds. They would buy shares in the slave ships—rich food and wine, beautiful women, soft beds, fine houses, were almost within their grasp. But it was a pity they had to pass by the village they had raided. A pity one could not guess these things and see into the future. He saw it as they had left it —the huts in flames, the dead lying scattered as they fell, dead warriors, spear in hand, old men and women, the children all killed like cattle for these were useless, neither strong enough to march loaded with ivory nor worth much if they happened to survive. Still, they had been killed humanely, with clubs. Being Christians they were against torture and left that to the savages they employed when they hunted men alone. But it was a pity that there was no other way but through this little plain where these Kaffirs had once lived. However, perhaps he could turn it to good account by saying, "See, what a good thing I am with you, because without me you might have run into trouble." He would say he had known of this massacre. That it had been done by the knob-nose Kaffirs who had gone on, running like wild hunting dogs, and would not return this way since they had killed every living thing in their patch.

This was the story he told Flip as they rode towards the ruins of the village. Flip was jaunty. A young leader riding with his gun butt on his hip, his hat on the back of his head. Behind him rumbled the wagons, behind them came the stock. As they got closer to the village the devastation became more apparent. The wooden bones of some of the huts had not burned completely but stood out like the calcined ribs of some strange beast. On the ground were the bones and skulls of the dead. The skulls and bones, too, of the Kaffirs' dogs and the remains of chickens, goats and sheep and cattle. On tall poles driven into the ground skulls were mounted as a warning to those who would pass by. These were already pecked clean by the crows and bleached white by sun and wind. This had been da Silva's idea. It was his trademark. Tomaso had always been against it, saying it served no purpose and was not Christian, but then to each man his own idiosyncrasies. These decorations were da Silva's and certainly they lasted a long time. Six months ago they had come upon a kraal that had been destroyed five years and only the skulls remained to mark it. Provided the posts on which they were mounted were of hard and ant-resistant wood, and that the skulls were sufficiently impaled, there seemed to be no reason why they should not last indefinitely. He pointed them out to Flip as if he could not see them.

"Senhor," he said solemnly, "when you see that you know that the Knob-noses have passed this way. That is their mark. Their spoor. If we were not in haste it would be in my heart to tear them down and bury them as if they were Christian men, for all men, white or black, are created by God." He took off his hat in a reverent manner as they rode by and thought how well he had got out of this difficulty.

Flip was thinking of the women and children in the wagons who must see and smell these horrors, for the smell of death still lingered here. Then, as they rode past a hut, the very last one that was only partially destroyed, an old woman staggered out. Her skin was drawn tightly over her ribs, her face was a black skull in which the burning agates of her eyes blazed hatred as, gathering her remaining strength, her lips drawn back in a savage snarl, she sprang at Tomaso, screaming with fury.

Tomaso, white with fear, beat her down from his rearing horse, as with a hand on his belt she tried to scramble up his body. His Kaffir who walked at his side leaped upon her and drove his knife into her heart as Tomaso, turning his horse, galloped back past the wagons in the direction from which they had come. The Kaffir ran too, dodging in and out of the scrubby bush like a hare pursued by dogs.

Flip turned in his saddle to watch them as if they had gone mad.

35

THE ASSASSIN

THAT IT should have happened this way infuriated Tomaso. Why had he lost his head? He should have been able to explain the attack by some story or other. How had the old woman escaped? She must have been hiding under a heap of skins and let the hut burn over her. The treachery of some people was unbelievable. But for him to have to run for it as if he was a Kaffir. What a pity he had lost his head. Luckily, the Boers had been too surprised to shoot or pursue him. They had not really understood what had happened—it had taken place too fast. The woman's attack and his retreat had all been part of a single movement. His Kaffir had been quick, too, with his knife. A good boy who must be rewarded. He would see to it when they got back. He was not a man who forgot a favour or an injury. A true Romero with the temperament of a Quixote. A tilter at windmills, a man who, had he been born rich, quite white and more handsome, would unquestionably have carved himself a niche in some great hall of fame. It was all there. *Si*, all the qualities of greatness, but he had never had a chance; fortunately, the whole world knew this, so he was never blamed. Known! Indeed, his name was a byword from Maputo to Mombasa. If you want slaves, they all said, see Tomaso Romero. There is no better man. No man more bold, more kindly or more straightforward in all his dealings. With these thoughts to console him, Tomaso galloped till he was out of sight and waited for his Kaffir to join him. Then hiding the horse among the trees, they lay down to recover themselves, after which they went on again, somewhat carelessly for they had nothing to fear, having escaped the Boers who, as far as they could see, had made no effort to pursue them. So careless was their progress that they almost ran into Barend following the spoor of the wagons.

Pushing his Kaffir down in the grass Tomaso said: " It's the young man who rode off to spy out the land." He wondered what he had seen. But even if he had seen nothing, here was a chance to kill a Boer and reduce the party by one good gun. Then, he thought, the Boers might hear the report and come seeking its cause. They had better remain hidden. The young man would ride by, and he would have had the horses not smelled each other and begun to neigh. Now he would have to run again. Tomaso mounted and spurred his horse. What a good thing he had rested him. His Kaffir would lie hidden—as he, with his usual courage, drew off the danger.

Seeing Barend's horse thundering down upon him, the Kaffir fired one wild shot, dropped his gun and fled. Tomaso saw this, for he ran at an angle to his own line of flight. Then he heard the Boer's shot and the Kaffir's scream. These Boer heretics were devils indeed, as apt to shoot from the saddle as from the ground. But it had given him time to get away. His man had not died in vain, for now he was free and beyond pursuit.

When Tomaso got to the site of the proposed ambush, making a long sweep round the Boer laager on the following day, after having spent a night of terror in the veld, Carter was not pleased to see him. He did not congratulate him upon his escape. He merely cursed him for a fool who had, by his clumsiness, allowed the Boers to become suspicious. Why had he not faced the thing out? They would have guessed nothing if he had not run away. Why had the old woman not been killed? Why had the huts not been utterly destroyed, or even properly searched? Why this? Why that? He acted as if he was their leader, as if the coffle and the raiders were under his command.

"I give you all this," Carter raved, "gold, cattle, guns, lead, powder. There it all is in your hand and you throw it away like a child that has never learned to obey. And your Kaffir, a first-class fighting man whom you have lost, whom you left, deserting him in action. Something for which you should be shot. By God," he said, "two of you, both armed, and put to flight by a Boer boy in his twenties." He stepped up to him and slapped his face.

He, a Romero, had been slapped in public! He raised his gun only to have it knocked out of his hand, and fell screaming with pain as Carter kicked him in the belly. This man was a devil and no Christian.

Carter seized his hand and pulled him to his feet.

"Stop that row," he said. "I know you are a Romero—a half Romero. That you have been insulted. That your honour has been impinged and that you will never be the same man again, which is true because this time if you do not obey my orders I will kill you."

"Senhor," Tomaso said. "You have but to command. My life is yours, my house, my horse."

"You have no house, but the horse I will take," Carter said. "I am a cavalryman, a *caballero*, and do not care to walk. But you," he said, "you must walk, and walk far and fast. Go off and collect your Kaffir friends, all the naked ones. Collect them and bring them to me quickly. Promise them loot. Cattle and iron and other things. Let them come and wash their spears in white men's blood. Say: ' Let us

see if you are as brave as you pretend and can face gunfire.'
Now go," he said, " and hurry."

" Food," Tomaso said. " I have eaten nothing."

" Then eat, but eat in haste for we have no time to lose."

What a fool the man was, Carter thought as Tomaso left
him. What a windbag. What a coward. Still, with enough
men he could take the laager by storm. It made him laugh
to think that only a few months ago he had been with the
Boers, fighting off the Kaffirs. Now he was with the Kaffirs
fighting the Boers. A true soldier of fortune, fighting where
it suited him best, where there was the most profit for himself. He thought of the profits, of revenge on those sancti-
monious bastards, revenge on Harry and his little finger
pickled—worth the ransom of a king. And the girl—his
while he wanted her, and when he had done with her there
were many who would pay for her—a white, golden-haired
girl fit to be a queen. He felt no doubts. If he could not
get what he wanted one way he always got it another.

He laughed as he thought how Tomaso had been surprised
by his language. By God, he thought, education comes
in handy sometimes. Sometimes it was useful to talk like a
bloody lord.

At the laager Barend was talking to Oom Willem. It had
been hard for him to control his temper.

" So," he said, " you could not wait?"

" We knew you would find us. We have not gone far."

" Ja, Oom Willem. But you are not safe in a laager, and
suppose I had not come back? Would you have guessed
that something was wrong and proceeded with greater
caution or have gone blundering on with your God-sent
guide? Guide!" he shouted. " The man was a spy sent to
lead us into ambush."

" He has run away," Oom Willem said.

" I saw him, and I killed his Kaffir."

" You saw the ruined village?"

" Ja, I saw and smelled it as I followed your spoor. I saw also an old woman who was newly killed."

" That's it," Oom Willem said. " She sprang upon Tomaso, our guide. His Kaffir killed her with his knife and then they ran away. Can you tell me why they ran?"

" What do you think?"

" I have no idea what to think. Perhaps that the old woman was mad. But why should they bolt? It was the work of the knob-nosed Kaffirs. He told Flip so as he rode beside him. Those skulls on poles, he said, proved it. They were a sign of the Knob-noses."

Barend, standing beside his horse with his arm over its neck, began to laugh.

" Oom Willem," he said, " he ran because that old woman recognised him. She knew who he was—what he had done."

" How could she?"

" It was he and his friends who destroyed the village. They are slavers. I ran into them. If they had seen me they would have killed me as they killed Ullman—I found his body and those of his boys. And Carter is with them. It was he who commanded the ambush the guide would have led us into!"

" No, not Carter. He must be dead. I have prayed for his soul. I have wondered if we did right to cast him out to die."

" He is not dead, I tell you. He lives and looks more evil than ever among these evil men. And now that this plan has failed he will make another. I know that man. Therefore we will make a strong laager now, at once, and this place is as good as any, with a fair field of fire, water and good grass for the beasts."

" If you think so," Oom Willem said.

" Think! I know!" Barend said.

" Very well then, give the orders."

Barend mounted his horse again and shouted: " We will laager here," and told Hendrik, Oom Willem's driver, to swing his wagon to the left as a signal that all could see and halt.

" Give me your horn," he said to Oom Willem. The long blast he blew sounded over the veld.

Barend now paced out the laager. The total length of the wagons, when closed up, was three hundred and sixty feet—one hundred and twenty yards. Dividing this by three gave him forty yards. He took twenty paces from Oom Willem's wagon. This was the centre. He threw down his hat to mark it and measured off the position of the other wagons as they came up. It was a small laager, too small to hold many of the beasts—each needed four square yards for comfort—but safe, for the smaller the laager, the safer it was.

Barend was a good wagon master and glad to show his skill. On the trek he had thought of it a great deal. Once the wagons were in place and the cattle sent off to graze and water, the tree and bush cutting began. Every space between the wagons and the wheels had to be filled, the bushes lashed fast and the wagons chained to each other so that they could not be pulled apart. This was the strongest laager they had ever made. The tightest. A solid ring that would have to be taken by storm, it could not be pulled apart. But Barend knew Carter. He knew his hatred and his skill, and did not underestimate him. The man had been a soldier and a brigand. He was brave and resourceful. How else could he have survived his ordeal in the wilderness and at the end of it, apparently by sheer force of character, have taken over the command of a slaving gang? This was to the death. The fight would not be broken off when the Kaffirs found no easy pickings.

Then the guns. All the spare guns were loaded and the ammunition prepared for immediate use. Powder was poured into tin plates, piled into them as if it was black sugar. In an attack no one measured their charge. They just threw a handful down the barrel and banged the butt on the ground so that some of the powder flowed out of the touch hole into the pan. Beside the powder plates were heaps of buckshot cartridges, the shot being sewn into soft greased leather bags that dropped down the barrel without difficulty. In action the ramrod was never used. This enlargement of the touch holes had been Oom Willem's idea, and it enabled a very rapid fire to be kept up, the minimum number of shot in a cartridge being sixteen, of a size that went two hundred and twenty to the pound. The range was seventy yards and the bags burst like small shells in the air. Thus, as the effective range of an assagai was only fifty yards, the Boers had the advantage. The speed of fire was five to six shots a minute, so that a good man could fire three times while a Zulu charged a hundred yards. But here again, the situation was not the same as it would have been with wild Kaffirs. These slavers were armed with guns as good as their own.

At last everything was ready, and now there was nothing to do but wait and pray.

Tante Maria had broken the news of Ullman's death to his wife, who had taken it well since that was the fate she had foreseen.

The second day of the laager passed and nothing had happened. There had been no sign of Carter or his people. Fear had been overcome by boredom. The edge of the men's alertness was blunted, so to pass the time profitably and to keep the Boers' guns in their hands, Barend suggested a Jukskey shoot. In this game two yoke skeys, a foot long and two inches wide, were set up some yards apart, fifty yards from the firing point. One man had to run forward and kick over one of the skeys before the other could load his muzzle loader and shoot down the second one. For their competition they used bullets wrapped in vet lappies—greased linen patches that allowed the bullets to go down the barrel easily yet held them firmly in place.

The noise of the shots and the running of the competitors put everyone in a better frame of mind. It had taken their minds off things, and in addition had got their eyes and hands into rapid firing again. If they had had to wait till they were attacked it might have been too late. Barend had the feeling that with Carter there would be no delay, no preliminaries. He would drive the attack home and try to overrun them with the first charge. Harry Bates stood near him.

" Harry," he said, " how will Carter attack?"

" He's a brave man," Bates said, " but he has a twisted devil's mind. A cruel man. How he has survived I do not know. I only know that I should have died. I lack his resolution."

" Ja," Barend said, " you would have been ashamed in your heart if you had been he, and have died of it, but he has no shame. He has only his rage which gives him strength and nourishes him." Barend paused, certain that he was right. That hate gave a man power, as love did, or fear, as all great emotions did. Then he repeated his question.

" What will he do, Harry? You are a soldier too. What would you do?"

" If I were he I should post my riflemen on that ridge." Harry pointed to his left, " and tell them to fire as fast as they could into the laager while I brought up my wild Kaffirs and threw them into the attack from two sides."

"Ja," Barend said, "that would be a good plan. We must ignore the bullets and face the spearsmen. The others will never charge. No Kaffir with a gun will charge as long as he can lie safely in cover and fire off his piece."

The people were about them trying to hear what they were saying. Once again they were restless and uneasy.

"We must give them something to think about," Harry said. "Let us compete, you and I, in shooting at a mark. We are the two best shots. Let us see who is the winner, and we will shoot for a prize. My hat," he said, "the hat that is my pride and the envy of all who behold it." He laughed and held it up. A fine hat of leather with a leopard-skin crown in which were stuck two short black ostrich plumes.

"And if I win," Harry said, "I'll take your hat, and then I'll have two, one for every day and one for Sunday."

"Ja," Barend laughed. "And if I win I shall have yours, but I will not save it for the Lord's day. Nee," he said, " I'll wear it every day so all men shall know that I shot it from your head. Kom, kerels," he said, "set up the mark. Two ox ribs at fifty paces."

They set them up. Bates fired first, hitting the rib fair and square, knocking it down in splinters. Barend took careful aim. His rib flew shattered into the air.

"Now try seventy paces," Oom Willem said. He had joined them and was directing the shoot.

At seventy paces the result was the same. At eighty both men missed their first shot and struck the bones, breaking them to pieces with the second.

" A hundred," Oom Willem said.

This was indeed a test. The white bones were only as

wide as two fingers, and at this distance were scarcely visible. Lying down they could not be seen.

Bates took the first shot sitting. With his elbows on his knees he sighted his gun with the greatest care. Everyone held their breath. If he hit the target this would be a notable shot, one of which men would speak for years to come. He fired. The bone trembled but did not fall. It was a miss, but a miss by only a hairbreadth. A shout went up: "Well done! Man, but that was good!' Harry looked round smiling; it was a good shot and would take some beating.

Barend loaded slowly, tamping down his wad and bullet with his ramrod. Then he, too, sat with his elbows on his knees. Twice he brought the gun down again and resettled himself, wriggling his buttocks into the ground. The third time he put up his gun he did not hesitate, but fired almost at once.

"A hit, by God, a hit!" they cried as the rib sprang into the air like a living thing.

Harry clapped him on the back and said: "We can shoot, you and I, but you are the best. Here is my hat. I only ask but one thing of you—that you tend it carefully and do not wear it in the rain if you can help it." The two men shook hands and laughed.

"Coffee," Barend cried. "Let us all have coffee. Let us celebrate to-day and lace it with a soppie of good Cape dop."

Carter had led his men to the vicinity of the wagons. He did not much care if they were seen. By now, thanks to that fool Tomaso, the cat was out of the bag. He should be coming back now, at any moment, with reinforcements of wild Kaffirs, eager for blood and loot. In the meantime, he thought he would go and have a look at the laager himself.

It would be easy to hide at a safe distance and watch their doings. If only he had had a spyglass it would have been easier. He might even have been able to watch the girl. That was the only danger with the Knob-noses and blood Kaffirs. They might kill her if he did not reach her first. Of course he would tell them and they would understand his orders. No women to be killed till the fight was over. But once their blood was up they killed everything. There was no staying them; as long as anything moved they would drive their spears into its body. Still, he would manage somehow.

He smuggled down behind a bush and watched the Boers. It was a strong laager, he could see that from here. And all the shooting there had been to-day. What had it been about? There was no sign of disorder. Just practice, no doubt. That was the kind of thing Harry would think of, or Barend. That Barend was no fool. It was a pity Tomaso had not killed him. He lay quite still. It was restful to lie like this, and useful too. He was absorbing the lay of the land, placing his men, seeing from where they would attack. He watched the horses and trek oxen grazing nearby. The main herds were farther off. As darkness fell they would be driven in, and out of habit and fear of the wilds about them, settle down to rest near the wagons that were their masters' homes. The horses and pick of the oxen would sleep within the laager. It would not hold them all, so only the leaders, the wheelers and the best other pair or two of each span was held in safety. With these a new span could be broken in quickly and be ready to work in less than a week.

How lucky it was that he knew these people and their habits so well from having lived with them for months. By God, he thought, they can't surprise me. Not Freddie Carter. He knows the lot.

Then he saw a man walking towards him, alone. Some

man just out for a stroll. And why not? It should be safe
enough so near the laager. A man. It was Harry. Harry
without his big Zulu. Harry alone, delivered by the devil
himself into his hands. He would pass within thirty yards
of him.

He raised his gun slowly, flattening himself still lower
upon his belly. " Harry, by God, Harry!" he was saying to
himself. The saliva ran out of the corners of his mouth as
if he were hungry. Now, he thought, now. This was the
moment. He pressed the trigger, saw Harry fall, and ran
forward, drawing his knife, as he ran. A quick slash and the
little finger would be off, neat as a whistle at the knuckle.
And before anyone could say Jack Robinson he would be
away. If he was followed, so much the better. He'd lead
them on to his Kaffirs. Then they'd drive those they didn't
kill back to the laager, pursuing them closely and over-
whelming the wagons all in one swift action.

He saw it in his mind as he ran, crouching like a crab,
towards the fallen man whose legs still twitched convulsively.
He jumped on to him, put one knee on his belly, raised his
knife and seized his hand. The wrong hand, by God, he
thought, as he dropped it. It was the left hand that had
the crippled little finger and the ring. He raised the right.
It was the left, he knew. The left. The left. He dropped
the hand. This man had no crippled little finger, no
ring.

He looked at the dead man's face, pushing back the hat
—Harry's hat, that had fallen forward to hide his features.
Barend. Good God! He had shot Barend. The disappoint-
ment brought tears of rage into his eyes.

Cries were coming from the laager. He must run for it
now. He jumped to his feet and picked up his gun, but he
had hardly turned before a bullet in the shoulder knocked
him down. They've got me, he thought. This time it

would be the end. His gun was unloaded. He had only his knife. He took it in his left hand—his right was useless now, and lay waiting. With luck he would kill one of them as they bent over him thinking he was dead. He closed his eyes and waited, like a viper with its fangs hidden flat against its gums, for a hand to touch him.

36

THE PREPARATION

HARRY'S ZULU joined him. Flip came running up. "What is it? What has happened?"

"Your brother has been killed," Harry said. "Carter killed him in my place. It is my fault that he died."

"What do you mean? How did it happen?"

"The hat," Harry said. "He was wearing the hat that he had just won from me and Carter killed him. He thought it was me. And I killed Carter. I heard the shot, saw Barend fall, and having my gun in my hand fired at once."

"It was a good shot," Flip said. "At least he is avenged."

The Zulu touched Harry's arm. "Baas," he said, "he is not dead. A dead man does not sweat." He raised the knobkerrie he was carrying.

"No," Bates said, "you cannot hit a wounded man."

"I cannot kill a wounded snake? I, a Zulu, who kills his friends if they are sorely hurt and beyond cure?"

Harry looked at Carter. What had he done to this man? Why did he hate him so? Because he had saved Francina? But it went back further than that. He bent over him as if hoping to discover the secret. Carter, who had been breathing so softly that the rise and fall of his chest could not be seen, managed, in spite of the pain it gave him, to strike upward towards Harry's belly with his knife. A stroke that would have disembowelled him had he been able to send it home. But the Zulu was faster than he, as the mongoose is faster than the striking snake. As Carter's knife rose the kerrie fell, smashing his wrist and sending the knife flying in a shimmering arc across the veld.

" Can I kill him now, inkoos? Now I can kill him, can I not?"

Harry put his hand on Nzobo's shoulder.

" Once again you have saved my life," he said, " but Carter must not be killed."

" Why not?" Flip said. " We should have done it long ago. We should never have let him go."

" Because I want information from him. Who are these people who threaten us? Why does he hate me?"

" He will talk," the Zulu said. " I will smear his face with honey and peg him out on a broken ant heap. Then I will stir them with a stick. He will talk or he will die. Or else I could . . ."

" Now you will carry him back," Harry said, " for who knows what will happen now."

The Zulu picked Carter up as if he were a child, but without tenderness, so that he gave a scream of agony. Harry and Flip between them carried Barend, one at his head, the other at his feet. The hat that he had worn for so short a time was balanced upon his body. People crowded out of the laager towards them. Louis ran to his brother.

" Barend! Barend!" he cried. " Speak to me!"

" He will speak no more," Flip said.

Francina burst into tears, regretting her every unkindness. Tante Maria stared at Carter in the Zulu's arms.

" Why did you bring him back? Why did you not kill him?" she said.

" Because I was forbidden, lady," the Zulu said. He had a great admiration for this immense woman.

" Well, I will not nurse him." She followed behind the group as it went to the wagons. " Let him die," she said. "He will die anyway, with a wound like that. But let him die untended, like a dog on the veld. Die thinking about the evil he has done and the men he has betrayed."

An hour later she found Francina washing out Carter's wound with vinegar and water, and tying up his shattered wrist in splints.

" You," she said. " You can touch that man. The man who dishonoured you. Take the hand that tore the clothes from your body and dress it," she screamed, her fist raised as if to strike the girl.

" He is still a man, Ouma, and he can do no more harm. Surely it is written that it is right to turn the other cheek and succour the distressed?"

Tante Maria turned away, quivering with fury. That girl. There was no knowing what she would do. Not ever. Not even God could know.

Francina did not know herself. It was not as she had said. She was not being a good Christian girl, not turning the other cheek. In her heart she was ashamed, for she was in some way drawn to this man who had so nearly violated her. Also, she hated him. Also, she regretted the death of Barend, and was sorry she had not been more kind to him. But also she was glad to be quit of his attentions. Now no one stood between her and Harry. There was only his aversion to her. That she must overcome. Somehow she knew that he would come to Carter. Knew that he must come to this man who had once been his comrade and was now his murderer, or would have been but for a trick of fate—the exchange of hats in a game such as might have been played by children. And she was right, for hardly had she bandaged Carter's wrist and shoulder before Harry Bates walked up to her.

" That is a most Christian act, Francina," he said.

" No," she said, unable to lie, " No, it is not. I would not lie about such a thing to you. I hate him, but somehow had to dress his wounds. He could not be left alone to bleed to death."

" Why not?"

" He must live to speak, Meneer, so that we shall learn something about the band he leads and why he killed Barend."

She knew he had thought it was Harry, but she wanted to make him tell her so in his own words. Wanted to hold him near her, talking.

" It was not Barend he sought to kill, but me," Harry said. " Barend wore my hat."

" But why you? What had you done?"

" Have you forgotten?"

" That you saved me from him? Oh no. Oh Harry, how could you think that?" She put her hand on his forearm, holding him so that he could not back away. " But there must have been more than that, because in the fight on the koppie he said he had always hated you and should have killed you long ago. But why? Why?" She stamped her foot. " Why should he have wanted to kill you? When you are good and he is bad?"

" I do not know, Cina," he said. " I have no idea."

Carter, who had been lying still again as if he was really dead, now opened his eyes, bared his yellow fangs like a snarling dog, and said: " No idea, hey? . . . Ye've no idea, 'Arry? Well, I'll tell yer. It's your pinkie I want. Your bloody little finger and your ring, pickled in a little bottle of tiger's milk it'd bring me a thousand golden smackers at the Cape from a certain party. And I wanted the girl and I'd 'ave 'ad 'er but for you."

" You're mad, Fred."

" Mad, eh? Never knew you was worth so much, did you? Dead or alive, but worth more dead, and your little finger the proof of it."

Francina stood beside Harry, her arms about him, frozen with horror. His little finger. To prove he was dead. Pickled in a bottle of gin. She took his hand in hers to look at the distorted finger that wore the golden ring. " Who?" she said, " who?"

" Who? You silly little bitch. Who but his bastard brother?"

" My brother? My half-brother, John?"

" Who but he? Who but Mr. Bloody Captain Jack— Captain Jack Robinson of the Tenth Dragoons. He wanted you dead because his ma was never married." Carter began to laugh. " Mustn't do that," he said, " mustn't laugh, it hurts too much. Christ, it's funny to think I'm pegging out, kicking the bucket, and I'll never laugh again. That this is the bloody end of Freddie Carter. Hurts to laugh, though," he said again. " Where was I, 'Arry? Oh, yes. Captain Jack. Look, 'Arry, your dad thought he had a mock marriage with your ma. Thought the parson was a cheap actor all decked out in a parson's gear. But it weren't so. He was a regular parson of the line. A long service chap, he was, and he put it in the book. In his bloody register. Their names, I mean. Your dad, Sir Bloody Robinson, and your ma, whatever her bloody name was, and so when he, your dad, married Captain Jack's ma, rich and great as she was, they weren't married at all, and so his ma's a whore and he's a bastard. You're it, 'Arry boy, the heir. Sir bloody 'Arry." Carter began to laugh. " Christ!" he said, " oh, Christ!" He caught a piece of his red and yellow neckcloth between his teeth to bite on.

" Then you are a ' Sir,' " Francina said. " Sir Harry Bates."

" Sir 'Arry Bates, Bart.," Carter spat. " That's what he'll be when the old man pops off. And a laugh that is too, because 'e'll be dead. Aye," he went on, his voice rising to a kind of chant, " the 'ole bleeding lot of you'll be dead, dead as bloody doornails. All but Miss Dainty 'ere, an' I've no doubt she'll wish she was when Don bloody Sousa y Madrigo I Kiss the Monkey's Tail gets 'old of 'er. Aye," he said to Francina, " it might 'ave been better with me, seein' as I'm white." Again he laughed. "A slaver's moll, our proud lady a half-caste slaver's moll . . ." He fell back in a faint.

" What does he mean?" Francina said. " Oh, Harry, what can he mean?"

" It means that we were right to go into laager. He has persuaded the slavers to attack us. He was going to lead them."

" But why? What could they get?"

" You. He wanted you for himself and the loot of the wagons."

" And he'd fight? People would be killed so that he should have me?" Francina was shocked. That two men should fight with their fists for a girl's love, ja, that was reasonable enough, even with knives among the coloured people. But that white men with guns should start a war . . .

" A war," she said, " they would make a war for a woman?"

" It's been done before," Harry said. " There was Helen of Troy—the face that launched a thousand ships."

" Helen—who was she? Why did they launch ships?"

" To sail the sea, to fight in a foreign land."

" Had they no girls of their own, and how could she be married to a thousand men? Meneer, King Solomon had a thousand wives, it is said, but with men it is different."

" Yes," he said, " it is different. And it was not only for you. There is the gold that is carried in the wagons, and the guns, the powder and the ball, the cattle and horses, all the loot of such a caravan as ours."

" What shall we do?"

" Prepare and wait for them. What else is there to do?"

Near them Oom Willem sat with the Bible open in front of him. Now there was another grave to be dug. Two graves in fact, for Carter would not live long, and there might be more if the Kaffirs attacked. But that Barend should die before he did was almost incomprehensible to him. Accidents and fatalities were natural enough under the conditions in which they lived. But Barend. He had pinned his faith to Barend. Barend was to be his successor. His heir, too, in that he was to marry Cina. That he should die first was still, though it had happened, unthinkable. Who had he to rely on now? Flip? Flip was too young, too reckless. There was only the English soldier—Harry Bates. How strange that it should be he. A rooinek, a dragoon, and yet he was the man who had changed all their lives in the very beginning with the stallion he had brought them.

About him the life of the laager went on. The children played near him at games of war, the boys rescuing maidens from imaginary Kaffirs, the maids helping the boys to repel attacks and nursing the wounded with tender care. So did the coming reality and the children's games impinge upon each other, the coming battle being presaged by the cries and shouts of simulated combat till Tante Maria appeared and slapped the children down.

" Little fools, " she said, " you are brave now. Just see that you remain brave later. Get you to work like real Boer children preparing for battle instead of playing such infant's games."

She gave the boys long narrow bars of lead to be cut into small chunks by striking a knife blade into them with a hammer. She set the girls to rolling the lead squares that they cut on a stone to round them off, and others, the bigger ones, with Miemie at their head, to sew the little soft tanned-leather bags that would contain the slugs.

Thus she went from wagon to wagon to see that the women had the spare guns loaded. That they had ball and powder suitably dispersed, ready for immediate use, and strips of old linen rolled for bandages.

Flip was in a fever of nervous fury. His brother was killed —Barend who had saved his life. Moreover he was not a man who could wait. Where were the Kaffirs? Why did they not come?

"Let us go and find them, Harry," he said. "If I must be killed then I must. I can wait no longer."

He began to make his way out of the laager. Francina stopped him. Flinging her arms about him she pressed her body into his. "Must I lose you, too?" she whispered. She knew she could hold him, calm him, but that she had had to do it in front of Harry whom she loved upset her, and she began to cry. Flip put his arms round her. She flung away from him. What would Harry think now? Think of a girl who took a new lover before the first was even buried?

Now that the news of Carter's capture had come in, Tomaso was for abandoning the project, leading his handful of slavers back and dispersing the Kaffirs. But they would not go. They stood about him shouting, gesticulating, waving their guns and spears.

One, a sub-chief, wearing the tail feathers of a widow bird in his hair, said: "It is simple. You will lead us to battle. If you run away we will kill you. If you refuse to lead us we will kill you. For now our spears must be washed in the blood of a white man. That is what we have promised them." He held his assagai to his lips. "Beloved one," he said, "you shall drink white blood." He jumped towards Tomaso raising the spear, "Shall it be yours or theirs?"

"I will lead you," Tomaso said, but his knees trembled.

This was not an unsuspecting Kaffir village to be surprised in the dawn. This was a laager. The Boers were fine shots, bold men waiting and ready to fight, entrenched behind their wagons. He might get killed. It was said they could kill a man at two hundred paces. Some of his own men, the trained slave catchers, might be killed. This would be a severe loss. It took time to train a slave catcher. The slaves had to be handled like livestock, like cattle. It was important to know how to feed, water and rest them. The routes they followed had to be learned. Above all, a slave catcher must not lose his head. Some, when they were new to it and inflamed by the smell of blood and the cries of their victims, could not cease from killing till all were dead. *Madre de Dios*, a slaver's life was not an easy one. But at least it had been straightforward till this damned English heretic had come to tempt them. That was it. He saw it clearly now. This man had been sent by the devil to destroy them, so that they should catch no more slaves and save no further pagan souls for God.

His religious train of thought was ended by the sub-chief, who pricked him with the point of his spear. " Lead on, inkoos," he said, " lead on, for you are the induna and must go before us who follow so humbly behind. Run away," he hissed, " and my spear will go into your ribs."

Tomaso set off towards the laager, with his slave catchers behind him and the Knob-noses and blood Kaffirs on either flank. He was now impressed with his qualities of leadership. This was something these Kaffirs could not do alone. They needed him. " *Si*," he slapped his belly and shouted, " here runs the best blood of Portugal, the blood of soldiers, adventurers, and sea captains." The Kaffirs yelled in unison and beat their weapons upon their shields, delighted to hear the war cry of their leader.

It was Francina who, having climbed to the top of the

wagon, saw the Kaffirs first. "They come," she cried,
"they come!"

The Boers stood to their guns and waited for the attack.
They were not going to ride out against Kaffirs as well
armed as these. With his spyglass Oom Willem could see
Tomaso directing operations, waving his hands this way and
that. He could even hear him shouting orders in the Kaffir
tongue.

Harry, at Oom Willem's shoulder, said: "He has been
told what to do by Carter, or he has done it before." This
was when he saw Tomaso dispose his sharpshooters behind
rocks and bushes and send the Kaffirs under their own chiefs
to either flank.

The Kaffirs had now forgotten Tomaso. Let him and his
handful shoot at the laager if that was their method of fighting, but they, the real warriors, would storm the white
man's kraal and carry it by the spear. They waited, grouped,
nervous and excited as hounds on the leash for their leaders
to give the word. The leaders waited for the slavers to open
fire. With the first ragged volley, they charged, leaping in to
the attack. They had expected to hear the Boers' answering
fire, but it never came. On Harry's advice they had ignored
the shots of the slavers. "They'll never move," he said.
"They haven't heart, least of all Tomaso," whom he saw
directing his part of the battle from behind a giant antheap.

At fifteen paces a savage fire met the Kaffirs, killing and
wounding many, tearing their ranks apart, but they plunged
on with the wild courage of their kind, like dogs, their fury
blinding them to danger. Here was loot, glory, blood. This
was war, their favourite sport. Some reached the wagons
and were blown apart as they shook the spokes of the wheels.
None breached the laager, and then as a wave of the sea that
has dashed all its wild majesty of tossing spume against the
rocks falls back into itself and withdraws, so did the Kaffirs.

The Boers had been ready for them and were too strong. But their herds remained, so picking up their wounded and leaving the dead scattered upon the veld, the Kaffirs withdrew, and the swiftest of them ran towards the herds whose spoor showed so clearly in the trodden grass.

"To horse," Harry cried, and jumping on their saddled horses a group of boys and men swept out of the laager, galloping to outflank the running Kaffirs and save the stock. Only when the big grey thundered past him did Harry realise that Francina was with them, leading them in fact. Francina was somewhat surprised herself. She had gone with the others because whatever happened she had no desire to be left behind. But that she should lead was Bloubooi's fault. He was a horse that could not bear to see a flying tail in front of him.

Behind them the noise of the attack began again. They heard more firing, but could not turn back now. The galloping Boers now dropped their reins on the horses' necks and fired on the Kaffirs who were running from them—killing several. Reloading again, Harry's party cut still further into the Kaffirs' line of advance, driving them back whence they had come, so that they could not escape into the hills and come at the cattle by another route.

Just as they were congratulating themselves that they had routed the enemy, a bullet took Hendrik's horse behind the shoulder and brought it down dead. Pulling Bloubooi on to his haunches, Francina shouted: "Hendrik! Hendrik, are you hit?"

He got to his feet. "I am all right."

"Jump on my horse," Harry said. Hendrik got up behind him as another body of Kaffirs leaped up out of the long grass. The Boers would have been ambushed if one of them had not fired at Hendrik. This running battle had taken them into some low, treeless rolling hills. The laager was hidden from them, but from it came the sounds of renewed and much hotter fire.

Harry turned on Francina who now rode at his side. " You little fool," he said. " You could have been killed and may be, yet."

" Ja, Meneer Harry," she said. " That is true for all of us."

" You are a girl," he said.

" That is also true, and there are times that I do not regret it."

" Well, you should look like one and behave like one," he said. He was furious with this child.

" On Sundays, in my dress and kappie, I am a girl,' Francina said. " On weekdays I am free."

" And act like a silly boy," Harry said.

" I am never like a boy, Harry. I am just free. Is a bird in the air, when you see it fly, a cock or a hen? No," she said, " it is just a bird. It is free. Thus am I free on my horse like a bird."

Harry held up his hand and stopped. The others closed in on him.

" Now," he said, " we will attack the Kaffirs from the rear. We must see where the Kaffirs are and how to take them." His words were checked by some wild cries and another burst of firing.

" Come," he said.

They advanced at a slow canter.

37

ATTACK

As soon as the Kaffirs saw the Boers ride out after the cattle thieves they attacked the weakened garrison again. Success, and revenge for their losses, now seemed certain. In the laager all were fighting desperately. The women and children were doing more than load. They were firing guns that some of them could scarcely lift. Miemie, her face black with powder, loaded her gun with the slugs she had been sewing into bags an hour before, and resting the barrel on the spokes of a wheel, fired as fast as her small brother could reload and hand her a fresh gun.

Oom Willem had lost his hat. His white hair and beard awry, he fired his biggest elephant gun, a four to the pound, into the thick of the charging Kaffirs. If only they would come back, he thought. If only Harry got back in time. But he had been right to go. The stock had to be saved. To be left without beasts here would be to die immobilised and helpless.

Tante Maria was fighting beside him. " Ha," she said, " ha, if I can kill lions I can also slay men. But that girl. Before God, Oom Willem, that girl has ridden out with the men. She is like one possessed. Ja, like a Gadarene swine she flings herself over the cliff into that black sea of Kaffirs to revenge the death of her lover. It is a fine thing, to demand justice, to demand an eye for an eye and a tooth for a tooth, but she goes too far."

She fired her gun. " Now you will come no more, you naked black devil," she cried, and went on, " But that a girl should ride out to war on her horse like that . . ."

" As long as she gets back," Oom Willem shouted. " As long as they all get back. As long as they get back in time! We cannot stand another charge." He peered through the smoke. " Pull out the gate. They come!" he shouted.

" They come!" Tante Maria shouted as Harry, Francina and the others galloped in, the cloud of red dust thrown up by the horses' hoofs mixing with the smoke of the black powder. The wagon that closed the laager was lashed back into place.

Francina jumped from her horse, leaving him to run loose, and seized a gun.

" Thank God you're back," Oom Willem said. " And the cattle?"

" They are safe," Francina said. " Safe for an hour or so at least. We killed three and turned the others back."

" That's good," Oom Willem said. " And no one was hurt?"

" No one, but Hendrik's horse was killed. Harry Bates picked him up and brought him in. I stood beside him," she said, as the Kaffirs came on again. More men seemed to have joined them. Another contingent must have come from somewhere, hearing the sound of battle and smelling loot. This time they got up to the wagons and, leaping on their own dead, reached the tent tops, driving their spears into the triple canvas and pulling themselves up. Two jumped down into the laager and were killed by the spears of the tame Kaffirs before they could do damage. Spears came raining into the laager. There were wild cries, the screams of the wounded, and the panic-stricken lowing of the cattle as they milled round and round in terror.

Then from the Kaffirs came the sound of a horn. There

were more shots. A sharp volley and the Kaffirs fell back.

As the smoke cleared Oom Willem let out a shout. "White men," he cried. "A rescue! The Lord God has seen fit to save us once again!"

"It was near," Tante Maria said. "Magtig! The Lord always saves us. That is to say he has, up till now. But sometimes he leaves it till very late!"

Their rescuers, eight in number, swept down upon the Kaffirs, taking them in the flank.

"Mount!" Harry shouted. "Mount and charge!"

A moment later every man was on his horse and out of the laager again, Francina on Bloubooi among them.

They swept up to the retreating Kaffirs, firing from the saddle, halting to reload and riding on. Francina rode at Harry's heels, holding Bloubooi back. She had no gun but held a pistol in her hand. Many Kaffirs fell. The rest were in full flight. Tomaso's men fired a volley at the Boers which hit no one and then fled too, with Tomaso in the van.

Now, their horses blown, the Kaffirs dispersed, the two groups of Boers came together. Who were these strangers? These Boer men and boys, evidently part of another trek which had followed in their spoor in time to save them. One rode forward. Francina knew him at once. His black hair and beard were longer, his face burned browner, but his bright black button eyes remained the same. The smous. The smous was back among them. Francina spurred towards him.

"Meneer," she cried. "It is Meneer Rosenberg, our smous!"

He took off his hat and bowed from the saddle.

"The same," he said, "but older and somewhat worn with travel"—he looked down at himself—"and also stained."

"Oh," she said, "this is good. Good."

" Ja, it is good to see so lovely a maiden again, riding like a man among men with a valuable silver-mounted pistol in her hand."

Francina laughed. " You want to buy it?"

" I will buy anything. I am a Jew." He laughed back at her. " That is why I came. Ja, magtig!" he said, " all my best customers went on this picnic to the North so I had to follow."

" Who leads your trek? Who are these people?" Harry asked.

" Swellendamers," he said. " I lead them. I told them I knew the way."

" You never told us you knew the North."

" My little flower, I did not know it then, but it is not hard to pick up and follow the spoor of a trek like yours."

" Thank God you came," she said. " Thank God you came in time."

" Thank God," he said. Then he laughed. " When we heard the gunfire I, being a Jew and cautious, said to my friends: ' Let us stop here and hide.' But they being bold Christian men said, ' That is the sort of counsel a Jew would give,' and they insisted upon joining the fray. Ja, my pretty one," he said, " but if I had said, ' Come on, they are in trouble, let us go to the rescue,' they would have thought: Ah, the Jew, what will he get out of this? Why should he wish to run into danger? and hung back. My heart," he said, " men are very contrary and because they trust no one they will always act against all counsel, even the best."

A big fair man had come up to them.

" A lie, a lie," he said. " It's the Jew who said: ' Make haste, ride like the devil,' and he who led us." He clapped Rosenberg on the shoulder, almost knocking him from his sweating horse.

" And you, Meneer," Francina said.

" I am Fourie, Jappie Fourie of Swellendam."

" I am Francina Marais." She held out her hand.

" A girl! I thought you were a boy!"

" Do I look like a boy?" Francina stared at him with big gold-flecked eyes, her bosom heaving with a mixture of exhaustion, excitement and anger. What a big, stupid fool!

Harry rode up. " This is Meneer Bates," she said, " our leader under my Oupa."

" An Englishman?" Fourie said. " Man, but this is a funny trek, led by an Englishman and a girl-boy armed and mounted on a blood horse. Man!" he said, " what a horse! What a horse!"

" He's mine," Francina said, leaning over to pat Bloubooi's neck.

" And Salome?" Rosenberg said, " what of her? She is well, I trust."

" Ja, she is well. She is at home." Francina nodded towards the laager.

" Salome?" Fourie said.

" My love," the smous said, " who left me for another."

" And she is here?"

" Ja, she is a donkey," Francina said.

" You see," the Jew said, " she had to be. Only a donkey would leave me for another." He nearly fell from his saddle with laughter as, swinging their horses round, the Boers all rode back together.

Fourie said: " We will bring our wagons up and join you, if we may."

" The more the better," Harry said. " If you agree to follow our leader, Oom Willem."

" He sounds good enough for us," Fourie said. " We wish to hunt and trade and then return to the Colony."

" Then you have no women with you?" Francina said.

" No women. Only a minister."

"A predikant? Where is he?"

"In charge of the wagons. He will not fight unless he is attacked, but he is a good man, one of the best of his kind. Though I must say I do not care for his kind. Man," he said, clapping Francina on the shoulder—they were riding side by side—"all predikants and ministers depress me. They make me afraid with their talk of hellfire. Man," he said, "I do not like the idea of being frizzled like a boerewors at a braaivleis—after all a man is not a sausage."

Francina laughed. "You are a funny man," she said.

"Ja, I am funny. I love to laugh. That is why I do not like to be made sad."

Oom Willem came to welcome them. "You saved us," he said. "God sent you to save us."

"God!" Fourie said, "the Jew. Ja," he said, "that smous made us hurry all the way, as if he knew . . ."

"I knew," Rosenberg said. "I knew that more men would be needed. And they are good men." He introduced them.

"Meneer Jappie Fourie—" he said, "Meneer Herman Smit—Meneer Jacob du Toit—Meneer Franz Theron—Meneer Manie Botha. And the two boys, Johannes and Boetie, the brothers of our leader, Jappie Fourie."

"Leader!" Fourie said. "Before God, I do all the work, but it's you, the Jew, who leads, for it was he who tempted us away from our comfortable farms."

"You still have the farms and you will go back rich as I promised you, or you will die up here as I also promised you. Meneer Prinsloo," he said to Oom Willem, "these are all hot-headed young men. Had I only promised them wealth from hunting they would not have left their firesides. So I said: 'There is danger, my friends. Of those who set out not all will return.' That was enough to set them on fire."

Everybody laughed. By now they had dismounted and sent their horses to water. Their sweatstained saddles stood on their flaps against the wagon wheels to dry.

"Food," Oom Willem said, "coffee. This is a great day for us."

"With a few more great days," Tante Maria said, "our dainties will all be eaten. As it is the melbos and konfyts are almost done."

"Brandy," Oom Willem shouted, "and wine, even if it is the last of it!"

When they had eaten they mounted fresh horses and rode off to escort their wagons in. The smous drew Harry aside.

"Harry," he said, "do you know what has happened at the Cape?"

"Carter, whom I wounded and who is likely to die, told me that I am my father's heir and that my half-brother, Captain Robinson, is illegitimate. Something I find hard to believe."

"All this is true, and more than true. You are Sir Harry Robinson. Your father is dead."

"Me, a Baronet—an English Baronet? You mean I am Sir Harry Bates, Bart." Harry began to laugh.

"Not Bates. Bates is no more. You are Sir Harry Robinson."

"Rosenberg, my friend, I am Harry Bates, the English Boer, and Harry Bates I will remain."

"The title and the money," the smous said. "There is a fine place—a great house, horses, objects of art, servants and much wealth."

"Let it go. It is not for me. It has come too late."

"Too late?"

"Yes. I am a wild hawk now, used to a hard life, to danger, to change. Do you think I could ever turn myself into a dunghill cock?"

" It is a fine dunghill, with sixty rooms, they say, and a pack of hounds and running horses of the best English strain."

" I am happy here, and here I will remain. This is now my land. But tell me the story."

They sat upon a large flat rock.

" You knew that your half-brother plotted your death?"

" I knew, but only to-day did I find out why."

" When your father died it all came out. Perhaps he was ashamed of the trick he had played your mother. Perhaps he hated your half-brother. The son who had so often mocked him. Which it was no one will ever know, but he left a letter. In the letter was the proof—the famous Captain Jack of the Tenth was a bastard. He had to send in his papers. To retire. He had no friends as you may remember. He had sycophants because he was rich, but not a friend. These men deserted him at once. He challenged three men to fight, but none of them would accept his challenge. They did not fight with bastards. They had learned about you, about you being his half-brother, and remembered how he had hounded you, had you flogged and would have had you shot or hung had he had his way. This was the end of Captain Jack. Even his doxy left him in public, saying that a bastard she did not mind, being one herself, but a man who would slay his own brother and torture him was not for her, and with that she spat in his face and left him on the arm of another."

" And Jack? What became of him? Where is he now?"

" Now?" Rosenberg echoed. " I have no doubt that he is now in hell. After all this he had nowhere to turn, so he robbed a merchant at pistol point. He hoped to escape to England in some disguise and needed money to bribe his way. But he was caught and condemned to the gallows, but later he escaped and was shot down."

" So he's dead?" Harry said. " His life of debauchery is over."

" Ja, Harry. It is all over for Captain Jack."

They returned to the laager together in time to see the newcomers' wagons being drawn into place. The defensive circle was now an elipse.

That night, as they sat round the fires, the smous told more of his party's trek. Of how they had found the graves along the road and stopped to pray, the predikant reading the funeral service.

" So it was read after all," Oom Willem said.

" Ja, it was read, and hymns were sung at the place of the Christmas laager."

They had first become aware of the battle that had taken place when the iron tyres of their wheels had crunched over the bones of the dead Zulus that were hidden in the grass. Then they had halted to search the veld, had found the Van der Merwes' graves and piled the Zulu skulls in a heap beside them.

Oom Willem said: " We have more dead here, more to be buried. A good man is gone and a man more evil than any I have previously encountered or even dreamed of is about to die if he is not already dead."

" In birth and in death all men are equal," the predikant said. " That is my belief, even of murderers, for they know not what they did."

" Then you think we should bury them together? The murderer and his victim? That they should lie side by side and have a single service for the two?" Oom Willem asked.

" Why not, Meneer? Are they not joined in death? The good and the bad, the black and the white. Can there be white without black, Meneer, or the light of day without the darkness of night? The living we can judge, the dead we must leave to God."

At dawn next day the graves were dug beside the trek pad. Two deep graves, three yards apart, and the bodies wrapped in blankets, lowered into them on a sling of riems. Dressed for Sunday, the women in their bonnets instead of kappies. The men who had beaver hats draped them in crêpe. The crowd stood with bowed heads listening to the funeral service; to the oration which followed, and then, as the graves were being filled in, changed back into their habitual clothes, inspanned their oxen, and with loud cries and whip cracks continued their advance. A man of theirs was dead, but eight more had come. They now saw men as guns, as stalwart arms, to work and fight. While Barend had lived they had loved him, he was their brother; to defend him they would have died. But dead he was dead, and none really mourned him but his brothers and his father's second wife. Francina was sad but able to forget her sadness in watching Harry talk to the smous, and riding first with one of the new arrivals and then another. Flip sulked because, having led him on, she now preferred the strangers. No one thought of Carter save to say that had they shot him sooner Barend would still be alive.

Behind the wagons the long snake of trodden grass wove its way past the bare red earth of the graves. A light wind stirred the veld, stroking the grass tips, smoothing them into waves of light and shadow as soft as a woman's hair. A steenbok came out of hiding to stare with dark eyes and wide-spread rabbit ears. A long-tailed widow bird hovered in uncertain, dipping flight. A beetle fell into a rut dug by a wagon wheel and, unable to climb out, followed the trek.

For the first time wheeled traffic had passed here. Now

that the white men and the wagons had gone, the slow
rhythm of the veld began again. The merging of life into
death and death into other forms of life. There was no
time here, since but for the road there had been no change
for a thousand years—nothing to differentiate to-day from
yesterday or yesterday from to-morrow.

38

THE PROMISED LAND

THE MOUNTAINS were before the Boers. They had begun as hills, and the way through them, through poort after poort and valley after valley, had seemed clear. Oom Willem spoke with confidence, that some now thought to be assumed, about how near they were to the Promised Land. But all knew that there was no turning back now, for the Kaffirs were behind them. That they did not attack here in this broken ground could only be due to protection of the Lord and the fact that these hills frightened them, for these were not mountain Kaffirs. Indeed, there were none here, for the mountains were too bleak, and the flats below them too rich for the tribes who lived there ever to leave them. So the Kaffirs left the mountains alone—an abode for spirits and devils. Nevertheless, they followed the Boers at a distance, ready to take advantage of any mistake that they might make.

And since there was no turning back and the land he sought must lie in front of them, Oom Willem made the best of things and put on this bold front of confidence, the expression on his face more calm than the questions in his heart. Their direction was right, of that he was sure, but what of the obstacles? He had gone wrong somewhere. There had been big mountains, he remembered them well, but he had not crossed them. They had passed them by to the right, to the east. He had not struck far enough west. It was the flood that had done it, and the Kaffirs, and the half-caste who had confused him with soft words and promises. But at the time he had indeed seemed God-sent. How else had he been able to describe the lands that he sought so well? Who could have imagined that Carter, who had heard him tell the story of this hunters' paradise by a hundred fires, would have instructed him in every detail? Carter, whom all had assumed dead, and who was dead now and buried beside his victim, the fine young man, Willem's almost son, whom he had struck down. How should he have suspected this man Tomaso? How should he? Yet Barend had, and he had brushed Barend aside. But Barend had been right, as all now knew to their cost. But how great the total cost would be none yet knew. Not the full price that they might have to pay for error.

Each day the wagons and loose stock climbed. There was never a place large or flat enough for a laager. The most they could do was to draw three or four wagons together to form some defensive triangles, or squares, and this only with some of the wagons. The others lay alone like anchored ships held only by the stones behind their wheels. There was water, plenty of it, in rushing mountain torrents, and grass, too, on the slopes between rock faces that towered up into bare, sharp grey peaks. All this was good, at least not too bad—to-day, now. But what of to-morrow?

As the dead must bury their dead so the to-morrows must take heed for themselves. Who knew what each day might hold? Each was like a cup, like an open hand, palm upward, filled with events, with unpredictable hours, that brought love to one and death to another. Disaster and success were but two sides of the same rix dollar. Disaster to them would be success to the Kaffirs who pursued them. God's face was on one side of the coin, and the devil's on the other, and each day that a man lived it was spun in the air of his years.

These were the thoughts of the old man. The wisdom of his years that he could pass on to no one. But this was a strange thing—that the good should so often turn to ashes in a man's mouth and the gall change suddenly to honey. Even this, this terrible climb that was bringing hardship and pain to all, might in the end prove good. But now it was not good.

" Now," he said aloud, " truly now I could cry: ' Call me Mara, for the Almighty hath dealt very bitterly with me.' "

But having cried this aloud he regretted it. For who was he to question the ways of God? And loudly, as if to dispute his own thoughts, he cracked his great whip with echoing shots across the backs of his oxen, sending the hawks that rested in the kranses screaming into the air.

Now everywhere the scene was the same as the spans faced the mountains. Oom Willem had been the first, but now every whip cracked. The drivers screamed their oxen's names: Witman, Rooiland, Bles, Witpens, Swartjie, Stompie, Bluikman, Bosveld, Geelbek, Donker, Ireland, Scotland, Engelsman, Klinkie.

The names and the whip claps came echoing back from the empty cliffs. For this was an empty world, bare of bush and trees, of life, clothed only with sparse harsh grass and spiked blood-red aloes, grouped like men and as tall, to illuminate the desolation with the candelabra of their flames.

Double spans of oxen, thirty or more to a wagon, belaboured with sjamboks, flung themselves into their yokes, their frightened eyes bursting from their sockets. One of Oom Willem's pole oxen died from its exertions, blood pouring from its mouth as it fell. This delayed the wagon line, and the wagon had to be held by hand till stones were found to prevent it slipping backward; the dead ox was dragged away and roughly butchered, while another was

inspanned. Then, after the delay, welcome enough to both
man and beast, they started off again, and the near silence
of the halt was broken once again by the sounds of their
advance. Men and women, even children, flung themselves
upon the great rear wheels of the wagons, and seizing the
spokes in their hands, forced them to turn. No one rode,
even the sick and the pregnant walked. The small children
staggered, clinging to their mothers' skirts, or were carried
in their arms. This was the assault of a mountain, a climb
that attacked these heights as if they were enemies, which
indeed they were, for to fail might mean death, something
that even the children seemed to understand.

Ahead, silhouetted against the sky, those below saw Oom
Willem hatless, his white hair blowing in the mountain
wind, his body swinging as he cracked his whip above his
beloved span. Hendrik was leading, for Willem Prinsloo, in
this crisis, preferred to drive himself. When others cursed
their beasts he called them endearing names—beloved, my
love, my heart—and not one of their skins was whip-
scarred. The voorslag of his long giraffe-hide whip clapped
above their backs, for these oxen were like children to him
and a man does not strike a child, and his heart was sore for
the brave ox that had died. Behind his wagon Tante Maria
plodded. A mountain climbing a mountain. Her face was
purple, her breath, like that of the draught oxen, came in
great gasps. She held her belly with both hands to support
it, while Francina, as light as a buck at her side, was torn
between laughter and tears at her Ouma's plight. All the
riding horses but Bloubooi were running loose with the
horse herd. Bloubooi's rein was held in Francina's hand as
he scrambled along behind her. Beside him came Salome,
who refused to leave him. About them were the dogs and
the rams, sometimes before and sometimes behind.

Harry Bates and the smous both pushed on the wheels of

the Prinsloo wagon when it seemed about to come to a shivering stop. Children, excited, frightened, or exhausted, according to their natures and strength, laughed, screamed and cried, demanding to be carried, demanding to be put down, ran forward or dropped back to be collected by the wagons in the rear where there was an eddy of lost children, a tail of them, like the tail of a kite.

Harry Bates was walking beside Francina when he noticed the first drift of mist. About them the long whips cracked over the backs of the straining oxen. The sjamboks lashed the wheelers as they leaned against the pole, sometimes almost on their knees so great their endeavour. Their flanks heaved, great gasps came from their open mouths. This was the worst ascent the trek had made. Finding this new range in front of them without a break, they had been forced to attack it frontally, like an enemy that could not be outflanked. The air still rang with the shouts of the drivers, with cries of encouragement, of anger, of despair, the barking of dogs, the lowing of cows that had lost their calves and calves crying for their dams, sheep and goats bleated, the tail of children laughed with the excitements or wept because of them. As the column climbed—wending its way between great rocks, crashing down through gulleys cut by the rains of a thousand storms, all wondered when it would end and how—for mountains had no end—and what lay beyond them.

They could not turn back now, though the fears and dangers of yesterday seemed like security when compared to those that they faced to-day. Below them, on their right, was a void, a deep cliff.

Looking down, Francina said: " An eagle, Harry. Have you ever seen an eagle from above before and looked down upon its back?"

" Yes, Cina, and I have seen something else before also, in

the mountains of the Cape." He pointed to some wisps of mist drifting like feathers below them.

"Mist," Francina said.

"Yes, mist, and I do not like it, not in the high hills. Not here."

And slowly, as they watched, it increased. The light, ephemeral drifting feathers, that had been almost ghostly and transparent, thickened and grew. The feathers became wool, became sheep, the sheep closed into solid flocks; into white blankets that hid the dark emptiness of the gorge, drew apart for a moment like curtains, and then closed again. But this was not all. The mist came down from above, also. At first it, too, was a light, a whirling drift that did no more than blur the outline of the surrounding peaks. Then it thickened and Harry sprang into action. Jumping on Francina's horse, tearing the reins from her astonished hand, he forced Bloubooi up the hillside to Oom Willem's wagon.

"Stop!" he shouted. "We must stop while there is still time."

"Stop? Why must we stop, jong?"

"The fog is coming down. Soon we shall not be able to see more than a yard. Stop now! While we can still see to find stones to put behind the wheels and outspan our beasts."

Flip, who was beside Oom Willem, did not wait for his order but ran back shouting: "Stop! Get stones beneath the wheels while we can still see. Span out and tie the beasts."

The drivers began to whistle to stop their oxen. The voorloopers threw small stones into their faces and the oxen halted on the steep incline, leaning into their yokes and holding the load. Horses or mules would have run back, Harry thought, as he helped to collect rocks to push behind the wheels of the heavily laden wagons.

It was only just done in time. Before the last ox was

tied to the trek tou the fog was over them. A thick white blanket that enveloped man and beast, so that each was alone, isolated, trapped, unable even to see the ground upon which it stood, or a man his own hand if he raised it to his face. And so night fell, none daring to move, all remaining still in the mist, as if they were dead men with weighted feet standing erect in water, and all, even the boldest of men, afraid, for this was beyond their experience, as was the loneliness of it, men being separated from their wives, and children from their mothers. And then, seeing there was no end to it, that the mist grew even thicker, weaving new blankets about them, wisp by wisp, they lay down, sinking to the ground where they stood, the men beside the wagons, the oxen beside their yokes.

Harry Bates, the smous, Francina, Bloubooi, Salome, the dogs and the rams, lay down beside each other, each listening to the breathing of the other.

Putting out his hand towards Francina, Harry touched the grey horse's skin. Bloubooi whinnied with pleasure, for he too was afraid. Francina lay against his flank, getting warmth from him. The dogs had their heads in her lap, the rams were pressed between her and the horse.

" It is like being blind," Harry said, " but everything is white instead of black."

" Ja," the smous said, " but also we know that above us the stars are shining and that in the morning the sun will burn up the mists, consuming them as fire burns up chaff. So, in the meantime, let us consider our own lives, for perhaps the Lord God had wrapped us each in his own blanket of fog for that purpose."

" What are you thinking about?" Harry asked.

" The same as you—girls," the smous said. " But you have a beautiful girl, separated from you only by the body of a friendly horse. Whereas I . . . "

"There are plenty of girls," Harry said.

"There are no girls for me," the smous said, laughing. "No girls with breasts like two young roes that are twins which feed among the lilies, whose necks are towers of ivory, and eyes like the fish pools of Heshbon."

"I have never seen a girl like that," Harry said.

"You have never seen a Jewish girl," the smous said. "They are all like that except the ones that are fat and ugly, and bad-tempered like the women of other races all over the world."

They all laughed. Francina said: "We must find you a wife, Meneer Rosenberg."

"You know very well that I think only of you, Francina. That having smelled the rose I am unlikely to pluck the thistle."

The smous was pleased with the effect he was creating. He had taken her mind off their situation, which he personally considered disastrous. Why should there be a way out of these mountains? And whether Oom Willem was the prophet that he appeared to be, a man inspired by God, or just a silly old fool in his dotage, time alone would show. But till it showed, they might as well make the best of things. This, he felt, this making the best of things, was one of his race's most valuable characteristics. If we Jews had not had this ability, he thought, we should have died out long ago.

Girls. He had not been thinking of girls, but to talk of them always turned men's thoughts from other things. He had been thinking of God. Of how each man was now alone, and able, did he so wish it, to do the arithmetic of his life, to balance the books, check the credit and the debit of his deeds. How few men ever remember, he thought, that "we brought nothing into this world, and it is certain we can carry nothing out."

As the sun rose the mist became paler, whiter, though no

less opaque. Then it began to dissipate from above in the same manner that it had risen from below the previous evening, getting more wispy and less dense. Soon the people could see each other and the wagons, though not their wheels nor their own feet on the ground. They looked as if they were wading through a sea of wool, and afraid to move since they still could not see where they were going, they merely shouted greetings to each other. The oxen had all stood up, arching and stretching their backs like dogs. Everything was beaded with moisture. Francina's hair and eyelashes were hung with diamond drops. The sheep's wool was wet. The men's clothes were soaked. The wagon tents dripped as if it had been raining. First, the highest peaks about them emerged. Then others. At last they could see where they stood, but they were upon an island, one of many that stood out in a white, woolly sea.

A cry of terror came from behind them. " Come! Oh come, someone! Help!"

Harry and the smous joined in the rush.

There was a wagon with one wheel over the white world below. Another yard and it would have gone over. The oxen had only just stopped in time the previous night and the driver had seen nothing. The beasts stood calmly on the edge of the precipice, unmoved, chewing the remnants of their cud. Below each ox was the dry black outline of its form. Within a yard of the span on the off side, the world ended and the void began.

" Quiet, you fools," Harry shouted. " Stand still! If you frighten the oxen all is lost. Where is their leader?"

A frightened Hottentot came forward.

" Speak to them," Harry said. " Call them by name softly, and swing them inward, but not enough to move the wagon."

" *Kom*," the boy said, and took up the riem that was still

looped about the two leaders' horns. They followed him.
The other oxen moved with them, inward and back.

"Now outspan," Harry said.

Slowly, and with infinite precaution, the oxen were made
loose. Now the wagon had to be off-loaded. It took an hour
before everything was out upon the veld.

In the meantime Harry Bates and Flip had been looking
at the wheel that overhung the cliff. The rocks here seemed
loose and the edge most insecure. It they pulled the wagon
forward by hand, swinging the disselboom inward, the off
hind wheel sticking over the cliffside might bring it down,
a fall that would include the wagon.

"The wheel must come off," Harry said.

"Ja," Flip said, "but that will not be an easy job."

Harry said: "It must be done."

"Ja, my friend, but by whom? It is not a job I want,"
Flip said. "Nor will I tell a boy to do something of which I
am myself afraid."

Oom Willem and Francina joined them. "It must come
off," Oom Willem said. "We cannot lose a wagon."

Harry took off his coat.

"What are you going to do?" Francina asked.

"Take off the wheel. Bring me riems, good ones, and a
hammer."

With a hammer in his hand, Harry crept under the wagon.

"Hold down your wheel," he said, "in case I tip it when
I lean upon the axle."

Four men held the wheel. With his left hand on the axle,
his body over the emptiness below, Harry knocked up the
lynch pin with the hammer, put his hand between the
spokes and picked it out from the nave. Now he fastened
two long riems round the felloes and the tyre and passed
them back under the wagon bed to Flip.

"I want a crowbar now," he said. "I am going to knock

the wheel off the axle. It will fall and swing, so be ready.
Don't let it go, and don't let it pull you over, for it will be
heavy and fall suddenly."

After three sharp blows the wheel trembled on the edge of
the axle. " Be ready," Harry shouted. " Now pull!" and
he struck. The wheel fell, jerking the men who held the
doubled riems forward. Then it swung like a pendulum
below them dislodging rocks as it rubbed against the cliffside. At last it stopped and was pulled up. Now the wagon
was drawn in upon three wheels, and all doubt about Harry
Bates as a man and a leader vanished from his companions'
minds.

The mist was going now, but still the valley below them
was hidden. It lay like a white lake at their feet. Then
a sudden wind sprang up, striking them with an icy hand
and sweeping the remnants of the fog away like dust before
a broom.

Oom Willem gave a great shout. " Canaan!" he cried.
" The Promised Land! We are here!" Like Moses he had
led his people through the wilderness.

They were there! There it lay, a thousand feet below
them in its rich green and fertile glory, but between them
was the mountainside that was almost a cliff. Baboons,
goats and perhaps the boldest of men could descend into the
Promised Land, but neither the big stock nor the wagons.

A gasp went up from the Boers. Oom Willem threw his
hat upon the ground and knelt. " Pray," he said. " Let us
pray. The Lord has led us here and He will show us a way
down."

Many followed his example, falling on their knees at once.
Harry turned on those who still stood, whispering. " Pray,
you bloody fools," he said, his cavalry past taking charge
of his tongue. " Pray," he said, " for without God's help
we'll never reach the bottom!"

39

THE DESCENT

WITH MIXED feelings the Boers set about making their camp. A laager was neither possible nor necessary up here. But they had arrived. Their Moses had led them out of the wilderness. The Promised Land was there, and from this distance fully up to their expectations, but never had so near a place seemed so far away. In distance, before God, ten yards. Stand on the cliffside, drop a stone, and it fell into this earthly paradise. But a man was not a stone, and for a man there was an almost vertical descent of a thousand feet.

Children were warned to keep away from the edge. Cattle and horses were herded away, but the goats and sheep ate along the crest, and even over the side of the krans. And why not, for these were mountain animals, created by God to climb among the rocks.

Leaving the others, Harry went off alone to explore. They were on a saddleback. On one side was a deep kloof filled with trees, with a raging torrent at its base. On the other lay the valley that Oom Willem had described so often. But his party must have approached it from another quarter and forgotten this great krans that cut it off from the outer world. Or, and this was also a possibility, this was not his valley at all, but another that resembled it and looked as if it would do, if ever they got down to it, quite as well. It was well watered and full of grass. No more could be asked than this.

Shading his eyes, Harry saw elephant, buffalo and herds of zebra and wildebeeste. He saw four giraffes and knew there must also be much small game invisible from this distance.

He walked on slowly. The hog's back or neck ran straight for two miles and then ended in a mountain running into it at right angles. This ended his search. They could go no farther, so the descent must be made between the place where he now stood and the outspan where the wagons waited. If the worse came to the worst they could get down there by taking the wagons to pieces and carrying them down a plank and a wheel at a time. Much stock would be lost, and men too might fall, but it could be done. The only problem left, one which must be dealt with too when the time came, was how, when they did get down, would they ever get out again? If Oom Willem had made a mistake and there was no other road, and this instead of being an open-ended valley, was only a great cup in the hills, in which, by some cataclysm, the wild beasts he saw had become enclosed in the distant past and had remained, breeding each according to its kind in seclusion ever since. This seemed unlikely, and he felt that since the beasts had found a way to come and go, they would do the same, following some elephant path till they reached the open plains to the south again. Usually a wagon could go where an elephant had gone before, since they were most adept at choosing the easiest way and lowest gradient. Strange roads they made, like keyholes through the forest, narrow at the bottom where they walked but wide above where the brushing of their great bodies against the bush in their passage had pruned the branches to accommodate their bulk.

With these thoughts in his mind Harry came slowly back, walking on the very edge of the cliff and pausing every few yards to look down. At last he found a place. Not good.

In fact, had the others not been so bad, impossible. It was merely better than the others, no more than that, and still impossible to any but the boldest drivers forced by desperation to take their chance. He went swiftly back.

" Well?" Oom Willem said.

" I have found a way."

" A good way?"

" No, a bad way, as bad as can be, only the best there is. With ten men in a week we can make a road of sorts. With picks and crowbars we can cut out the mountainside and move the smaller rocks. Then, with such skills as we have and God's help, we shall be able to get the wagons down, slowly, one by one."

More than a week passed before the road took shape. First, in order to get over the ridge, a cutting had to be made. Then, working sometimes in the steepest places with riems on their belts fastened to pegs driven into the cliff face, the men levered away rocks that went rolling and bouncing down to land with a crash in the valley. They cut into the krans and dragged down trees that were set up like corduroy at right angles to the face. They were inset on the cliffside, lashed to posts sunk into the outer slope and then covered with branches and earth and stones from above. It was never a road and could never become one.

A toboggan track was how the Reverent Charles Gordon described it. " Aye," he said, " with a bit of snow upon it, what a fine slide it would make." But he worked at it with the others. So did the smous, but with many complaints: " Man," he said to Harry, " fancy me working with my hands. Me, a Jew! Do you know that this makes me very remarkable among my people, for we only work with our heads, calculating our profits and working out the rates of our usury."

They all laughed, for he was among the most skilful at the more delicate and dangerous tasks.

Before they begun the road, Harry and Flip climbed down the cliff to explore the valley and found that it led out past lesser hills to the south. They had come upon it from the worst quarter where it ended abruptly in the krans they were going to descend. The game was plentiful; the soils of two kinds—black and red—and both were deep and plentiful. There was a strong stream that ran down the valley, beginning in a vlei that was fed from springs in the hills, which would make watering lands a simple matter. Eventually many morgen could be irrigated. The two men had now become infected with Oom Willem's dream. They saw farms here and a little township—a dorp, with a village street, a church, a courthouse and a school.

They returned, jubilant with their news of plenty, withholding only one item. That there were many lions about—many more than they had met elsewhere. This spot seemed to suit lions to perfection. It was true that in the camp they had heard an occasional roar coming up, muffled from below, but the amount of spoor when they got down had surprised both men and they had seen lions, some alone, some in pairs, and one pride of eight—a family of various ages. This had been a splendid sight. First, stalking out of a reed bed, had come a great black-maned male, then a lioness with two grown cubs. Then came another lioness with three smaller cubs, loose-skinned, big-footed creatures, plodding doggedly along after their mother like immense spotted kittens.

But even the lions were a good sign, for you did not find so many lions in bad country. It had to be rich to support them, and lions could be shot. "Ja," Flip said, " we will have much sport in hunting them."

Bates said: " We will have to get Tante Maria to show us

how to kill lions." for such had been their good fortune she alone had had an adventure with the king of beasts. Still they said nothing. Why frighten people? When they got to the bottom they would find out. They did not even tell Oom Willem. Nor did they tell him that it was not his valley. There were no five little hills. There was no great rock outcrop rubbed smooth as marble by scratching elephants. But having come so far and found this, it was good enough. It was the best, the fairest and most private place they had yet seen. It was Canaan, and if there was another one—the one Oom Willem had described—let others have it. This was theirs by right of adventure, of blood, and occupation.

In the camp the girls were both excited and bored. Miemie looked over the men as if they were cattle while she swung her hips and made eyes at them from under her kappie which she often allowed to slip back and hang from her shoulders. She no longer wore her leather mask, and her pretty face was soft, smooth and white as milk. Of the men who had come in the wagons only one was married. They had come with the smous to hunt elephants, but if they liked the country, they said, they would return, bringing new wives and stock with them.

The youngest among the newcomers was Adriaan Theron, and it was at him that Miemie set her trap. Very tall and strong, with blue eyes and almost yellow hair and, from his clothes, guns and servants, rich. It was him or the predikant for her. If she could get either of them she would be content, she told Francina.

"You know what I said to Meneer Theron, Cina, last night when he returned from working on the road? I said: 'Meneer Theron, why go back to the Colony for a wife? Surely you could find one among us? We are pioneer girls, voortrekkers who know the wilds and are inured to danger. What would a little bread-and-butter miss do up here?' He did not answer me," she said, " but I could feel his eyes upon me. Ah," she said, " there was nothing he missed, and my bowels turned to water."

" Ja," Francina said, " I am sure they did, and also for all the other young men. It is in my heart you see nought but men."

" And you nought but horses. Surely it is more maiden-like to think of men? But that is not true either, for you play with men as if they were toys, sending them mad and not knowing what you do, as if you were still a child. Mag-tig, if I sent a man mad I should know what to do. If I sent him mad now, with a predikant sent to us by God Himself, I should make him marry me, and . . . "

" And if there was no predikant?" Francina asked.

" Then I should lie with him and bear him a son to bind him to me, and we would be married in the eyes of God and our people till a predikant came our way. Do you think, Cina, that here, beyond the English, and beyond the law, men and maids will wait? No, no," she cried, " they will marry themselves in the eyes of God first and the laws of the Church and man will follow later."

Francina put her hand on her friend's arm, drew her to her and kissed her. " I hope you get him, Miemie. I hope you get him."

" But which, Cina? And while I seek the one I may lose the other. This is what I fear—to fall between two stools. And since one is the predikant, can he marry himself to me, do you think?"

To prevent the children running quite wild and turning into white Kaffirs, Tante Maria had begun a school for them. Slates had been brought out and a cane with which to beat manners and letters into the rude, the stupid and recalcitrant. Their clothes were washed, the knots combed out of their hair and the oldest set to teach the younger. Miemie was inspanned to instruct arithmetic and teach the tables which she scarcely knew herself. But the plan was good and the adults grateful for the respite they were given.

Tante Maria taught geography and history, both some-what vaguely, for she only knew that the English had come from over the sea to take their country from them and liberate the slaves. And that about Africa was the sea which, for those who had not seen it, she described as a big dam so salt as to make it useless. For her the world was flat and the sun went round the world. In the end, what she taught was of little importance, for the children would read nothing but the Bible and calculate little beyond the numbers and value of their stock when they grew up.

Hardihood, courage and resource were of more value here than book learning, and Tante Maria's tales of hunters, Kaffir fighters and heroes would live in the children's minds till they died. The school was conducted among the rocks and the children called by the ringing of a bell. The bell was, in fact, the most academic aspect of Tante Maria's school for young voortrekkers.

At last the road was finished. Oom Willem, Flip and Bates believed that by exercising the greatest care the wagons could be brought down the mountain. But they had to be prepared for the hazards of their descent, and kraals built at the bottom to hold the stock when it was driven down. In order to avoid a multitude of small enclosures, big ones were made and the herds amalgamated. Despite the losses there still remained one hundred and eight horses of all kinds, seven hundred and forty cattle, not including two hundred trained working oxen, and over two thousand fat-tailed sheep and goats.

Oom Willem's wagon was to be the last one down. It was decided that the Beyers' should be the first and they set about the preparations that were needed. It was first emptied of all small things that could be carried down by hand. The cases and barrels of provisions and furniture were lashed securely to the wagon rails. Holes were bored into the planks of the wagon bed through which extra riems were passed to hold them still more firmly in place. The wagon was then jacked up and the great rear wheels removed. Two selected trees were drawn under it by oxen pulling them forward from the rear by their trunks till they could go no farther. The trunks were then made fast under the wagon, the jacks removed and the wagon stood supported by the springy branches of the thorn trees upon which it lay like a sled on runners. The front wheels were now lashed so that they would not turn, and riems were tied to the near rails so that the men who went down with it could pull it towards the mountainside if it began to veer over the cliff's edge. All this was done ten yards from the beginning of the ramp. Just enough room was left to inspan the two pole oxen—the wheelers who alone would drag the wagon, now more of a sledge than a wheeled vehicle, down this terrible road where destruction was certain if the smallest error was made.

The Beyers' wagon was chosen because of Flip's boldness and skill as a driver, and the quality of his pole oxen, two immense beasts that Barend had trained five years ago, which stood sixteen hands and were as tame as dogs.

Flip led them to the disselboom himself, raised the yoke, dropped it upon their willing necks, and fastened the strops on to the skeys. Then he gave the lead riem to his bushman voorlooper and climbed on to the wagon, his long whip with the lash rolled round the bamboo stock in his hand. By touching either ox with its tip he could guide them.

About the wagon were grouped the whole trek, with Oom Willem, the predikant and Harry nearest to the cliff's edge. Facing the people, the predikant raised his hand. " Let us pray," he said. " Let us pray for a safe descent for our brother and his leader, and for the brave oxen, too."

Everyone knelt down, men, women and children. The smallest children, too small to kneel, stood beside their mothers. The babies the women put on the ground in front of them, beside their husbands' hats.

" Oh Lord," the predikant began. " Oh Lord, who so far has blessed this trekkie, saving it time and again from danger and death, extend Thy hand once more, we pray Thee, to support this frail wagon in its terrible descent. Support it, Lord, that these Thy children, when they reach the promised land below may raise a tabernacle to glorify Thy Holy Name. Amen."

" Amen! " echoed the people.

" Amen!" said a child who had been dreaming, after the rest had done.

" God bless you, Flip Beyers," the parson said.

Oom Willem shook his hand. " You will be the first," he said. " Ja, the first man in Canaan."

Flip called to his boy. The boy, who had been squatting by the wet black noses of the oxen, rose, turned his back on them, and faced the road ahead. The men who were going to hold the wagon from falling grasped the riems. " You are ready?" Flip cried, looking round and raising his hat.

" We are ready."

" Then loop!" he cried. " Loop! Rooiland, Rooiman, loop!" His voice rose to the scream that the cattle knew and loved. They leaned into their yokes and stopped, surprised, as if they could not understand their failure to move the wagon.

" Loop!" Flip shouted again. The oxen pulled harder, the bound front wheels scraped along the ground, cutting a furrow. The trees behind them swept the veld bare as if it was a broom as the oxen moved slowly forward. Now they were off the flat, down the ramp and on the road. They disappeared. Only the end of the tent, cocked up into the air like the back of a great grey sheep, was visible against the skyline as the people crowded forward.

Two men ran to take the riems that trailed behind to help hold the wagon back and prevent it from overrunning the oxen in the steepest parts, for there were places where the fall was less than two in one. From above they heard Flip's voice calling to his beasts, " Rooiman, Rooiman!"— he was the outer ox—to bring him inward towards the face of the mountain. They heard the men on the riems shouting as rocks fell, bounding down into the paradise below.

One by one, at a rate of two or three a day, the other wagons followed. Some of the riding horses had to be blindfolded before they could be led down. Milk cows and working oxen were driven down with blows, their tails twisted and even bitten by their herders, when too terrified to go on they hesitated and came to a stop. The smaller objects of household gear that had been left above were brought down by hand. And one woman, too sick to walk, was carried, tied into a roughly constructed stretcher.

From above where Oom Willem's wagon stood alone among the rubbish and desolation of the earlier encampment, his party looked down upon the new settlement, upon the tops of the white tented wagons, the kraals, the livestock smaller than toys and the people, unrecognisable, no larger than small ants.

Flip, Harry Bates and four others had climbed up to help Oom Willem with his descent. By now all were practised; deep ruts that held the sliding wheels had been carved out of the road, and the worst danger spots were known. With Oom Willem driving and Hendrik leading, while Flip and Harry held the riems and shouted encouragement and advice, the great wagon—the last of the trek to descend— slid to safety.

Only the horses remained above, because being wilder than the cattle, men could not yet be spared to herd them in the valley. Up here they could not go far and the grass that the cattle had eaten sufficed them since they liked it short. Francina remained with them, with some servants and tame Kaffirs, watching Oom Willem's wagon go down.

Then her work began. She was going to bring the horses down.

At last it was done. Now everyone was down and every beast.

" I'll water him," Hendrik said, taking Bloubooi's riem from Francina's hand. The stock watering place was at the stream half a mile away. The people drew theirs from near by.

" Thank you, Hendrik," Francina said, sitting down. ' I'm tired." She had worked hard rounding up the main horse herd, forcing them to the edge of the road, and then riding Bloubooi through the mob to the front, where she dismounted and holding him by the nose band of his head collar had led him down. Seeing him go, the others followed. But she had been frightened. Not afraid of falling herself, but that Bloubooi should slip or that the others would bolt suddenly, urged too hard by the men behind them, and overrun her.

She watched Hendrik lead Bloubooi off through the trees.

There was stock scattered everywhere—horses, cattle, flocks of sheep and goats. The wagons lay at rest now in a sea of grass that came up to their axles but was being swiftly trampled down and would soon disappear. Already it was a wagon village—a street, for they each had their appointed positions, equidistant from each other, and some of the Boers, the first down, had already raised the framework of Hartebeeste houses and were cutting sods to wall them. This was the way Oupa had said it would be. Ja, the way he had seen it. First wagons and rough turf houses, and then cottages, whitewashed and neatly thatched with grass. The blue smoke that now rose from the cooking fires in front of the wagons which would one day be a street, would then pass out of chimneys into the sky. It was a chimney and a hearth that made a home. There would be gardens and fruit trees, and a church with a bell. It would be wonderful to live in a village like this with all her friends.

She wondered how she had ever stood the isolation of the farm at the Cape. I stood it, she thought, because I knew no better, for like all women I like the company of my kind, the life of a town, for to her their line of wagons, now permanently encamped, was a town. The picnic was ended. She began putting her boy's clothes away and dressing as a girl. In the last few hours she seemed to have grown up. She felt that the descent of the mountain was her last adventure. Everything would be peaceful now. The farm seemed very far away. The wild rides, the horse pistols, the trek, had all fallen from her. She had crept out of the past like a snake casting its skin, and now sat resplendent in her new pink cotton dress with a quilted pink kappie on her head, her hair brushed up in a golden crown about her brow as if it was Sunday. She was thinking of Harry Bates—Sir Harry—and how wonderful he was. A man who could have gone back over the sea and been important, but who had given it all up to remain with them—a Boer like themselves. "All that I care about is here," he had said. What could he have meant?

Hendrik had led the horse away from his nooi to water and was bringing him back to the klein meisie whom he loved like his own child. His children had gone, his wife was dead; Francina was all that was left to him, she and Oubaas and Tante Maria, the woman that was so like a queen ant in appearance, or a great maggot wriggling along, but strong. Ja magtig! She was strong, both in mind and body. And the horse. He loved the horse, Bloubooi, who had the intelligence of a man. The dogs were at his heels for they seldom left the horse, since he and Francina were usually together.

The long rooigras parted before Hendrik's feet. So high was it that its heads brushed his thighs. This was a rich, fat land. They would be happy here. Over the crook of his left arm he had his double-barrelled gun, for no one since the trek had begun was permitted to move out of the camp unarmed. To his right was a bunch of horses with a mare and a foal somewhat apart from them. Hendrik looked at them, recognising them as the Oubaas's stock—a blue roan mare with a dark foal that would one day be grey and finally turn white like the horse he led, that was its sire. As he looked at the mare, a lion sprang upon her and she screamed.

The riem was torn out of Hendrik's hand as Bloubooi charged, his lips drawn back, his teeth bared. The riem had burned through Hendrik's palm drawing blood from it. He leaped after the horse. The lion had the mare down. It had jumped on to her back, and with its left paw had pulled her head round as it crouched upon her withers. Bloubooi attacked with chopping hoofs. The lion reared and leaving the mare seized his muzzle, dragging him down.

Hendrik, now only a few yards away, put up his gun and fired. There was only a hollow click as the hammer struck the flint. As the lion turned on him he pulled the second trigger. The gun misfired again. He drew his knife. This was the end. No man could face a lion with nothing but a knife. But no man would run away, to be killed running, like a fleeing buck. The dogs now flung themselves upon the lion. With one blow of his paw he killed Wolf, striking him in the head and tearing it half off his body. Wagter closed with him, seizing his mane and hanging on while the great beast turned on Hendrik, who, thrusting his left arm down the lion's throat, seized and twisted his tongue as he drove his knife into its heart. But as he struck the lion moved. The knife killed Wagter, who fell dead at his feet. Hendrik knew his end had come. The lion's foul breath was in his face as its jaws closed over his neck and throat. He gave a gasping cry and died.

40

THE PLOUGH

FRANCINA WAS not the only one who had heard the screams of both man and horse. With the others she ran down the track that led to the water. She was the only woman and was the only one unarmed. Harry Bates led the way. The smous behind him; so were Fourie and his brothers. Other men followed behind them.

Again Harry was furious with her. "Why are you here?" he shouted over his shoulder.

"It is my horse and my man."

"This is no place for you. If the lion is there, do not move. Do not run away or scream."

"What do you think I am, a frightened woman?" Francina panted, wishing she had on trousers again instead of her pink dress.

"I do not know what you are—a boy or a girl—only that you are a nuisance, always causing trouble and in the way."

Her reply was never made, for they had come on the scene of the disaster before she could reply.

In a little dell, a cuplike depression in the veld, they found them all. The big grey horse, his silken coat blotched with blood. Hendrik dead across his body. One of the dogs lying a few yards away where it had been flung, its head crushed by a blow from the lion's paw, the other beside Hendrik with his knife in its body. The mare the lion had killed lay still farther off, her foal, disconsolate, was nuzzling her body.

"Stay there, and do not move," Harry said.

Move! She could not have moved. She stood as if frozen as horror overcame her. Thinking of all the love here that was lost. Her love for this man and these beasts and theirs for her. The years they had lived together. All that they had seen and shared. The wild hunts and gallops, the camps, the memories of home—and Hendrik. Hendrik who taught her to ride and tend a horse. Hendrik, the brown man who had been a kind of elder brother to her. All were gone. Their lives run out upon the veld. For blood was life. How odd that it should be all mixed here—the blood of man, horse and dog. She put up her hands to cover her face to hide the sight, and leaned back against a tree.

Harry said: " I'll kill the lion. Hendrik will be avenged."

" Ja, Harry," Francina said. " But it will not bring him back, nor my Bloubooi nor my dogs."

Sobs now shook her badly.

" I'll take you back," he said, and with his arm about her heaving shoulders Harry led her home.

What could one do with a girl like this? What could he do? How could he tell her he loved her when she did not seem to know whether she was a girl or a boy? She had teased poor Barend. She had sent Carter insane, and Flip was following in his footsteps. But what went on in her mind and heart? Too much had happened to him for him to risk more hurt. If he must love her let it be as it had been before on the koppie after his fight with Carter. Love her, he thought, yes, but only as a child—a beautiful wayward child.

Behind them the other men were carrying Hendrik home.

Tante Maria laid out the body with the aid of the girls who sobbed and wept as they worked. Francina, now recovered, came to look at Hendrik.

" He was good and brave," she said.

Both girls let out piercing shrieks and renewed their tears. Tante Maria stopped them gently.

"I loved him, also," she said. "Ja, and before God I even love you, too, though it is hard to believe, and might even shed tears if either of you were eaten by some wild beast."

This failed to calm the girls who now flung themselves into each other's arms and wept even more bitterly.

Eva said: "I wish we were home. Why did we ever come?"

Sara said: "We loved him and he loved us both. We bear his fruit," she patted her swollen belly.

"So it was he!" Tante Maria said.

"Ja, ja," echoed the girls.

"Well, it is better than a stranger, I suppose, but you are bad, wicked girls."

"We are just girls," they said.

Francina went to her Oupa.

"Oupa," she said, "we have suffered a great loss."

"Ja, my child."

"Hendrik my friend, my horse and my dogs."

"Ja, a tragedy."

"We must do him honour," Francina said. "The first man to die here in our new home, the first to lie in our own graveyard."

"I have decided where it will be," Oom Willem said. He pointed to the two big trees that grew near the cliff they had come down. "But I had thought I should be the first," he said, almost with regret.

Francina said: "Oupa, I want your coffin."

"My coffin?"

"Ja, for Hendrik. We must do him honour. You said so yourself."

"It is too big," Oom Willem said. "He would rattle about in it like a pea in a saucepan."

" I will pack him up with fresh herbs and flowers,"
Francina said. " Oupa, give me your coffin. I will arrange
with the smous to bring you a new one from the Colony.
It will come in time, for you are like a great tree that will
live for ever."

" Maria," Oom Willem shouted. " Maria, get all that
rubbish of yours out of my coffin. I need it."

" Unfortunately you do not need it yet."

" I need it, I say. And anyway, what right have you to
fill my coffin with rubbish? I never complained, I never
even complained of you sitting on it, rubbing the grain off
it with your great behind. Ja, for a thousand miles you sat
upon my coffin . . ."

" I polished it," Tante Maria shouted. " Is that all the
thanks I get for polishing your coffin?"

" But all in one place, Maria, and you have done more
than polish it, you have warped, you have dented it.
Anyway, empty it at once and get it out. We are going to
bury Hendrik with honour, for he is the first of our dead
in Canaan."

So it came to pass that Hendrik, his body surrounded with
grass and flowers, packed in Oom Willem's great coffin,
was laid to rest between the two enormous marula trees at
the foot of the krans. And for the first time, so far north in
this wild land, the solemn words were spoken, " Man that is
born of woman halts but a short time to live and is full
of misery. He cometh up and is cut down like a flower . . .
The Lord hath taken the soul of our dear brother unto
Himself. We therefore commit his body to the ground . . .
Earth to earth, ashes to ashes, dust to dust. The Lord gave
and the Lord hath taken away. Blessed be the name of the
Lord."

A salvo of shots that echoed up into the hills were fired
over the grave, and the first part of the ceremony was com-

plete. The minister, dressed as a minister, the people in their best clothes, now stood watching as the child born upon the trek was baptised into the Church of God. So, in one ceremony held in the shade of the two great trees under the African sky were their first dead in this place ushered out of this world and their firstborn welcomed into it.

All men were there but the hunters, Harry Bates and Nzobo, his Zulu.

With Hendrik and Bloubooi dead, the man and the horse that had been so much in her life, and the dogs gone, Francina felt empty, as if she had been made of water and had cried herself away, so that her skin held nothing, so that she was lighter than air—a seed that could be blown anywhere at any time by any wind and did not care. All that was left to her now was Harry, and he did not like her. He would not meet her eyes or look at her. He had been tender when Bloubooi died. Ja, just as he had been tender before on the kopje—tender, but holding her like a child.

She stamped her foot and shook out her hair. A child! A child! Before God she was a woman and able to bear him a child, and now the fool had gone out after the lion with his Zulu, as if two dead men were better than one. He had said: "Hendrik was my friend, too, so I will kill the lion and avenge him. Besides," he had gone on, "we cannot have man-eaters about, not in this new paradise." He had laughed and had patted her again, as if it was a joke. This verdompte Englishman was beyond understanding. What could one do to such a man, to a man so blind that he could not see a maiden's love? Or saw it and refused her in disgust. Others might have acted thus, thinking of Carter, but he knew. He knew she was untouched. He had been there to save her.

Somehow she must attract him. Make him love her.
How her heart ached, and now she could not even ride over
the veld with her dogs at her heels to ease the pain. Her
horse and dogs were dead. Now she must sit like the other
women whom she had always despised, nursing her wounds,
licking them like a dog with the tongue of her memories.
She thought of Harry on the day he had brought the great
horse to the farm, and how she had stood beside her Oupa
staring at him with her finger in her mouth. Had she loved
him even then? Had her love for Bloubooi been another
part of her love for this man, so that she had felt nearer to
him when she was upon the horse's back? Two men he had
killed for her—the man on the mountain who would have
taken her, and Carter. Why had he done this if he was
without feeling for her? Why? Why?

Oom Willem sat beside his battered wagon upon the
sea-cow's skull that had served him for a seat as it had his
father before him. It was one of the things Tante Maria had
wished to leave behind, but he had refused. "It was my
father's," he had said.

They had arrived at last. He had led his people through
the wilderness. A thousand miles and more in a year of
travel. Ja, he thought again, like Moses leading the Israelites. That is what I am like. The idea pleased him. He was
also glad to have arrived alive. At times he had not thought
to do so. Verily, death's angel that had hovered over him
like an aasvoel so many times, and had now left him, thanks
to God's mercy.

In front of him on the veld was his English plough.
Smiling softly he gazed at it. Then he got up and patted it
as if it was alive.

Tante Maria, a little thinner than she had been, looked
up from the fire where she was cooking. "Well," she said

with a loud sniff, " now that we are here, if indeed we are here, I hope that you are satisfied."

" I am satisfied, woman," he said. " God has brought us to the Promised Land."

" Ja," she said, standing with her hands on her hips. " Ja, the Promised Land, but is that a name for a place? Where is it? That is what I wish to know. Where are we? It is my belief that we are in Egypt, having passed the source of the Nile a month ago. Or in the moon, perhaps, so strange a land is this, so wild and savage, with my baby crying her heart out because her horse is dead, her dogs are killed, and the boy who brought her up torn to pieces and eaten by savage beasts. Willem," she said, " that is something to think about. A good Christian boy in a lion's belly, and as if that was not enough, pursued by the Englishman whom she loves. Ja, ja," she cried; " and our Hendrik inside the lion bobbing up and down as he runs. The Englishman and his Kaffir chasing him, and as like as not, to join Hendrik should these beasts attack them . . ."

" We have buried Hendrik so he is not in the lion's belly and there was only one lion," Oom Willem said. " I saw the spoor."

" Ja, one. But why should he remain alone? Without doubt he has wives and friends, all hungry for human meat. And you, you silly old man, you stand there patting a plough as if it were a horse or a woman."

Oom Willem was not upset. Nothing could upset him now. He regretted Hendrik's death, he had been a good and faithful servant. But death now seemed to him more of a friend than an enemy. He had arrived at the place where he would die. He would never go hence. He never wished to. He looked at the mountain they had come down. At the road the Englishman had carved in its side. That was where he would lie buried between the great marulas that

F.H.

grew there, beside Hendrik, master and man lying side by side. He pointed. " That is where we shall lie. That is where all who die here will lie, in the shade of the trees at the foot of the berg."

" Me lie? Me dead? Magtig, Oom Willem, it is I who will lay you out. I even have the silver coins in my kist that I set aside to put upon your eyelids. Ja," she said, " and a silk scarf to tie up your sagging jaw. I have made provision for everything. In death you are my Jan's brother and must have the best."

" I did not say you would die first, Maria. I wish to be the first, and then you can lie beside me at last, thus achieving in death something you have wanted ever since you first laid eyes upon me."

" Oh! Oh!" Tante Maria screamed. " That you should say such things as that to your deceased brother's wife!"

Harry and the Zulu had no difficulty in picking up the spoor. The lion, when he had been driven away from Hendrik's body, had made for a sluit that ran only in the summer rains and there on its sandy bed were the marks of its great pugs. Both men had guns and walked in single file. Bates leading the way with caution. This was not a beast to be trifled with. They had a good dog held on a leash with them—one on whose nose they could count if they were at fault. When night fell they had gone ten miles. Harry had expected to come up with the lion much sooner. It looked as if he knew they were after him. Perhaps they should have taken more precautions, waited till the next day, brought food and blankets. But they had thought they would find the lion laid up nearby in some clump of lala palms or scrub. Now it was dark and the lion, if he chose to exert it, had the advantage over them.

Quickly, before the full night fell, they collected wood.

Fortunately, there was much of it nearby, trees washed down by storms and wedged against the rocks or lying loose on the stream bed. So with a fire in front of them, their backs to the bank and their loaded guns across their knees, the two men waited, dozing when they could, for the dawn.

Harry stared at the stars, bright in the spring sky. Barend gone, and now Hendrik. These two men he had admired greatly. Hendrik's devotion to Francina had been like Nzobo's to him, a bond as great or greater than that of blood. The horse, too. The horse that he had brought to the farm all those years ago, and that Francina had loved with such passion. Both the boy and the horse must be avenged.

He wished he knew what Francina felt about him. It seemed to him that since that day on the koppie she had avoided him. That she was ashamed because he had held her almost naked in his arms. At that instant he could have taken her. He knew it and so did she. This was the key to her shame. What stood between them. That she, a virtuous maid, had offered herself. He had loved her, but she had been going to marry Barend. Now, with Barend dead . . .

He spoke to his man. " If you loved a maid what would you do?"

" Take her, lord, unless she ran too swiftly. Oh, my chief, and my friend, I see into your heart and know your love. That is why we pursue this lion so that you may lay its skin at her feet. But fear not the outcome, lord, for I have seen her eyes. They are soft for you, like those of a calf in its pen, crying for its mother's milk. Lord," he said, " a maid runs from a man in two ways, either like a klipspringer leaping among the rocks, risking her life and never looking back, or she runs not so fast, looking over her shoulder, towards a mealie field where the plants are tall and the ground soft to fall upon. These, lord, are the two ways of a maiden. There are no others. It is my heart that the maid you desire desires you also, and will seek a private and soft place when you pursue her."

He got up to put more wood upon the fire.

When the morning came they drank water from a pool— the lion had stopped there too, to quench his thirst— tightened their belts against their hunger, and went on. Sometimes they lost the spoor, then the dog, whimpering between fear and excitement, found it again. The lion remained in the sluit which at last ended in a wooded cleft that separated one of the foothills of the berg from another. Here the dog, shivering with fright, lay down and refused to move.

"We are near," Harry whispered.

Their guns cocked at the ready, they went forward. Before they had gone ten paces the lion charged, coming downhill with tremendous leaps, roaring his fury, his mouth open, his eyes blazing, his tail erect above his back. Harry fired the bullet in his right barrel and missed. With his second barrel, loaded with buckshot, he struck the lion in the foot, but the beast still came on. The Zulu could not fire till Harry threw himself down as the lion leaped at him. Finding that he had missed him, the great beast sprang at Nzobo, one of his hind feet ripping Harry's back to ribbons as it strove for purchase. The Zulu's bullet caught it in the throat and it fell dead at his feet.

Harry scrambled up. "A near thing," he said, "if you had not been there it would have been the end."

"Your back, my God, your back, my lord!"

"Yes, my back," Harry said. "It can still be the death of me from the poison in his claws." He was almost fainting now with shock and pain. He sat down.

"Make a fire," he said.

"A fire?"

"Yes, a fire, a good one, and while it burns we will skin the lion."

"How are we to get back?" the Zulu said. "I can carry you. That will be the only way. Carry you as far as I can and then fetch a horse."

"That's a good plan," Harry said. "Now for the fire."

They lit it and began to skin the lion. At last it was done and folded, the hair side inward, into a kind of parcel which Nzobo tied with bark torn from a vaalbos growing near them.

"Bring me my gun," Harry said. Taking it by the small he pushed the barrels into the ashes of the fire.

"What are you going to do, O Chief?"

"I?" Harry said. "Nothing. It is you."

"I? What am I to do?"

"Help me strip off my shirt to begin with, and now take the gun, holding it by the stock, and burn the wounds upon my back."

"I cannot do it. Lord, I cannot do it."

"Would you have me die? This is our only chance."

There were three great scratches, and three times the Zulu laid the almost red-hot barrels along the bloody stripes. The air smelled of burning flesh. Harry was sweating with pain. The brown skin of the Zulu was almost putty-coloured as he put his hand on Harry's shoulder. "Lord," he said, "forgive me. That was a terrible thing to have to do."

Harry took his hand and gripped it in his agony. He could not speak. At last he said: "Water, bring me water."

There was a small spring in the kloof. They had both noticed it before the lion charged. The Zulu ran to it and brought back a hatful. Harry gulped it and splashed some on to his face.

"Now we will go," he said.

"Get on my back, O lord."

"I will walk. Give me your gun and take the skin."

"Surely we can leave the skin and come back for it?"

"Leave it for the hyenas? No, it goes with us, and we will see which is the biggest, ours or Tante Maria Prinsloo's." He tried to laugh. "Yes," he said, "bigger or not, she is the better hunter. The lion did her no damage."

At last, when they were more than half-way back Harry said: "Leave me here and go and get our horses. Both of them. But say nothing to anyone of my plight."

"I must tell no one?"

"No one at all."

Harry sat in the shade of a tree to wait, with the lion skin and the gun beside him. At last he saw the horses coming.

Near the wagon one of Tante Maria's hens cackled in the bush. Her hens had all survived, and now, as glad as the people to be settled, they stole their nests and began to lay. The red cock stood on his toes and crowed.

Francina ran towards the hen that she saw coming out from behind a clump of high grass. She had wondered where she laid. There were two eggs in the round depression she had made. Two lovely, milk-white eggs.

Tante Maria came waddling towards her. "Good girl," she said. "You have found the nest. Now I can make a custard."

"I want them," Francina said. "Ja, I want them. I have them and I shall keep them."

"Give them to me."

"Try to take them and I'll smash them on the ground."

"So that is what we have come to, is it? An egg thief—a girl who steals eggs like a snake."

"Let me have them, Ouma," Francina said. "Just these two."

" What for?"

" To wash my hair with the yolk."

" So you are really going to become a girl again. I have never heard of a boy, no matter how golden his hair, using an egg upon it."

Francina stamped her foot.

" Can I have them?"

" Ja, my child, ja, and a hundred eggs besides if you will for that purpose."

In her heart Tante Maria was glad the great grey horse was dead, for it was he who had taken her little girl from her. She had always known it, and this only proved her right once more. The horse had bewitched the child. Now, with it dead, Francina was turning into a girl again, wearing dresses and washing her golden hair with egg yolks. She was going to say as much to Francina but when she looked round the girl was gone.

She had gone to find Miemie, and half an hour later both girls were washing their hair, their heads, dark and fair, bent over two tin basins set upon a table made of planks mounted on four posts stuck into the ground. It was the last thing Hendrik had made, and only because it was complete had he taken Bloubooi's rein from Francina's hand. Chance. What was this strange chance? This hazard that selected men for death, blindly, as if they were chickens fluttering in a fowl house. Barend had been shot because he had won Harry's hat. Hendrik had died instead of her because, having finished the table and thinking her tired, he had wished to help her. Tears came into her eyes. Hendrik, Bloubooi, and the dogs, all gone in a few minutes. And Harry? Suppose he did not come back? This was no ordinary lion.

She squeezed the water out of her hair. Miemie, who had knotted hers on top of her head, said: " You are crying,

Cina! What's the good of crying for a servant, a horse and two dogs when they can all be replaced?"

" I'm not crying," Francina said. " It is the soap that has got into my eye." Then she sprang at her friend in fury, slapping her face. Kicking her feet from under her, she flung her down and, seizing her ears, she beat her head up and down upon the ground.

" You! You! You!" she screamed. " You are no better than a woman!" Having lived among men so long Francina found it hard sometimes to believe she was a girl.

Miemie yelled with pain. " My ears!" she cried. " You will tear off my ears!"

Tante Maria ran towards the struggling girls. " What are you? Children of three years or nubile girls to fight like this?" She stood over them, poking at Francina with her foot.

Then she cried: " Oh God! Oh God! Look who comes!"

At the sound of horror in her voice the girls broke apart. Harry was back. Sitting straight in the saddle, with the seat of a British Cavalry trooper, he was riding down the wide road in front of the wagons and the huts. His face was as white as paper, his chest was bare and bloody. On his head he wore the famous hat. The Zulu walked beside him, holding him up and leading his own horse.

Francina ran to him. " Harry! Harry!" she cried. "' What is it? How badly are you hurt?"

Staring straight before him, he rode on, as if he would ride for ever, through the camp, up into the mountains down which they had come, on . . . on . . .

" Hendrik is avenged," he said. " The skin is on the other horse."

Francina saw it, neatly folded, lashed to the saddle as Harry swayed and fell into Nzobo's arms.

" Bring him to me," she said. " This man is mine!"

Carrying his master gently in his arms, the big Zulu brought him to the wagon and set him down upon the bed, laying his back upward. Francina saw the deep scratches of the lion's claws and the welts of the burning gun barrel that had been laid upon them.

"He made me do it," Nzobo said.

About the wagon now was a crowd of people. Those behind were saying: "Is he dead? Will he die?" Those nearest to him saying: "No, he is not dead yet, but he is like to die."

Tante Maria pushed her way through them, using her hands as if she was swimming. Having been the first to see Harry Bates she was the last to arrive, not being able to move as fast as the others; the crowd had come between her and the wagon.

"You will cure him, Ouma?" Francina asked.

"Ja, I will cure him. I have cured worse than this with my salves. Get back, you fools," she cried, turning on the people from the steps of the wagon. "I must have room and he must have peace." They fell back from her, all but the Zulu.

"He will live," he said to Francina. "My lord will live."

"If he does not live, I shall die," she said.

"Aaie," he said, "it is as I thought. The maiden does not run far or fast, and it is my lord who lies ready in the mealie field."

"What did you say?" Francina asked, for he had spoken in his own tongue.

"I said, inkoosikaas, I am glad that my master is in such good hands, for he is a great man and a chief."

41

WILLEMSDORP

It was a month before Harry Bates was well enough to go abroad. He had lain for nearly thirty days in the tent that had been attached to the Prinsloo wagon, upon a mattress of fresh grass, in a bed that his man had made of riems strung on a frame of posts. Nzobo slept on the ground beside him, and between the three of them—Tante Maria, the Zulu and Francina—his life was saved. The terrible burns upon his back that had prevented his death from blood poisoning were cured with Tante Maria's salves. The fever that had almost sweated the life out of him was held at bay by Francina's love. She hardly left him to eat, herself, and fed him the strong soups and other food she cooked for him, a spoonful at a time.

Now, at last, as he stood swaying on his feet, he said: " Thank you, Francina, for all that you have done. But why did you take such pains to save such a useless man?"

" Useless, Meneer?" she said. " Useless, Harry? Don't you know that all the men count on you to lead us? That after my Oupa, who is near to his death, you are our leader?"

She came up to him and stood staring up into his face, her eyes wide open, her lips parted.

" Don't you know by now that I am a woman, Harry? That I love you?"

His arms went round her, holding her close against him.

"My heart," he said, "my beloved. I have loved you since I first saw you—a small girl with your Oupa, staring at my grey horse. Then you came to me like an angel upon the mountain, and I loved you more. Love," he said, "day and night for years I have loved you."

Francina slipped out of his arms.

"What!" she cried. "All this time and you have said nothing, while I broke my heart?" She burst into wild tears and flung herself into his arms once more.

"Ja magtig," Tante Maria said, peeping into the tent. "It is a good thing the predikant is here, for was it not said by the Apostle Paul that it was better to marry than to burn? And it is in my heart that there is much inflammable material here."

Oom Willem was behind her. "Ja," he said, "we will have a wedding soon."

Tante Maria said: "It is natural for you to want to see a grandson before you die."

"Ja, ja," he said. "A grandson, and a son too, perhaps, for Magdalena Beyers is going to marry me. Now we will have a double wedding that will balance the double funerals we have had—those of the poor Van der Merwes and of Barend and his assassin. Ja," he said, "and we will have it under the trees in the cemetery, for the trees can also be a church and the mountain an altar to the glory of God."

"You!" Tante Maria cried. "You old satyr! An old man like you wanting marriage!"

"I am following the Word, woman! Do you not know what God said?" he asked. "Are you so ignorant of the Holy Writ? God blessed them," Oom Willem said, "and said unto them: 'Be fruitful and multiply, and replenish the earth and subdue it.'"

"Men!" Tante Maria said. "Men are all the same.

They want only one thing, and like the devil they quote the Scriptures to get it. To think that I was once married to the brother of such a man! To think that had we lived in biblical times I would have gone to him, to this monster, for in the Book of Deuteronomy, Chapter 25, Verse 5, it says very clearly that the wife of a brother shall not marry a stranger. Her husband's brother shall go into her and take her to him to wife and perform the duties of an husband's brother to her." She burst into loud lamentations and wails, crying: "Just think from what I have been saved. Had I lived then, the horrors I must have suffered. And then for you to marry a stranger!"

"Why cry, Maria," Oom Willem said, "since you are alive to-day and safe from all molestation?"

The marriages took place, and in their appointed time both Francina and Magdalena became great with child. There had been other births but no more deaths, and some of the rough Hartebeeste houses built of sods had been replaced with whitewashed cottages of unburnt brick. The church at the end of the village street served for both a fort in case of attack and a place of worship. It was lit by loop-holes set above the rammed clay benches against the walls, upon which the congregation sat, and upon which the defenders would stand to fire. The street ran east and west, so on entering it one either went past the church on one side or the other or faced its narrow door.

Fruit trees had been planted, grown from the peach and apricot stones that had been brought up from the Cape and cuttings of figs that had made the journey in pots, vegetables and flowers from seeds they had brought with them, and others given to them by the smous.

The stock had prospered, and the hunters and the smous were preparing to return, their wagons loaded with elephants' and sea-cows' teeth, with lion and tiger skins, rhinoceros horns and other products of the chase.

The wagons were being loaded in the wide space left for this purpose—the outspan in front of the church.

Tante Maria was preparing more soap, surrounded by her adopted brood. She looked from the simmering cauldron to the church and the wagons. Ja, she thought, these are the sources of civilisation—the church, soap, and the wagons that wend their way across Africa and link us to the lands across the sea. Now that she was settled and busy again, she was content. Things had turned out much better than she had expected, and though there was not the comfort here to which she had been accustomed on the farm at home, there were compensations. It was not so lonely living in a dorp like this, surrounded by people and with a church at your door. Besides, the comforts would come. The smous had said he would return next year and bring everything they needed.

They had decided to call the village Willemsdorp after the old dotard who had, by the Lord's guidance and a great good fortune, managed to lead them here. It was certainly odd that such a man should be her husband's, Groot Jan's, brother. Well, she had done her duty by him taking care of him for years, and the loose woman he had married was welcome to him. One day she would find him out. Tante Maria stirred her pot with vigour. Ja, she thought, for a while he will deceive her, but it cannot last. How Oom Willem would deceive his wife was not clear in her mind, only that he would do so and that Magdalena Beyers, now Prinsloo, would find him out.

Francina was happy with her Harry and her baby that was to come. They had decided to call it Willem. Before long there would be many Willems here, for all the women wished to honour their old leader. The girl Francina had been was forgotten, lost in the woman she had become.

Oom Willem sat upon his sea-cow skull smoking his pipe, watching the oxen draw his English plough. The first furrows were being turned. It had all come to pass as he had hoped and prayed. Here he was, old but honoured, and happy with a young and beautiful wife, with his Francina married. He had a son and a great-nephew on the way, for certainly they would be boys. What more could a man ask of God?

First they had beaten their ploughshares into swords to fight their way north, and now they were beating them back into ploughshares again to cultivate the lands that they had won. The long span of oxen turned the grass over. The rich black earth beneath looked like velvet behind the plough.

Ja, he thought, it has indeed come about as it was written. " Then did they till their ground in peace, and the earth gave increase, and the trees of the field their fruit."

It was for this we trekked, for a new land and peace. We, the voortrekkers—those with the fiercest hearts and the greatest love.

GLOSSARY OF
SOUTH AFRICAN WORDS

Aasvoel—vulture

Allewêreld—exclamation: all the world

Assagai—native spear

Biltong—sun-dried meat

Blouboi—Blue Boy (Francina's horse)

Bobotie—dish of curried meat with rice

Boer—South African farmer

Brey—to tan leather

Dassie—rock rabbit

Disselboom—pole of wagon or cart

Dorp—village

Groot—great

Hok—animal pen

Impi—regiment

Induna—lesser chief, often of royal blood

Inspan—to harness

Jong—young man

Kappie—sunbonnet

Kaross—skin rug

Kartel—bed in wagon made of criss-crossed rawhide strips

Kerels—fellows

Kloof—valley or cleft in the hills

Konfyt—sugar-cured preserves

Kop—mountain

Kopje, koppie—hillock, a small kop

Krans—cliff

Laager—defensive camp of wagons locked together

Lappie—cloth, rag

Magtig—abbreviation of Allemagtig, Almighty

Mooi meisie—pretty girl

Morgen—land measure (two acres approx.)

Nagmaal—Communion

Nooi—young lady

Oom—uncle

Ouma—grandmother

Oupa—grandfather

Outspan—to unharness

Poort—a pass in the mountains

Predikant—preacher

Randjie—ridge

Riems—rawhide thong, reins

Rooibok—impala

Rooinek—red necks, Englishmen whose necks turned red instead of tanning

Sjambok—heavy rawhide whip

Skey—yoke peg

Sluit—ditch, washout

Taal—Dutch dialect, now obsolete

Trek tous—traces made of twisted rawhide, for fastening of yokes to each other

Veldschoen—home-made rawhide shoe

Vlei—marsh

Voorlooper—boy who leads the oxen

Voortrekker—pioneer, one who went in front

447